"I loved this book! I didn't think I could possibly enjoy another book as much as I did Craig Parshall's first novel, *The Resurrection File*. But I simply couldn't put *Custody of the State* down! In it, Craig Parshall tackles issues that every citizen should be concerned about. I can hardly wait for the next in the Chambers of Justice series. I'm addicted!"

—Diane S. Passno
Executive Vice President, Focus on the Family

❨   ❨   ❨

"This is not only a great mystery, but also a deeply moving, redemptive book. Craig Parshall has a terrific writing style. The characters take on flesh and blood, and the situations become compelling. Although few novels make it into Hollywood movies, this is one that deserves translation to the big screen. Bravo!"

—Ted Baehr
Chairman of the Christian Film & Television
Commission and publisher of MOVIEGUIDE®

CUSTODY of the STATE

CRAIG PARSHALL

HARVEST HOUSE™ PUBLISHERS

EUGENE, OREGON

Unless otherwise indicated, all Scripture quotations are taken from the New King James Version. Copyright ©1982 by Thomas Nelson, Inc. Used by permission. All rights reserved.

Verses marked NASB are taken from the New American Standard Bible ®, © 1960, 1962, 1963, 1968, 1971, 1972, 1973, 1975, 1977, 1995 by The Lockman Foundation. Used by permission.

The following Scripture quotations in this book are not identified in the text:
    page 9: Joshua 24:15
    page 250: Matthew 14:10-12
    page 283: Psalm 91:4 NASB

Cover by Left Coast Design, Portland, Oregon

CUSTODY OF THE STATE
Copyright © 2003 by Craig L. Parshall
Published by Harvest House Publishers
Eugene, Oregon 97402

Library of Congress Cataloging-in-Publication Data
Parshall, Craig, 1950–
    Custody of the state / Craig Parshall.
        p. cm. — (Chambers of justice ; bk. 2)
    ISBN 0-7369-1026-3
    1. Custody of children—Fiction. 2. Child abuse—Fiction. 3. Georgia—Fiction. I. Title.
PS3616.A77 C87 2003
813'.54—dc21   2002013757

Printed in the United States of America

04   05   06   07   08   09   10   / BC-MS /   10   9   8   7   6   5   4   3

To John DiFrancesca, my friend and brother-in-law:

for his dedication to his children—
and his faithfulness to Him who created the first family
and who beckons us all to join His eternal family

Acknowledgments

I am deeply indebted to Marilyn Clifton, my administrative assistant, for her tireless legal research that helped to inject reality into this fictional story; to Barbara Henderson for her painstaking keyboard work on the manuscript, as well as general research on everything from meteorology to geography; and to Sharon Donehey, as always, for her faithful handling of countless details that attend the preparation of a book, from inception to the final rush to make the deadline.

A special thanks is due, again, to Paul Gossard with the editorial staff at Harvest House Publishers—his eye is keen, and his sense of the story and of the characters involved is ever insightful.

My wife, Janet, and my four children made a massive contribution to this story, simply by teaching me the primacy of parenting and the essence of family.

The inspiration for this story really springs from my experience, during a 27-year practice of law, representing parents and families who found themselves at the blunt end of government abuse. We have the greatest legal system in the history of the world—but when our courts and our law enforcers aim their considerable power at dedicated parents and law-abiding families, the results can be tragic.

And in that regard, I am also thankful to those attorneys around the nation alongside whom I have had the privilege of fighting to help protect the integrity—and the sanctity—of the family.

1

THAT MORNING BROUGHT THE usual sounds and smells as the family gathered for breakfast inside the kitchen of the white farmhouse—the one with the long, dirt driveway that wound through the soybean fields and that eventually connected to the county trunk highway.

Buried in the rural quiet of the Georgia countryside, the family gathered for the rituals of the routine and the mundane. Within the house, it all felt familiar. The daily patterns of their home had sheltered them. The life of the Fellows family had become predictable, the only major variations being those of weather, season, and the market price of soybeans, and occasionally Mary Sue's schedule as a part-time nurse. Though their life was lived on a farm with the usual machinery, tools, and field chemicals, it had been a safe one.

At a quarter after six, there was only the slight heaviness of early-morning fatigue, but nothing else. The family was beginning the day in the usual way. They were cradled in the details of the normal. They were safe.

Outside, the house was tidy enough, but the careful eye could detect signs of minor neglect. The paint was peeling slightly. The red shutters set the white wood siding off nicely, but one hung a little off-kilter, the casualty of a storm. Joe Fellows, a thirty-year-old farmer who managed his sixty-acre soybean farm almost single-handedly, had promised Mary Sue that he would get to those odd jobs. But he never seemed to be able to find the time.

Joe, Mary Sue, and Joshua, their four-year-old, were halfway through breakfast. Joe had been up since a quarter to five. After an hour's work he'd ducked back into the house, tossed his International Harvester baseball cap down, stripped off his red plaid coat, and sat down for breakfast. Now he was slurping from a mug of coffee.

Mary Sue was dancing between the stove and Joshua's place at the barn-board table where her son was catapulting food off his plate with glee. Like a baseball player caught between first and second base, bowl in hand, Mary Sue moved slightly toward the stove, then toward the table, then toward the stove again. With one hand she was trying to scoop more scrambled eggs into the bowl from the frying pan, and with the other she was reaching out toward the table, pointing her index finger at Joshua.

"Joshua, no!" she yelled. "Don't throw your food."

Joshua, a skinny, pale boy with big hazel eyes and brown hair, was grinning widely. He tossed more eggs off his plate.

Mary Sue stopped and pulled a long strand of her strawberry-blond hair away from her face. As she stared at Joe, who was reading the market prices in the paper, her pale blue eyes, usually soft and inviting, started to flash into anger, as they could do in seconds.

"I could use a little help here," Mary Sue snapped out to her husband.

"Joshua, don't," Joe said nonchalantly from behind the newspaper.

"That was a great help, thanks," she shot back, her pretty features starting to flush. "Will you reinforce the rules at the table, please?"

"Okay," Joe responded, smiling. Then he slowly lowered the paper from his face as Joshua watched intently. As his face was revealed, Joe crossed his eyes, bared his teeth, and growled in a bearlike voice, *"D-o-n-'t t-h-r-o-w y-o-u-r f-o-o-d!"*

Joshua rocked with giggles in his little chair.

Mary Sue tried to muster up the appropriate anger, but gave up as she started laughing a little herself.

"You're hopeless," she said to Joe, who seemed pleased that he and his son had waged a small but successful rebellion together.

As Mary Sue walked over to her husband with the bowl of eggs, he pushed himself away from the table.

"You haven't finished your plate," she said.

"I've got a lot of work to do."

"How about your work in setting a good example for Joshua?"

"What are you talking about?"

"Eating habits. Children pick up bad eating patterns by watching the parents."

"Whether I finish my plate or not has nothing to do with Joshua not eating."

"Then what *is* the reason? The doctor doesn't know. I can't figure it out. And when he does eat, sometimes he throws up. That isn't normal. He's not gaining weight. I think there's something serious going on."

"Look," Joe said, "you're the medical expert—"

"I'm a nurse. That doesn't make me an expert."

"I've got a farm here that doesn't take care of itself. Soybean prices are going down. Weather reports don't look good. I'm not trying to blow you off, honey, but I've got a lot going on."

"Your family is your first priority," Mary Sue replied sharply.

"You want my two cents' worth?" Joe said. "I don't think that Dr. What's-his-name knows what he's doing with Joshua."

"What *is* his name?" Mary Sue asked, her eyes narrowed and her arms folded across her chest.

"I don't know..." Joe searched his memory for a minute, "Dr....What's-his-name. I can't remember. What's the difference?"

"When was Joshua's last checkup?" Mary Sue asked.

Joe gestured as if he were going to answer, then stopped. After a second he said, "Last week."

"Wrong. *This* week. Two days ago," Mary Sue replied. Then she added, "No further questions, Your Honor. Mr. Fellows is found guilty of being too busy for his family."

Joe sauntered over to his wife with a stern expression of his own. Mary Sue gazed into Joe's blue eyes, looking over his square jaw and the dark blond hair that framed his face with an unkempt swatch that hung down to one side. They stared into each other's eyes until a smile began turning up the sides of Joe's mouth.

He quickly touched his index fingers to the tickle spots on her rib cage until she started laughing and pushing him away.

"Making me laugh is not an answer," Mary Sue protested.

"I know that, darlin'," he said. "Look, I'm worried about Josh just like you."

"And when are we going to talk about what the social worker said?" Mary Sue added.

"Okay, now you're moving onto subject number two. We have to talk about that later."

"It's all related. That Liz Luden woman from Social Services said that if we were insisting on getting a second opinion, then they wanted us to get it done by today."

"Today—or what?" Joe said, his voice rising slightly. "*Or what?* You told her a couple of weeks ago that you were going to get a second opinion about Josh from another doctor. That's it. That is the end of it. No Miss Social Worker What's-her-name is going to meddle with our right to decide what's best for our son."

"It's too late. They're already meddling, Joe. Besides, the two of us have to talk about where I'm going to get the money for the second opinion."

"This is all that doctor's fault."

"Maybe Dr. Wilson meant well," Sue countered.

"By calling Social Services? Just because you wouldn't agree with everything he was saying? This doctor has tried how many tests on Josh? He's grabbing for straws. We tell him that we want a second opinion, and then the next thing we know he calls a social worker from the county on us."

"We've got a decision to make," Mary Sue pleaded, grabbing Joe's arm as he tried to pull on his coat. "The social worker said if we don't cooperate with everything they're asking, they might actually try to get a court order. Joe, I don't want anyone coming after my baby."

"This is really ridiculous," Joe fumed. "Just think about it. Why are they picking on us? We're your normal, average parents. You must have done something to tick off that Dr. Wilson. I bet it was the way you stopped following his orders."

"Josh was getting *worse!*" Mary Sue cried out.

"I thought you just said you *weren't* the medical expert!"

"Please, just give me five more minutes so we can decide this right now," Mary Sue pleaded.

"I'll give you my decision," Joe shot back. "We don't check in with the Department of Social Services on medical treatment for our son. Period. We'll get a second opinion *when we have the time, and when we have the money, and not a minute before that.*" He put his cap on, but before he swung the door open his face softened slightly. "Besides, if they take us to court, you'd whop them all bare-handed. You could wrestle wildcats, baby doll."

As he was walking through the door, he turned, pulled something from his coat pocket, showed it to Mary Sue, and shouted back to her, "I've got the walkie-talkie with me if you need to get ahold of me."

Joe closed the door behind him. As he buttoned up his coat he glanced at the familiar little plaque at the side of the porch. It bore a Bible verse from the book of Joshua:

"...As for me and my house, we will serve the LORD."

In the kitchen Mary Sue sighed and tried to smile. She gazed over at little Joshua, who was leaning sideways in his chair. His eyes were closing and his head was nodding as he started to doze off.

"You are so tired all the time, aren't you, precious one?" Mary Sue said.

She walked over to the counter to retrieve Joshua's sippy cup. After hunting for it for a few seconds, she found it behind the toaster and gave it to Joshua. But after a sip, he made a face and spit it out. Then he rubbed his eyes.

"No, momma, no…"

"Don't you want any more?" Mary Sue asked, moving her hand along his baby-soft cheek.

Outside, Joe fired up his tractor and drove out along the track that led to the barns and outbuildings. He was already past the buildings and beside the back forty acres when something caught the corner of his eye.

He put the tractor into neutral and studied the horizon.

Off in the distance along the road leading to their house, he saw a cloud of dust spiraling up into the air from three cars that were approaching. He could see the squad lights on top of the first two. As he looked closer, he could see they were from the sheriff's department. The third car was plain brown, and it looked like it was one of the Juda County government vehicles.

Joe snatched the walkie-talkie.

"Mary Sue, listen up—we've got trouble coming down the road."

"What do you mean?"

"Two squad cars from the sheriff's department—and another car from the county. Heading right toward the house."

"Joe, we've got to do something."

"I've got a bad feeling about this. I'd be willing to bet they've got some kind of legal paper for us. That's the way it happened when my uncle's farm got foreclosed. Just like this. Double squads from the sheriff's department."

"What do they want?"

"I don't know," Joe said, his voice tense.

"No one's going to take Josh away from me, you hear? No one!" Mary Sue cried out.

"Mary Sue, calm down. Nobody's talking about taking Josh. I'm just going to tell them to get off my property until I can talk to a lawyer."

"Joe, what if they're coming for my little boy? You don't know—we can't take any chances."

Joe paused for a second. He knew that this was a defining moment. One of the make-or-break events that jumps into your path like a deer at night, right in front of your car while you're doing sixty. With little warning, and barely time for anything except instinctive reaction.

"Until I find something out..." Joe said—and by now he had his tractor in fourth gear and was heading back to the house at a healthy speed—"you'd better take Josh out the back door. Take the truck, and the two of you get off the property through the back pasture and across the creek. Head out to the state highway. Then call me later to make sure the coast is clear before coming home."

Mary Sue grabbed Joshua, who already had been startled by the tone of the conversation. She snatched the truck keys and headed for the back door—but thought better of it and ran upstairs.

Sprinting into Joshua's bedroom, she picked up his soft-sider bag and threw in some of his t-shirts, training pants, and jeans. Then, carrying her little boy under one arm and his bag under the other, she hurried down to the master bedroom, where she grabbed her make-up case, some underwear, and a pile of unfolded clothes that lay in a laundry basket and stuffed it all in a laundry bag.

Running to the window, Mary Sue could see the three cars stopped at the fence in their driveway. A deputy was jumping out of his squad car and going to the gate. She could make out two women in the third car, which had the Juda County insignia. She grabbed a pair of yellow child's binoculars that were lying on a dresser. She squinted through them—now she could see the social worker Liz Luden behind the wheel. Another younger-looking woman was in the passenger seat next to her.

In less than a minute the caravan of cars would be in front of their house.

Bounding down the stairs with Joshua bobbing up and down in one arm, the bags in the other, Mary Sue rushed to the door. With the few fingers that were still free, she snatched her Bible off the kitchen table, ran out the back, strapped Joshua into the car seat in their pickup truck, tossed in the bags and Bible, and jumped behind the wheel.

Fumbling with the pile of keys, Mary Sue nearly jammed the house key into the ignition by mistake.

"Please, God—please, God…" she muttered as she fished for the ignition key.

She found it, started the truck, and lurched forward down the road that led to the back side of the Fellows farm.

She and Joshua bounced from the jolts of the rough road beneath them as she increased speed, the truck tires spitting dirt and gravel.

Glancing in the rearview mirror, Mary Sue looked back at the house she was leaving. Tears were streaming down her face. All she could manage was, "God, protect us…protect us…."

"Why you crying, momma?" Joshua asked.

There was no answer. Mary Sue leaned her head into her left hand, trying to control her sobs as she steered with her other hand and headed the truck toward the creek and the state highway that lay beyond.

All she could think about now was the little creek and whether it had dried up enough for her to cross it without getting stuck in the mud.

2

Okay, I read the story. Then I read it again. The facts are plain enough. A young mother. Scared. She believes she has to save her child. So she flees from the authorities."

"Is that all there is to it?"

"No. But I'm just sticking to the basics. I'm trying to be objective."

"That must be the trial lawyer in you talking. So what does your objectivity tell you?"

"That the mother believes in what she is doing. Thinks she has heard the voice of God."

"What do you think?"

"I'm not sure. Part of me believes it. Most of me. But I'm conflicted."

"You're trying to resolve the conflict?"

"Exactly."

"How are you going to do that?"

"That's why I'm talking to you. You're the one with the theological degrees, Len, not to mention that you're my favorite law professor. I'm just a trial lawyer."

"Look, my degree isn't what's important. Or my teaching credentials. Let me put it to you plainly, Will. Ultimately, it gets down to miracles. Is the Bible God's revealed Word?"

"I accept that. But that doesn't end the debate."

"Well then, is it just the miraculous birth of Jesus that you're struggling with? Or is there something else?"

"The nativity story. That's what I've been focusing on. The virgin birth. Angels start appearing. Magi traveling from far

13

away arrive on the scene. King Herod sends out the edict against the children. Visions and dreams. The mother, her husband, and the baby flee to Egypt.

"On the other hand, let me say this. I do know that God does miracles. Look at me—a former agnostic ACLU attorney, now studying the Bible. Going to church. In love with a gospel singer."

Sitting across the table in the small, silver-sided roadside diner, Len Redgrove chuckled a little at that.

Will Chambers stopped for a second to appreciate the irony in what he had just said.

"But still," Will continued, "I'm wondering if we have to believe in the mass of supernatural detail that the Bible lays out about these events—that's all. Do we *have* to take it literally? Maybe it was meant to be symbolic."

"Okay," Redgrove said. "Then start with the innkeeper as an example. Let's establish the circumstantial facts. What do you think he saw when he encountered that young pregnant woman sitting on a donkey, with her exasperated husband standing next to her?"

Will reflected for a moment. "Probably thought, *Here are a couple peasants who can't come up with enough money to get a decent room.*"

"That's just the point. The Bible doesn't actually refer to the innkeeper. But he's implied in the text. The town of Bethlehem was jammed up with travelers who had to return to their town of origin for the census. No room. He looks at these two. What does he see?"

Will was listening closely.

Redgrove continued. "Relying just on his senses—his naturalistic bias, you might say—what did he see? Just another impoverished Jewish couple. He missed the miracle unfolding right in front of him."

"So miracles aren't for everyone? Some people are incapable of understanding them? Is that what you're saying?"

"Understanding miracles," Redgrove explained, "does not demand that we suspend our objectivity. Just the opposite. It requires *true* objectivity. God is the only *real,* objective source of information. His Word gives us the big picture. Otherwise, if left to ourselves, down there at ground level with the innkeeper, we end up merely shutting the door."

As the waitress dropped the check on the table, Will scooped it up. "You paid last time. I'll get it."

"By the way, how is your law practice?" Redgrove asked.

"Busy. Thriving."

"And how about *you?*"

"A little restless." Will gave it another moment of thought, then added, "Actually, I'm pretty discontented. Sometimes I wonder if I ought to stay in the law. If God is working on me, I question the value of what I'm doing as a lawyer."

"I always thought you would make a gifted lawyer—even back when you were my student. Look at the victories God has given you. He's used your legal talents."

"That's what Fiona tells me too."

"And how is she?" Redgrove asked.

"She's just finished a concert tour. She's coming back tomorrow and we have a date tomorrow night."

"Haven't proposed to her yet?"

"No," Will's voice dropped slightly. "I…really don't know that she'll have me. There seems to be some hesitation on her part. So…" His voice trailed off.

"Give it time. And give it to the Lord. He's the ultimate matchmaker. If he wants the two of you together, it will work out."

Will nodded. But those words did not give him any comfort. He shook hands with his old friend and they agreed to meet for dinner again at the usual time next month.

The attorney climbed into his '57 Corvette and motored home to his large log home which was perched on the rolling Virginia countryside. The sun was setting when he arrived, so he sat for a while on the broad porch that wound around the house and admired the scarlet and orange colors that were fading around the contours of the Blue Ridge Mountains on the horizon. Then he walked inside and turned on the television set.

Punching the channels, he stopped at INN—International News Network. He liked to catch the daily *Slice of Life* news summary.

After the world news, he was reaching for the remote when something caught his eye. On the television, he saw a blond man in an orange jail jumpsuit shuffling across a courtroom with manacled feet, hands in handcuffs.

"The Georgia farmer is being charged with obstruction of justice and felony child abuse," the announcer said. "His wife and their four-year-old child are still missing. It is alleged that Fellows aided in their flight from sheriff's deputies."

Will studied the desperate look on Joe Fellows' face as deputies led him up to the judge's bench.

"Buddy," Will said out loud to the television, "I hope you have a good lawyer."

3

I<small>N THE</small> J<small>UDA</small> C<small>OUNTY</small> J<small>AIL</small>, in his orange jumpsuit, face unshaven, hair greasy and tangled, Joe Fellows sat on the prisoner's side of the glass window. At the bottom there was a metal tray that could be passed between the prisoner and the visitor, but only when the jailer unlocked the opening.

Seated on the other side of the glass, a tall American Indian was looking intently at Joe. His black hair was worn in two long braids that hung down his back. On his head was a black baseball cap with the gold letters "WWJD."

"As I told you," the Indian explained slowly and patiently, "I am Flying Eagle White Arrow, a chief of the Lakota tribe. My Christian name is Andrew."

"And you have seen my wife, Mary Sue?"

"All I can say is that she is safe. That's all."

"And you came here to tell me *that?*" Joe asked, still unclear as to how this big Indian man fit into the recent turn of events that had forced him into jail and had sent his wife fleeing with their son.

"Yes. Don't worry. The Lord will not leave you or forsake you."

"Thanks," Joe said.

"But please do not ask me anything else."

Joe eyed the stranger and nodded his head. He had no other choice now but to trust Andrew White Arrow.

"My mother was here just before you arrived," Joe added. "She's got the name of a lawyer. Can you get this attorney's name and telephone number to Mary Sue somehow?"

17

With that, Joe lifted up a small piece of paper. He was about to motion the jail guard to come over and unlock the tray, but Andrew lifted a hand of warning and shook his head.

"Don't give it to me. Just show me through the glass."

"Are you going to remember it?"

"I've got a good memory," Andrew said softly, and smiled.

Joe held the piece of paper with a name and telephone number against the glass. Andrew studied it for a few seconds. Then he gestured for Joe to pull it back. Something in Andrew's expression told Joe that he recognized the name on the piece of paper.

"You know this lawyer?" Joe asked.

"Never met him," Andrew said. "But I've heard about him."

Joe added, "Tell my wife we're going to fight this tooth and nail. Take no prisoners. All the way. Will you?"

Andrew stood up from the folding chair to his considerable height. Joe got up quickly, and he put both of his hands to the glass. Suddenly, his expression of determination had dissolved. His face was sunken, and his eyes were like of those of an animal startled at night in the woods.

"Anything else you can tell me? Anything?" Joe said in a voice that was now almost pleading.

"Yes," Andrew said, "there is."

He spread his arms out with his palms up and closed his eyes. And then he said in a deep, calm voice, in a chanting cadence,

> Hear my cry, O God;
> Attend to my prayer.
> From the end of the earth I will cry to You,
> When my heart is overwhelmed;
> Lead me to the rock that is higher than I.
> For you have been a shelter for me,
> A strong tower from the enemy.
> I will abide in Your tabernacle forever.
> I will trust in the shelter of Your wings.

Andrew smiled at Joe and said, "Psalm sixty-one, verses one through four."

As the guard led him away, Andrew turned and added, "New King James Version."

Outside the locked unit, in the jail lobby, the head jailer was waiting for Andrew. Seated behind an ancient-looking desk, he was wearing the brown uniform of the sheriff's department, which was stretched tightly over his immense girth. He was bald, and his thick neck was rippled and jowly.

The jailer was mopping the sweat from his brow with a paper towel, and he glanced at the visitor sign-in clipboard, then spoke to Andrew as he entered the lobby.

"Andrew White Arrow. Would that be you?"

"Yes," Andrew answered simply.

"The prosecuting attorney for Juda County wants to talk to you. Take the elevator down the hall to the third floor. Second office on the right."

"Can I get my driver's license back?" Andrew asked.

The jailer leaned back in the swivel chair, but only slightly. He crossed one of his legs with great difficulty and stared for a moment at the tall Indian.

Then he said in a low grumble, "You'll get your ID back when the prosecuting attorney is through with you."

Andrew made his way upstairs to the lobby of the prosecutor's office, where he sat for a few moments before being led to an inner office. He was shown to a seat across from a large walnut desk. The office walls were lined with law books and a scattering of plaques and certificates, and on one wall there was a framed picture of a stumpy cartoon character with a big cowboy hat and a long handlebar mustache, and a huge six-gun in each hand. Across the top were the words "WE GET THE BAD GUYS!"

Suddenly a short, stocky man in a suit and tie rushed into the office yelling something over his shoulder. He stopped in his tracks next to Andrew and eyed him.

"You're Andrew White Arrow?"

Andrew nodded.

"I'm Herodius Putnam, prosecuting attorney for Juda County. Friends call me Harry. You can call me Mr. Putnam. You're a big one. You're some kind of Indian chief?"

"Lakota tribe."

"Don't say. Your driver's license says you live in Santa Fe, New Mexico. What are you doing here?" Putnam asked as he sat down at his desk.

"My brother. He's been living in Atlanta. I went there to pick him up and move him."

"What kind of work do you do in Santa Fe, Mr. White Arrow?"

"I teach at a community college."

"What exactly?"

"Philosophy and comparative religion."

"That would make you an educated man. So you'll be able to understand what I'm about to tell you. Joe Fellows is charged with obstructing a criminal investigation. We were investigating the possibility that his wife has been slowly poisoning their little boy." Then Putnam repeated the words again. "*Poisoning their little boy*. You visited him today in jail. You'd better be real careful about having contact with Mr. Joe Fellows."

Andrew said nothing. His face was expressionless.

"Why'd you visit him? You know him?"

"Not really."

"Then why were you here?"

"I heard about his being in jail. I thought he might need some Christian encouragement."

Putnam looked up at Andrew's cap with the "WWJD" lettering. He was about to say something but thought better of it.

"Listen to me real careful. I've got a question for you, and I want the truth. Do you know the current whereabouts of Mary Sue Fellows or her little boy?"

"Current whereabouts of Mary Sue Fellows or her little boy," Andrew repeated slowly.

"That's right. Joe's wife. Where she is *this very minute*. Same for her little boy. Do you?"

After listening intently to the question, he said, "No."

"She's fled the jurisdiction. Anybody harboring her is a criminal. And they will be prosecuted. So, is there anything you want to tell me? This could be real serious."

"This does sound serious," Andrew noted.

"Yes sir, it is."

"Then maybe I ought to talk to a lawyer," Andrew said.

Putnam jumped up and walked around the desk to Andrew. Even while standing, he was only slightly taller than Andrew sitting down.

"So you want a lawyer?"

"I don't know—do you think I need one?"

"Why ask me?" Putnam barked out.

"Because you are a lawyer. I thought you might be able to tell me whether I need one."

"Don't play games with me," Putnam said, pointing his finger at Andrew. Then, after staring at him for a few seconds, the prosecutor walked over to the window that overlooked the park across the street. He gazed over at the swings and play structure, which were vacant in the cold weather.

"Let me tell you something. We had one murder in all of Juda County last year—*only one*. Most prosecutors would love a record like that. But not me. You know why?"

Andrew shook his head.

"Because that murder involved the death of a little girl. Child abuse of the most horrible kind. All over the newspapers. Child welfare folks from the state house came down here. That will never happen again in my county if I can do anything about it. *It will not happen.*"

Putnam strolled over to Andrew and put his hand on his wide shoulder. "Mary Sue Fellows needs help. I want to give it to her. And that little boy needs protection. So one day he can grow up healthy and play on the swings like a normal little boy."

But Andrew still made no response.

"You have any information about Mary Sue Fellows or her little boy, you'd better get it to us immediately. Savvy?"

"I understand," Andrew replied.

Andrew was escorted out. Harry Putnam picked up the phone and punched the extension number for the detective in the children's unit.

"Get someone to tail that big Indian who was visiting Joe Fellows. He knows something about this, I'm sure of it. We've already called the airport in Atlanta, and he's scheduled to be on a flight back to New Mexico in a couple of hours. Have some local law enforcement ready to pick up the tail in New Mexico when he lands."

Then Putnam smiled a little. "I have a feeling that Mr. White Arrow is going to lead us right to Mary Sue Fellows and her boy."

Andrew was led back to the jailer. He was still seated at his desk, and now he was reading an *Amazing Mysteries* magazine. As Andrew strode in, he put it down.

"I suppose you want your ID back?"

"Yes," Andrew said.

The jailer pulled it out of the drawer and fingered it with his meaty hand. Then he tossed it on top of the desk.

As Andrew picked it up, the jailer leaned forward, breathing noisily. Then he spoke. "You being an Indian chief and all, I figure that makes you Tonto. So where's the Lone Ranger? I don't see him anywhere." And with that, the jailer chuckled in self-satisfaction.

Andrew looked the jailer in the eye. "Oh, don't worry." Then he broke into a large smile and added, "I think he'll be here soon."

4

INSIDE THE LAW OFFICES of Will Chambers, PC, in Monroeville, Virginia, the meeting was coming to a close. Will was finishing up his agenda. Next to him Jacki Johnson, a diminutive black lawyer, was taking some notes. At her right was Todd Furgeson, the youngest associate.

"So," Will continued, "the cases keep rolling in. That's the good news. Let's make sure we keep up-to-date with our deadlines calendar. Jacki, you're going to cover that hearing in Richmond for me. And Todd, talk to me later today about the research I need from you on that new case."

"The one against the government of Sudan?"

"Yeah." Then Will turned to Jacki. "I need to talk to you about this. It just came in. The Sudanese government allowed some American missionaries to be rounded up by terrorists, right in front of that General Kurtzu Nuban. I'm sure he's on the take. We'll be suing the government on the grounds that it knowingly permitted the terrorists to kidnap and murder innocent Americans."

"Sounds like one of our average small-claims cases," Jacki said wryly. "So it's the three of us against the government of Sudan?"

"I know," Will replied, "the odds are a little uneven. But I promise we'll take it easy on them."

Jacki chuckled. Then she added, "Don't forget, I'm taking some time off with my hubby. Howard and I are taking a long weekend. If any emergencies come in, count me out for a few days."

Will nodded. He was about to rise, but he noticed a mysterious smile on Jacki's face.

"All right—what am I missing?" Will asked.

Jacki's smile broadened. "Nothing about the case. Just an observation."

"Well, *what?*" Will probed.

"I was just thinking—ever since you stopped coming into the office smelling like booze…and stopped single-handedly insulting most of the legal community in Virginia, D.C., and the surrounding Eastern seaboard—you've kept yourself generally out of trouble…"

Will was amused, but Todd was not. Though his face was stone, his eyes had widened.

"Ever since those days," Jacki went on, "it's almost been *boring* around here. I can actually practice law now. I don't have to be your nursemaid anymore!"

Jacki noticed the shocked look on Todd's face and quickly added, "Hey, Todd—I'm exaggerating. Don't worry. Will was never that bad."

"Yes, I was," Will said without hesitation. "But those days are gone. No more bailing Will Chambers out of trouble. We practice law now, and we don't expect you to sweep up after the elephants. We run things like professionals here."

Todd was nodding in relief.

"But we also don't take ourselves too seriously, Todd," Jacki added. "A little levity is good for the soul."

As they began to disperse, Will put his hand on Todd's shoulder. "Nice work on that brief you turned in yesterday."

Smiling, Todd gave a quick nod of appreciation and then headed for the law library down the hall.

As Will walked past the reception desk, Hilda Swenson, the blond secretary with the big hair, was waving a pink telephone message in his direction.

"Urgent call, Will. This woman is frantic. She needs to talk to you right away. I bet you could be so much help to her. Poor woman—she was crying on the phone. She's really stressed."

Will took the slip and studied it.

"There's no number for me to call."

"She insisted on calling back."

"Where's she from?"

"Well," said Hilda, "she didn't want to tell me."

"What's this about?"

"Wouldn't tell me that either," Hilda said with a smile and a shrug.

Handing the pink slip back to Hilda, Will said, "I don't think I have time to play twenty questions. When she calls back, tell her that I'm really pretty busy. Maybe we can have Todd do a preliminary interview over the phone."

"She insisted on talking only with you."

Will paused. Then he said, "Okay. I'll talk to her if she calls. But tell her I really don't have a lot of time. Hilda, this Sudan case is going to occupy my schedule for the foreseeable future." Then he headed into his office, and closed the door.

He was already more than an hour into the stacks of documents from the State Department and the Gospel Missionary Alliance when his intercom buzzed. He looked on the little computer screen. The message read, "Will, this is the woman I told you about. Is calling back. I told her your schedule. Says it's urgent."

After picking up the phone, Will asked who was calling.

"My name is Mary Sue Fellows."

"Your name sounds familiar. Have we talked before?"

"No—but it's been all over the news."

"What's the situation?"

"Child-abuse charges. We're in Georgia. My husband has been arrested."

"Is he a farmer?"

"Yes."

Will thought back to the news report on INN. "Yes, I heard about it. I'm sorry about your situation."

"We need a lawyer desperately."

"I'm not sure I can help. My schedule—"

But before Will could continue, Mary Sue interrupted. "I know. Your secretary told me. But we're innocent. This whole thing is insane—we love our little boy. Please help us."

"I've got two other lawyers here in the office who might be able to talk to you—"

"It has to be you. My mother-in-law knows about you, has read about your cases—she insisted that it be you. She's the one raising the money for our defense. From what she told us, you're the only one—"

But Will interrupted her. "There are a lot of good lawyers out there who could probably help you. I'm sorry. My time commitments are such that I really don't think I could jump right into your case right now."

There was silence on the other end.

"Mrs. Fellows?" Will asked. "Are you still there?"

"I'm on the run right now. The police are looking for me this very minute. My child needs medical help. But I will not turn him over to Social Services, because they have this ridiculous fantasy that I'm some kind of monster. My husband in is jail. We've been wrongly accused of this thing—the farm is being neglected—our lives are falling apart, Mr. Chambers."

Will heard her choking back tears. But before he could say anything else, Mary Sue said through her tears, "God wants you to take this case. I know it. I'll just wait till you can see that too."

Then he heard the click as she hung up at the other end.

After putting the phone down, Will swiveled his chair slightly until he could see the spire of the old St. Andrews Church across the street through his second-story window. He gazed at the Revolutionary War–era edifice for a few moments.

"Oh, boy," Will sighed to himself. He rubbed his forehead, thinking about how much pain and injustice was out there. And how he was just one lawyer, with a small firm. He could only do so much. He decided to say a short silent prayer for the Fellows family.

When he was done, he turned back to the tall stack of documents that lay on his desk. As he flipped each page, he jotted down notes on the legal pad in front of him.

After a few minutes he buzzed Hilda.

"Do me a favor, will you? Before you leave for the day, order some dinner in for me. You know the stuff I like. It's going to be a long night."

"Are you kidding?" she replied.

"Huh?"

"You're supposed to be out with Fiona tonight. I made the reservations myself."

"Oh, yikes. You just saved my hide. That's right. Thanks for reminding me, Hilda," Will said sheepishly.

He glanced over at the picture of Fiona on his bookshelf. He liked that one the best. She was beautiful from any angle, of course, in any picture, with her dark auburn hair, piercing dark eyes, and cover-girl features. Her smile set the whole room aglow.

But unlike the studio pictures she used for concert promotions or autographing for her fans, this photo was different. She'd been caught in mid-laugh at a party the two of them had attended. It was impromptu, unabashed, and bursting with life. That was Fiona.

Will wondered how he could have forgotten about their date. However, for him the whole business of getting back into the matters of the heart—rather than the issues of the mind—had been laden with complications. Ever since he'd met Fiona he'd felt a tidal pull toward her—falling in love with total abandon. His life was starting to come together. The old demons were gone. His law practice—which he'd constantly questioned—was undeniably successful.

Nonetheless, his relationship with Fiona kept running into quagmires—sinking under the weight of his problems with relationships or her seeming impatience with the slow growth in his spiritual faith. *Tonight,* he thought to himself, *we're going to communicate. Really communicate. We need to move things to a deeper level. After all, I want to marry this woman. This is going to work—I've got to make sure of that.*

5

ON THE NINTH FLOOR of the International News Network building—the tall glass tower that was its headquarters in Atlanta—Crystal Banes, host of prime-time television's *Inside Source,* was holding court.

In the small conference room she was swiveling slightly back and forth in her red leather chair, bobbing her foot. Fortyish, with a blond "Prince Valiant" cut, she was attractive in a hard-featured way, but she had a habit of curling her lip from a smile into a smirk, ever so subtly.

Around a small table that was strewn with newspapers, magazines, faxes, a few government bulletins, half-empty coffee cups, and press releases, her team was gathered. Her producer, assistant producer, chief writer, and regular camera man were all there, busy taking notes—all except the camera guy, a man in his late twenties whose flat-top hair was dyed a little on the orange side: He was giving a blank stare out the window.

"Come on people, let's go," she chided. "Ideas. I want ideas."

"There's always the parking permit scandal with that congressman..." the assistant producer chirped out.

"Please," Banes groaned, "don't give me that."

"How about doing something on Max Mulligan, the radio talk-show host from Baton Rouge with ties to the KKK?" the writer said.

"Legal department says we'd get creamed on that one," the producer shot out.

There was silence.

Then the camera guy, who was still looking out the window, spoke up. "How about that lady who's on the run from the cops with her little boy? Child-abuse charges. The kid is being poisoned, supposedly. The husband is in jail, saying this whole thing is a travesty—we're innocent, blah, blah—the police can't find her. She's still out there with the kid, out there in the wild blue yonder."

"Where'd you hear this?" the producer asked.

"On the news. *Our* news. On *our* network. *Duh…*" he said with a laugh.

"Don't talk to me that way," the producer shot back. "I consider that harassment. And camera guys are a dime a dozen."

"Let's all just stand down," Banes said with an air of superiority. "Actually, I think Spike may have something."

"Crystal, these criminal cases take a long time to develop. We don't know which way this case is going to turn," the producer said.

"I'm not thinking of this as a criminal case—not exactly," Banes said. "That would not be the real hook. The hook would be…" And with that she paused a minute to think about it.

"The hook," she continued, "would be to *locate* this mother who's on the run. To get to her *before* the cops get to her. *Talk about a scoop!*"

"What if she doesn't want to talk?" the writer asked.

"Hey, give me a break. Everybody wants their fifteen minutes—especially on *Inside Source*," Banes said. "Besides, who says that we need to get her permission to find her? Let's track her down. Get the scoop. Stick a camera in her face before the authorities can even locate her."

"This is going to be expensive," the producer chimed in. "We may have to get some extra budget approval."

"Then do it," Banes said. "Go. Go. Whatever you have to do. I think I like this. I'm going to track down the *poison mom* on the run with her little baby boy. Spike, get your equipment ready. The rest of you talk to research immediately. I want background.

The names of the lawyers involved. They always want to blab if we promise them face time. Get names of relatives of the mom. Any leads on folks who may know other folks who just may know where she is."

As the crew started rising, Banes was still talking.

"I'm gonna locate this lady..." she said, glaring at the memo she held in her hand. It spelled out dismal news about the ratings of *Inside Source*. "Hey, little mommy," she said, seeming to address the air, "I'm coming to find *you!*"

6

FIONA CAMERON WAS SLOWLY rotating her water glass between her hands, clinking the ice slightly. Will could see that she was tired. In the candlelight of the corner table at Churchill's, their favorite restaurant, he saw the fatigue in her eyes, which were drooping. Her face, usually bright and electric with enthusiasm, was drawn—and a little pale.

"This concert tour really wore me out," Fiona said.

"You do look tired," Will responded. "Maybe it wasn't a good idea to take you out tonight."

"Oh, no," Fiona countered, brightening up. "I'm glad you did. The concerts went well. The Lord really blessed us. Wonderful crowds—receptive and warm."

There was a pause—and then she added, "I missed you."

"I missed you like crazy," Will said. "I kept telling myself that when you came off this tour you wouldn't have to travel for a while. Then we could start spending more time together."

Fiona looked down at the starched white tablecloth.

"Yes—before you went on tour my schedule was super heavy. That trial went on a week longer than any of us had planned. And, well…"

"And you missed the dinner we had scheduled…"

"I am so sorry," Will said, his voice dropping.

"In fact, you were supposed to take me out here."

"Which is why I brought you here tonight."

"Your apology is accepted," Fiona said, trying to smile again. "It's no big deal. I understand that your schedule gets harried when you're in trial. I guess the thing that hurt the most was having to leave on tour without so much as a goodbye from you."

"Look," Will said, reaching over and taking both of her hands in his, "this is an important stage for us. I feel that. I hope you do too. You are incredibly busy. And so am I. But somehow we need to find a way to cut through the busyness. To focus on the really important things. You and me. Us. Where we are going in our relationship."

Will paused for a second, and then he added, "Fiona, I don't want to lose you. More than anything in the world, I want you in my life."

He was going to add something else, but as he gathered the words, the waitress came over to the table and refilled their glasses. Will pulled his hands back.

"How are we doing?" the waitress asked. "Can I get you anything else?"

After smiling and waving her off, Will tried to recoup. But before he could, Fiona spoke up.

"There's something I need to tell you."

The look on Will's face must have been obvious because she quickly added, "Oh—it's nothing really that big. Just more of the same scheduling demons coming out…My recording company contacted me on the road," she continued. "They reminded me that I need to finish the studio time on that CD."

"What's the deadline?"

"They want me to go to their studio—either the one in New York or the one down in Nashville. I think I'll go to Nashville. Anyway, it needs to be done right away."

"You're kidding!" Will exclaimed. "Tell them to back off. You're exhausted! You want me to call them?"

Fiona laughed. "Whoa. Will—it's okay. I'll tell them I need a couple of days of down time first."

"How long will you be gone?"

"Probably a couple of weeks," she said hesitantly.

She could see the disappointment in Will's face and quickly added, "Will, I don't want to be separated any more than you do." Then after a few seconds of awkward silence she changed the subject.

"Tell me about you. Any new cases?"

"I already told you about the Sudan case with the murdered missionaries. I'm starting to dig in on that one." Then Will added as an afterthought, "I turned down a child-abuse case. Never got much about the details. I told the parent I couldn't take it because my plate is pretty full right now."

Fiona's eyebrow arched slightly. And then, after a moment, she spoke. "Where did you say that child abuse case was?"

"Well, the case is pending in Georgia. Why?"

"Oh, just something I'd been thinking," Fiona replied, her voice trailing off slightly.

"What is it?"

"It's just that—if you'd have taken the case—that would have been typical, I guess."

"Typical of what?" Will asked, starting to feel irritated.

"I know something about your law practice from when you handled my father's case. The trials you're involved in take you all over the country—sometimes to different parts of the world. They're very demanding, I know. So, I guess I've just been thinking…"

"Fiona, I'm not following you."

"Will," Fiona said after hesitating, "when we met…we weren't exactly young kids in college. I was pretty established in my music ministry. And you had been practicing law for a lot of years. People develop routines—they develop whole lives living by themselves. And then when it's time for a relationship…It's just that I want to know that I'm valued. That you look at our relationship as something more than just a bachelor's life but now with a woman that you go out with regularly. In a relationship, the way I see it, one and one don't make two. One and one make *one*. And every so often I get the feeling—maybe it's unfair of me to say this—that you're not making a lot of accommodations in your career, and your life, for *us*."

Will, stung by that comment, sat up straight in his chair and leaned forward slightly.

"There's something I just don't see here," Will said. "I tell you about a case I'm *not* taking—a case that happens to be in Georgia. And then you use that as a basis for talking about how I haven't made any accommodations in my life. I told you I didn't take the case because I've got too much on my plate. Doesn't that mean that I'm trying to create a place for us?"

"No," Fiona said bluntly. "I heard you saying that you couldn't quite fit it into your schedule, not that you had me in mind when you made the decision. Not that you should think about me every time a new client walks in the door—what I'm talking about is not the details of this case. I'm talking about our relationship. I just want to make sure that you're making a place for *us*. That you're willing to make sacrifices and adjustments in your life."

"Sacrifices?" Will asked, his voice rising. "While we're on that subject, how about your recording session, which is going to take you out of state? And it's going to separate us—at a time when I thought we would really be able to start spending some time together. I'd never heard about this until you just dropped it on me, just now."

"Will," Fiona said, her voice filled with distress, "I told you about this recording session weeks ago. Don't you remember?"

Will shook his head with some embarrassment and shrugged.

Fiona managed a half-smile and reached out to touch his hand. "Will," she said, "I want this to work just like you do. It's just going to take a lot of sacrifice—and a lot of adjustment. And it's going to take some change. Just like when you came to Christ. There's still a lot of change that has to take place there also."

Will bristled. "So you're saying that I'm spiritually immature because my conversion came later in life than yours?"

"I didn't say that."

"But I think that's what you meant," Will replied.

Fiona was still holding his hand, and she squeezed it. "Will, darling, listen to me. God is doing great things in your life. I look at you—and I see nothing but a miracle. Please believe me when I say that."

After a moment, Will looked up and smiled.

Then Fiona remembered something. "Oh, I almost forgot," she said, reaching into her purse and pulling out a piece of paper. "You wanted me to make sure to remind you of the date we were arranging for the dinner at church for my dad—on the anniversary of Mom's death. We're scheduling a luncheon at the church, and here's the reminder."

She passed the note over to Will, and as he glanced at the date and time, his countenance fell.

"What's wrong?" Fiona asked.

"Well…I think I've got a problem with this date," Will said hesitatingly.

"I mentioned this date to *you* before I started making plans to set it up," Fiona said, her eyes full of hurt.

"Well, if you did, I don't remember it," Will said. "I don't have my calendar with me—but I'm absolutely certain this is the date that we've set up an all-day meeting between the State Department and the families of all those missionaries we're representing in our case against Sudan. It's taken us months to set that up. We've got people flying in from all over the country. A few people are even coming in from overseas." Will leaned his head on his hands. "Man, this is a disaster."

Fiona simply closed her eyes and shook her head.

The waitress appeared again.

"Any dessert?" she with a professionally cheery demeanor. "Mud pie is delicious. Berries and cream? We have a chef's specialty—"

"How about the check?" Will snapped.

After the waitress was gone, Will looked across the table. Fiona's eyes were filled with tears. She was resting her head on her hand, and her lip was quivering a bit.

"I think I'm just overtired. Would you please take me home?" she asked.

Will nodded. He searched for something to say. But not finding the words, he turned in silence to watch the waitress hustling over to the table, bill in hand.

Inside, he was trying to ignore it—the pull of the swirling whirlpool, sucking the two of them down. Into the unspoken vagaries of miscommunication and broken trust, into the carefully plotted romantic plans that always seemed to go awry. Down into the ocean graveyard of drowned intentions. To the sandy bottom, where the failures of love rest in the dark, like some rusting vessel.

7

JUDA COUNTY PROSECUTOR Harry Putnam was pacing back and forth behind his desk, his short, stocky frame occasionally bouncing on the balls of his feet to punctuate a point as he lectured the small circle of county staff assembled in his office.

"One—we still don't have our hands on Mary Sue Fellows or little Joshua. Two—we've got a hearing coming up in Joe Fellows' case at the end of this week. Three—like I said, we still haven't located the Fellows woman or her kid. Are you all starting to see a pattern in my comments this morning?"

Putnam stared at Otis Tracher, the tall, thin plainclothes detective with a bland expression and an unruly tuft of hair that seemed to defy combing. Tracher sat up a little straighter and volunteered a thought.

"I know that finding the perpetrator and her victim is the number-one priority here," the detective said. "I've got two other officers working this in addition to myself."

"I am not happy," Putnam snapped out, bouncing up with the last word. "In fact, I am very unhappy. I asked you to tail the Indian—"

"Harry, we did. The Indian didn't take the flight."

"And why not?"

"Maybe someone tipped him off. All I know is that when that plane landed in Albuquerque, he wasn't on the flight," Tracher explained.

"Where does that leave us?"

"Wherever he came from, he returned by another route."

"He disappeared?"

"Yeah."

"Like magic?" Putnam rapped out sarcastically.

"We're going to get him. Just a matter of time," said the detective in a voice that struggled to carry conviction.

"Let me remind you," Putnam continued, "that it really isn't about the Indian. It's the Fellows woman and the kid I want. The Indian is just one clue."

"I've got the PD out there in his hometown in New Mexico checking with the community college where he teaches. Talking to his neighbors. We're running all the leads. We'll get a bead on where the guy is."

"When are you going to be finished interviewing all of Mary Sue's relatives about her whereabouts?"

"Maybe a couple days."

"That brings me to point number two," Putnam said. "Joe Fellows' bail hearing is coming up at the end of the week. I'm not sure what the defendant is doing about an attorney, but the judge is going to make a decision about bail. I need *you* there at the hearing"—and with that, Putnam pointed at Liz Luden, the social worker.

"I've got it in my calendar."

"You've got to really spread on the ghoulish stuff. We're fighting bail because the mommy is still out there with the kid. Daddy isn't stepping up to the plate to tell us where the kid is so we can save him from his abusive mother. Liz, you've got to be able to hammer the stuff we talked about so we can keep Joe in jail till he breaks and tells us where they are."

"Right," she said. "We've got the medical information."

"Yeah—that's dynamite. But I don't want too much out of the bag. Just enough to let the judge know that we've got absolute medical proof that she's been slipping the kid brake fluid instead of orange juice."

The social worker continued. "I've also got some policy ammunition we can use at the hearing." She turned to the young intern sitting next to her and motioned for the notebook on her lap. The intern quickly handed it over to her supervisor.

"Thanks, Julie," Luden said while she was turning to a page she had marked with a yellow sticky note.

"Here it is. Part IV of my CRAM—"

"Your *what?*" Putnam blurted out with arched eyebrows.

"CRAM. Child Risk Assessment Manual," Luden explained. "It lists standard risk-assessment modalities for evaluating children suspected of being neglected or abused. Or their families. Risk factor seven says the index of suspicion rises with 'parents who hold rigid, authoritarian religious beliefs. Be on the lookout for absolutist child-rearing strategies that are potentially harmful—such as corporal and physical punishment, spanking, or verbal abuse cloaked in religious language.'"

"So?" Putnam asked.

"This Fellows woman is rigidly religious," the social worker continued. "Fundamentalist. Bible-this and Bible-that type. The medical records from her primary health-care provider indicate that she made statements that God is the ultimate healer—or something like that—and she believes in spanking and does use that form of discipline on Joshua. I think we can argue that she meets the criteria for a heightened risk of being a child-abuser."

"No," Putnam said slowly, squinting his eyes as he paced, "let's leave that one alone right now. Play that one close to the vest. That courtroom may have reporters crawling all over the place. I don't want any of these civil-liberties types to say we are antireligious down here in Delphi, Georgia. After all, we are all good, God-fearing, churchgoing folks."

Luden nodded with a smile.

"We'll wait till some of the medical evidence starts coming out—when people start seeing that she must be some kind of monster. That's when we start talking about her being a Bible-banging psycho."

Putnam leaned over his desk, giving his final command. "Let's get this woman, take her and her husband to trial—and then let's get a double conviction."

He straightened up and added a final thought. "No reason why we can't wrap this whole case up by Christmas. No, sir. No reason at all."

8

Hilda poked her head into Will's office. "Want some coffee?"

Will looked up from the papers on his desk. "Sure."

"How'd it go last night?"

There was a pause before Will replied.

"I take mine black."

"Uh-oh. That bad?" Hilda said.

"How long have you and Bruno been married?"

"Thirty-five years," she said, smiling.

"What's the secret?"

"He's a wonderful man. And I'm a very patient woman. And we both love each other." And then she added with a hearty laugh, "And also, he keeps loaded weapons away from me!"

Hilda turned to go, but then looked back and said, "Don't lose her, Will. I just love that gal. Fiona is one in a million. You just have to know what women want."

"I thought I knew."

"Women want you to stop acting like an expert on *what they are saying*—and want you to start listening to *how they are feeling*."

"That sounds a little mysterious."

"That's what makes us women so fascinating! Actually, I just read it in this great book—*Men Are Aliens—Women Are Earthlings.*"

As Hilda left, Will thought for a moment about what she'd said. But whatever it meant, he knew it was too late to salvage last night.

Before he could collect his thoughts, Jacki Johnson walked in and sat down across from his desk. "I took a call for you this morning from the State Department. One of their legal counsel contacted us before you got here. They wanted to talk about our plans to file suit in that Sudan case."

"What did they want?"

"Let me ask you this—how is your relationship with State nowadays?"

"As you know," Will said, "there was a time when we didn't exactly see eye-to-eye."

Jacki smiled. "Yeah, I remember."

"But that's another story. Presently we have a very good working relationship. Why?"

"They have a favor to ask."

"Oh, this ought to be interesting."

"They want us to hold off on filing suit—just for a while."

"What's the reason?"

"Apparently," Jacki explained, "the State Department is engaged in some very delicate negotiations. A couple of relief workers were recently kidnapped in Sudan, and they're trying to get them released. The captors are a fringe group doing their dirty work with the blessings of the Sudanese government."

"And they're afraid that any outside agitation—like our lawsuit against General Nuban—may rock the boat?"

"Exactly."

Will pondered the question for a moment.

"I have been thinking," he said, breaking the silence, "about the jurisdictional problem in this case. The only way to avoid a real cat-fight over jurisdiction is to get service of our Summons and Complaint on General Nuban personally."

"And doesn't he have to be tagged with service within the borders of the U.S.?" Jacki asked.

"He does, if we want to be absolutely certain about getting good jurisdiction."

"Where does that put us?" she asked.

"I think it means that buying some time now—before we file suit—might actually be to our advantage. We can figure out the jurisdictional quirks first. Work out the legal kinks about getting General Nuban served. Besides, I don't want to jeopardize the lives of those relief workers. I think I'll call the clients and let them know today."

"Oh, one other thing," Jacki added. "The State Department is going to have to cancel the meeting with you and the families of the missionaries. Which is probably a good thing."

"Why?" Will asked.

"Two of the families called the other day. They said they couldn't make the date that had been scheduled anyway."

After some reflection, Will's face brightened. "Yeah. That is a blessing."

"Oh?" Jacki asked. "What's up?"

"Well, I inadvertently set that meeting on a bad date," Will replied. "It was on the same day as the luncheon honoring Fiona's dad, Reverend MacCameron—which is also on the anniversary of the death of Fiona's mom. The whole church is turning out for it. A friend of the family is coming all the way from Scotland."

Jacki stared at Will. "Wow. You really hit the trifecta on that boo-boo."

"You talk like I'm not a caring guy. I am—right? I mean...I foul things up occasionally with Fiona, but it's never intentional."

"You really want me to answer that?"

"Sure—give it a shot."

"Well, like I told my hubby the other night—I said, 'Howard my love, I know you didn't forget our anniversary *intentionally*. On the other hand—*intent* is merely the difference between first-degree murder and second-degree murder.'"

Will tried to manage a smile as he pondered his associate's remark.

After Jacki left, Hilda swept in with a smile and a cup of coffee, placing the latter carefully on Will's desk.

"Oh, I could have gotten that," Will said. "Thanks, Hilda. Say, would you get the Gospel Missionary Alliance on the line for me? We've got a new development in the Sudan case."

"Anything I need to tell them when I get them on the phone?"

"I'll explain it to them. It looks like that case may have to go on the back burner for a while."

"I see," Hilda said with a smile. She stood looking at Will for a second, as if she knew something he didn't know.

"What's up? You look like the cat that swallowed the canary," Will said

"Do I?" Hilda remarked, a little too offhandedly. Then she hurried out of his office.

Within the hour Will connected with his clients' representative. Yes, they would certainly defer to the State Department's request and Will's recommendation. The filing of the lawsuit would be postponed for a while.

For the next two hours Will prepared for some upcoming depositions and went through the mail. It was getting close to lunch, and he was planning on running some errands in town. As he prepared to rise from his desk, his intercom lit up.

But there was no message on the video screen.

"Yes?"

"Will?"

"Yes?"

"This is Hilda."

"Yes, Hilda. I recognized the voice. Aren't you the same one who was kind enough to bring me coffee this morning? You're the same one who works about twenty feet from my office, right?"

Hilda giggled.

"What is it?"

"I've got a call for you."

"Yes?"

"Should I put it through, Will?"

"Hilda—who's calling?"

"You want to know who is on the line?"

"Yes, Hilda. Who wants to talk to me?"

"It's a woman."

Will brightened up. So Fiona had decided to call. She wanted to let Will know how much in love she was with him—how sorry she was that things got off to a bad start at dinner. She'd been thinking about the two of them—and she wanted to talk about fixing the situation between them. Will paused for a few moments. He finished playing out the scenario and grinned.

"Absolutely—put her through," Will said cheerily.

"Mr. Chambers?" said the woman at the other end.

"Yes," Will answered, surprised that it didn't sound like Fiona.

"This is Mary Sue Fellows."

"Who?"

"The woman who called you the other day. About the child-abuse case."

Will remained silent.

"Do you remember?"

"Yes...what can I do for you?"

"Mr. Chambers—I don't mean to be presumptuous. Really. But I need your help awfully bad. And I believe God has picked you to deliver me from the hand of those who are pursuing me."

After another silence, Mary Sue added, "I am just going to keep pestering you, I'm afraid. Just like the parable in the Bible about the widow pestering the judge for justice—I believe you are the man to bring about justice for me. This is the worst thing that has ever happened to me. To my family. Ever. The truth has to come out."

"I know we talked once before...and I told you I couldn't help you—"

"Yes. Your schedule was very busy, from what you said," Mary Sue interjected, "I remember that, but—"

"Something has come up," Will broke in. And then he added, "My schedule has opened up. Maybe you should tell me something about your case."

"Oh. Oh!" Mary Sue cried out. "Yes. Absolutely. The authorities are saying something about my trying to poison Josh—my little four-year-old. It is absolutely not true. I can't imagine ever doing something like that. It's unthinkable. Insane. Josh has had some medical problems…"

"What kind of problems?"

"We can't figure it out. I've taken him to the doctor multiple times. I was getting impatient. Dr. Wilson wasn't able to diagnose it. Josh was losing weight. Vomiting. Not eating well. I stopped following the doctor's orders because Josh looked like he was regressing. I insisted on a second opinion. That's when the doctor contacted Social Services."

"Child abuse is a serious charge. What do they base it on?"

"I have no idea," Mary Sue said, her voice rising.

"Where are you now?"

"I have to be honest with you, Mr. Chambers. I really don't know if I should tell you that. The police are looking for me and Josh. I was hoping you could get these charges dropped first. Then I'll come back."

"That may not be as easy as you think. Look, I want you to call me back in thirty minutes. I will put you on the speakerphone. Todd Furgeson, an associate attorney in the office, will also be with me. We will get a complete factual background from you then."

Mary Sue thanked him several times, said "God bless you!" excitedly, and then hung up.

Will walked into the lobby.

Hilda looked up from her computer with a sheepish smile.

"Did you know she would be calling this morning?" Will asked.

"I guess I did."

"So my own secretary is conspiring against me!"

"Will, I'm so glad you're going to help that poor woman!" Hilda exclaimed.

"Any other calls while I was on the phone?"

"No, Fiona didn't call."

"Why do I get the feeling you're getting way too far into my head?" Will said with a rueful chuckle.

Which got him to thinking about the child-abuse case in Georgia he'd just agreed to take on. *The Mary Sue Fellows case—* Will mused to himself—*I don't think I'll be rushing to tell Fiona about that one.*

9

WILL WAS WRAPPING UP his jail conference with Joe Fellows. He had been trying to reassure the young farmer, but he wasn't sure he was succeeding.

"Just so you understand—the fact that I will be representing Mary Sue, but not you, doesn't mean I believe you are guilty of anything—or that I believe her but not you. It simply means that there is a potential conflict of interest if I represent *both* of you at the same time. And if I get conflicted out of the case, then I can't represent either of you."

Joe nodded. "Yeah...I think I understand. Looks like I need a local lawyer of my own."

"Have anyone in mind?"

"I think my mom knows a guy here in Delphi," Joe said, mustering up a small measure of enthusiasm. "He's a good guy. Stanley Kennelworth. We'll get ahold of him. I'd best do that pretty quick so he can be with me at my bail hearing."

"Good. I'll be in touch with him too. I want this to be a team effort. I plan on working closely with him to coordinate a joint defense strategy."

Will wished Joe well and told him that he would do his best to make sure Mary Sue was well-represented. Then he left the jail and headed to the county prosecutor's office.

Harry Putnam was out for a long lunch, so Will told the secretary that he would be back to visit him shortly. He decided to spend the lunch hour investigating the local venue. He strolled through the old Juda County Courthouse, a brown-brick structure from the turn of the century—four stories high—rising up over the main street of Delphi. The marble floors were worn and smooth, and the ceilings were high, with painted murals. The sounds of footsteps and voices echoed up and down the hallways.

Outside the courthouse Will walked down Main Street. It was his custom to size up the demographics of every out-of-state community where he was going to try a case. What kind of agriculture supported the area? What were its industries? Did they vote Republican, Democrat, or Independent? Who were the founding families everybody knew?

He noticed some posters along the street for a city-council election. Some announcements for the local high school play. The Honorary President of the state Rotary Clubs—a handsome, prosperous-looking fellow who appeared to be in his thirties, named Jason Bell Purdy—had his name and picture on flyers in the store windows. He was inviting the townsfolk to the annual pancake breakfast and fundraiser for Project Child Care—"offering affordable day care for low-income families." Next to his name were the words "Delphi's Favorite Son."

Will also noticed a few for-sale signs and for-rent signs up and down the street. Most of them were listings of the Jason Bell Purdy Realty and Development Company.

A few blocks down, at the corner, there was a large Catholic church—St. Stephen the Martyr—with a sign outside listing Father Harold Godfrey as the rector. Beneath his name were the words "A Clear Conscience Lets in the Light." Across from the church was a Nickel, Dime & Dollar Store, on a cross street that bore the name "Stanfield Purdy Avenue."

As he walked back to the courthouse, Will decided that he was starting to get a good feel for the town.

By the time Will returned to the prosecutor's office, Harry Putnam was back from lunch. He greeted Will with a firm handshake and a hearty welcome.

"You're a bit outside of the Commonwealth of Virginia, Mr. Chambers. What brings you to our fair city of Delphi?" Putnam asked, leaning back in his desk chair.

"I've just been retained to represent Mary Sue Fellows."

"Well, that is very interesting. You licensed to practice here in Georgia?"

"No. I've got local counsel. I'm filing a motion for pro hac vice admission for her case," Will replied.

"Don't say. Then I've got a question for you."

"Fire away."

"If you represent her—you must have been in touch with her."

"That's right."

"Where is she, Mr. Chambers? Where is your client? We've got a warrant out for her."

"I really don't know."

"You don't know," Putnam repeated, nodding his head a little as he said the words. "Counselor, did you bother to ask your client that? Did you ask where she's got that little boy of hers hidden away—that little Joshua who is being poisoned by his mother?"

"Mr. Putnam, you know better than that," Will countered. "Even if I knew that, to disclose that conversation would be to violate attorney–client privilege."

Putnam's face was now twisted up, his eyebrows down low over his eyes, which were reduced to mere slits.

"Counselor, you may want to think about heading back to old Virginny. Otherwise, you'd better be ready for some old-fashioned bare-knuckle boxing here in Delphi. We're mighty serious about child abuse. I'm not about to let some outside counsel ride in here and tell me he's going to hide a fugitive from justice—while that fugitive is slowly killing her little boy. Not going to happen. Not here. Not with me. You read me?"

Will nodded, managed a smile, and rose to say goodbye. As he was leaving he turned and said, "I do read you, Mr. Putnam," squelching the temptation to add what he was already thinking—*I'm reading you like a fifty-cent comic book.*

10

Mary Sue Fellows had been at the ranch on the Sioux Indian reservation for only a few days. Yet she already felt a strange sense of belonging. The geography of the place gave her a feeling of shelter and safety. She would take Joshua out on walks through the canyons of the South Dakota Badlands. They would stop and gaze at the high plateaus of brown stone and tan earth that jutted up, surrounding them with sheer rock walls that towered up into the open sky.

At the end of the afternoon, as sunset was approaching, the shadows would begin creeping over the rock formations, casting strange shapes over the canyon walls where darkness was meeting the last light of the day. Along the high plateaus that were flat as tabletops, the rims would create iridescent slashes of brilliant orange and red as the fireball of the sun would illuminate a few streaks of clouds like painted horse's tails.

Though Mary Sue still felt the lonely desperation of her plight, she was also convinced that she had witnessed the hand of Divine Providence—like a guide that was going on before her.

When Mary Sue had accelerated away from their family farm in the truck that day, her mind had been racing. How could she and Joshua be safe as long as they remained in the state? Why not get out of Georgia—at least until she found out why two sheriff's squad cars and the case worker from Social Services had descended on their home with no warning? That was when Mary Sue settled on a plan—she would get to the airport and take the first flight to Iowa. She had an uncle there. She would ask to stay with him until she learned something from Joe. Mary Sue had never been close to her uncle, but now she was desperate.

But then, a few miles from the airport, her truck unexpectedly shuddered violently and started slowing down, and the oil light and the engine light went on. Mary Sue pulled over to the shoulder as smoke poured out of the front. She buried her face in her hands and cried out to God. Then, after wiping her face with her blouse sleeve, she leaped out of the truck, lifted the hood, and climbed back into the cab to figure out what to do.

That was when a dusty Suburban with South Dakota license plates pulled up behind her. There were three men in the front seat—all of them appeared to be American Indians. Mary Sue also saw a woman in the back seat.

She had a momentary sense of fear. But then one of the passengers walked up to the window with a broad smile. She instantly recognized the letters "WWJD" on his baseball hat as he began to introduce himself and ask how he could help.

Andrew White Arrow, along with one of his brothers—Tommy White Arrow—tinkered a bit with the engine. As they worked, the two of them seemed to be muttering together. Andrew smiled and appeared to be urging his brother to do something. Tommy, who was shorter and stockier than Andrew, was shaking his head "no" and glancing occasionally at Mary Sue, who stayed in the cab.

After a few minutes, the two came around to the side of the truck. Mary Sue rolled down her window.

"As best as we can see, this engine is shot—you may have thrown a piston," Andrew said. "Can we give you a lift? There has to be a gas station not too far from here."

Mary Sue shook her head. "Thanks anyway. I don't have time to get this fixed. I'm trying to make a flight at the airport."

Andrew's face brightened. "I'm headed there too. My flight doesn't leave till tomorrow—we could at least take you there. Which flight are you taking?"

Mary Sue looked away. "I'm not sure which flight."

"You're not sure what flight you're taking?" Tommy asked suspiciously from behind Andrew's tall frame. "Check your ticket. You have a ticket, right?"

"Not exactly," Mary Sue replied.

Tommy threw his hands up, said something in another language, and began walking away. Andrew told his brother to hold on. Then the tall Indian man turned to Mary Sue, looking her full in the face. "Are you are in some kind of trouble?"

She hesitated for a moment. But she had no choice now. Nothing short of complete trust would do.

"Yes," she said. "I'm in some kind of trouble with Social Services. Maybe the police. I don't know all of it. I just know that I have been wrongly treated. My child may be in jeopardy. I have to get out of the state before something terrible happens to my little boy. Before they take him away from me."

"How can we help?" Andrew asked.

"I don't know," she said. "Maybe you can't. All I know is that I called out to God in the middle of this disaster—and that's when you drove up."

"I'm a Christian," Andrew said. "I know God works like that—strangers coming from far away—being led to his children when they are in trouble."

Then Andrew stepped back from the truck window. He walked over to his brother and spoke with him for a while. Tommy seemed wary of Mary Sue. Whatever it was that was being said, he didn't seem to be persuaded.

Then Andrew gestured and seemed to be making another point. As he did, Tommy looked back at the truck, and his face softened. Finally, Andrew strode over to Mary Sue and said that Tommy and his brother Danny, who had been sitting in the back of the Suburban with their sister, Katherine, would be willing to take her to the family ranch in South Dakota. She could stay for a few days in an empty cabin they had there. Andrew added that

Katherine lived on the ranch with her husband, though Tommy, who owned the ranch, ran things.

Mary Sue hesitated, and she pursed her lips as she struggled with her decision.

"My brother Tommy is a good man—he's not a Christian, he follows the old Lakota religion—but he is a trustworthy man. I will pledge my life on that," Andrew said. "And I think you will like Katherine—and Danny too. But it's your decision."

Mary Sue finally agreed to go with them, though she still felt a healthy measure of caution.

They took Andrew to the motel across from the airport in Atlanta. He was scheduled to fly to Minneapolis the next day—he had left his car there after attending an educational conference. Since he was still on sabbatical from his small college in New Mexico, he planned on driving from Minneapolis to Tommy's place in South Dakota, where he would visit for a few weeks.

On the way to the airport, Andrew probed the background of Mary Sue's problems with Social Services. He listened intently, asking pointed questions that Mary Sue was quick to answer.

Suddenly Andrew remarked, "I heard on the radio, just before we saw your truck, that a farmer from some city—a city with an ancient-sounding name…oh, what was it—Delphi, that's it. The man was arrested for child abuse."

"Delphi?" Mary Sue said, her voice rising.

Andrew nodded quickly. "They said they were looking for the mother and a child."

"That's Joe. Father in heaven, they've arrested him," Mary Sue said, her eyes closed and her voice trembling.

Andrew suggested that perhaps he could give some encouragement to her husband. Perhaps he could visit Joe in jail—rent a car and drive over to Delphi—before his flight left.

Mary Sue approved—and asked Andrew to make sure to tell Joe that Joshua was fine, that she was in good spirits, and that she loved him. Then they dropped off Andrew at the Airliner Motel.

The drive to South Dakota was tense at first. Mary Sue tried to engage the group in conversation, as Joshua dozed off and on in his car seat. Gradually, after a few hours, she started feeling more at ease.

She learned that Andrew and Tommy and their sister, Katherine—a midwife with some nursing training—had come to Georgia to secure custody of Danny. Many years before, Danny had suffered a head injury on a construction site and had been left mildly brain-damaged. But for reasons that were too complicated for Mary Sue to understand, Andrew and Tommy had had to wage a several-year administrative battle to gain Danny's release from the state institution and into their care.

Because of their mutual nursing interests, Mary Sue was quick to relate to Katherine, whose warm, quiet voice and round pleasant face were set off by an infectious smile.

On the other hand, Tommy seemed angry—and he was fiercely protective of the political rights of his tribe and of the Native American religion that he practiced.

During the long ride to South Dakota, Tommy vented his anger in long diatribes about—among other things—General Custer, the breaking of treaties by the American government, the squalor on American reservations, discrimination against Indians in American movies, the failure of American Indians to coalesce into a strong political force, the massacre at Wounded Knee in 1890 and the uprising by Indian activists at that same site in 1973, and finally, his distrust of white police officers.

Mary Sue concluded that it was this last grievance that must have motivated him to help out an unknown woman and her sick child.

On the other hand, she found Danny to be a delightful person. His relaxed, smiling demeanor was a welcome contrast to Tommy's angry political speeches. Danny was fond of reading the highway signs, reciting them with glee. He also had a remarkable knack of hearing an advertising jingle on the radio only once and then repeating it in toto, complete with mimicked intonation—sometimes even songs. Clutching a crystal-blue yo-yo in his hand—which he played with expertly—he kept Joshua entertained for hours in the back seat of the Suburban.

《　　《　　《

That trip to South Dakota now seemed, not days, but years away. They had arrived at the ranch, and it hadn't taken Mary Sue and Joshua long to settle in.

Tommy's ranch consisted of several acres of horse enclosures and a few houses. The main lodge housed Tommy, his sister, Katherine, and her husband. There were two other smaller cabins fifty yards down the road. One was a guest cabin left open for visitors—mostly relatives of theirs. The other was Andrew's when he came to stay for a few weeks at a time.

The lodge and the two small cabins had been built by Andrew and Tommy by hand—fashioned from split logs that had been cleanly cut and varnished. The houses were on high ground, up from the floor of the canyons near them, so that during the occasional torrential rainstorms they were never in danger of being flooded.

Today, Mary Sue and Joshua were walking through the canyons.

As they strolled, Mary Sue mused on how she and Joshua had come to be there—and why. And she also thought about Joe, locked in a jail cell, alone and separated from her. When she thought of that, she had to struggle not to cry.

The October air had turned chilly, and Mary Sue closed up the neck of the thick red blanket jacket that she had been given by Katherine. Mary Sue's attachment to her had grown quickly. She loved her Indian name, "Walking Song," and she had, in just a few days, learned much about life on the reservation from her.

Mary Sue had even learned a few words in the Lakota tongue. The family, she was told, was of the Sioux *tunwan*—"nation."

Within that group, they were also of the *oyate,* or tribe, of the Lakota. And within that, they were also of the Oglala "band," or *tiyospaye.*

As she walked with Joshua, she stopped and pulled the strings tight on the hood of his snow jacket. The little coat was vinyl, with a torn sleeve and an elbow mended with a brown leather patch. Katherine had donated that too.

Mary Sue glanced at her watch. In a few minutes she would meet Katherine, who would drive her to the pay phone five miles down the highway next to a gas station. She wanted to call Will Chambers' office and check in with him. She knew there was a chance that Will might not have returned from Delphi yet, where he was going to interview Joe in jail. But she had to call. She needed the reassurance of being in touch, perhaps being able to find out even the smallest morsel of information about the criminal charges that had been filed against her and her husband.

Joshua was holding Mary Sue's hand and trying to kick the stones that littered the canyon with his small feet. He was even breaking into an occasional silly rhyming song. Mary Sue was happy because he'd gone an entire day without throwing up after eating. Yet she knew she would soon have to get him to a doctor and pursue a diagnosis for his mysterious medical condition.

But at that moment it was enough that she was safely out of reach of the authorities, that her little boy was happy, and that the two of them were hidden within the canyons of the Badlands.

Mary Sue and Joshua went back to the small guest cabin after their walk. She had given Joshua a very light breakfast, which he had been able to keep down. She thought she would wait to feed him lunch until after their trip to the phone booth.

After they'd waited only a few minutes, Katherine pulled up in her station wagon. They strapped Joshua into the car seat and headed down the long road that led to the highway. Katherine smiled at Mary Sue, but said little on the drive to the phone booth.

Deep in thought, Mary Sue was wondering what news Will Chambers' office might have. They pulled up to the phone booth, which stood alone along the highway at the corner of a small gas station with a lone pump. Next door was a small grocery store. Katherine pulled the car off the highway and parked in front of the gas station.

She turned to Mary Sue. "You make your phone call. Joshua and I will stay here in the car. I want to work on the new clapping game I've been teaching him."

With that, Joshua started clapping his hands furiously from the back seat and giggling. Mary Sue got out and walked over toward the phone booth, looking down the highway in both directions. No signs of traffic in either direction. She paused to feel the crisp breeze against her face and gazed out to the stark, rolling brown hills that stretched out to the horizon, broken only by a few pockets of dead vegetation and scrub.

After dialing Will Chambers' number, she heard Hilda's voice. Hilda explained that Will had not yet returned from Georgia where he was working on her case. She connected Mary Sue to the office of Jacki Johnson.

"Mary Sue, I am one of the other attorneys in Will's office," Jacki explained. "He has told me a little bit about your case. He was planning on talking to the prosecuting attorney after he talked to your husband. But he hasn't returned yet, though he did call back once to brief me on the case."

"Did Mr. Chambers tell you how Joe is doing?" Mary Sue asked.

"His spirits are high. He says he wants to fight this all the way—that he'd rather rot in jail then confess to something he didn't do, particularly when it comes to little Joshua."

"That's just like Joe," Mary Sue noted.

"There is one little technical glitch," Jacki went on.

"Glitch? What's the problem?" Mary Sue said, suddenly tense.

"Will decided that he can't represent both you and Joe at the same time. It presents a potential conflict of interest—and with everything else going on in your case, you don't want to invite that kind of problem. So Will decided that he is going to represent only you, and Joe is going to get his own lawyer."

"Oh—I don't feel good about that," Mary Sue responded. "Joe and I are together on this. I don't like being split up."

"I'm sure it won't be a problem. Will is used to working with other attorneys on a team basis. I'm sure he will help Joe get good local counsel—someone he can work with while still officially representing you."

"Has Mr. Chambers gotten to the bottom of this—why they are making such a crazy allegation against me? Saying that I am actually poisoning my son? Where are these lies coming from?"

"He's not sure yet," Jacki said. "As he works further on the case he'll get discovery from the prosecutor. I'm sure those questions will be answered at that time."

"And what about the court appearance later today?"

"Joe has his bail hearing this afternoon—possibly with his new attorney, whoever that happens to be. And at the same time, Will plans on entering an appearance in your case."

After a pause, Jacki added, "You know, Mary Sue, you are going to have to tell us where you are. And eventually you will have to give yourself up. The law is going to require it. I'm sure Will has talked to you about that—and if he hasn't, he probably will."

There was silence for a moment. "Miss Johnson?"

"Yes?"

"Are you married?"

"Yes, I am."

"Have you ever been a mother?"

"No, not yet. But I do look forward to that. Howard, my husband, and I would like to have a baby. Why?"

"Just wondering," Mary Sue said, looking over at the station wagon where Katherine was playing a patty-cake game with Joshua.

Then she continued. "Talk to me about turning my child over to Social Services when you've carried a baby under your heart for nine months. When you see him born—and nurse him when he's got a temperature of a hundred and three. When you're the last thing he sees at night and the first thing in the morning. After you hold your child when he is scared and kiss his tears away—then come to me. Then talk to me about what the law requires, Miss Johnson."

11

WILL WAS SITTING in the attorney's bench in a Delphi court-room—that of Judge Wilbur Mason. At the front, the bailiff was chatting with another court worker. Except for a couple in the back, no one else was in the room.

After glancing at his watch, Will looked around the court-room. In the back row there was a blond woman in her forties, well-dressed, who looked mildly familiar. Next to her was a younger man in a denim shirt, with hair that had an orangish tint to it. He had an MTV look about him.

It was now 1:15 P.M. The hearing in Mary Sue's case had been scheduled to start at 1:00.

Then the door to an anteroom opened, and a small flood of people entered the courtroom. In the lead was prosecutor Harry Putnam, striding quickly, file in hand. He was grinning.

The court reporter was next, lugging her stenographic equipment.

She was followed by a woman wearing a bland suit jacket and a pair of jeans, with a plastic tag dangling from her neck on a little chain. She was carrying a pile of papers. Will assumed she was a county worker—probably Liz Luden from Social Services.

Finally, a rumpled-looking woman in a pantsuit entered the courtroom. She had a briefcase and shouted a husky hello to the bailiff as she walked over to him. The two enjoyed a loud laugh about something until the judge entered in his robe, a thick file under his arm.

The courtroom fell silent as everyone rose.

"State of Georgia versus Mary Sue Fellows—child abuse— one count—everybody here?" the judge asked.

"Herodius Putnam, prosecutor, for the State."

"Harriet Bender, recently court-appointed to act as attorney ad litem for the child Joshua Fellows," the woman in the pantsuit barked out with enthusiasm.

"Liz Luden, Social Services, Your Honor."

Will Chambers moved forward to the empty counsel's table.

"Your Honor, Will Chambers, from the Commonwealth of Virginia. I have filed my motion for admission, pro hac vice. I am here, entering a special appearance on behalf of Mary Sue Fellows."

"Perhaps you could enlighten us," the judge asked with a smile, staring up at the ceiling, "what's so *special* about your appearance today, Mr. Chambers?"

Putnam and Harriet Bender laughed loudly. The bailiff and the court clerk were resisting the temptation to join in the mirth.

"The special appearance is to let the court know that we are objecting to jurisdiction over my client. A *general* appearance, Your Honor, would have waived any jurisdiction defects—"

But Will was interrupted by the judge. "Oh, now don't lecture me on the law of criminal jurisdiction, Mr. Chambers. Before we get down to the nitty-gritty legalities of the situation—you're asking this court to permit you to practice here in Georgia for purposes of this case?"

"That's right. I filed my motion for admission, which has been endorsed by Alexander Armstrong, former Chief Justice of the Georgia Supreme Court and presently the president of the Georgia Bar Association."

"I know who Mr. Armstrong is, counselor. He and I just had dinner together at the state bar meeting not three weeks ago," the judge said. "So let's not get off on that." He paused for a few seconds, eyeing Will.

The judge turned to the other two lawyers.

"Any objections to Mr. Chambers' motion?"

"No objection," Harry Putnam snapped out, then sat down.

"Ms. Bender?"

Harriet Bender rose slowly.

"As guardian ad litem for the minor child, I take no position on Mr. Chambers being admitted. However, if I get a whiff of any funny business from out-of-state counsel that interferes with the best interests of my client—Joshua Fellows—I will be back in this courtroom in a heartbeat. And Mr. Chambers," and with that she turned to face Will, "this court knows that I will tolerate no attorney who takes any action that impedes my representation of my children."

The judge smiled. "Mr. Chambers, Ms. Bender is one of our best attorneys ad litem for minor children. This court knows well how she represents them with the kind of zeal that a mother bear would show for her little cubs."

Will decided not to comment on that metaphor, and he nodded politely. Though he couldn't help thinking that the part of the mother bear had already been cast in this drama—and Mary Sue Fellows was the one playing it.

"On the criminal case number 04-CR-169, Mr. Chambers, is your client here?"

"No, Your Honor."

"Why not?"

"To divulge that would be to reveal attorney–client confidences—which my client has not authorized me to do."

The judge tapped both hands on the bench like he was playing a bongo drum. When he finished he addressed Will again.

"Do you know where she and little Joshua are?"

"I can candidly say that I don't know where they are. But even if I did, I would probably not be able to reveal that based on my ethical duty to preserve client confidences—"

"You seem to be singing the same song again, Mr. Chambers. I'm hearing a broken record. If this isn't live—then it must be Memorex..."

Putnam and Bender were chuckling.

"Let's hear something new," the judge said impatiently. "Like this—when can this court expect Ms. Fellows to be *present with you* in court so we can take a plea—and proceed with this criminal case?"

"I'm not sure, Your Honor. If Mr. Putnam would see clear to dismiss these charges—or at least file a nolle prosequi—I am fairly confident that I could produce Mary Sue Fellows, and the prosecution and I could then discuss getting to the truth—"

Putnam jumped up, his arms flailing.

"The State of Georgia will not be dismissing these charges, Your Honor. As the court knows from the ex parte hearing we held in closed chambers before opposing counsel got here, this is a very serious case. You will recall the substantial evidence of child abuse that we have already presented."

"Ex parte hearing?" Will asked incredulously.

"Yes," the judge said, "our code does permit that. Section 9-27-315 specifically authorizes an emergency hearing without attendance by the parent or her counsel—and even without notice to them—in order to transfer custody of the child—"

"Your Honor," Will said, "section 328 in that same code chapter requires a finding by the court, based on an *emergency* situation, that the health and safety of the child have made such a drastic hearing—in the absence of the presence of the attorney—absolutely necessary—"

"I've been satisfied by the evidence. In fact, I'm more than satisfied that Mary Sue Fellows has got some mental issues—at least according to the evidence I've seen. And *my land*, Mr. Chambers—giving her little boy hydraulic brake fluid to drink—do you think that's *not* a danger to health and safety..."

But before Will could respond to what was apparently just a rhetorical question, the judge continued.

"The code has been satisfied. I have, today, entered an order transferring custody of Joshua Fellows to the care of the

Department of Social Services. Ms. Luden, have you secured a proper foster home for the child?"

Luden nodded.

"Now, all we need is the mother and the child. The criminal case cannot proceed without Ms. Fellows appearing personally to enter her plea and submit to the jurisdiction of this court. Instead, Mr. Chambers, this court is proceeding on the civil case—on the petition filed by Juda County for a permanent transfer of custody of Joshua out of the care of Ms. Fellows—the basis is child abuse. Because that action is civil—not criminal—we can proceed without Ms. Fellows' personal appearance."

"I don't have a copy of that petition," Will noted.

Putnam tossed a stapled packet of papers onto the counsel table in front of Will.

Will glanced at it and then addressed the court.

"We enter a denial to these allegations."

"Noted," the judge said casually. "The court clerk will be advising you all—when you come up to the bench after the hearing—of the date for the adjudication hearing on the issue of child abuse as grounds for transfer of custody."

"Your Honor," Will said.

"Yes?"

"The ten-day Georgia law hearing."

"What about it?"

"Under section 19-13-3, subparagraph (c), 1, we have a right to a hearing within ten days to challenge this court's ex parte order transferring custody."

"Fine. You'll get your hearing."

"When?"

"Right now, Mr. Chambers. Go ahead and argue. Persuade me that what I did fifteen minutes ago in my office was legally incorrect."

"I've had no time to prepare for that argument," Will countered. "I've just received the petition."

"It's all in there, Your Honor," Putnam said, joining in. "The affidavits. Everything. Mr. Chambers should be able to respond to that right now."

Will grabbed the packet of papers and flipped to the back. There was an affidavit from Dr. Wilson, the family's doctor. He had written that Mary Sue had impeded his proper treatment of Joshua, disregarding his advice. That she had become belligerent when he inquired about Joshua's medical history and her feeding schedule. And further, that he had personally reviewed the medical records from the hospital, where he had submitted Joshua to blood tests. Those test results, he concluded, had noted the presence of ethylene glycol—the main ingredient in hydraulic brake fluid—in Joshua's blood. Any further ingestion of that chemical could be fatal to Joshua.

A second affidavit was signed by Detective Otis Tracher. The detective indicated that after the arrival of the sheriff's deputies— and the arrest of Joe Fellows—he and a member of the evidence team had swept the kitchen for evidence. They had taken samples from the kitchen counter and had seized a child's drinking cup. The state crime lab results all indicated that there was hydraulic brake fluid on the kitchen counters and—most importantly—*on the child's cup.*

Of the final two affidavits, the first was from Liz Luden, Department of Social Services. It indicated that an anonymous caller had reported that Mary Sue Fellows was poisoning her son with hydraulic brake fluid. The second was from Dr. Parker, a local pathologist, who had performed the test on Joshua's blood that verified the poisoning.

"This evidence is complex and technical in nature," Will said after reviewing the documents. "I need time to secure expert witnesses to rebut this."

"Not here you don't. This is only a ten-day probable-cause hearing. Save that for trial."

"Your Honor, this is all hearsay evidence—"

"Which our code *permits* in an *emergency* hearing," the judge emphatically noted. "Read it yourself."

"I have," Will said. "That applies to emergency ex parte hearings—like the kind that you held in my absence earlier today— *but it does not apply to the ten-day probable-cause hearing.*"

"Well," the judge said, leaning back, "that's what makes a good lawsuit. Differences of opinion. You can appeal that if you want—at the end of this case. Your objection is noted. This court affirms its prior ex parte order in this case."

"But Your Honor," Will added, "the county's entire case rests on expert-opinion evidence. But there is no evidence of the qualifications of the experts in these affidavits."

Putnam was preparing to jump in, but the judge responded first. "I'm taking judicial notice that each of the folks in these affidavits is an expert. What else you got?"

That is when Harriet Bender rose to her feet.

"We want Mr. Chambers to be ordered to either produce the child or inform this court—as well as my office—where Ms. Fellows is hiding *my client* Joshua Fellows."

"I have serious objections to that—" Will began to counter.

"I'm sure you do, Mr. Chambers. Now, here is what I am going to do," the judge continued. "Mr. Chambers, you will have a period of time to either produce the child or find out from your client where the child is located." Then the judge looked to Putnam.

"How long do you want, Harry?"

"Well, maybe seventy-two hours," Putnam replied.

Bender stood up and rapped out, "*Twenty-four hours*, Your Honor. No longer than that. This little boy is fighting for his life."

Before Will could respond the judge leaned forward and ruled.

"Here's what I'm going to do. I'm a fair man. Mr. Chambers, you've got five days. Five days. Either the boy, or his exact whereabouts—so our law enforcement folks can pick him up and place him in the safety of a good foster home."

Will clenched his jaw and nodded silently.

"I want your verbal acknowledgment to that—*on the record,* Mr. Chambers," the judge demanded.

The purpose of that was clear to Will. The court was preparing the way to find him in contempt if he failed to comply.

"Do you fully understand each of the things I have ordered you to do today?"

"Yes," Will said.

"Do you have any questions for the court at this time?" the judge added in a formal tone.

"Yes," Will said. "I do have one. But I think I'll save it—I'll save that question for the trial on the merits, Your Honor."

The judge gave him a quizzical look. Then he gaveled the court hearing to adjournment.

Harry Putnam scooted over to Will and held out his hand.

After Will shook it, Harry gave him a parting shot.

"Welcome to the fine city of Delphi, Mr. Chambers."

12

After Judge Mason had adjourned the court for a short recess, Will grabbed his briefcase and turned around, surprised that the courtroom had filled up during his brief hearing on Mary Sue's case. Reporters flocked to Harry Putnam for comments. Two of them asked for Will's card while dashing toward the prosecutor for a quote.

In the back of the room, Crystal Banes and Spike, her cameraman, hung back. Banes quickly approached Will and introduced herself.

"Mr. Chambers, I'm Crystal Banes, host of *Inside Source*. I'm letting these local reporters have a crack at the prosecution. Frankly, Mr. Putnam does not interest me. I know where the *real* news is, and that's why I'm talking to you."

"And what news is that?" Will asked.

"You are in touch with Mary Sue Fellows on a continual basis, I would imagine," Banes said.

Will did not respond. He studied Banes intently.

"Mary Sue Fellows has got to be in a really tough situation. This poor mother and her sick child, scared to death, on the run—what a tragedy," Banes pointed out.

But Will did not take the bait. The TV host tried another approach.

"You mentioned in court the possibility of Harry Putnam dismissing the charges or…what was the phrase you used?"

"You mean 'nolle prosequi'?"

"Yeah, what's that?"

70

"That is when the prosecution voluntarily withdraws the charges before the criminal case has really begun."

"Well, let's assume Putnam should change his mind and decide to withdraw the charges—at least temporarily. How quickly could you really get Mary Fellows back here to Delphi?"

"In other words," Will responded, "you want to know how close, or how far away, Mary Sue is from Delphi right now?"

Crystal Banes eased into a crooked little smile and tilted her head in anticipation.

"As I said before the judge, I do not know where Mary Fellows is. But even if I did, my client would probably not authorize me to release that information."

Banes straightened up, her expression changing quickly.

"Mr. Chambers, would you like to step out into the hall? I would love to get a statement from you on camera."

Out in the hallway, Spike slung his shoulder-mounted camera quickly into position, and with a click, the floodlight washed Will's face. Banes jumped in.

"Will Chambers, defense attorney for Mary Sue Fellows—a fugitive from justice—you suffered a series of setbacks in court today. Judge Wilbur Mason overruled your objections to his order transferring custody of the little child, Joshua Fellows. He appeared persuaded by the evidence the prosecution had presented in the closed hearing—and he flatly overruled your objections based on attorney–client confidentiality by ordering you to either produce Mary Sue Fellows or tell the court where she is. Are you discouraged by so many defeats in such a short period of time?"

"I am wondering if you or I could imagine, Ms. Banes," Will said calmly, " what it would be like for a mother to be wrongfully accused of poisoning her own child, a child she loves, protects, and for whom she would lay down her life. I wonder what that would feel like. You and I probably have no idea what turmoil that would create for a loving mother."

"And are you going to obey the court order issued by Judge Mason today?" Banes interjected. "Are you going to tell the court where Mary Sue Fellows is? Are you going to produce her to the authorities?"

"I'm going to do my job, which is to zealously defend my client against these unjust charges. I plan on doing my job—just like you will undoubtedly do yours."

"Oh yes," Banes responded, "You can bet I'll do my job, Mr. Chambers. You can take that to the bank."

By the time Banes had made her last statement the floodlight had clicked off, and Spike was already packing up his camera equipment. Banes quickly scurried into the courtroom and elbowed her way to the front, through the reporters, where she introduced herself to Harry Putnam.

Will took a seat in the back of the courtroom and waited for court to convene.

A few minutes later, Judge Mason entered and called Joe Fellows' case. Joe was led in from a side door. He was in his jail suit, handcuffed and manacled with ankle chains. Next to him was attorney Stanley Kennelworth, a diminutive man in an orange plaid sport coat that clashed with his red golf pants, which he was wearing though golfing season, even in Georgia, had long since passed. He had slightly receding hair and wore black horn-rimmed glasses.

Joe Fellows shuffled up to the front of the courtroom in front of Judge Mason. Next to Joe, Stanley Kennelworth was struggling to pull his file out of his briefcase.

"Appearing on behalf of defendant Joseph Fellows, Your Honor," Kennelworth stated.

"We're here on a bail motion by defendant for release from custody pending trial—and also on the motion of the prosecution to withhold bail release until defendant meets certain conditions," Judge Mason said.

"That's right." Harry Putnam popped up to his feet. "But the prosecution and defense counsel have conferred, and we think we've got the bail issue resolved."

"That's wonderful," said Judge Mason with a wide smile.

Putnam glanced at his legal pad for a few seconds, and then he spoke. "Your Honor, defense counsel, Stanley Kennelworth, has agreed that the defendant can be released as soon as Mary Sue Fellows is presented, along with little Joshua, to the authorities—or as soon as defendant advises us of her whereabouts, whichever comes sooner," Putnam explained.

Joe Fellows whirled around to face Kennelworth, who was by then nervously peering down at some papers in his hand. Joe had a look of utter amazement.

"Your Honor," Joe blurted out, "I'm *not* going along with this deal. I do not know what Mr. Putnam is talking about...or my own lawyer, for that matter."

"Mr. Fellows," the judge said sternly, "as long as you've got counsel with you, you will not address this court—unless it is to answer a question that *I* pose to *you*. Your lawyer is going to do the talking, not you."

The judge then turned to address Kennelworth.

"Stanley, I'll count on you to make sure your client understands that release on bail is being denied until such time as he reveals *everything* he knows about the whereabouts of Mary Sue Fellows, his wife, and his child, little Joshua."

Kennelworth nodded somberly. Next to him, Joe shook his head in bewilderment.

Then the judge added, "Stanley, the court is expecting you to advise your client accordingly. And we are anticipating that he is going to play ball and abide by the court's decision in this case—and help us locate little Joshua so that his life can be protected."

"I certainly will," Kennelworth responded. "I will be continuing to discuss this matter with Mr. Fellows. He certainly doesn't want to jeopardize the health or welfare of his child."

Two deputies escorted Joe Fellows away from the bench. But before departing the courtroom, Joe turned and gave one last furtive and desperate look to Will. And then the side door was opened, and Joe, along with the two deputies, disappeared into the jail corridor beyond.

Will was stunned. He had probably seen a *more* lackluster defense of a client at some other time in his career, but no examples came to mind.

Stanley Kennelworth had been recommended by a farmer who, along with Joe was a member of the local agricultural co-op. Kennelworth had handled a traffic ticket for him. When he'd heard that Joe might be retaining him, Will had followed up with a short phone call from his motel room and talked to Kennelworth personally.

Kennelworth had seemed friendly, cooperative, and enthusiastic about defending Joe. But Will had no way, on such short notice, of verifying his competence to handle such an unusual case. Now, after the court hearing, Will was feeling somehow responsible for Joe's substandard defense.

One thing was very clear to Will—Stanley Kennelworth was offering no resistance on behalf of his client to the prosecution steamroller. And Kennelworth himself was lying down like a road happily preparing to get tarred.

Most of the reporters were quickly exiting the courtroom as Will pressed his way up to the front. When Kennelworth finished packing up his briefcase and turned, his eyes widened at the look on Will's face.

Will stared him in the eye. "Stanley, I've got some case law I could send over to your office on this bail issue. I would strongly suggest that you take a look at it, consider asking the court to allow you to withdraw your stipulation, and get the court to vacate its bail condition that requires Joe to divulge the whereabouts of his wife and child."

"Oh, thanks anyway," Kennelworth replied meekly. "But I've got my own strategy that I'm pursuing here."

"And what strategy would that be?" Will pressed. "Changing Joe Fellows' permanent address to the Juda County jail?"

Kennelworth adjusted his glasses nervously and groped in vain for a response.

"Look," Will continued, "I didn't mean to come at you like that—but I do believe that you have some strong arguments that you can use, constitutional and otherwise, to get his release on bail without requiring him to locate his missing wife and child. In fact, I think I remember a Supreme Court case a few years ago—"

"I think I'd better handle my case myself," Kennelworth said, summoning his fortitude, "and you'd better handle yours."

With that, Kennelworth grabbed his briefcase and sprinted over to a local newspaper reporter who was about to leave the courtroom. He smiled and handed the reporter one of his cards, then quickly exited into the hallway.

It was clear to Will that Kennelworth's performance in the case would be a problem not only for Joe, but for Mary Sue's case as well. Will had hoped to forge a strong defense alliance with Joe's counsel. But that possibility was evaporating. It appeared that Joe would have to overcome not only Judge Mason, prosecutor Harry Putnam, and guardian ad litem Harriet "mother bear" Bender—but now, Stanley Kennelworth as well.

13

WHEN WILL RETURNED to his motel room, it was late afternoon. Before he headed out for some dinner, he wanted to make a few calls.

The first telephone call, of course, was to Fiona. She picked up her cell phone on the second ring.

"Hey, beautiful!" Will said, greeting her with an optimism that was designed to ignore how their last, dismal dinner had ended.

"Hi, Will," Fiona replied, a little too cool for his comfort.

"What's wrong?"

"Nothing. How are you?"

"Wait a minute," Will pressed in. "Something's bothering you."

"Will, look at your watch."

"It's five-thirty in the afternoon."

"Remember I left a message on your voice mail—telling you the only time we would have a break, all day, was at two o'clock? And you called me back as you were heading down to Georgia, agreeing on that."

"I couldn't call. I was tied up in court."

"Then you should have called me and just left a message saying you couldn't touch base. As it was, I was sitting here for half an hour with my cell phone in my hand, waiting for your call.

"We made a point of agreeing to connect with each other at two. Will, are we ever going to start getting serious about putting the other person first?"

"Being two relatively intelligent people," Will said, groping for a balm for the hurtful moment, "I think we just can sit down and work out a way to stay in touch. Fiona, I'm sorry. Maybe I should have left you a message saying I couldn't call when I thought I could."

He heard someone in the background yelling Fiona's name.

"Things are not going very well here," Fiona said with a sigh. "New producer. That's him shouting for me, right now. Folks are not being cooperative. One of our regular backup singers has the flu—and the other got in a car accident. We're trying to finish the recording session with pickup singers."

The voice in the background grew louder.

"I'll pray for you," Fiona said sounding rushed.

"And I will do the same for you," Will said.

There was a pause, and he wanted to say something else. Something tender. And intimate.

The voice shouted out Fiona's name again, louder.

"Got to go, 'bye," she said quickly. Then she hung up.

Will paused and sat on the motel-room bed, staring at the telephone on the nightstand where he'd just hung it up.

If love is so grand, he thought to himself, *then why isn't it easier?*

He then called his office and was able to catch Todd before he left. He gave him an urgent project on Mary Sue's case, asking him to prepare a research memo on the legality of Judge Mason's order imposing on Will the duty to divulge information on the whereabouts of his client—in a situation in which he didn't possess that information, and even if he did, in which his client would undoubtedly order him not to do so.

For good measure, he also asked Todd to research the validity of the court's order holding Joe Fellows' bail release hostage until he disclosed the location of his wife.

"The judge has really got me in a corner on this one," Will said. "I need this as quickly as you can get it, Todd. You know, really put the pedal to the metal."

Todd agreed to dive right in and e-mail the results to Will's laptop.

Before leaving the motel, Will had one other piece of business. He had been thinking back to Stanley Kennelworth and his performance in court. Will kept returning to Stanley's cheerful willingness to cooperate with the prosecution's request that he squeeze information about Mary Sue's whereabouts from Joe Fellows as a condition of his release on bail.

What if that was something other than simply bad lawyering?

Was there a possibility that Kennelworth was being improperly influenced in his representation of Joe Fellows? And if so, who was doing the influencing?

With the local lawyer now representing Joe, Will was prohibited from contacting him directly without Kennelworth's consent. Though Will needed to get more information on Kennelworth's background, it appeared that Joe was not going to be a source of information for him.

But Joe's mother had come up with Kennelworth's name as a possible defense attorney, so Will called her. She picked up immediately.

How much did she know about Kennelworth, and what did she know about his law practice?

Madeline, Joe's mother, said she knew Kennelworth because he'd represented another member of the farmer's co-op on a traffic charge. She had heard a little bit about the cases that he did: traffic and drunk driving mostly. From what she knew, the only criminal cases he handled were strictly misdemeanor—no serious felony charges. She had also heard that he did collections work for local professionals in Delphi—a few doctors, dentists, and accountants. And the farmers liked him because he came cheap.

Before Will said goodbye, Mrs. Fellows changed the subject. She asked Will where he would be staying while working on Mary Sue's case. Will told her that he would probably be staying at the local motel in Delphi where he was now.

Madeline kindly suggested somewhere else. There was a woman from church who owned a houseboat on Eden Lake. It was comfortable and well kept-up, and her friend was looking for someone trustworthy to house-sit for the next month or two while she and her husband were traveling. Why didn't Will just use the houseboat while he was in town, rather than having to pay for a motel room? After all, she added, the pier where the houseboat was moored was only about fifteen minutes from downtown Delphi.

The idea of staying on a houseboat appealed to Will. He liked being near the water, and it sounded like a tranquil spot, with plenty of privacy and room for him to work on the case.

After accepting the invitation and thanking Madeline, Will jotted down the spot where she told him the keys would be waiting for him. He hung up, still not knowing what to make of the information about Stanley Kennelworth. But he figured that the local attorney was just one more factor he would have to grapple with in trying to effectively defend Mary Sue, and he left it at that.

Then he left for dinner. He found a place called Denny's Log Cabin, apparently a popular eating spot with the locals. It was located on the main highway into town.

During dinner, he went over the affidavits that had been filed by the prosecution in Mary Sue's case. They were all troublesome, but the one that bothered him the most was the one alleging that, shortly before the police had obtained a warrant, Mary Sue had taken out a large insurance policy on Joshua's life.

She had never told Will anything about having the life insurance policy.

The importance of that evidence was obvious. While the prosecution was not technically required to prove motive, as a practical matter they would have to do so in order to convince the judge or jury why Mary Sue Fellows, an otherwise loving mother, would poison her son with hydraulic brake fluid. It simply didn't make any sense unless the mother had a serious emotional problem. There was no evidence of that—thus, the life insurance policy provided the missing component of motive.

In his early analysis of the case, Will felt that the prosecution would build its case first on motive, secondly on the scientific evidence. Even though the scientific evidence, at least on the surface, appeared to clearly show that Joshua had ingested small amounts of brake fluid—and the toxicology report had also indicated that there was brake fluid on the kitchen counter and on the boy's cup—there might be other explanations for that.

Perhaps Mary Sue had been accidentally exposed to brake fluid—particularly living on a farm—and in turn might have accidentally exposed her son to it.

However, the driving force—the life insurance proof—tended to prove that the exposure was intentional rather than accidental.

And then there was the additional problem of the burden of proof. On the criminal child-abuse case, the standard was "proof beyond a reasonable doubt." But now the county was proceeding on the case of the custody of Joshua, based on child abuse as the grounds. That case was civil, and the prosecution could prove its case by a much lower standard.

All of this boiled down to one thing. Will had to come forth with an aggressive, clear explanation for Mary Sue's innocence. He could not rely on any presumption of innocence as his defense. He would have to get down to the bedrock truth about Mary Sue's conduct toward her son and be able to cogently argue that to the court or the jury. That was no small task in a community already sensitized to the horrors of child abuse because of the tragic death of a young child the year before.

As Will was paying his bill at the counter, he started chatting with the restaurant manager.

"I'm here from out of town, and I'm trying to get some information about one of your local attorneys—Stanley Kennelworth," Will said.

"Sure," the manager replied, giving Will his change, "I know old Stanley. He's an okay guy. Does traffic work, I think. He's in small-claims court quite a bit." Just then, one of the patrons sitting at the counter spoke up.

"You see that new sports car that Stanley was driving the other day?"

The manager smiled and said, "Yeah, that's a beauty, isn't it?"

"That's no sports car," said another fellow sitting next to the first one.

"Well, what would *you* call it? Brand-new Jaguar. *I* call that a fancy sports car."

"Naw," the second man replied, "that's no sports car. Sports cars are cars that are high-performance, ya know—NASCAR, racing potential. You ever see a Jaguar in a NASCAR race?"

"NASCAR!" the first man said, laughing loudly. "There ain't *ever* no sports cars on the NASCAR circuit."

"You know what I'm talking about," the second man said. "What's the name of that European racetrack where they got them sports cars, foreign built…"

"You mean Le Mans?" Will said, joining in.

"Yeah," the second man said, "that's what I'm talking about. Racetrack potential. I ain't ever seen a Jaguar on a racetrack."

"Well," the manager said diplomatically, "whatever. The point is, he's driving a brand-new Jaguar and it's a beauty."

"What was he driving before?" Will asked.

"Some old piece-of-junk station wagon," the first man at the counter said.

"Yeah," the manager added, "old Stanley must be doing pretty good for himself. I wouldn't never have figured him to be making that kind of money."

"Interesting," Will said, scooping up his money.

He tucked the file under his arm, thanked the manager, and headed out to his car, unable to help thinking *I'd take my '57 Corvette over a new Jaguar any day*. Will had the lingering feeling that Stanley Kennelworth was important to Mary Sue's case— and not just because of the car he was driving.

14

Jason Bell Purdy's spacious personal office took up most of the fourth floor of the historic Purdy building in Atlanta. Built by his father, Stanfield Purdy, famous Georgia entrepreneur, twice candidate for governor, and direct descendant of the Purdys who had helped settle that part of the state in the early 1800s, the building was a landmark in the city's history.

Purdy was sitting at his massive mahogany desk and playing with a crystal golf ball, which he was tossing from hand to hand.

Across from the desk, a young, attractive secretary was tapping her pen gently against her steno pad and gazing out the window behind Purdy.

"Let's see…" Purdy said, his voice meandering. "Where was I?"

The secretary looked down and then said, "You were talking about getting the invitations out for the golf tournament and making sure that they did a better job this time of bringing in some congressmen and federal judges, not just the regular group from the statehouse and the governor's office."

"Yeah. Yeah. Yeah. That's right. Okay, you finish the rest—you know what I want," Purdy said, now holding the golf ball in his fingers and pretending to throw it like a baseball. "Hey, how about dinner tonight? We can make it a working dinner. We've got all of the Eden Lake stuff to go over."

The secretary shifted slightly in her chair and closed her steno pad. "I don't think so, Mr. Purdy."

Purdy's eyes widened, and he cocked his jaw slightly in a forced smile. Placing the golf ball on its wooden stand on his desk, he straightened up a little in his chair.

"What's with the 'Mr. Purdy' stuff? Since when?"

The secretary leaned forward a little and said, "Since this," and she raised her left hand to display a diamond ring. And then she added, "Since I've been engaged—that's when."

"Well," Purdy said, "I mean, that's no big deal. We can still be friends."

"That's what you said the last time," the secretary replied. "I'm sorry, Mr. Purdy, but I don't feel comfortable mixing business with your personal life."

Purdy squinted a little at his secretary and clicked his upper and lower teeth together ever so slightly. After a moment he continued.

"That's fine. You know, Beth, I would never want to do anything to make you uncomfortable."

The secretary smiled politely, rose from her chair, and left the office, closing the door behind her.

Purdy rocked back and forth in his executive chair for a few minutes, gazing out the window. Then he touched the instant-message button on his video screen.

The face of a female employee in the payroll department appeared on the screen.

"Hey," Purdy said.

"How can I help you, Mr. Purdy?"

"Would you do me a favor?" Purdy asked. "Check Beth's personnel file. I'm sure we've got some warning slips in there for her being late to work, don't we?"

"I doubt it, Mr. Purdy," the woman answered. "Beth is always very prompt. She has an excellent work record."

"Oh, I'm sure that's not right. I'm sure we'll see at least three or four late slips and some other warnings. Please check her file to make sure that it's up-to-date, will you please?"

The woman on the video screen paused for a minute, looking down. Then her eyes returned to Purdy.

"I understand. I will get right on it, Mr. Purdy."

Picking up his private line, Purdy rapidly punched in a telephone number. "Hey, this is Jason. What did you find out?"

"Just the usual stuff, but nothing like you're looking for."

"Have you checked all the folks who have access to his box?"

"Yeah," the other voice said. "I don't think anyone took any of the papers out."

"I think that just about does it."

"I'd say so," the other voice said. "He was pretty predictable. Kept all of his stuff in the same places, same routines every day. No mysteries, no surprises with a guy like that."

"Yeah," Purdy said. "Typical bank president, may he rest in peace."

The other voice chuckled, and Purdy hung up the phone.

Purdy flipped open his Palm Pilot and accessed his monthly calendar. On the calendar date three days hence, he tapped in the message: *Beth, bye-bye.*

He flipped the cover closed. Then he fished in the bowl of hard candy on his desk, ripped the plastic off a piece and popped it into his mouth.

"Giving up cigarettes is hard," Purdy muttered into the air. "But then—I'm doing it for myself. I deserve a long, healthy life." And he smiled at that thought.

15

I'M SORRY," THE FBI AGENT at the other end indicated, "but there is nothing we can do immediately. As I explained to you, we'll have to forward your request to the U.S. Attorney's office. The decision will be made there, and I'm sure he'll go through the usual evaluation."

"Can you get this expedited for me?" Otis Tracher asked.

"Doubt it," the special agent replied. "There are no federal charges outstanding, no federal warrants, and as far as I can see, no probable cause to believe that a federal crime has been committed. As far as I can see this is purely a state matter. But as I said, it's for the U.S. Attorney to decide. He'll give me a directive as to whether we should assist in trying to apprehend this...what did you say her name was?"

"Mary Sue Fellows," Tracher said.

"Right. Whether we'll give any assistance in locating and apprehending Mrs. Fellows. As soon as I hear something, I'll let you know."

The detective hung up the phone and turned back to his memo book, where he jotted down some notes.

Tracher was no brilliant investigator, but he was known for his persistence and stubborn dedication to the cases he handled. He was also capable of detaching his emotions from his work. He left questions of right and wrong, justice, and equity to Harry Putnam, his prosecutors, and the judges. His job was to locate, apprehend, and bring in the culprit—and to gather sufficient evidence to convict.

Tracher had not been discouraged by his lack of results so far. When he had contacted the college in Santa Fe where Andrew White Arrow taught, he was informed that Andrew was on sabbatical for several months. The administration did not know where he was going to be spending that time, other than at an educational conference in Minneapolis. Contacting the conference center, Tracher was told that Andrew had indeed attended, but they did not know how he had traveled there, or what means of transportation he was going to take afterward, or his destination after the conference ended.

The college administration in New Mexico did have on file an "emergency contact" person listed by Andrew when he'd first starting working at the college some years before—a Susan Lee Tacoma. Tracher located her and learned that she was a former girlfriend of Andrew's. But they had broken off their relationship about two years earlier when Andrew had gotten "too religious," as Susan put it. However, she did recall Andrew mentioning that some of his family was located in either South or North Dakota.

That information was the best lead the detective had received thus far. When he checked with Mary Sue's relatives, as well as the extended family of Joe Fellows, a few of them had indicated they'd had a phone call or two from Mary Sue. But none of them had caller ID on their telephones. None of them indicated they knew where she was located or where she was calling from.

Armed with the information from Susan Tacoma, the detective telephoned the U.S. Department of the Interior, Bureau of Indian Affairs. A woman answered, and Tracher recited the initial details.

"What law enforcement agency did you say you were calling from?" the agent asked.

"Sheriff's Department, Juda County, State of Georgia. This is Otis Tracher, Chief Investigator for Crimes Against Juveniles," the detective replied.

"And who is it…what tribe…what were you looking for?"

"The man's name is Andrew White Arrow, Sioux nation, Lakota tribe."

"Detective, do you have any idea how many square miles of Indian reservations there are in North and South Dakota? And how many Lakota you've got located there? Look," the intake officer continued, "from what you've told me, this isn't even a federal issue. No federal charges. You haven't alleged a violation of law by any Indian on a reservation—"

"Well," Tracher replied, "this Andrew White Arrow is under suspicion of possibly aiding and abetting the flight of a felon out of the State of Georgia."

"Suspicion? Look, I'm no expert in criminal investigation, but we deal with law enforcement agencies pretty often. You're going to have to have something more than that for me to put this on the top rack. I will send your request to locate this Andrew White Arrow over to my supervisor. That's all I can promise."

Tracher thanked her and hung up the phone. He stood up, stretching his tall frame, and looked at the papers, files, and notes that were scattered all over his desk. Scratching his head and yawning, he glanced over at the bulletin board that hung in his office. On it were pinned the pictures of missing juveniles and juvenile offenders he'd recently been investigating.

Tracher snatched up a photograph lying on the mess on his desk and lumbered over to the bulletin board. He thumbtacked it dead center in the middle of all of the other pictures. The photo showed Mary Sue Fellows cradling Joshua in her arms, smiling. The detective had located it in the Fellows house the day he had arrested Joe.

He stared at the picture. Something from his background—perhaps a phrase from catechism, or a homily delivered by Father Godfrey at St. Stephen the Martyr Church—touched his memory.

Tracher continued staring.

"Madonna and child..." he muttered. Was that a famous painting...or was it sculpture? It was a strange thought, and

Tracher dismissed it. Looking at his watch, he saw he had just enough time to grab some lunch. After that he would go on-line to do some research about Indian reservations in North and South Dakota.

His job was to apprehend Mary Sue Fellows and her young son, Joshua. He was going to do that. He was going to do it without hesitation. He would do it because it was his job, and his job was to enforce the law.

16

WILL WAS DRIVING DOWN A LONG, wooded country lane on his way to the houseboat where he planned on staying while he worked on the Mary Sue Fellows case. A small sign at the side of the road—"Public Landing 1 Mile"—gave him hope that he was driving in the right direction.

Two issues in the case had been haunting his mind. One was immediate—and it was threatening to Will's professional career. The other was a more transcendent issue, involving Mary Sue's guilt or innocence—and his need to get some answers to her seemingly unanswerable dilemma.

The first issue lay right at Will's doorstep. In two days, the deadline imposed by Judge Mason would expire. The judge had ordered Will to produce the whereabouts of Mary Sue or to arrange her turnover to the authorities, and pursuant to that, he had noticed a status hearing on the fifth day to ensure that Will was before the court to explain his response in person. Every step that Judge Mason had taken on that issue confirmed Will's suspicion that any disobedience to his order would result in a finding of contempt of court. The sanctions for contempt could run the gamut—from a fine to imprisonment. For Will, the stakes couldn't be higher.

Todd had reported in promptly with the results of his legal research, but they were less than definitive. The obligation of a lawyer to disclose the location of a client who had fled a jurisdiction in anticipation of an arrest warrant or an adverse order from a court was murky at best. On the one hand, an attorney was bound to protect the confidences of a client—and that would include confidential communications by a client that informed the attorney of his whereabouts. On the other hand, an attorney had an obligation to disclose ongoing or anticipated criminal conduct that a client mentioned to the lawyer.

If Will chose wrongly by withholding the information, it might not only jeopardize Mary Sue's case—it could result in his disbarment, and a contempt order sending him to jail.

On the other hand, if Will were to discover Mary Sue's whereabouts and then disclose them to the court *against* her desires, that also would be an ethical violation. And if Mary Sue was then located and Joshua was wrenched from her care, he could well be in danger if Mary Sue was correct in concluding that he was suffering from an undiagnosed and mysterious medical problem. Indeed, his condition had appeared to be deteriorating under the care of the family physician. Now, ironically, according to Mary Sue in her last telephone contact, Joshua now seemed to be improving somewhat.

The second issue was equally troubling, but for different reasons. As Will lined up the pieces of evidence from the prosecution that proved Mary Sue's complicity in poisoning her own son, they were chillingly consistent.

His client did not have a good explanation for why she took out a $100,000 insurance policy on Joshua at the same time his medical problem started surfacing. When Will had questioned her about it in their previous conversation, her only response was that she'd thought the policy was only $10,000, the premiums were rather cheap, and the insurance broker was a friend, who was starting out in a new job. She thought she was doing him a favor. She honestly had no idea—or so she explained it to Will— that the face value of the policy was actually $100,000, not $10,000.

In addition to this, the forensic evidence from the scene showed hydraulic brake fluid in the kitchen and on Joshua's cup. There were several potential explanations for how the toxic fluid might have accidentally ended up in the kitchen. Mary Sue might have had it on her hands, or detective Tracher and the other officers might have picked up some of the fluid while searching the garage and then inadvertently contaminated the kitchen. Or finally, the forensic lab might simply have been mistaken in its finding that the substance was hydraulic brake fluid and not something else. The latter option, while possible, seemed the least likely. And though detective Tracher might have contaminated the kitchen, it was very unlikely he would have thoughtlessly touched Joshua's cup—a prime piece of evidence in such a case—with hands or gloves that had already been exposed to another substance.

That left only the first option—accidental exposure by Mary Sue. Up until now, Will's client could not remember any instance, in the time frame shortly before Joe's arrest, when she would have handled brake fluid on the farm.

Will considered the final piece of evidence was the most powerful. The Delphi Community Hospital had concluded that Joshua's blood contained poisonous amounts of ethylene glycol, one of the main ingredients in hydraulic brake fluid.

Before driving out to the houseboat, Will had taken a side trip to this hospital. It was relatively new and surprisingly up-to-date for a small community. In the medical library, he'd done some preliminary research on ethylene-glycol poisoning. The results, at least initially, were not promising.

Ethylene glycol was most commonly associated with child poisoning by engine coolant—antifreeze. Will reviewed the *Index Medicus*, but a quick check revealed no medical-journal articles dealing with hydraulic brake fluid poisoning.

Will also knew that law enforcement officers would occasionally make errors by contaminating or misinterpreting forensic evidence. But as a general rule, the rate of error among medical personnel was even smaller. Personally, he had found that particularly true when the evaluation was done, not by a lab technician, but by the chief pathologist.

According to the affidavit of Dr. Parker, the pathologist, the levels of ethylene glycol in Joshua's blood could *not* be accounted for by incidental exposure, such as a small amount of brake fluid on the fingers, that was then ingested by a child. The amount consumed had to be substantial in order to account for the levels he had measured in Joshua's blood sample.

Will's concentration was interrupted as he crested a hill. The road dropped down steeply to a sloping boat ramp at the lake. A sign off to the right read simply "Private Piers." Will turned right and glanced quickly at his scribbled directions. Coming to the third landing, he slowed down and saw a houseboat. He pulled into the short driveway that dead-ended where the aluminum pier began.

The houseboat was a simple affair with a walk-around deck and square living quarters in the center. There was a small wheelhouse on top. Parking his car, Will boarded the houseboat and looked out over the lake. It was clear, with a cloudless sky, and the lake was a deep blue. As a light breeze rippled over the water, Will took a minute to gaze out, listen to the lapping of the water, and enjoy the gentle swaying of the pine trees that rimmed the lake.

It all took him back to his days as a boy, when he would spend his summers on a lake in Maine. His father, an editor of a Massachusetts newspaper, would come up to the little cabin and join Will and his mother on Thursdays and then leave again on the train the following Monday.

Though Will was just a "summer kid," over the years he'd developed close relationships with the "townies." He would spend his summers fishing, hiking through the white-pine forest, or hanging out at the little log-cabin store.

Somehow the houseboat on this lake was bringing those idyllic summers back to him. This, he thought to himself, was a beautiful and peaceful place to spend his time while he was preparing for Mary Sue's case.

After a few minutes, he unlocked the door and brought in his bags. He'd just begun unzipping them, when the phone rang. Picking up the phone, he recognized Mary Sue's voice at the other end. No doubt she'd been relayed by his office.

"I heard you're staying on a houseboat—that sounds nice. Eden Lake?"

"Yes," he replied. "It's beautiful out here. How are you and Joshua doing?"

"Pretty good, considering the circumstances. He's not throwing up nearly as much, and he's eating a little bit better. I've tried to keep a diary of what we're feeding him out here—it might be different. Maybe that's a factor."

"Are you going to get him to a doctor soon?"

There was a pause. "I'm working on that."

Will knew that his time was running out regarding Judge Mason's order, and he had to confront Mary Sue about it.

"I've been ordered to discover your location and reveal it to the court, or to produce you and Joshua to the authorities."

There was a silence on the other end for close to a minute. Finally Will spoke.

"Mary Sue, I can't encourage you or assist you to disregard an order from the court, no matter what my personal feelings may be about the inappropriateness of that order. Will you tell me where you are, or will you surrender yourself and Joshua to the court or to the police?"

Mary Sue sighed at the other end and cleared her throat. When she spoke her voice was quiet but firm.

"Will, I can't do that. I'm absolutely innocent. Joshua has some medical problem that is not going to be diagnosed properly if they grab him from me and put him in a foster home. You are simply going to have to prove my innocence so I can return. I want my family back together again. I want my husband out of jail…" At that point Mary Sue's voice began trembling.

"You realize how difficult this is going to be for me? Your case is going to be hard to defend with an empty chair next to me in court rather than my client."

"I know that, Will. But I have to do what is right. I have to do what I believe God wants me to do. I have to take care of my son and my family. Just protect me, please. Be my defender. Deliver me out of the hands of those who are after me."

In the background, Will could hear the sound of an occasional car or truck roaring past his client. It sounded as if she were at a phone booth on the highway somewhere.

He glanced down at the phone and suddenly noticed it had caller ID. He saw an area code on the display.

His heart sank.

"Mary Sue, I want you to listen very closely to this next question." Then he thought through what he was going to ask her.

"This phone has caller ID," Will said. "I see your area code right here in front of me, as well as the number. Are you instructing me *not* to divulge your whereabouts to the court? Are you demanding that I withhold that information?"

"I can tell by what you're saying—by your voice—that this is an important decision, isn't it?" Mary Sue replied. "What I tell you next is going to have an impact on *you*, isn't it, Will?"

"I'm not the issue here—you and Joshua are. I need you to tell me straight—what is your decision?"

"Okay, then." There was another pause, and then Mary Sue gave Will his marching orders.

"Will Chambers, you are my attorney. I am instructing you *not* to tell the court anything about my telephone number or where I called from, or where I might be located. That's my order to you." She paused and then added, "And may God help you when you deliver that message to the judge."

Will then said his goodbyes and hung up. He thought of the old black-and-white adventure shows he'd watched on Saturday mornings as a child. The ones where the hero is caught in some forbidding dungeon—and the walls are being cranked closer and closer together as the hero holds his hands and feet out in a vain attempt to stop the slow, massive pressure of inevitable doom.

Head down, he stepped out onto the deck of the houseboat and put his hand on the railing. Feeling the breeze from the lake wash over his face, he looked up. Off in the distance, a gull flapped its wings, then dove down into the water, grabbed something with its beak, and accelerated up with aerodynamic ease.

Will sensed the walls slowly grinding in toward him. If he were going to escape, he would have to learn how to fly. Somehow—some way—he needed to find some wings.

17

INSIDE THE CORRAL, Tommy White Arrow was leading a pinto stallion by a rope around the inside of the ring. On its back, a young woman with blond pigtails was studiously erect and poised in the saddle. Her mother, on the outside of the ring, was watching her intensely.

On the other side of the corral, about forty feet away, Mary Sue Fellows was sitting on the ground with Joshua cuddled in her lap. Her son was staring, bug-eyed, at the horse in the ring. His little arms were raised up as if grasping the reins and were bouncing methodically with the movement of the horse. Though his dad ran a few head of cattle on his farm and once had had some goats, Joshua had had very limited contact with horses. But since he and his mother had come to the ranch, Joshua had been enthralled with those of Tommy's.

Mary Sue turned and noticed the tall, lanky frame of Andrew striding toward her. Katherine was next to him, along with Danny, who was doing "cat's cradle" with his yo-yo. Suddenly he blurted out, "Yogi's Pizza—It's Better than Yum!" Andrew smiled and explained it to Mary Sue. "That's the newest one Danny heard on TV. Now he's doing it ten times an hour!"

"Mary Sue, why not let Joshua go with Danny to get a closer look?" Katherine asked with a twinkle in her eye.

"Oh, I'm not sure that's a good idea," Mary Sue replied. "I don't think that Tom appreciates us watching him."

"Don't let Tommy's gruff ways fool you," Andrew said. "He's like a cactus—prickly on the outside, but sweet on the inside when you get to know him."

"If you'd like, I'd be glad to keep an eye on him so he can stand next to the corral and watch Tommy work with the horses," Katherine suggested.

Joshua's face lit up, and he shouted out, "By the horses, Mommy!"

Mary Sue smiled, shrugged her shoulders, and nodded to Katherine, who scooped Joshua up and walked with him to the training ring, with Danny close behind.

Andrew reached down and helped Mary Sue up off the ground. He suggested they go sit down at a picnic table that was about a hundred feet away. Mary Sue could tell that there was something on his mind.

"How's Joshua doing?" he asked.

"All things considered, very well. He's eating better, he's not throwing up as much, even though he's still running a low-grade fever. But he's very happy—although he asks for his daddy a lot."

"There's a doctor in town—he's semiretired and runs the medical mission for the reservation. Dr. Kendoll. He's a very learned man, the kind that really loves to try to solve medical mysteries. You ought to take Joshua in to see him."

Mary Sue looked skeptical but nodded politely.

"I bet you miss your husband too," Andrew added.

"Very much. I've just realized that in the years we've been married, this has been the longest we've ever been separated. I long for the sound of his voice. His hugs. His sense of humor. His strength. And now I can't even call him or talk to him."

"I'm sure you've thought about the future—what you'll do depending on how the case turns out," Andrew commented, obviously moving toward a point.

"Sure. I think about that all the time. And I go back and forth. I can't stand to be separated from Joe. This has to end soon. But I'm terribly worried about Joshua and a legal system that seems to be blind to the truth. I can't allow them to steal my baby away from me. I don't care what their motives are—I don't even care why they did what they did. I will not allow them to take Joshua away."

Andrew was quiet for a minute. He and Mary Sue watched Tommy while he exerted his expert control over the horse with the young woman rider. Then Andrew spoke up.

"My brother Tommy says something about the horses he breaks. He says that all wild horses first look at every human as just another predator. They look at you and size you up, and they try to determine whether you'll attack them—whether you are an enemy."

Mary Sue studied Andrew's face as he pressed his lips together. He thought a moment before he continued.

"But once a horse decides you're no longer a predator, they're willing to accept you as a friend. I think that's a little bit like you, Mary Sue. You feel that the legal system—that the police and the lawyers and the judges are all predators. You see them as the enemy because they came after your child and they're coming after you. Maybe that's so, but there's a big difference between you and that pinto in the ring."

Mary Sue tilted her head a bit and smiled thoughtfully. She had an idea where Andrew was going.

"You are a child of the great God. You can't just divide the world into friends and foes. It isn't like that. You know what I'm saying. You love Joshua—I watch you with him and I know that in my head, my heart, and in my soul. All of us here know that, even Tommy. He watches you, and he sees the way you want to protect your son. But you have to take your orders from the King of heaven. God says to trust him. And he also says, with only a few exceptions, that you must obey the laws of the government, because he has established government and laws."

Mary Sue's face became animated. "When Peter and the other disciples were forbidden by the religious establishment of their day from preaching the gospel—did they obey that law? No! They continued to preach and to teach boldly, in the marketplace, in the streets, everywhere. Some laws cannot be obeyed," Mary Sue declared.

"I know that well," Andrew responded. "In the comparative religion class that I teach, we study how the various religions answer this simple question: How should I live my life? Every religion has beliefs and principles, and many—if not most—have a sacred text that the believers accept as binding and authoritative. But there is one difference with Christians."

Mary Sue had narrowed her eyes, and they were riveted on Andrew.

"Only the Christian has the indwelling Spirit of the great God. Like the reins on a horse, the more trained you are by the Holy Spirit in obedience to God, the less he has to yank your head or snap the reins against your haunches. Read his Word— study it—keep your mind and your heart pure. Listen to the quiet voice of his Spirit within you. Be prepared to take chances. Be ready to be surprised by the High King of the universe."

The two of them fell quiet as they continued to watch Tommy work the pinto. Joshua was standing on the fence, with Katherine grasping him tightly from behind. As Tommy strode past, without breaking so much as a glimmer of an expression he swept the cowboy hat off his head and plopped it on top of the head of a delighted Joshua. Joshua whirled his head around to show his mother and waved wildly, grinning hugely with joy and excitement.

Mary Sue waved back energetically and then threw him a kiss. Then she clasped her hands, prayerlike, in front of her mouth, and bent her face against them. She closed her eyes and sighed. Andrew reached across the picnic table and put his right hand over her hands, enclosing both of hers in his palm.

"Your husband, Joseph, gave me his blessing—to be your protector, along with Will Chambers, in his absence—until he is released from jail. That is what I will do," Andrew said. "You are like family here. But we always tell the truth to family. We don't always agree—but we tell the truth." He rose and walked back to his cabin.

Mary Sue knew how a simple decision could change everything. She could make one phone call—and Joshua would be apprehended and placed in a foster home, and she would be placed in jail. Perhaps it was her lack of faith that was keeping her from making that phone call.

Or—on the contrary—was she obeying some greater call from God? She could not resist the conviction that a process had been set in motion by dark forces that she neither understood nor was able to deter. She knew that the legal system, the social workers, and police all had their roles. As a nurse she had seen abused and neglected children—children with cigarette burns, and malnourishment, and severe, unexplained fractures. She was repulsed by the thought that any adult could victimize a helpless child.

But this was different. Now she felt like the victim. Though innocent, she felt incapable of stopping the great, grinding machine that seemed inclined to deprive her of her son and find her guilty of a crime she had not committed.

Was she lacking in faith? If Daniel, the prophet of the Old Testament, was willing to face man-eating lions, what right did she have to resist confinement in a jail and a trial on criminal charges?

Then Mary Sue's thoughts turned to Will Chambers. She knew that she had placed Will in a dilemma. In two days—unless she changed her mind—her lawyer might be defending her cause from the inside of a jail cell.

18

"So the bottom line, Joe Fellows, is that you really don't know where your wife, Mary Sue, is, or your child, Joshua?" Crystal Banes asked.

Joe Fellows squinted under the glare of the camera lights that had been set up in the jail conference room. Spike, the cameraman, stood with his shoulder-mounted camera pointing at the imprisoned man. Joe thought about the question and then answered.

"Like I said, I really have no idea where Mary Sue and Joshua are right now."

Banes leaned back in the metal folding chair and flipped her notepad closed. She brushed a fleck of dust off her silk pin-striped suit.

This was not the first time that the TV host had interviewed a jail inmate. Throughout her career, she had been in and out of prisons and jails on a number of assignments. But she always found them to be loathsome places—filled with metal cages for humans, the dank odor of perspiration, and a low-level but constant din from the prisoners yelling from their cells.

The Juda County jail was no different. She gazed at a reflection on the floor. It—and the walls and the ceiling—had all been painted with the same glossy grey enamel, like the bottom of a battleship.

And, as usual, Banes had decided that she had definitely over-dressed for the occasion.

She smiled vaguely and looked once more at Joe before she stood up. She knew that this prisoner was different. She added him to her own very small group of inmates—the ones for whom she felt some sympathy.

On another assignment, one dealing with the legalization of prostitution, Banes had interviewed a number of prostitutes and call girls in prison. She personally supported legalization of the practice and felt that these tawdry women with their cheap make-up, dull eyes, and ripped hosiery didn't belong in jail. If they had to make a living with their bodies, then so be it. And further, she felt that most of the drug addicts she'd interviewed in prison deserved to be in a hospital rather than in a cell.

But with only those exceptions, she had concluded that the majority of convicts and prisoners she had interviewed during her career ought to be kept in cages to protect the public. If they weren't guilty of their *present* offense, then they were probably guilty of many other crimes for which they had simply not been caught. Even those on death row she had little pity for, unlike many of her journalistic associates.

But there was something about Joe Fellows that she knew rang true. He didn't belong in jail. That wasn't saying that his wife wasn't a child abuser—but only that this quiet young farmer was probably getting a raw deal.

Not that her opinion on that score would change anything. She was going to track down Mary Sue Fellows because her job was to get the story—and to get it before anyone else. After all, there was a ratings war going on. Crystal Banes did not intend to be a casualty.

As Banes stood up and straightened her suit, Stanley Kennelworth, who had been sitting patiently through the interview in the corner of the jail conference room, jumped to his feet.

"Okay—you going to get some interview time with me? On camera? Like you said?"

Banes broke into a small crooked smile.

"Sure," Banes answered. "Spike, let it roll." Then Banes took the microphone, pointed it in Kennelworth's direction, and asked, "What do you think the outcome of this case will be, Mr. Kennelworth? Innocent or guilty?"

"Well…that's a real good question—real good. Now what I say is—" Kennelworth paused—"what I say is, we're going to let the justice system decide. I'll just do my best and we'll let the court make up its mind."

"Sharp," said Banes, turning to her cameraman with a smirk, "Don't you think, Spike—wasn't that a sharp comment?" Spike turned off the floodlight and lowered his camera. He said nothing, but stared at Banes without expression.

"Well, that's a wrap," Banes concluded, motioning to Spike and quickly heading for the door, where the two deputies stood on the other side of the glass. She gestured for them to unlock the door, and when they did, she and Spike quickly scurried out.

In the background, Stanley Kennelworth, in a louder than usual voice, yelled out, "So when's this gonna be on television?"

"We'll be in touch," Banes said, tossing the comment over her shoulder but not turning around.

In the parking lot, Spike worked on loading his equipment in the trunk of the car. Banes had a self-assured look.

"So—you think it went okay?" Spike asked.

"Sure. Most of it was a lot of zero. Except for one thing. One very important, small little thing. Something that Joe said. Let's see if you caught it."

Her cameraman thought for a moment. "Probably the bit about the state hospital." He paused for a few moments and then added, "Where that big Indian's brother had been hospitalized and where the big Indian had gone over to get him out and bring him back to the reservation. That's the connection. That's where you're going to go to start tracking the big Indian, and the reservation, and the rest of the Indian family—and find out Mary Sue Fellows' location from there."

Banes cocked her head, and raising an eyebrow very slightly, and responded. "Good, Spike. Good for you. You're learning, I'm proud of you."

"So tell me," Spike asked, "exactly why did you have me set up my camera, turn on the floodlight, and never roll film on that interview? What's the deal on that?" As the two of them climbed into the car, with Spike behind the wheel, Banes stretched back her arms behind the seat and began her short tutorial.

"Important note to file, Spike," she said. "To get interview with prisoner in jail, first get permission from lawyer. Now, how to get permission from lawyer? By promising televised interview and face time for attorney on television. So I call Kennelworth, I give him the pitch, I tell him we are coming in with cameras rolling, Kennelworth jumps like a catfish at a smelly bait ball."

"But that still doesn't answer my question," Spike pressed.

"The point was not to do an interview on tape anyway. I was just getting leads from farmer Joe to track down his wife. He didn't know that of course. Besides, at this point I don't want *anything* on tape. If you don't have it on tape, there is nothing for a court or a prosecutor to subpoena."

"What about your notes?" Spike asked.

"What notes?" she snapped back.

As they drove out of the parking lot, Spike glanced over at Banes with a quizzical look.

"What? You have another question?" she asked.

"Yeah, I do have one."

"Well, what is it?"

"You're a sophisticated, internationally known, globe-trotting television-magazine news host."

Banes smiled and her eyes widened slightly. She wasn't used to Spike stringing that many words together. Perhaps there was more to her young cameraman than met the eye.

"Well—what's your question?"

"Just this—how do you know so much about catfish bait?"

Banes parted her lips as if she were going to offer an explanation, but then thought better of it. Instead, she reached into her briefcase, retrieved her cell phone, and rapidly began punching in the number of the INN studio line.

After a few seconds, she spoke.

"This is Crystal—give me research. I'm trying to track down the address of a state hospital in Georgia."

Spike was still looking over at her, naively waiting for an answer to his question. But Crystal Banes had already closed the door and locked it. This was one of her golden rules—*never* get too personal with the techies. *Ever.*

19

THE INSURANCE COVERAGE ISSUE had to be dealt with head-on. Will knew that. The fact that Mary Sue had taken out a $100,000 insurance policy on Joshua's life provided proof for the prosecution that she had a motive to poison her son.

Will pulled up to a small, single-story house. Outside there was a large sign that read, "Bob Smiley Insurance—Life-Health-Auto."

As Will climbed out of his car, Harriet Bender, the court-appointed guardian ad litem for Joshua, was striding out the front door. She swung the strap of her briefcase over her shoulder and then lit a long, slim cigar, pausing for a moment to blow a large smoke ring. She then pulled her Palm Pilot out of the side pocket of her briefcase, snapped it open, and punched some information into her schedule.

As she caught sight of Will walking toward her, Bender cocked her hand back, the cigar resting in two fingers. She watched him approach, and when he was just a few feet away said, "Fancy meeting you here, Chambers."

"Now, I suppose you might be here to update your health-insurance policy," Will said with a smile, "But I doubt it. So that means you were talking to Mr. Smiley about the Mary Sue Fellows case. Learn anything?"

"I have a practice, Chambers, that when I am doing guardian ad litem investigations, I never tip my hand until I complete the investigation, arrive at my conclusions, and file my report with the court."

"So I take it," Will said, "that you are willing to give Mary Sue Fellows the benefit of the doubt—that she is innocent of child abuse until proven otherwise?"

"Oh, I'm way past that." Bender said. "This lady is guilty—and she needs help—and I need to get that kid back in the State of Georgia. Are you going to play ball with the court tomorrow?"

"I suppose that means we've got something in common—because I don't like to tip my hand either. But I will tell you this—I consider the judge's order inappropriate. If it's appealed I believe it will be reversed. And more than that, I believe Mary Sue Fellows wouldn't harm that child for anything on this earth."

"You can save that for your closing argument to the court," Bender responded. "I've looked at the evidence and I don't buy it. Ms. Fellows may come across like the sweet-looking little-mother type with a tear in her eye. But I believe she's been slipping brake fluid to her son for breakfast. I want little Joshua in a safe, loving home with lots of support systems in place. I don't know what you think about the city of Delphi, Chambers, but we've got very up-to-date resources and services here for this child."

"There is one support system I am interested in."

"Let's hear it," Bender said. "Maybe there's something we could work out. You turn the kid over, bring in Mary Sue Fellows, and I'm sure we could provide whatever services you need. What resource are you thinking about?"

"The Fellows family unit. You know—mother, father, and child. Back together under one roof. Raising their own child. Making their own decisions. Not having to worry about arrest warrants, police tracking them down, or ex parte hearings where custody orders are issued without notifying the parents or their lawyers. That's the kind of resource I'm looking for."

Bender took a long drag on her cigar, blew the smoke out, and then reached for her car keys.

"This just confirms my suspicions. As long as you approach this case with that kind of ride-'em-cowboy attitude, I don't think we have much to talk about."

Will was going to respond, but Bender went on. "I've got some summer reading for you, Chambers. *It Takes a Village* by Hillary Rodham Clinton. You need to start joining the twenty-first century. Children aren't the chattel of parents anymore. That went out with the Industrial Revolution."

"That's true," Will responded, "but educate me a little on one thing—exactly when did the state adopt the presumption-of-*guilt* rule? I must have missed that."

Bender didn't bother to reply, but turned and walked away.

Will entered the small insurance building, coming into a pinewood-paneled anteroom that had one empty desk and a few chairs scattered around the room. On the walls were a few plaques commending Bob Smiley for "Highest Sales in Delphi for a New Insurance Agent." Another plaque recognized Smiley as a member of the Rotary Club. On another wall, a large painted sign read "Why Take the Risk? Get Insured!"

The lawyer heard some movement in an adjacent office, and he tapped the bell that sat on top of the empty desk.

In a moment, a man stepped into the room, quickly thrusting his arms into his sport coat and straightening his tie.

"Yes, sir—sorry to keep you waiting. Bob Smiley. What can I do for you, sir?"

Will shook hands and gave Smiley his card. "I'm Mary Sue Fellows' attorney."

Smiley's head bobbed back slightly, as if someone had just tugged gently on a string attached to the back of his head.

"Well," Smiley said, straightening his suit coat, "what's up?"

"I'd like to talk to you about the life-insurance policy that Mary Sue Fellows took out on Joshua, her son."

"I did just give a statement to that guardian lady, she was just in…"

"Harriet Bender?"

"Yeah, I think that was her name. I just went over all of this with her."

"I hope you don't mind—I'd like you to share that information with me too."

"I do have a meeting I've got to get to," the agent replied, "so I don't have a lot of time—"

"I'll be quick. How long have you known Mary Sue Fellows?"

"I've known Joe and Mary Sue for a lot of years—going back to high school here in Delphi."

"Who did you know better—Mary Sue or Joe?"

"Probably Mary Sue—I didn't know Joe that well in school. I mean, it was a small high school, so everybody knew everybody. He was a good football player. I'd watch him play. I had a few classes with him. That sort of thing."

"And Mary Sue?"

"Well—everybody knew Mary Sue. Cheerleader. Lot of guys were always after her. A real cute girl, full of life, as smart as a tack. Mary Sue was definitely Miss Popularity."

"Did you ever date her?"

"No, it was never like that. Not that I would've minded it. I always liked Mary Sue a lot, but—it was never really like that."

"After high school, did you keep in touch with her?"

"Sure, I'd see her around Delphi. I'd run into her from time to time after high school. Back when she was dating Jason Bell Purdy."

"Mary Sue dated Jason Bell Purdy?"

"Sure, not for long—I'm not certain why it ended. I think a lot of folks were surprised that they didn't stay together. Jason always liked Mary Sue. He went to a nearby rich, private high school of course. He officiated at the Rotary Club pancake breakfast the other day. We made him our Honorary Chairman because he's always been treated like a local Delphi boy."

Will jotted down a few notes, including Jason Bell Purdy's name. He underlined it. "So about the insurance policy. I'm sure Ms. Bender asked you some questions about that?"

"I really can't remember what we talked about, but it was mainly about the policy, the amount, when it got issued—that sort of thing."

"Do you remember the details of how you came to write up that policy for Mary Sue? Did she call you—did you call her? How did that happen?"

"You know," Smiley said, thrusting his hands in his pockets, "I wonder where I put my car keys. I'm going to need my car for this meeting." With that Smiley began looking vaguely around the room.

"So tell me, Mr. Smiley," Will repeated, "why did you end up writing a policy on Joshua's life? Did you approach Mary Sue, or did she approach you?"

"Like I told Ms. Bender, I really don't remember a lot of the details. I write a lot of policies. Once they go into effect, I don't really spend a lot of my time thinking about what went on before they got written."

"With all of the policies you write for folks—life, health, auto—I'm sure it's quite a task keeping all of the information straight and organized."

"You bet. It's a major job indexing and keeping all of your files up-to-date."

"There is just one file I'm interested in. I'd like you to pull the Mary Sue Fellows life-insurance file for me so I can take a look at it. Would you mind?"

"Hey—here they are!" Smiley exclaimed, walking over to one of the chairs in the anteroom, where his keys were resting.

"Would you mind if I took a look at that file?" Will said with a little more emphasis.

"I would like to help, but I'm going to be late for my Rotary Club meeting. Give me some time to hunt down that file and I'll get back to you." Then Smiley pulled Will's card out of his pocket and asked, "Is this your number? Should I call you here?"

"Actually, I'm staying here in Delphi. Why don't I give you a call later today?"

"You know—I don't think that's going to work. I won't have enough time to look through my files. Why don't you call me tomorrow afternoon?"

Will studied Bob Smiley carefully and then reluctantly agreed.

They shook hands, and Will headed out of the little house with the big insurance sign out front.

Unfortunately, he was leaving his meeting with the agent with more questions than he had answers. More than that, Smiley's discomfort with the interview scored a magnitude of 7 on the Richter scale. Of course, Will knew that few people enjoy being interviewed by a lawyer, particularly regarding a pending court case. And no one enjoys being dragged into litigation involving a former high-school friend accused of child abuse.

But what Will had to figure out was whether there was more than that lying under the surface. He had the distinct sensation that there were some tremors underfoot—and he could only wonder if he was getting close to a major fault line.

20

Law professor Len Redgrove paused a few seconds on the other end of the line. Then he asked his next question.

"What constitutional arguments did you raise in your written brief to the court?"

"The Sixth Amendment—impairment of right to counsel," Will answered.

"But Will," Redgrove went on, "I thought you said this was a civil hearing brought by the Department of Social Services to take custody of the child based on alleged abuse? The Sixth Amendment is not implicated in noncriminal proceedings."

"Exactly," Will responded. "But there's still an outstanding criminal warrant for her—and criminal child-abuse charges have been filed. If and when they apprehend her—or she turns herself in—those criminal proceedings will kick in to full gear. And I represent her in both the civil child-abuse and the criminal child-abuse cases. So I think the Sixth Amendment does apply."

"Good point. How about the Fourteenth Amendment—did you raise that also?"

"Absolutely. And in addition to the due-process argument, my position is that if the court forces an attorney—an attorney who has taken an oath to preserve the confidences of his client—to violate that oath and disclose the whereabouts of his client when his client has instructed him not to, that's the same as if the client was 'compelled' to incriminate herself."

"Alright. Let's go to the other prong of the Fifth Amendment test. Even if there is 'compulsion' against a client, how is the disclosure of her whereabouts 'incriminating' against her? How does it create a reasonable apprehension that she could be found guilty of a criminal offense?"

"I think we've met that test as well, Len," Will responded.

He pressed on with his argument. "Suppose the client says to the attorney, 'Well, here I am, in a grass hut on such-and-such a beach in Puerto Rico.' And she further verifies that she has the child with her in violation of the existing court order that she turn the child over to the Department of Social Services. And the lawyer divulges this to the court. That information sets her up for possible contempt-of-court citation. The court could conclude that she willfully violated the court order—and could impose a jail term upon her for her violation."

"Was that the ex parte order that you told me about? No notice to you or the parents?"

"Yes," Will said, "the court entertained that secret hearing without notice, on the grounds that there was an emergency in regard to the child's welfare."

"Amazing," Redgrove remarked. "But local judges have a tremendous amount of discretion in determining whether emergency circumstances warrant an ex parte hearing. My experience with that mostly involves injunctions, where one party is alleging there's going to be an imminent disaster to its rights if an immediate injunction is not issued. You know, a typical temporary restraining order for twenty-four hours or so."

"But Len, here we have Mary Sue Fellows' rights as a *parent*. You can't get more fundamental or more important that that. Her rights are being trampled by a judge based entirely on circumstantial evidence, with no notice to *either* parent. Besides, Social Services had access to the medical records before—why didn't they intervene sooner if it was such an emergency?"

"Look, Will," Redgrove said, "that's the advocate in you talking. I can respect that. You had the heart and mind of a trial lawyer when you were in my Constitutional Law class all those years ago. But one thing about being a law professor—it's like being a judge. You have the luxury—if you can call it that—of being more objective.

"Let's assume you have a father who has been beating up a child—or you suspect it. And each time the child goes into the hospital he has more and more bruises. Finally one day the child shows up with an unexplained fracture. And you also have some evidence that the father has threatened, 'If this kid spills his milk one more time I'm going to take a baseball bat to him and finish him off.' Now, what do you do as a judge? Do you say, 'Let's wait for more evidence'? Or do you err on the other side—in other words, save the child and worry about legal niceties later?"

"I'm not saying it would have been an easy call," Will continued, his voice rising in passion. "But what I am saying is this—I find it uncomfortably convenient for the court to have ended up on the side of issuing an order at the request of a local prosecutor based on flimsy circumstantial evidence without notice to the opposing party or her attorney. Doing the right thing in court becomes the most important when doing the right thing is the *hardest*. People need justice the most when the decisions are the toughest—not when they are the easiest."

"I love to see that fire in your belly for justice," Redgrove responded warmly. "Our legal system is a fragile thing. In a way it's like a fine instrument that has been properly calibrated so it can be operated adequately only by the hands of a skilled and conscientious artisan. The clumsy, the dishonest, the politically minded, or the tyrannical—once they lay their hands on the levers of justice, they can do a great deal of damage. That's the challenge you have, Will. Firmly but respectfully reminding the judge that the levers of this great machinery don't belong to him personally. They belong to everyone—including Mary Sue Fellows and little Joshua."

"Thanks, Len," Will said.

"Now, on a personal note, let me tell you this—you are in one tough spot. I hope you're prepared for the consequences. You know what I'm talking about."

"I do," Will affirmed. "I could end up doing jail time on a con-tempt-of-court citation."

Both men paused, and then Redgrove spoke up again.

"One thing you and I haven't talked about. One option. You've probably thought about it. Your representation of Mary Sue Fellows—"

Will shot his response back immediately. "I'm not going to withdraw from representing her. I'm not walking away from this. That would do nothing except help preserve my own hide. I'm not throwing Mary Sue and her family to the wolves."

"No," Redgrove noted with a little resignation in his voice. "I didn't think you would. What time is your hearing tomorrow?"

"Nine o'clock in the morning."

"Does Fiona know about all of this?"

"No…she and I have been playing phone tag for a while. She's in Nashville at a recording studio, working on her new CD. We've been missing each other, leaving messages. It's probably just as well. We're still making some adjustments."

"Will," Len Redgrove said in closing, "I am honored as usual that you wanted my advice on an issue. I wish I had some snappy, all-purpose answers. Some quick bright-line legal test you could argue. But the fact is, you've got one foot on firm ground and the other in quicksand. The next move you make is going to be critical."

After Will hung up the phone, he pondered Redgrove's tone of voice. He knew it when he heard it. Real concern. It was the concern not just of an ex–law professor—or even a professional and spiritual mentor—but of a friend who cared deeply for Will.

In law school, Len Redgrove had recognized Will's potential as a trial advocate. He'd worked with him on law review, person-ally assigning complex issues for his research. He had coached Will on the moot-court team that went to the national finals.

Yet Will often thought back to one class in particular that Redgrove had taught. In his class on jurisprudence, the professor had laid out the variety of legal philosophies that could serve as a basis for the idea of justice. But he was most eloquent when he discussed the Judeo–Christian roots of law—in the identity of a personal Lawgiver whose combined attributes of mercy and moral perfection created the only credible foundation for a consistent philosophy of law.

Will had kept in touch with Redgrove over the years of his practice. And he'd often spoken to him on a personal level. When Will's wife, Audra, had been murdered, aside from his uncle Bull Chambers—a retired North Carolina judge—Len Redgrove had been the only other person to whom Will had confided the terrible details of that day.

After Audra's death, Will's contact with Redgrove began to wane. But when Will had undergone his recent spiritual awakening, he'd rekindled his relationship with the law professor. Now they would discuss the Bible together, both theological issues and very personal ones as well.

Will walked into the tiny houseboat bathroom, splashed some water on his face, and looked into the mirror. He didn't know what it was that bothered him the most about the impending court hearing before Judge Mason. Was it his own unyielding, often unreasonable, drive for legal perfection? If so, then it might be merely arrogance or pride that ignited his anger at the thought of being cited for contempt in the Delphi courtroom.

Or perhaps it was something else. The ghost of something long past—deeply buried. The need to prove something—to someone, somewhere.

But Will also knew there could be a simpler explanation. He knew the way he was built. He had always found it intolerable to see the weak victimized by the strong. Whenever he saw the great, toothed gears of the law grinding up the innocent and the powerless, Will knew that his task was obvious—he needed to grab hold of the gears and stop the mangling and the maiming.

Perhaps that's all he was—all he would ever be—as a lawyer. A brake in the wheels of the justice system when it threatened to crush the quiet people—the ordinary folks—the meek and the decent. And that was all right by Will. Unless, of course, it was his flesh that was getting fed into the big machine.

21

THE AIR WAS COOL THAT MORNING, and there was a haze on Eden Lake as Will carried his files from the houseboat to his car. He loaded them into his trunk, closed it, and was about to climb in behind the steering wheel when he remembered something.

He went back in and made his way into the bedroom, snatching the pocket New Testament off the nightstand and sliding it into the side pocket of his suit coat. He glanced into the bathroom, found his toothbrush and travel-size tube of toothpaste, and put them into the other pocket.

In approximately an hour, Judge Mason would be ruling on whether Will would be in contempt of court, depending on whether or not he decided to disclose what he knew about Mary Sue's whereabouts.

Will believed in being prepared. In this case, he was trying to think of anything else he might need for a possible stay in the county jail.

As he pulled away from the pier where the boathouse was moored, he realized he'd misplaced the directions back to Delphi. He studied the landmarks along the road and tried to remember a few that would lead him into town.

He recognized the sign that led him away from the marina area and soon found himself on the county highway, feeling confident that he was heading in the right direction. Will glanced around for a sign that he'd noticed on his last drive out to the boathouse. It marked a turnoff onto the main highway that led to Delphi.

After a few minutes, he saw the sign situated next to a pole that was flying a red windsock. It read,

TEX—THE FLYING COWBOY
Crop Dusting
Aerial Photography
Stunt Flying
Private Charters

He made the turn onto the main highway, and after five minutes or so he noticed the sign that read,

Welcome to Delphi!
We're Glad You're Here!

Trying to give himself a mental reprieve for a few moments, he turned on the car radio and punched the buttons until he located the national news. The announcer went through the usual litany of events. Hostilities in the Middle East. Oil prices. Some hopeful signs in the unemployment rate. A possible nationwide strike of airline pilots. And the final story about the Justice Department's seeking to extradite American billionaire Warren Mullburn from Switzerland as a material witness in an ongoing investigation into international bribery, political corruption, the suicide of a former Undersecretary of State, and the murder of Mullburn's bodyguard.

That final item held a particular interest for Will. Mullburn had surfaced as a shadowy presence in a case Will had taken to trial the preceding year. Through an extraordinary series of events, Will had actually met the billionaire face-to-face at his mega-mansion in the Nevada desert while Will was representing Reverend Angus MacCameron, Fiona's father. That case was what had brought him and Fiona together.

Musing on the recent course of their relationship, Will soon saw the buildings of downtown Delphi. He parked two blocks down from the courthouse, but still in full view of the activities outside. There was an INN television truck with a tall satellite antenna parked across from the courthouse. Behind it was a remote-broadcasting truck for the Atlanta stations. A handful of TV reporters were milling around the trucks, and a group was forming on the front lawn of the courthouse. He could spot Harry Putnam talking to a reporter with a notebook. Next to him, Harriet Bender was occasionally gesturing broadly and adding comments.

As Will sat for a moment, a green Jaguar pulled over to the curb about a hundred feet in front of him. He saw the driver grabbing furiously around the inside of the car for something. Then the door swung open, and Stanley Kennelworth got out. He had a thin file in his hand and began walking quickly across the street without looking. An oncoming car screeched on its brakes, narrowly missing him, and he raised a quick hand of thanks and then scurried across the street to the courthouse lawn, taking his position on the other side of Putnam. After the reporter walked away, Putnam, Bender, and Kennelworth huddled quickly.

Joe Fellows' case was not scheduled to be heard this morning. The only order of business that Will was aware of was the Mary Sue Fellows prosecution. Judge Mason was going to demand information on the whereabouts of Mary Sue Fellows from Will. But as far as Will knew, no other motions were scheduled in either case.

He climbed out of his car with his briefcase and began striding towards the courthouse. He glanced at the Jaguar and noticed it had temporary plates. He looked at the date. Kennelworth had obtained the car within the last ten days. On the back of the new car he also noticed a small dealership nameplate for "Continental Motors."

As Will neared the courthouse, the group on the front lawn was beginning to break apart and file into the courthouse, with one notable exception. Crystal Banes was hurrying directly toward Will.

"So, counselor," Banes said, "truth or consequences?"

"Are those my only two options?" Will asked. "How about truth or justice?"

"You haven't answered my question."

"No, I haven't." Then Will added, "But you will get the answer inside this courthouse in a matter of minutes."

"So you don't know what you're going to do? You're walking into this courtroom with no idea what you are going to say?" Banes asked sharply.

"No," Will said, "I didn't say that. I have a battle plan, but just like any other incursion into hostile territory, the battlefield here is a fluid environment. Besides," Will noted, "this may be an important skirmish, but it isn't the war."

Banes tilted her head, studied Will for an instant, and then turned and hurried ahead of him into the courthouse.

22

WILL WALKED QUICKLY into the courthouse and headed directly to Judge Mason's courtroom. Suddenly—and for no apparent reason—Will became aware of his surroundings. He noticed a glass display case in one of the walls dedicated to community safety. And how his shoes were making echoing click-clack sounds off the marble floor. He laid his hands on the dull brass handles of the courtroom, pulling the tall, chipped, and imperfectly varnished oak doors open.

As he opened the doors, he saw a courtroom that was full. Most of the audience was news reporters, but there was a handful of what Will presumed must be community onlookers and perennial courthouse hangers-on.

Putnam was already situated at the counsel table, and next to him, Harriet Bender. Behind both of them, social worker Liz Luden presided with her file on her lap. In the bench behind her, Stanley Kennelworth was seated, staring off into space.

Will glanced around quickly for any member of Mary Sue's family, but saw none of them. As he walked through the small wooden gate that separated the audience from the counsel tables and the bench, he concluded that this legal struggle—at least today—would be witnessed only by the hostile forces of the prosecution team, a few curious onlookers, a few curious court watchers, and the professionally curious members of the press.

There was no rooting section, no cheerleaders, and no home-team banners to cheer on Will's defense of a family torn asunder by the brute force of the state. This legal battle—and Will's fate—were about to be decided in this miniature coliseum packed with unfriendly faces.

Unpacking his briefcase and setting out his file, Will glanced over at the opposing table. Putnam looked away. Guardian ad litem Bender was staring straight ahead.

At the front of the courtroom a bailiff with a holstered revolver shifted his weight as he stood at semi-attention with his hands behind his back. In a moment the stenographer hurried into the courtroom with her steno machine, put it in place, and took her seat with her fingers ready on the keys.

Right after the court clerk brought the court file out, dropped it on the bench, and took her seat at the clerk's desk, Judge Mason strolled into the courtroom. His black robe had been unzipped down to the beltline, revealing a white shirt and a cowboy string tie. He took a casual look around the courtroom with his hands in his pockets and smiled. The clerk bent over and whispered something into his ear, and the judge zipped his robe up to the neck, brushed himself off a bit, and then mounted the stairs to the bench.

"Good morning, all," he said cheerily. "We are here on case number 05-65667—Juda County Department of Social Services versus Mary Sue Fellows. Are counsel ready?"

Harry Putnam stood up quickly.

"Herodius Putnam for the County."

"Guardian ad litem Bender for the minor child Joshua Fellows," Bender snapped out and then resumed her seat.

"Will Chambers for the defense."

Will was still standing when the judge began addressing him. "I see, Mr. Chambers, that you are sitting alone at counsel table. That is quite unfortunate. That's a real shame. I want to know where your client is. Let's start talking."

"I filed our written arguments with the court yesterday and provided copies to opposing counsel."

Before Will could elaborate, Judge Mason cut him off. "Right. I have read your arguments. Counsel has read your arguments.

Let's go. Where is Ms. Fellows—where's Joshua—what do you have to tell me today, Mr. Chambers?"

"Your Honor," Will began, "this court—in its order—has thrust my client's defense onto a bed of needle-sharp nails. No matter which way we turn, the defense will suffer irreparable harm—constitutionally, ethically, and legally."

"Well, Mr. Chambers, maybe someone should have told you in law school that the practice of law out here in the real world can get mighty tough. Sometimes when you take a position of arrogance and defiance toward a court, you've got to pay the piper. You're going to get a split lip once in a while. Is that what you're here for? To complain about the split lip you're going to get from this court? If you don't produce the information that you have been ordered to turn over regarding your client—"

"I am here," Will countered, "to remind the court—with all due respect—that I have a privilege of confidentiality in my conversations and contacts with my client. That is a sacred trust, and I am not about to breach it. This court has ordered me to breach it—but that I cannot, and will not, do. I am also here to remind the court that the Constitution gives my client a Fourteenth Amendment right of due process, and a Sixth Amendment right to the assistance of her legal counsel, both of which are endangered if this court orders me to do what I cannot do.

"Now if I *do* know something about my client's whereabouts, I am here to tell this court that I have no liberty nor permission from my client to divulge it. On the other hand, if I do *not* possess information about my client's whereabouts, then this court would have me do the impossible—and suffer potential imprisonment when I have failed to carry out that impossible task."

"Where is Mary Sue Fellows? Where is Joshua Fellows?" Judge Mason bellowed, his face no longer with a warm and pleasant smile but purpling in anger.

"To repeat myself," Will continued calmly, "I cannot answer that question, Your Honor."

Harry Putnam jumped to his feet.

"Your Honor," Putnam said, "I take no position on what the court should do with Mr. Chambers at this point. I would point out, however, that guardian ad litem Bender may have some information for the court."

"Oh yes, Your Honor." Bender rose slowly with a confident smile on her face. "I have some important evidence that I want to present right now. May I call a witness so that we can make a record for the court?"

Judge Mason was still staring at Will. He diverted his eyes only momentarily in the direction of Bender, giving her a quick nod of approval.

Bender waved in the direction of Stanley Kennelworth, who nervously rose and inched his way along the side of the courtroom and up to the witness stand. She began examining him.

"You are Joseph Fellows' attorney?"

"Yes," Kennelworth answered in a low, quiet voice.

"You have talked to your client on numerous occasions regarding his case—as well as the case involving his wife, Mary Sue Fellows?"

"Yes, that's true."

"And yesterday, did you invite me to meet with your client, Joe Fellows, to talk about Mary Sue's case?"

"Yes, ma'am, that's correct. You, and me, and my client Joe Fellows met in the jail, and we had a talk."

"And in that discussion, the three of us—we talked about Mary Fellows' case, and how much Will Chambers might know about where his client is?"

"Right. We talked about that. Sure."

"And Joe Fellows told you and me—"

"Hearsay!" Will exclaimed, jumping to his feet. But before Judge Mason could rule, Bender pushed on.

"And what did Joe Fellows say?"

"He said his mother had told him that Will Chambers knew the area code that Mary Sue was calling from."

"Double hearsay!" Will added, his eyes riveted on the judge, waiting futilely for him to make a ruling.

"And where did Joe Fellows' mother hear about Will Chambers knowing the area code?"

"She supposedly learned it from a recent conversation with Mary Sue Fellows."

"Triple hearsay!" Will exclaimed. He stretched his arms out in front of the judge, shaking his head in disbelief.

"Are you asking for a ruling, Mr. Chambers?" the judge asked.

"I certainly am, Your Honor," Will said firmly. "We have three layers of hearsay—and I don't hear anyone arguing one of the exceptions to the hearsay rule."

"How about this," the judge said. "Maybe this is not being offered to prove the actual truth of the hearsay statements. Maybe guardian ad litem Bender is trying only to set the stage to prove one of the exceptions—like intent, or state of mind. Isn't that right, Ms. Bender?"

"Oh, that's true," Bender chimed in. "That's exactly why I'm asking the questions."

"Whose intent? Whose state of mind? How is any of this relevant?" Will demanded.

"It's your intent—your state of mind, Mr. Chambers," the judge replied, his jaw clenching slightly. "You're an inch-and-a-half from the county jail. I'm trying to find out whether you are being contemptuous of my order or not. So your objection is overruled. Anything else, Ms. Bender?"

Harriet Bender smiled and shrugged happily. "Nothing else, Your Honor."

Stanley Kennelworth started to rise from the witness chair, but Will stopped him in his tracks.

"You can remain seated, Mr. Kennelworth," Will said. "I have a few questions for you."

Kennelworth sat down, but quickly shifted in his seat as if someone had placed tacks on it.

"Mr. Kennelworth, do you still represent Joe Fellows?"

"Yeah. I still represent him."

"Do you acknowledge your ethical duty to defend your client zealously?"

"Sure. I know all that."

"I look around this courtroom, Mr. Kennelworth, and I don't see Joe Fellows anywhere. Is he still down in the county jail at this very moment?"

"Oh, yeah. He's still down there."

"Whose idea was it—yours?—to invite guardian ad litem Bender down to talk with your client?"

"I can't remember."

"But you know that if the conversation had been just between you and Joe Fellows that it would have been protected by attorney–client privilege? You wouldn't have been able to disclose it because it then would have been confidential?"

"I suppose so. I knew that."

"So, knowing that, you brought Ms. Bender into the conference so that you could deliberately break the attorney–client privilege by bringing an outsider into the conversation—thus waiving the confidentiality of your client and allowing you to testify in court today that I knew something about Mary Sue Fellows' whereabouts?"

Bender and Putnam both simultaneously jumped to their feet, shouting out objections made indistinguishable by the confusion.

"Out of bounds," the judge said loudly. "Mr. Chambers, you're way out of bounds."

"Your Honor, I think we need an answer to my question. My client deserves an answer to this question. The integrity of this court requires an answer to the question."

"I'll be the judge of what this court needs!" Judge Mason roared. "You're overruled!"

Will whirled back to face Kennelworth and kept slugging.

"Are you concerned at all about being sued for legal malpractice for what you've done in court today?"

"Objection!" Putnam and Bender both howled, jumping to their feet.

"Sustained!" the judge barked.

Will's natural impulse was to keep slashing. Keep pushing ahead. Keep punching and grabbing until he could squeeze the truth out of Stanley Kennelworth. But that was when he stopped. He knew he had to resist that visceral instinct. All of his years in trial—all the questioning of all those witnesses in all of those courtroom battles—had taught him to resist what his natural bent would otherwise cause him to do. He slowed down. He took a few breaths. And he calmly addressed the attorney in the witness chair.

"By the way, I noticed your new Jaguar as I drove up to court. Beautiful automobile," Will said with a smile.

Kennelworth brightened up and leaned back slightly in his chair. "Thanks. I'm glad you like it, Mr. Chambers."

"Is anyone paying for your time in testifying today?"

Putnam and Banes both jumped up and objected.

Before the judge could snap out a ruling Will decided to remind him of the playing field.

"Your Honor," Will said calmly, "I think it's important for me to establish a *very good record* so that when this case goes up on appeal the reviewing court will have an adequate foundation on which to evaluate your ruling."

Judge Mason leaned back in his chair, drumming his fingers on the bench. "Answer that question. And only that question. Are you being paid to testify today?"

"No, absolutely not," Kennelworth answered.

Will stepped back in. "Your new Jaguar—was that purchased as part of your fees for this case?"

Kennelworth jerked his head back slightly and opened his mouth, but paused before letting any words escape.

"I don't know what you mean. I don't understand the question."

"I think you do. Was that new Jaguar purchased as part of any of the fees paid to you in connection with this case?"

Kennelworth paused again. And then he answered. "What that car represents—that was a business deal. So it really has nothing to do with any of this."

"Did you receive that new Jaguar from Continental Motors in Delphi?"

"That's right. That's exactly where I got it."

"And was it a gift to you from someone—someone who has an interest in this case—perhaps someone who has an interest in what you would say about the Mary Sue Fellows matter?"

"Like I said, it was a business deal. I was given that car—it was in lieu of my fees on something. That's all. Nothing to do with this. Nothing at all."

"Give me the name of the client, Mr. Kennelworth," Will asked, his eyes riveted on those of the other lawyer, whose glance now darted away from Will's. But the judge intervened to ease Kennelworth's obvious testimonial torment.

"You don't have to answer that," Judge Mason said. "It's simply not relevant here, Mr. Chambers. Now I assume you are finished with this witness, is that correct?"

"Given the limitations on my ability to examine this witness, I don't believe I can ask any other question that this court will not overrule."

The judge quickly dismissed Kennelworth from the stand and then whirled back toward Will Chambers.

"Which brings us to the business at hand. What's it going to be, Mr. Chambers? My way or the highway?"

"I think there's a third alternative," Will said. "The third alternative is justice. Applying the law according to established legal principles."

Judge Mason turned to Harry Putnam.

"Mr. Prosecutor, what's your position on all of this?"

Putnam rose to his feet. The look on his face was now missing the typical Harry Putnam arrogance. His brow was a little wrinkled, and he looked a little perplexed.

"Your Honor, I want the court's order enforced. I want Mary Sue Fellows back in this jurisdiction so we can hear her side of the story. And I want Joshua Fellows back in this jurisdiction so we can place him in a foster home to ensure his safety.

"Now, this court entered an order prohibiting Joe Fellows from being released on bail until he told this court the whereabouts of his wife. But he's still sitting in jail, and that hasn't worked. I'm not sure whether placing Mr. Chambers in jail for contempt is going to bring Mary Sue Fellows and her son back into this jurisdiction. I just don't know. As a result, I'm not taking any position on what punishment this court should mete out against the defense counsel."

The judge stared at Putnam for a second as if he were going to engage him and then decided against it. He turned his glance toward Harriet Bender, and simply nodded. Bender rose quickly.

"Judge, I think Mr. Chambers is in willful disobedience to the court's order. He has no excuses. He comes down here from the Commonwealth of Virginia and disregards the honor of this Georgia courtroom. Furthermore, he has willfully conspired with his client to impede my ability to represent my client—Joshua Fellows. I have not had a chance to have access to Joshua Fellows, my client, because of Mr. Chambers' arrogant refusal to obey this court's order. Nothing less than commitment to our county jail is appropriate. I am afraid there is no other alternative for you, Your Honor—you need to send Mr. Chambers to the county jail immediately."

Judge Mason turned his eyes toward Will, who was seated at the counsel table with his handed folded in front of him, a stern look of unflagging resolve on his face.

"Mr. Chambers, do you have anything else you want to tell me?"

Will responded quietly but firmly. "Your Honor, I am an attorney who's taken an oath to zealously represent my client within the bounds of the law, including my duty to preserve attorney–client confidences. I have two things to tell this court. First, Your Honor, I do have information about the area code from which my client was calling me. Second of all, I shall not now, nor shall I ever, divulge that information to this court unless instructed to do so by my client or by the Georgia State Supreme Court. To do so would be to violate my sacred trust with my client and to violate my responsibility as an attorney."

Judge Mason leaned forward. His head was tilted slightly, as if he were straining to hear the horn of some approaching freight train still off in the distance.

The courtroom was silent, with one exception only—a creaking sound that was coming from the chair of the court clerk. Her upper torso and head were at rigid attention, her eyes riveted on Will, but she was shifting slightly in her chair in anticipation.

"Mr. Chambers, please rise," the judge intoned.

Will rose to his feet.

The creaking sound stopped.

"Mr. Chambers, do you know what I am going to do now?" the judge asked.

"Whatever it is," Will said quietly, "I'm prepared to hear it."

"By the authority vested in me by the State of Georgia, and pursuant to the laws of this state, I hereby confine you to an indefinite term of imprisonment in the Juda County jail. You shall remain there in the custody of Juda County until such time as you purge yourself from the contempt of court that you have willfully and flagrantly committed. You can purge yourself from this contempt and end your imprisonment by simply giving the word to the jailer that you wish to be brought back to this court-room and divulge to me everything you know about the where-abouts of Mary Sue Fellows and her son, Joshua. Until that time, you are an inmate of our local jail. Bailiff, take Mr. Chambers away."

The armed bailiff quickly stepped over to Will's position at the counsel table. As he did, Will rapped out quickly, "Your Honor, I'm asking this court to stay the execution of its order for a sufficient time for me to file an immediate appeal."

"Motion denied!" the judge responded.

The bailiff took Will by the arm and began leading him from the courtroom.

Will turned to the judge one last time. "Your Honor, I move that this court recuse itself from any further proceedings in the Mary Sue Fellows case on the grounds of manifest bias and prejudice in its conduct of this hearing."

"Mister, that motion is denied!" the judge exclaimed, now rising to his feet with both hands on the bench, his face flushed with anger.

As the bailiff led Will to the side of the courtroom Crystal Banes reached over the audience railing and thrust the microphone of a small tape recorder in Will's direction, yelling one final question to him.

"Mr. Chambers, what's your next move?"

The bailiff was opening the side door to the jail corridor that lay on the other side, his hand tightly on Will's arm, and Will had time for only one last comment as he disappeared through the doorway.

"I guess I'll catch up on my Bible reading."

Then the door that led from the courtroom to the Juda County jail closed with a bone-jarring bang.

Banes turned to Spike, her cameraman, who was standing next to her in the front row of the courtroom.

"Bible reading, I'm sure!" she said with a sneer.

But Spike was not smiling. His lips were pursed and his brow was furrowed as he stared at the door that had just slammed shut.

23

As Will sat on the metal cot, his back against the wall, he found it difficult to believe he was an inmate in jail. He had his pocket New Testament in his hand and had been trying to do some reading, but he couldn't focus. He was distracted by the constant stream of profanities being yelled by inmates, the din echoing down the gray corridor.

Will had no idea how long Judge Mason was going to hold him. For that reason, he knew he had to be mentally prepared for the long haul.

Somehow, he had thought that, as a lawyer, his confinement might be different. There he was wrong. Whether permitted by the judge or required by jail regulations, he was treated no differently than any other inmate.

He had been taken to a holding cell, where a uniformed officer introduced only as guard Thompson stood ready with an impassive expression and surgical gloves on his hands. He was told to strip and leave his clothes in a pile on the floor. After that, he was submitted to a humiliating physical search. He was allowed to keep his New Testament, but he was not allowed to keep the toothpaste or toothbrush that he'd put in the pockets of his suit coat. He was also refused an immediate phone call.

"I am a lawyer, guard Thompson," Will said. "I don't want to hassle you—but I've got a right to a phone call and I need to make that phone call right now."

The guard did not change expression. He had heard similar requests from nearly every inmate who had been checked into the holding cell before being assigned to a bunk. His answer was always the same.

"You will get your required phone call when it is convenient for us—and *after* you have been processed and checked into your cell. Not before."

Will was issued an orange jumpsuit with the words "Juda County Jail" stenciled on the back. He was also issued a pair of paper shoes with stretched-out elastic at the ankles, which were barely capable of remaining on his feet.

Will found a blessing in the fact that the jumpsuit was soft and comfortable to wear. Yet he knew that was only because it had been worn by countless other inmates before him. He tried to keep that thought out of his mind.

As he sat on the bunk and gazed across the cell, he realized the other bed was unoccupied. He wondered whether he would be assigned a cellmate.

He did not have to wonder long.

Soon, another guard led an inmate to the door of the cell and opened it noisily. The inmate slowly shuffled in, the door slamming with a metallic bang behind him. He was of medium height, thin but muscular, with greasy, blond hair and long sideburns. His sleeves were rolled up almost to his shoulders, revealing a tattoo of a grim reaper that wound down his right arm from his bicep almost to his wrist.

The man's eyes focused like lasers on the little book on Will's lap, then he looked at Will's face and studied him for a moment. After a moment, he raised his right arm and pointed right at the attorney.

"What makes you think I don't want your bunk? What makes you think you ought to be sittin' there lookin' at me?"

Will leaned forward on the bunk, tensing for a challenge. "This is the bunk the guard assigned me. That means the other bunk belongs to you."

"How do I know you're not lying? Maybe you're a punk. How 'bout I take you down right now?" The other man steadied himself by planting his feet and tilting his head down, as if he were gazing at a caged animal through the bars.

Will stood up quickly—so quickly the inmate took a half-step back.

"I think that would be a big mistake—we both know that," he said authoritatively.

The other inmate took a step toward Will until he was eyeball-to-eyeball. Then he broke into a wide smile, showing yellowed teeth and a lifetime of dental neglect.

"Hey—I'm just messin' with you," the inmate said, laughing. "Lighten up."

Will eased back into his bunk and managed a modest smile.

"I'm Ivan. You got a name?"

"Will Chambers," Will replied and got up out of his bunk again, this time reaching out to shake hands with his new cellmate.

Ivan's smile disappeared, and he waved Will off with both hands.

"Oh no, man. You don't do that in here. You don't reach out to another guy's body—*ever*."

Will understood instantly and retreated to his bunk.

"See," Ivan continued, "all you got in here is *you*. Your body and your space. Now *The Man* controls your body. He tells you when to get up, when to get down. When to eat. But your space—your space belongs to *you*. Your space is that half-inch around your body that nobody better get into. *Nobody*."

Will acknowledged that he understood. Then he asked Ivan what his last name was.

Ivan studied him for a moment, as if deciding whether or not to answer. Then, very slowly and cautiously, he spelled it out— *T-S-O-U-G-R-O-S-K-Y*.

Then he added, "It's pronounced 'Sugrosky.'" He raised an index finger in the air as a warning. "Just don't ever call me Ivan Sue. That would not be a good idea." He stretched out on his bunk, two hands behind his head, staring at the ceiling.

Will eased back in his bed and flipped his New Testament open to where he'd marked the place with his finger. He'd been reading the second chapter of Matthew.

In that Gospel story, Joseph had been warned in a dream by an angel to take his young bride, Mary, and their newborn baby and flee to Egypt. Joseph had been warned that Herod—jealous for his throne—had been told of the birth of Jesus and now wanted to locate and destroy him.

But while Joseph, Mary, and Jesus had been staying in Egypt, Herod died, and so an angel in a dream once again instructed Joseph. This time he was told of Herod's death. It would now be safe to return to Judea.

"So—you're a Holy Roller, huh?" Ivan said, breaking the silence.

"You mean this?" Will said, raising the book up so that Ivan could see the text.

"I can smell a Holy Roller a mile away."

Will smiled and returned to his reading. After a few moments, the silence was broken again.

"So what part are you reading?"

Will gave a simple description of Joseph's return from Egypt with Mary and the young baby Jesus.

After a bit, Ivan chimed in again.

"So—let me get this straight—Joseph and his old lady and the baby—they go to Egypt 'cause they're runnin' from The Man—right?"

Will paused before responding. "Well…you might put it that way."

Another minute went by, and then Ivan offered his own homespun interpretation.

"So, that means—if I follow you—if I bust out of here and escape and run off somewhere to escape The Man, then I'm just doin' what Jesus' old man did. That right?"

"Not exactly," Will replied.

"Why not? What's the deal?"

"Joseph had specific instructions from God himself to escape to Egypt. He hadn't committed a crime—in fact, a crime was about to be committed against his family. And when Joseph took his wife and his baby away, he was under the guidance and protection of God himself. That's the difference between the hypothetical case you're telling me and what's in the Bible."

After a few more seconds, Ivan asked, "You're that lawyer, right?"

"Yes," Will replied. "How did you hear?"

"You'd be surprised," Ivan said.

Will put the book down. "What have you heard?"

"That you wouldn't give some information about your client even though the judge told you to. That you're protecting your client and the judge hammered you. And here you are, wearing the orange—just like the rest of us."

Ivan was now lying on his side, his head propped up with his arm, talking directly to Will. "No lawyer *I* ever had would do something like that for *me*—no way. My lawyers never did much for me—*ever*."

Will studied Ivan and then cautiously volunteered a rebuttal.

"So—are you saying that you're in here because of your lawyers? That's why you're in here?"

Ivan scratched his head furiously and laughed.

"No, man. No way. Let's face it—my lawyers were losers but that ain't why I'm here. I'm here because I was buyin' and sellin' stuff that was falling off the back of a truck—you know what I mean?"

"Receiving stolen property?"

"You got it," Ivan said.

"You just get in here?" Will asked.

"Naw—I've been in for a while."

"Why did they just move you into my cell?" Will asked.

Ivan paused and narrowed his eyes. He looked at the cell door, and then back to Will. Then, lowering his voice, he leaned toward Will and explained.

"I was in a cell with a guy they call Jumpin' Jack. His real name was Victor, but everyone called him Jumpin' Jack. He threw a food tray or something like that. Anyway, they sent him to the overflow pen."

Then Ivan broke into a strange sneer and shook his head.

"So? What happened?" Will asked.

"Well," his cellmate continued in a hushed voice, "when they finished with him at the overflow, they had to check him into the hospital. He's in a coma now, on life supports. He's breathing through a tube and his brain is all bashed in."

"How did it happen?" Will asked intensely.

"They said that he slipped in the shower and smacked his head. Of course, that ain't it. That's not how it happened."

"How do you know what happened?" Will asked.

"'Cause there's this guy that runs the overflow, this big guard. He loves messin' people up. This ain't the first time it's happened."

Will was trying to patch Ivan's story together.

"But I still don't understand why they moved you into the cell with me."

Ivan laughed. "I thought you were smart. Big lawyer man and you can't even figure it out," he said, still chuckling. "'You're a lawyer from Virginia. Your client's name is Mary Sue Fellows. She hit the road when the cops tried to arrest her for child abuse. The judge and dirty Harry Putnam—that's what we call him, 'dirty Harry' Putnam—want to find out where she is, they figure you know where she is, but you won't talk. Have I got all that straight, Mr. Attorney-at-law?"

Will was trying to piece together what appeared to be a stream-of-consciousness narrative from Ivan. And then the dawn broke.

Ivan must have seen the light go on in Will's expression.

"So here I am, and here you are. So you'd better watch out, anything you say *can* be used against you!" Ivan said with a laugh.

Will was surprised that he had not assumed on his own that the prosecutor would place a snitch in his cell in hopes of gaining information. The attorney suddenly recognized his own naivete.

"You owe me one," Ivan said with a half-grin. And then he added, "And I got somethin' else for ya."

"What's that?" Will asked.

"You're a Holy Roller—I got somethin' for you to pray about."

"Such as?" Will followed up.

"You better pray they don't ever haul you down to the overflow pen. You better pray to God that doesn't happen to you."

24

"WHAT'S THAT, MOMMY?" Joshua asked, pointing to a clear plastic cylinder containing ten sticks with cotton swabs at each end.

"They look like Q-Tips, don't they, honey?" Mary Sue answered.

Joshua was methodically walking around the doctor's examining room, inspecting each piece of medical equipment and all of the medical supplies.

Mary Sue glanced nervously at her watch. It had been at least fifteen minutes since the nurse had ushered her and Joshua into the office and said that the doctor would be "in to see you in a few minutes."

The fugitive had a rising fear that the delay had something to do with her. Perhaps a problem with the medical information she'd given the receptionist. Perhaps it was the fact that she'd listed no insurance company. But Katherine had accompanied her and assured the nurse that she herself would be paying for the visit.

Or perhaps the doctor was contacting the local sheriff's department—and they were on their way right now with multiple squad cars to arrest Mary Sue and snatch Joshua from her care.

"What's that, Mommy?" Joshua asked.

"That's a stethoscope."

Mary Sue looked at her watch again. She got up from her chair and quietly cracked the door open an inch, glancing through the hallway and to the lobby beyond. She could see Katherine seated in the lobby, reading a magazine. She could also see the main desk area, where the receptionist was typing calmly at her computer.

She closed the door and sat down. Joshua trudged over to her with a bored expression and flopped onto her lap.

"Can we go now? I'm tired of this room."

She set Joshua squarely on her lap and gave him a big hug and kiss.

"We have to wait for the doctor, Josh."

"Why? Why don't we go, Mommy?"

"Because we have to make you better and the doctor is going to help us."

Then there were voices outside the door, just down the corridor. A man's voice, and another voice that sounded like a woman's. And another voice. For a moment, Mary Sue began to feel the overpowering grip of panic.

She set Joshua down and quickly walked over to the window. She pulled back the curtain and saw that there was no screen on the other side. When unlatched and fully opened, the window would be large enough for her and Joshua to easily climb through.

The voices outside the door stopped. Mary Sue glanced out at the highway and the dusty, rolling hills in the distance. She stretched out her hand and touched the latch on the window. Then she felt a presence at her side, and she turned around. Joshua was looking up at her, watching her wide-eyed. He wrapped his arms around her leg and smiled.

She took her hand off the latch, bent down, and took him into her arms, feeling the sense of panic melt away.

Then she began walking around the room, telling her son about some of the pictures on the walls. She stopped in front of one of them that showed a farm scene, with a farmhouse not unlike theirs.

Out of nowhere, Mary Sue felt the empty, gnawing pangs of loneliness and fear.

She began praying. *Please heal my baby boy, whatever the problem is. Protect us. Let Joe know how much I love him. Bring our family back together. Make this nightmare end.*

Then after a few seconds she added, *And give your wisdom and courage to Will Chambers—wherever he is.*

The door to the room swung open suddenly. Caught off guard, Mary Sue was startled, and she clutched Joshua even closer to her as she spun to face the door.

Dr. Bill Kendoll, dressed in a white short-sleeved shirt with his tie loosened at the neck, holding a clipboard, was standing in the doorway.

He strode into the room smiling, reaching out a hand and cupping the side of Joshua's face. Joshua smiled back.

"Mary Sue, I'm Dr. Kendoll," he said, motioning for her to sit down on the chair he pulled up. "But everybody calls me 'Dr. Bill.'" He flipped through the documents on his clipboard.

"Okay, first visit for mother and child. The nurse indicates in her notes that there is some lethargy, some complaint of possible developmental delays—below the fifteenth percentile in height-and-weight bracket. Vomiting after meals. Lack of appetite. Temp is only slightly elevated. Any other symptoms you have noticed?"

"No, I think you've got it."

"I do note you feel that the vomiting and loss of appetite have improved recently—is that right?"

"Yes—in fact, I've been living with a family in the area for a little while and Josh has had a change in diet. I've noticed that his nausea seems to have decreased and his appetite is getting better ever since we came out here to South Dakota. In fact, I've written down a list of the things he's been eating in comparison to what he was eating before to see if that might be tied into a possible diagnosis." She handed the piece of paper to the doctor, who took it and looked at it with interest.

"Very impressive. That's very smart on your part."

"Are you going to be taking any blood?"

"Yes. No question about that. We've got to rule out some things. From the history you've given, this appears to be a problem that was getting progressively worse over the course of a year—until most recently, when you think there has been an improvement."

"How about the blood analysis?" Mary Sue asked, "Are you going to be doing a broad-spectrum evaluation rather than just a simple blood count?"

"Well," Dr. Bill said, smiling and looking at Mary Sue directly, "it is true that a broader blood test might pick up some of the more esoteric diseases—some of those metabolic disorders, though they're pretty rare. But I think we should be open to all kinds of possibilities."

Then, after turning to one of the pages in the notes and glancing at it for a moment, he looked up at Mary Sue again.

"So—what brings you to South Dakota?"

"Some family problems," Mary Sue replied.

"The chart indicates that you are staying over at Tommy White Arrow's ranch. Are you a friend of the family?"

"Actually, I've just gotten to know them recently. They're wonderful folks."

"Yes, they certainly are," Dr. Bill confirmed. "I've known them for a number of years. I've taken care of all of them, I think—Tommy, Katherine, even Andrew on occasion. And I'll probably be doing checkups on Danny, now that he's back here in South Dakota living with his brother and sister."

The physician glanced down at the piece of paper with Mary Sue's notes on Joshua.

"You say here that Joshua has been eating lower-protein foods and you wonder whether that might give us a clue?"

"Yes," she replied. "Katherine does the cooking, and she wanted to experiment with a low-protein diet she read about. So we're all her guinea pigs!" she added with a laugh. "And the other thing is, that he's been a little bit healthier—fewer colds and flu and that kind of thing—since I've taken him out of a one-day-a-week day care that he'd been in. I'm not sure if that makes any difference to coming up with a diagnosis."

The doctor leaned back in his chair and studied Mary Sue for a moment. Joshua was now squirming impatiently in her arms.

"You seem very educated on medical issues—do you have some kind of medical background?"

"Yes," Mary Sue responded. "I am a nurse."

"Well," Dr. Bill said, rising and walking over to the cabinet with the syringes, "let's draw some blood and see what we find out." And then he turned to Mary Sue and remarked, "As you know, it's amazing what you can find out from a little bit of blood."

25

THE LAST OF THE DINNER GUESTS had left Jason Bell Purdy's mansion outside of Atlanta. The cook, the two maids, and the housekeeper were cleaning up after the feast, which had been held in the grand dining room that seated forty.

Purdy was pacing in his study, in front of the French doors that led to a large veranda outside, and sucking on a piece of hard candy. He strode over to the Moroccan leather couch, plopped down, and punched the TV remote with his right hand while he flipped open his Palm Pilot with the other and began tapping into his calendar for the rest of the week.

On TV, a congressman was giving a press conference, sharing his comments on the potential airline pilot strike. Both the House and the Senate were closely divided on the question of emergency legislation to deal with the issue. The president had not yet commented on whether he would use executive power to order the pilots back to work if a strike occurred.

Purdy muted the sound on the TV and considered his own position on the issue—or more precisely, his difficulty in forming any position at all.

Ever since the death of Senator Jim Boggs Hartley, the political caucus had been seriously considering Purdy to finish out Hartley's term. He had money, connections, experience on several prestigious volunteer projects, and that golden commodity of name recognition. He even possessed local-hero status, having been all-state quarterback during his high-school days at the prestigious Exeter Academy. And what he lacked in raw IQ he could make up with cunning, charisma, and charm.

Purdy was quickly realizing that hiring political consultants and a group of PR experts to prepare him to fill Hartley's Senate seat had not been enough. Calling up his to-do list, he tapped in the message, "Hire political analyst/expert on the issues."

I've got to get me some brain boys to help me on these political issues, Purdy thought to himself. But a tap at the windows interrupted him. He whirled and saw a large figure outside the window. He smiled and gestured for the man to come in.

Howard John Jubb walked into the room. Six-foot-one, a broad-shouldered, beefy man with powerful arms and a thick neck, he sported a curly black beard and a Pittsburgh Pirates baseball cap. He was called "Howley" by most who knew him.

"Hey," Purdy called out.

"Hey," the visitor responded. "Nice dinner party?"

"It was alright," Purdy replied. "Man—what is it with the way you dress, Howley?"

Howley Jubb looked down at his outfit. He was wearing an expensive silk golf shirt on top and, on the bottom, a pair of camouflage pants with black leather military boots.

"What are you talking about?" Jubb chuckled. "This is the way I always dress."

"Yeah, that's just the point. That nameplate on your office says you're my real estate manager. You've got to do something about your image."

"What difference does it make? You have me slip in and out of your house at night—through the back door. You treat me like one of your housekeepers. Nobody ever sees me anyway."

"Do I hear resentment? Is there something about the work you do, or the money I pay you, that you don't like?"

"No, Jason. I'm not complaining. I'm just happy to have a job here on your plantation," he replied lightly.

Purdy studied Jubb's face and wondered if, underneath his smile, there was anything to worry about. He decided to laugh it off, and he slapped Jubb on the shoulder and invited him to sit down.

"I'm tired. Let's cut to the chase. Where are things with the bank examiners?"

"I don't think that's going to be a problem. They have no inkling that Pencup was anything more than a bank president. They don't know about the real-estate partnership. Their theory is that the two million was salted away by Pencup in some off-shore account. At least, that's the idea my contact is trying to sell to them."

"And you're telling me that Eden Lake has never come up in anything you've heard—right?"

"Jason, I'm telling you," Jubb assured him, "there is no talk *anywhere* about Eden Lake. They will not be tying you in with Henry Pencup—period."

"And what about the collar?" Purdy asked.

"I think we're alright on that. This guy is old school. Won't talk because it would violate the sanctity of the relationship. That kind of stuff. I've checked him out—very quietly, of course."

"And what if he talks? I mean, that's possible. Then what?"

"Well, then I got a backup plan," Jubb said, "a pretty good one. I'm proud of it."

"That's good. Backup plans are good. But not having to use backup plans is better. You follow me on that?"

"Sure," Jubb said, "but like I said, don't worry about it. I've got it covered. Now, how about a drink for me?"

"To tell you the truth, Howley, I'm tired—and I've got a busy day tomorrow. I'm hitting the sack."

Jubb stood up and glanced around the room.

"So, you're livin' alone nowadays."

"Yeah," Purdy remarked getting up. "You might say I'm in between ladies."

"How about Beth? She's not hanging around anymore?" Jubb asked.

"Like I said, I'm in between girlfriends right now. You know, busy with this and that. I've always got the regulars who call me, but I'm not much interested in them."

"Must be tough. You've got a tough life, Jason." Jubb snorted and swung around to give Purdy a high-five, then quickly headed for the door. Purdy called out after him.

"Hey, are you using that *mo-ron* Linus Eggers on this?"

Jubb turned and said, "Sure, I'm using Linus on this. But everything with him is always on a need-to-know basis."

"Well, I'm going to give you some advice right now—when it comes to Linus, there is *no need to know*, alright?"

"Sure," Jubb said, with his hand on the French-door handle. "Look, Jason, he's my brother-in-law. I picked him because I could trust him."

"Sure," Purdy replied.

Jubb closed the door and walked down the lighted Italian-stone path that led to the lower parking area of the mansion. There, he walked over to a black luxury Hummer with a silver skull-and-crossbones bumper sticker. A thin man—almost emaciated—with a prominent Adam's apple and deep sunken eyes was smoking a cigarette and lounging against the back of the truck.

"How'd it go?" he asked, flicking his cigarette into the air.

"You don't ask me those kinds of questions, Linus," Jubb replied. "Jason Bell Purdy is none of your business."

Jubb got behind the steering wheel and closed the door. As he fired up the engine, Linus quickly scampered to the passenger door and hopped in.

Inside the mansion, Purdy was calling the unlisted number of district attorney Harry Putnam. His wife answered cautiously but agreed to get him on the line.

"Jason, it's been a while. How are you?" Putnam asked.

"Fine, just fine," Purdy answered. "Hey, I wanted to personally invite you to the golf tournament that's coming up in a few weeks. It's going to be a great time. Some bigwigs, famous folks, well-connected—they're all going to be there. You are a local VIP there in Delphi. I thought you might enjoy hitting some balls around. It's over at my little project, the Eden Lake golf course."

"Jason, you know I don't golf. I've got those knee problems, remember?"

"Well, then ride in a golf cart and fake it. I don't think you'll want to miss this one."

Putnam laughed a little and said that he would think about it. Then Purdy quickly changed the subject.

"Something else—I know you are prosecuting Mary Sue Fellows. How's it going?"

"Jason, she's married. I know you dated her for a while a long time ago, but the woman is married. Besides—I intend to convict her and put her in prison. So I wouldn't show any sentimental attachment to this lady."

"No, that's all over. That was a long time ago. I'm just concerned that the right thing gets done. I want to make sure that you're considering all of the facts here, Harry. I'd hate to see the wrong thing happen."

"Well—for what it's worth—Mary Sue Fellows' attorney just got stuck in the Juda County jail for refusing to tell the judge where his client was. You can make out of that anything you want."

"Well Harry, just remember. I think you've got a great future. You don't need to be a district attorney the rest of your life. I talk to people. I've always wondered whether you ever thought about being a judge. Just thought I would mention that to you."

"Well, maybe we could talk about it sometime." Putnam said goodnight and hung up the phone.

Purdy flipped open his Palm Pilot again and tapped in the words "lawyer/jailer?" After that, he tapped in "background on lawyer—Suzanne?" Closing it, he turned off his television and padded across the plush carpeting in his stocking feet, out of the study and into the sprawling marble foyer, just as the housekeeper and maids were leaving for the night.

Each, in turn, said, "Good night, Mr. Purdy." Purdy said good night to them with a smile, enjoying the canopy of respect that covered him. He knew he was special—and he knew he had a beautiful future ahead of him. As he walked up the spiral staircase, he also knew that tonight he would have an excellent night's rest.

26

Y ou're sure that Will has not called into the office?"

"Fiona, I'm positive," Hilda said, trying to be reassuring. "He hasn't called in for the past two days."

"I really don't want to be a worrywart," Fiona continued, with an effort to be nonchalant. "It's just that we had only a short conversation at the studio. I thought he would call me back. But I haven't heard from him. It's just this feeling I have..."

"Look, honey. I promise to contact you as soon as he calls into the office," Hilda said in a positive tone. "I'm sure he is fine."

"Oh, I'm sure you're right, Hilda. I don't know why I get myself worked up like this over the man."

"Oh, well—I think I probably know," Hilda said warmly. "You are like me. You worry about your man—and then when things turn out alright, you don't know whether to hug him and burst into tears because he is okay—or get angry and go hunting for a rolling pin."

The younger woman laughed. "You know what the hardest thing is about men?"

"Sure," Hilda replied. "They are so *not* like us."

Fiona appreciated the secretary's good-natured humor. She had always figured that Hilda would bring a little levity to Will's high-octane approach to the practice of law.

Unfortunately, after Fiona hung up, she didn't feel much better than before. It was unlike Will not to check in with his office every day. She struggled with whether to call her father, Angus MacCameron, and ask him to pray. She couldn't shake the cloud of oppression she felt for Will, wherever he was and whatever he was doing.

On the other hand, she was worried about her father's health. Although it had been more than a year since his life-threatening heart attack and stroke, she still was very cautious about his health. He was a passionate and even volatile man on issues he felt strongly about. And he had developed a strong attachment to Will through the court case that had brought them all together. In a way, it seemed that Angus looked at Will as a long-lost son. For all of those reasons, Fiona hesitated to contact her father and tell him about her concern.

There was a knock at the office door, and it swung open. Fiona's producer was smiling somewhat tensely, and he tapped his watch with his index finger.

"I hate to bug you," he said, "but the band is off break, and we're ready to get back to work. Are you going to be ready soon?"

"Ted, give me just another minute. I have one more phone call to make," Fiona replied.

As the door closed, the singer picked up the phone and dialed her father's telephone number. She needed to hear the reassuring strength in her father's voice. And she needed to pray with him. Probably this vague sense of dread she felt about Will was nothing. But maybe it was something very real.

One thing she did know. As she listened to her father's phone ring, she had never been more aware that beneath the visible and commonplace textures of life, there was a spiritual world that was engaged in eternal combat over unseen kings and kingdoms. And she couldn't shake the feeling that Will was now caught in the front lines of that battle.

27

WILL HAD FINALLY BEEN GRANTED his demand for a telephone call. Guard Thompson escorted him out of his cell, down the corridor, through two locked steel doors, and into a day room, where there were a few linoleum-topped tables, some tipped-over plastic chairs, and a television in a ceiling corner. The TV was blaring, featuring a cooking show with a flamboyant chef who was effusively describing the delights of braised lamb with mint. In the far corner of the room, there was a wall phone. The guard punched a code into the phone and handed it to Will, then moved back a few steps and crossed his arms, observing.

"This is an attorney call—I need privacy," Will said.

"I understand, but I've got my orders. I have to observe you at all times during the phone call to make sure there is no destruction of the phone equipment."

Will gave a bewildered shake of the head, and he proceeded to punch in the telephone number of his law office.

Hilda answered and breathlessly asked where Will had been. Unfortunately, neither Jacki nor Todd Ferguson was in.

Taking a deep breath, Will attempted to calmly describe his circumstances and the legal assignments he wanted Hilda to deliver to Jacki so that his incarceration could be immediately appealed and challenged.

Hilda frantically wrote down his instructions but missed several key components, requiring Will to repeat each of the legal issues slowly. Before he could complete his second recitation of the research projects he was trying to communicate, Thompson interrupted and told him his time was up.

As Will walked back to his cell accompanied by the guard, his paper slippers making a shuffling noise, he was able to summon only one consolation from the phone call. Hilda had relayed the fact that Fiona had called, but had no idea where he was—and she'd assured him that she would call her immediately and fill her in. As he was approaching the door, he began chuckling.

Some great consolation—now Fiona can be told that her boyfriend is locked up in jail. I'm sure that will put her mind at ease.

Entering the cell, Will noticed Ivan perched on the side of his bed with an expectant look on his face. As soon as the guard left, Ivan said he wanted to show Will a few of his favorite card tricks.

Will smiled and obliged, stretching out on his bunk to watch. But Ivan was only into his second demonstration—something he called "the joker takes a wife"—when the two of them sensed a presence at the cell door. They glanced over and noticed guard Thompson standing there with his hands folded in front of him and a strange look on his face.

"Chambers, you gotta come with me. You got a transfer."

Will stood up, wondering what a "transfer" meant. As he approached the cell door, Thompson barked out, "Ivan, sit down. This doesn't concern you."

Will glanced over and saw that Ivan was standing a few feet behind him. He looked as if he wanted to say something or do something, but apparently was afraid of punishment if he did either.

Will's cellmate took a few steps backwards and slowly sat down on the edge of his bunk.

Thompson locked the cell door and began escorting Will down the corridor.

"What kind of a 'transfer' am I getting?" Will asked.

Thompson was quiet and didn't respond at first. Finally, as they approached the elevator at the end of the corridor, he answered.

"I've got orders to take you to the auxiliary jail."

"What's that?" Will asked.

"Look," Thompson replied, looking around nervously and lowering his voice, "I'm sorry—I don't make the rules, I just follow orders."

As the elevator door opened, Will heard Ivan's voice echoing down the corridor from his cell.

"You keep your eyes open, counselor! You watch yourself over there! You know what I'm talking about!" Ivan yelled.

Will looked Thompson in the eye.

"Tell me, guard Thompson, are you taking me to the overflow pen?"

"We aren't allowed to call it that."

As the elevator doors closed, Thompson added, "But that's what all the inmates call it."

When the doors opened two floors down, Thompson spoke again. "Like I said, I'm not the one that made this decision. I *am* sorry about this."

28

Dr. KENT FREDRICK PARKER, chief pathologist for the Delphi hospital, rushed into his office, his white lab coat unbuttoned and open, his top pocket crammed with pens. He swept a long, gray hair out of his face and then brushed his fingers over the coffee stain on his shirt.

Then he reached out a hand to greet Harry Putnam and Harriet Bender, who were already seated in his office.

Putnam led off by reminding him they were there to discuss the Mary Sue Fellows case. The last time they had met was at the beginning of the case, to quickly retain an affidavit, verifying his lab results on the blood sample taken from Joshua Fellows. As Parker situated himself behind his desk, he quickly acknowledged that, indeed, he did remember the case very well.

"Doctor, I sent you a copy of the affidavit that you signed for us previously. Did you get it?"

Parker nodded and retrieved it from a file that lay on the desk.

"We just want to go over your findings with you to make sure we've got it all nailed down. Your testimony at trial will basically follow the information we obtained from you on the affidavit," Putnam said.

"And when is this trial coming up?"

"I believe the trial date was mentioned in Mr. Putnam's cover letter to you," Harriet Bender chimed in. "Check your file, Doctor—I'm sure it's in the letter."

Parker glanced again at his file, retrieved the letter, and nodded in agreement.

"With the trial date only ten days away, we wanted to go through the questions that we will be asking then," Putnam continued. "So, the basics we want from you in your testimony are the identification that the blood sample came from Joshua during a hospitalization, the results of your lab test on the blood sample, the fact that the blood was determined to contain ethylene glycol, and the fact that ethylene glycol is one of the main ingredients in hydraulic brake fluid," Putnam concluded.

"On that last point about hydraulic brake fluid…" Parker said with some hesitation in his voice.

"We've got that covered," Harriet Bender said. She handed a stapled packet of papers to him.

"These are some technical papers from manufacturers of hydraulic brake fluid. They give its chemical breakdown, which includes the ingredients of ethylene glycol."

The doctor thumbed quickly through the packet of papers.

"Can I expect to be interviewed by anyone else before trial, other than you two?" Parker asked.

"I'm not sure. Possibly defense counsel for Ms. Fellows," Putnam said.

Then Bender tittered and added, "Although we're not sure about that—Mr. Chambers is cooling his heels in the county jail on a contempt-of-court order right now."

"Yeah, I think I heard something about that," Parker remarked.

Harry Putnam's gut instinct as a trial lawyer was to probe into Parker's last comment a little, but he resisted the temptation and decided to approach it from a broader perspective.

"Before we get into the particulars, Dr. Parker, is there anything you think you should share with us at this point that might be problematic concerning your evaluation of Joshua Fellows' blood sample?"

"Problematic in what way?" Parker asked.

Harry Putnam was jiggling his ballpoint pen in his fingers rapidly.

"Problematic in the sense that you believe it might undermine the validity of your conclusion that Joshua Fellows' blood contained ethylene glycol," Putnam explained, studying Parker carefully. "Or that might impact your credibility as a witness."

Dr. Parker removed his glasses and wiped the sweat from his nose, then calmly cleaned the lenses with the fabric of his lab coat.

Putting his glasses back on, he answered.

"I see nothing problematic, Mr. Putnam. Nothing at all."

29

At St. Stephen the Martyr Catholic Church in downtown Delphi, Father Godfrey, now 74, slowly plodded through his daily rituals and routines.

Early-morning prayer and homily. The leading of morning mass. Three days a week, one of the young assistants would drive him to the hospital for visitation.

On that day, though, there was no hospital visitation scheduled. But his mind was still preoccupied by the thought of one particular confession at the hospital.

The priest had taken confessions from dying men and women during the war in Vietnam. Desperate soldiers, their backs arched in indescribable agony, faces contorted, uttering their last words in hopes of absolution. And he had taken hundreds of deathbed confessions in peacetime as well. At the scene of car accidents. From the elderly, thin and languishing, in their beds.

Almost all of those confessions were attempts to tie up the loose ends of lives that had been unloosened by the impending reality of death.

But the confession of Henry Pencup had been different. Pencup had been a staid, reserved banker. Calm, respectful, and businesslike. He had quietly attended mass with his wife and had given generously to the church and its various charities. Occasionally he'd volunteered to help with the food drive and the soup kitchen.

But when the bank president had called for Father Godfrey from his bed in the Delphi hospital, it had not turned out to be an attempt to tie up the loose ends of his life.

To the contrary, what Pencup had told Father Godfrey held the threat of unraveling the social and political fabric of Delphi—and a good deal of the Atlanta establishment as well.

After the confession and sacraments, Father Godfrey had closed the curtain. Then there had been the awful sound from the heart monitor, the screaming tone that indicated total cardiac arrest. The nurse in the room had rushed to the bed and called for assistance.

That was the last that Father Godfrey had seen of Henry Pencup until his funeral.

But Pencup's last words to the priest had also unraveled something else. As a result, he had been left with a legal, ethical, and spiritual mess.

Pondering all this, Father Godfrey thought back to his young fishing days on the chain of lakes that fed into Eden Lake. Once in a while, the fishing line would become tangled in the reel. Any effort to pull it apart would only result in a more complicated, more impossible tangle. He used to call it a "bird's nest."

That was it. Henry Pencup had left a bird's nest of tangled threads in the old priest's wrinkled hands.

Whatever the resolution, Father Godfrey was not prepared to figure it out today. Instead, he would go out to his vegetable garden, a small patch of land behind the church. He would tend his tomatoes and check on his carrots. He would spend the afternoon seeing whether his small wire fence had kept out the rabbits that had worked mischief against his beloved vegetables.

30

SPIKE WAS SITTING BEHIND the steering wheel of the rental car parked on the shoulder of the highway. Stretched out before him across the dashboard was a highway map for South Dakota. He peered at the spider web of minor county highways and then glanced up at the sign some fifty feet down the highway.

"I think I've found it," he said out loud. And then he motioned to Crystal Banes, who was outside of the car, pacing on the shoulder of the road, and trying to get a better signal on her cell phone.

Banes ignored his gestures and turned away as she began connecting with her producer back in Atlanta.

After a few minutes, Banes got back in the rental car, folding up her cell phone. She threw a fatigued look at Spike.

"Excuse me," she snapped. "I've got a TV show that has to keep surviving. I've got other stories besides tracking down Mary Sue Fellows. So please don't interrupt me when I'm on the phone again, okay?"

"It's only that I found it. I thought you wanted to know."

"Found what?"

"The Sioux Indian reservation that we were looking for. I found our location. The reservation is only about twenty miles from here."

"Well, good for you, Spike," Banes said in a deliberate monotone. "So let's get there. Let's find out where this Fellows woman is. Let's get her on tape, and then let's call the cops."

"The cops?" Spike asked incredulously.

"Sure—what's the problem?"

"I thought you were after the story."

"Sure I'm after the story. I'm after two stories. First we get Mary Sue Fellows with a shock-of-a-lifetime look on her face as we click on the lights and get her on tape. Then we get the second story—we're right there when they arrest her, slap the cuffs on her, and grab her little boy away. That might be an even better visual than the first part."

"You never said anything about turning her over to the cops."

"Well, that's show business." Banes motioned for Spike to hurry up and start the car and head toward the reservation.

There was silence for ten or fifteen minutes. Then Banes broke the quiet.

"Don't get all soppy on me, Spike. I thought you were a tough, no-nonsense cameraman."

"So what happens after the cops grab her?" Spike asked.

"Well, she goes to jail. And the little kid goes to a foster home."

"And then what?"

"Spike, I don't know. She battles it out in court along with her lawyer—if he ever gets out of jail. And then there's an appeal, and then maybe we've got some more stories out of it."

"I've been reading the file," Spike remarked. "This mother has no history of child abuse. No criminal arrests. Her friends and family say she's a practically perfect mother. And then one day, an anonymous tip is called in. Nothing said about who the anonymous person is. But somebody says she's been poisoning this little kid. With brake fluid. So why that?"

"Why what?" Banes asked with a raised eyebrow, surprised by her cameraman's stringing so many thoughts together.

"Why brake fluid? Of all the things you're going to poison your kid with—why that? Doesn't that strike you as kind of strange?"

"Yeah. Poisoning your own kid strikes me as very strange, very bizarre, very sick."

"No, I mean the use of brake fluid," Spike continued. "If you're going to poison your own child—how about bleach, how about drain cleaner, how about even antifreeze? Besides, she's a nurse. She's got to know some chemicals that would do the job on her kid. If that's what she really wanted to do. Just seems strange to me—*brake fluid*. It's just really weird. Hard to believe."

"Spike, remember the news stories of the last decade—well, you're pretty young, so let's say the last five or six years? How many headlines with 'perfect little mothers' who say their children were kidnapped or murdered by some neighbor. And then you find out that these perfect little mothers were monsters and they killed their own children. C'mon, it happens all the time. Why not Mary Sue Fellows?"

"Because this is different."

"How?"

"Because as far as we know the little kid is alive and well. The mom has been taking good care of him. Remember how it all started. The boy is sick. That could be from a bunch of different things. And the police sweep down on the farm, she runs away out of fear. And her real story never comes out."

"Well, considering that Will Chambers is in jail," Banes said, "maybe you ought to be Mary Sue's attorney."

"What's going to happen to Mary Sue Fellows and that little kid—I mean, long-term?" Spike asked.

"Alright, I'll give you the straight scoop," Banes answered, "I've consulted with an attorney friend of mine in Atlanta. He handles a lot of these really bloody custody battles. You know what he told me?"

Spike just shook his head as he continued driving down the highway.

"He told me that once the kid is pulled out of the house and put in foster care, and they've fed him into the system, it's pretty difficult to pull him back out again. It's a little bit like reversing gravity sometimes. That's the bottom line."

The TV host and her cameraman fell silent for a while as they surveyed the long stretch of South Dakota highway ahead. The landscape was full of brown hills, with a handful of farmhouses and ranches scattered here and there.

"Keep your eye out for the next store. We'll stop and start asking if they know where this Tommy White Arrow's ranch is. We have to be getting pretty close. The first sign of civilization, the first little gas station or store, you pull in," Banes said. "Besides, I need to pick up some deodorant and some more toothpaste."

Sixteen miles down the highway there was a small grocery store with a sign on top that said "THE TRADING POST." A gas station was located on the other side of the store—with the pay phone that was often used by Mary Sue Fellows.

In the parking lot of the Trading Post there was only one vehicle right now—a Suburban. The Suburban belonged to Tommy White Arrow.

The vehicle was parked next to the Trading Post that day because Tommy had driven Katherine, Mary Sue, and Joshua to the store to pick up a few odds and ends. Tommy was busy trading jokes with the store clerk, an older man who wore sunglasses because of eye problems. Katherine was working down her grocery list, picking up canned goods in her small shopping basket. Down the aisle where the women's deodorant was kept, Mary Sue and Joshua were kneeling down. That was also where the coloring books and crayons were located.

For mother and son, the day had a calmness that came only with the routine and the mundane. Mary Sue had reluctantly adapted to her life at Tommy's ranch. Although she had longed to return home to her husband, she was tolerating her new, temporary life in South Dakota.

The Trading Post had become part of her new routine. She and Katherine had visited once a week.

Right then, she was not thinking about the case against her in Georgia, or even about Joe sitting in jail. She was looking at a coloring book and some cheap crayons—and wondering when she would find out the results of the blood test taken by Dr. Kendoll.

She was still squatting in the aisle with her little boy when the rental car occupied by Spike and Crystal Banes pulled into the parking lot, directly under the sign that read "THE TRADING POST."

31

BEFORE GUARD THOMPSON placed Will Chambers in the back seat of his squad car, behind the metal screen that separated him from the front seat, he locked his wrists in handcuffs and his ankles in manacles.

As the two drove to the overflow pen, Thompson glanced occasionally in his rearview mirror, studying Will.

On each occasion, Will locked eyes with him in the mirror.

There was a small part of Will that entertained a curiosity about Thompson's culpability. Was he only following orders in transferring Will to the auxiliary jail? And if so, who gave the order and why?

Will was certain this had nothing to do with Harry Putnam. Although Putnam was an aggressive prosecutor, perhaps even a street fighter, it was doubtful he would send a fellow lawyer into harm's way. This was confirmed as Will recalled Putnam's neutral position at the court hearing regarding Will's incarceration. And Harriet Bender, though her tactics were disproportionately vicious, lacked the authority to effect the transfer of an inmate.

That left Judge Mason as a viable suspect. There was one strong factor, though, that might eliminate him as responsible. A judge's order to the county jail could be easily traced. The judge would have to know—particularly in light of Will's final comments to the bench as he was being escorted out by the bailiff—that any additional or unreasonable punishment by him would be evidence of bias and prejudice. That evidence might suffice to remove him from the case and tarnish his reputation.

Working through the various scenarios, Will was left with two final options.

The first was that his transfer to the overflow pen was simply a matter of administrative convenience. Perhaps the county jail had received an influx of several new prisoners and simply ran out of bed space, and Will was the "lucky" winner. On the other hand, why not move existing prisoners to the overflow pen? That would seem to be an easier expedient and involve less paperwork.

The final option was beginning to look the most logical—that someone had pressured the chief jailer to make the transfer happen. If that was the case, then Will must have made some heavy-duty enemies in Delphi.

And that would necessarily involve his representation of Mary Sue Fellows. But how could a woman like Mary Sue Fellows make mortal enemies in Delphi? As Will finally completed his mental gymnastics, he realized that it was all an artful diversion. Beneath his curiosity about the transfer and the implications for the case, he was suffering from a growing sense of dread.

The information that Ivan had shared with him about the overflow pen was coming from a man with experience. Ivan had spent most of his life on the margins of society. In and out of jails, befriending those whose lives were spent in and out of jails, he was not the kind of man who would exaggerate the dangers.

Will was certain about one thing—this place to which he was being transferred was likely to be dark, and unspeakably violent.

That was when a thought struck him with such blinding intensity that he had to smile. He was smiling so broadly that when guard Thompson glanced at him in the rearview mirror, he took a second look.

Does God really protect us? Will thought to himself. As soon as he silently asked himself the question, he answered it. *Of course he does.* Then another thought: *Does he always protect us in the way we want, when we want it?*

And then he remembered something that Len Redgrove had once said to him.

"God's love for and protection of us are always consistent with his will for us—and his will for us is always consistent with what is best, not only for us, but also for a fallen world that he is always trying to rescue."

Those words had sounded so abstractly and logically true—and so consistently true with what Will had discovered in the pages of the Bible and in his own recent spiritual pilgrimage. But now it was something else entirely. Now, he was having to *live it out* in the middle of ugly and chaotic reality.

For Will, it was time to find out what he truly believed.

The squad car pulled into an industrial lane populated with dumpsters and dilapidated warehouses.

At the end of the lane there was a tall brick warehouse with cemented-up windows, four stories high and circled by double rows of barbed wire. The building was lit by several yellow overhead neon lights on metal poles. Guard Thompson parked the car, walked to the call box at the gate, and announced himself. The gate retracted. He parked the car within the barbed-wire fence and led Will to the single sheet-metal door which bore several chalk- and pen-marked obscenities that had been incompletely erased.

There was a clang on the other side as a bolt was withdrawn, and the four-inch-thick door cranked open. A tall figure in a deputy's uniform stood in the shadows on the other side.

"Here's the paperwork," Thompson said, handing a clipboard with several documents to the man in the doorway. The other man took it without comment. Thompson then gave him a small set of keys for the handcuffs and manacles, and as he passed by Will on his way out the door, he whispered, "Good luck," and then disappeared into his squad car and quickly drove away.

Will began to pray silently. *I don't belong to this place, Lord, I belong to you. I trust you, and I know that you are in charge.* He walked through the doorway, and the man stepped out of the shadow and into the light. He was big, with his hair shaved almost all the way down to the skull. His eyes were blank, his face expressionless. On the bridge of his nose there was taped a large piece of gauze with a faint spot of blood in the middle.

Will noticed that he was not wearing a nametag or a badge.

The attorney was led into a small vestibule with a desk and a compact TV, which was playing rock music videos. There was a small metal chair in the middle.

The guard with no name shoved Will down onto the chair and handcuffed him to it.

"Don't move," he said in a guttural command.

Then the guard ambled over to the desk and sat down, directing his attention to the music videos playing on the TV, which were followed by more music videos.

And followed by yet more music videos.

The common elements were raw—they all contained young men with ripped clothes, sunglasses, tattoos, and little pointy chin beards screaming into the camera from an assortment of bizarre angles.

Time dragged along at an excruciating pace.

There was a large, industrial-looking clock on the wall. Will had been sitting in the chair for two hours, listening to this miserable carnival of noise, banging, and screeching. During that time the guard had polished off several candy bars and two bottles of Mellow Yellow.

The room was hot, and Will was soaked in sweat. But the guard enjoyed a small fan, pointed directly at him, on his desk. Will's throat had become parched, and his back ached from his position on the metal chair.

He'd noticed that every fifteen minutes or so the guard would increase the volume a notch. By the end of the two hours the TV was blasting so loud that he figured the place could be cited for violating OSHA noise restrictions.

He knew that, for whatever reason, the guard was playing a sick game with him.

Another hour passed, and Will shifted minutely in his chair.

The nameless guard looked over at him and rose slowly. As he did, he put his hand in a drawer and pulled something out.

Then he sauntered over to Will.

"I thought I told you not to move," he said, standing directly over Will. "Stand up."

Will stood up clumsily, the chair still connected to him by his handcuffs.

His difficulty in standing had distracted him for a second. That was exactly the plan—as perfected by the guard through the many months of his tyranny in the overflow pen.

The guard reached out with his hand—the one containing the hand-held electric stun gun—and placed it hard against Will's neck.

There was a crackle–zap, and inside Will's head there was a flash and an explosion. A lightning bolt of pain and electricity ripped through his skull and down to his teeth, dropping him to the cement floor, his head bouncing off it like a bowling ball.

When Will regained consciousness the guard was standing over him, his boot placed heavily on Will's chest.

He saw the look on Will's face and bent down toward him.

"So—you don't like that, lawyer man—do you? You wanna do something about it? You wanna dance with me?"

He straightened up.

"We're gonna have some fun. I'm gonna give you dancing lessons."

32

CRYSTAL BANES WAS OUT OF THE CAR quickly and was walking toward the door of the Trading Post before Spike could turn off the engine.

Stepping into the little store, she approached Tommy, who was at the counter talking with the old man wearing sunglasses.

"Good afternoon," Banes greeted him. "I'm looking for a Thomas White Arrow. I'm led to believe he has a ranch somewhere in this area. Would either of you know where I could find him?"

The old man at the counter laughed and turned to the Indian.

"'*Thomas*'—I haven't heard you called that in a long time!"

Tommy studied Banes for a moment.

"I'm Tommy White Arrow. What can I do for you?"

Banes lit up in a bright smile.

"You're Thomas White Arrow? Honestly? That's you? We've come a long way to talk to you," she said, reaching out her hand to shake his.

Tommy broke into a sardonic half-smile.

"I didn't know that I was so famous."

"Well, if you aren't now, you will be when I get through with you," Banes declared, shaking his hand vigorously. "I'm Crystal Banes, host of *Inside Source*. We broadcast on INN—the International News Service—we're seen in every state of the Union, and in over two hundred countries around the world."

"And you want to talk to me?"

"That's right. You've got some very important information. A lot of people would like to know what you know, Tommy."

"And what is it I know that you want to know?" Tommy asked with a chuckle.

"A lot of people are looking for a woman and a child. The woman's name is Mary Sue Fellows, her son's name is Joshua. Some people think you may know where she's located. She may even be staying with you. You know, one story like this, and people make a career out of it. You could end up writing books, giving talks. Appearances on every major television station. All you have to do is answer a few of my questions."

"Make a career out of it?"

"Absolutely. Just think about it. Think of the famous cases in the last decade or two. All of a sudden, people nobody knew— now they're in the headlines, they're in the spotlight, they're writing books about their experiences. Everybody wants to get to know them. And there's money in that," Banes went on.

"I think I see what you're talking about. It's real clear now."

The TV host nodded enthusiastically. She tilted her head with a little smile and was getting ready to move in for the kill, when Tommy started speaking.

"You see what's going on, folks?" Tommy asked, addressing his comments to the handful of people in the little store.

"In the old days, they would come and offer the Indians Winchester rifles and firewater. Now they come to the reservation offering fame and fortune and a couple of minutes on national television," he continued. "Ms. Banes, I already have a career. I own a little ranch, I break horses, and I also give horse-riding lessons. I serve on the tribal counsel, I help support my family— here's my wonderful sister, Katherine," and with that he pointed over to Katherine, who was smiling and gave a little wave.

"I'm sorry if you took offense. I really didn't mean it that way," Banes said, trying to recover.

"I didn't take any offense. I just believe in speaking my mind."

"Good. It's refreshing to meet somebody who is a straight shooter. I appreciate people who tell you the way it really is," Banes remarked. "So, I'm wondering if you can give me the straight scoop on this Mary Sue Fellows and her child. Has any-body seen them, Tommy? The word has it that maybe your brother Andrew knows where Mary Sue is. Andrew visited her husband in jail."

She pulled a snapshot of Mary Sue holding Joshua out of her pocket and displayed it to Tommy.

"Do you recognize the woman in the picture?" Banes inquired. "She may be going by another name, of course."

"Why is this woman so important?" Tommy asked.

"The State of Georgia believes she's been poisoning her little boy, Joshua. They are searching throughout the country for her. They want to bring her to trial."

"Do you think she did it?"

"Honestly, I can't really tell you. I don't know," Banes replied, with a gloss of sincerity in her voice. Out of the corner of her eye she noticed that, during the interchange, Spike had sauntered into the grocery store and was listening intently.

"So this woman is supposedly poisoning her son? Is the little boy still alive?" Tommy asked.

"We just don't know," Banes responded. "But we think he may be in grave danger. He may even dying right now."

"Grave danger," Tommy echoed. "That sounds serious."

"It certainly is. And it's an important news story. And more than that—this little boy needs protecting," she added.

"I think I agree with you there. He certainly does need pro-tecting." With that Tommy turned and looked at Katherine, who was standing straight, not moving. In the aisle behind her, Mary Sue and Joshua were still crouching on the floor, out of sight.

"I've got a really great story for you," Tommy began. "Better than anything you had coming in here."

"I'd love to hear it," Banes quickly replied.

"Here it is. During the Kennedy Administration, way back in the '60s, a special study was done on the status of American Indians in this country. When the report came out, it indicated that most Indians were living in total poverty, suffering from malnutrition, lack of education, and lack of opportunity. Now, decades and decades later, what progress have we seen? What are you going to do about it? Are you going to air a show on the plight of American Indians?" Tommy took a step toward Crystal Banes, his voice rising.

"Tommy, that sounds like a great idea. Let's talk about this Mary Sue Fellows case, and then let's go to your idea. We'll do some filming down on your ranch, talk to some of the people on your tribal counsel. What do you say?"

"Yeah—you'd come down to my ranch, alright. And you'd do some filming. Maybe even do some interviews. But it would never show up on your program. You are interested in *your* story, not mine. So you can make all of the promises you want, but frankly, I don't believe any of them."

Banes had decided that this little grocery-store encounter had gone far enough. She turned to where Spike had been standing, but he wasn't there.

He had wandered down the aisle with the toothpaste and deodorant and children's coloring books. He was now standing directly in front of Mary Sue and Joshua, who were still crouching on the floor, and staring down at them in astonishment.

There was nothing that Mary Sue could say or do to save herself. But she didn't need to. In her look of anguish and silent pleading, Spike saw her dilemma in all of its confusion and heartbreak.

Having decided that Tommy White Arrow and his family were going to be of little help, Banes thought she might as well pick up some deodorant before they returned to their motel.

She glanced down the aisle where Katherine was standing but didn't see what she wanted. She went on toward the next aisle— the aisle where Mary Sue and Joshua were huddled on the floor. Spike was still standing in front of them. As he caught sight of Banes rounding the corner he quickly walked up to her, blocking her view.

"C'mon, Crystal. Let's get out of here," he said, taking her arm and turning her toward the counter. "I think this is the kind you use, right?" he asked, and he handed her two sticks of women's deodorant.

Banes walked slowly to the counter, studying Spike with a bewildered look.

"How did you know what brand I use?"

"I saw it spill out of your purse at the airport when they were doing a security check."

"Spike, you're pretty observant," Banes remarked, throwing some money on the counter.

"You'd be surprised how observant I am," he said with a smile.

As the two *Inside Source* people walked out the screen door of the Trading Post, Tommy reached out and grabbed Spike's wrist. Spike looked at Tommy, and they both shook hands, smiling and looking each other in the eye but saying nothing. They didn't need to.

Katherine watched tensely as the rental car pulled out onto the highway and sped off in the direction away from their ranch. After a few moments, she signaled to Mary Sue and Joshua that they could come out. Tommy suggested that they drive back to the ranch immediately.

Mary Sue was silent and trembling, still shaken by the incident.

She took a deep breath and quietly thanked God that their hiding place remained undiscovered. And she thanked him that the danger had passed—at least for now.

33

FIRST, THERE WAS THE SOUND OF WATER. Drops of water falling from a pipe in the ceiling and hitting a puddle on the cement floor. The droplets fell slowly, every thirty or forty seconds, as if they were timed.

Will opened his eyes. A flash of pain wrapped around his skull from ear to ear. He seemed to be lying on a metal cot, with the springs digging into his back—no mattress. Trying to move his arm, he found that it was handcuffed to the cot. Though the cell was only dimly lit, it hurt to open his eyes, so he closed them and tried not to think of the pain that surged inside his skull like lightning bolts. Everything was fuzzy and distant. His body seemed oddly removed from his thoughts. As if it were someone else's body that was racked with pain. Someone else's arm chained to the cot.

It was quiet, and the only sound he heard was the plopping of the drips of water into the puddle that was just a foot or so away from his face. He opened his eyes again and noticed a cot on the other side of the room, but that one had a mattress on it. Between the two cots there was a bucket. He was suddenly aware of the dank smell of urine and human waste.

The quiet was interrupted by two voices. There, at the opening of his cell, was the nameless guard. He was standing next to a large man with shaggy hair and a beard, who was wearing a denim vest with the sleeves torn off at the armpits, blue jeans that didn't accommodate his large stomach, and dirty black boots.

On the back of the man's ripped denim vest were the words "Hell Riders."

The guard said something quietly to him. Will caught the words "Mary Sue...location." The motorcyclist—which is what Will assumed he was—turned quickly to the guard, and then he looked at Will and grunted something. The guard opened the jail cell to allow him in, and closed the door behind him and locked it.

The guard left, and the motorcyclist shuffled slowly over to where Will was lying. He crouched down in front of Will and grabbed him by the hair, pulling his head up. Will opened his eyes slowly, and through his bleary semiconsciousness he saw the face of the man framed by a tangle of black hair that hung down on both sides of his face and his mangle of unkempt beard. His face was the face of destruction.

Then the motorcyclist began to speak.

"The guard tells me you are a lawyer."

Will did not respond. So the next words uttered by the man were in a deafening scream.

"I said, the guard told me you're a lawyer!"

Will nodded with the meager strength he had left.

"I hate lawyers. My ex-wife hired a lawyer in our divorce and he took away my Harley. Do you hear what I'm saying? That lawyer took away my Harley."

Will, surprisingly finding enough strength and lucidity to respond, was able to utter a few words.

"I don't do divorce cases," he said in a whisper.

"Okay—then how about a missing-person case? You got a client—some chick named Mary Sue. I'd really like to find out where she is. So you tell me. *Now.*"

"I don't handle missing persons either," Will mumbled.

Will pried his eyes open again, but this time he wished he hadn't. He saw the big motorcyclist drawing his fist back for a blow.

In the shock of that realization, time stopped. The thought leapt into his mind that the motorcyclist was capable of beating him to death. He knew that he was alone, in a place that was forgotten and forsaken.

In that instant that seemed to last so long, Will thought about Fiona. He felt bad for her that his funeral would have to be a closed-casket ceremony because his face would not be fit for an open casket.

There was an explosion of pain, and he felt like he was falling into a bottomless pit headfirst. A scene, perhaps from some movie, perhaps from his memory of the story, flashed into his mind for an instant. Jesus was hanging on the cross, head bowed down and hair dangling around his broken face. From the ground they were shouting, "Why don't you save yourself?"

And then there were no more pictures. No more sound. Just darkness.

34

THE SUN WAS BEGINNING TO SET as Mary Sue and Katherine were working together on the dishes from dinner. Mary Sue glanced out the window and saw Danny doing tricks with his blue yo-yo for Joshua, who was sitting, in rapt delight, on the ground. Andrew and Tommy were in the living room, laughing at something they had just seen on TV.

Katherine put her arm around Mary Sue and gave her a hug.

"You don't have to help me with the dishes—go talk to Andrew and Tommy."

"That's all right, I love helping you. You are so gracious, Katherine," Mary Sue replied.

"Let Katherine finish them—we need to talk to you about Joshua," Andrew called from the other room.

"Yeah—tell us what the doctor told you," Tommy added.

Katherine smiled and nodded.

Mary Sue wiped her hands off on the dishtowel, and sat down on a chair in the living room. The two men listened as she began to recount the findings from Joshua's blood test.

"Dr. Bill told me that this was only an initial impression. He can't make a final diagnosis. But he sees something unusual in Joshua's blood."

Andrew and Tommy looked at each other and then looked back at Mary Sue, both solemn and attentive.

"He understands why a doctor might have concluded…" And with that Mary Sue's voice trailed off and she looked down at the floor. She allowed herself to be distracted by the beautifully

179

embroidered rug, with carefully stitched white feathers, that Katherine had made for the lodge.

Tommy and Andrew did not try to prompt her. They waited for her to finish her thought.

"Anyway, the doctor said he could see why another doctor might have concluded that there was ethylene glycol in Joshua's blood."

"Wait a minute," Tommy chimed in, "tell me again what this ethylene glycol is."

"That's one of the chemical ingredients in brake fluid," Andrew explained. "And they are charging you, back in Georgia, with poisoning Joshua with brake fluid, right?"

Mary Sue studied Andrew's face for a moment. She was searching for distrust, for a change of heart in the man who had once said it was his job to protect Mary Sue and care for her until she was restored to her husband.

But in his eyes she saw only concern and friendship.

"Yes," she said quietly, "that's right. But the doctor also said something else."

Both men were listening intently. Tommy's face, brow furrowed, was resting in his hands.

"The doctor also said that the blood tests were consistent with a metabolic disease. He couldn't be sure—he's not a specialist—but he suggested we send the blood sample to someone he knows."

"Another doctor?" Andrew asked.

"Yes. Dr. Bill is a personal and professional friend of a world-renowned expert in childhood metabolic diseases. Dr. Forrester is his name. He practices medicine in London, but once he came to South Dakota to do a research project on pediatric diseases in Indian children. Dr. Bill called him and asked if he would take a look at the blood sample."

"Is he going to do it?" Tommy asked.

"He was getting ready to fly down to the Bahamas where he was going to work at a medical mission. Some kind of outbreak of liver problems with the children on Grand Bahama island. He said if we could wait until he gets back in a month or two, he would take a look at it."

"That long?" Andrew remarked.

"I feel the same way," Mary Sue said with resignation in her voice. "I don't think we should wait that long. We have to get Joshua diagnosed, and if he's got a major medical problem—and I really do believe he does—we need to get him treated as quickly as possible."

"But he's been doing so well," Tommy pointed out.

"I know," Mary Sue agreed. "And I'm not sure why that is. Maybe it's his diet here with your family. I mentioned to Dr. Bill that Katherine had us all eating that low-protein diet she'd read about. Maybe that's it. Or perhaps it's because he's not in day care anymore and he isn't being exposed to other diseases. I just don't know. But I don't think we can wait that long."

Andrew nodded in agreement.

"I think you have two decisions to make. First, you have to decide about getting that blood sample to Dr. Forrester. That means getting it to him down in the Caribbean. You'll have to get Dr. Bill to find out whether or not he'll have the necessary equipment down there to be able to evaluate it himself. But if he's doing medical-mission work down there, maybe he will."

Mary Sue nodded and looked to Andrew for his second point.

"And the other thing is this," Andrew continued, his voice dropping slightly. "You need to make a decision about returning home. Returning home for Joshua to get treatment in a hospital close to your home when we find out what his problem really is. And we need to talk about you going home to fight your case and support your husband."

Tommy came to his feet, his eyes flashing with anger. He pointed a finger at Andrew.

"That's a bad idea. You want to send her back to the White Man so they can trash her and put her in jail? And put Joshua in a foster home? That's what you want?"

"She may be able to defend herself better back home than she can on the run," Andrew suggested. "Besides, for Mary Sue, as a Christian, this is also a spiritual issue."

"Some friend you are!" Tommy retorted. "How many tongues do you have in your mouth? First you bring Mary Sue and Joshua into our family and pledge your love and support and friendship, and now you are ready to hand them over to the White Man."

"This is not a White Man–Indian problem we've got," Andrew replied, trying to reason with his brother.

"It isn't?" Tommy responded, his fists now clenched at his sides. "Do you remember what I told you—what happened at the Trading Post? That Crystal Banes is tracking down a news story. She is not just looking for Mary Sue and Joshua. She is trying to put us in the middle of this. This *is* about the White Man and the Indians, Andrew. Wake up!"

Mary Sue raised her hands in the air to silence her two friends.

"I appreciate both of you. I hear what both of you are saying. But this is something *I* have to think about. Something *I* have to pray about. This is *my* life—and Joshua's—and my husband's—that we're talking about here."

She stood up and put her hand on Tommy's shoulder.

"I understand what you're saying," she said. "There's wisdom in not trusting a system that seems to have really gone wrong in my case. And I know the mistrust you have for the police, and the lawyers, and the courts."

Then she turned to Andrew and smiled.

"I also hear what you are saying, Andrew. I need to put Joshua above everything else. And there is wisdom in the idea of turning myself in. But I just haven't made that decision yet. I know the time is getting short. I feel greatly burdened in my heart that I have to choose. I just need a few days to work this out."

In the kitchen, Katherine felt Mary Sue's burden in her own heart. She sighed heavily, wishing there were something she could do.

She glanced out the window to the backyard, where Danny was entertaining Joshua with his blue yo-yo. But then she noticed something. Joshua turned away from Danny with a strange look on his face, and he bent over on the ground and began throwing up.

Katherine whirled toward the living room.

"Mary Sue, Joshua is getting sick all over outside. We need to get out there!"

Then she turned back and looked out the window again, just in time to see Joshua collapse to the ground, and Danny reaching over to him with a look of terror and helplessness.

35

Mary Sue, I've been dying here in jail without you. But didn't Mom tell you that I didn't want you to risk calling me here?"

"I'm sorry, Joe darling. But I've been trying to contact Will at the houseboat and I get no answer. And I've been playing phone tag with Will's office. I'm getting really scared, not having any news about the case or how you're doing."

"You *know* they might be tapping this phone call—I'm using the pay phone in the day room. They could be listening to every word you're saying. They could be tracing your call."

"I guess I'm going to have to take that chance."

"Well, honey—I love you so much. I'm afraid I've got some bad news…"

"What is it?" Mary Sue asked, her voice constricting with tension.

"The judge really slammed Will Chambers. When he refused to give out any information about where you were, he got sent here to jail."

"Oh my heavens!" Mary Sue exclaimed. "Have you talked to him—how is he doing?"

"I have no idea. I was going to try to connect with him—but then, the next thing I knew, they transferred him out of here."

"Transferred? Where?"

"I think they shipped him over to someplace called the overflow pen."

"What's that?"

"You don't want to know," Joe said, lowering his voice. "I've heard some horror stories about the place. Things are really going from bad to worse."

At the other end, Mary Sue began crying softly.

"Listen, baby doll, our God is big enough to handle all of this. I don't know why this is happening. But you and I are going to stick together. We're going to beat this thing," Joe declared, trying to reassure her.

When Mary Sue had collected herself, she shared the rest of her heart with her husband.

"Joe darling, we've had a bad spell with Joshua. He's gotten real sick. He collapsed yesterday, and I had to take him to the hospital."

Joe struggled for words, but nothing came out.

"They've got him stabilized now. But we've got to get a diagnosis. Dr. Bill up here in South Dakota knows a specialist. He says he's one of the best in the world. We're going to try to get a blood sample down to him right away. But the problem is, he's on his way to some kind of medical mission down in the Bahamas. If we can get the blood sample down there to him, he might be able to take a look and make a diagnosis."

"It looks like things are coming to a head pretty quickly," Joe said with resignation in his voice. He paused, trying to decide whether to keep on bringing Mary Sue up to speed.

"You know our custody trial is coming up in a week. Mom probably hasn't told you—but I fired that worm Stanley Kennelworth as my attorney."

"What are you going to do now?"

"I was hoping that Will could represent you and I could represent myself at the hearing. I thought maybe we could work together. But I have no idea where he is right now."

"I've got to take care of Joshua," Mary Sue replied. "He has to be our first priority. I think that means I've got to get this blood sample out to that specialist. And I think it may mean I have to turn myself in. I'm struggling with that."

"I would have agreed with you a few weeks ago. But now that Will is sitting in jail and may not be able to represent you at trial, I just don't know."

Mary Sue was deep in thought and remained silent at the other end.

"If we go into court without Will," Joe continued, "and we lose this thing, I don't think we'll ever get Joshua back. And if you come back and they get custody of Joshua, then they'll go after you with the criminal charges that are still sitting there, waiting to be served on you. I see this whole thing exploding right in our face."

"I am talking to Andrew about it," Mary Sue said. "I am praying about it. So is he. And if I can ever get in contact with Will, I'm going to ask his advice too."

"I think Andrew is a good man. And I know Will is someone who's going to give you the straight scoop...I just miss you so much..." Joe said his voice trailing off as he choked back tears.

Husband and wife exchanged a few final, tender words, and then Mary Sue hung up the receiver of the pay phone next to the Trading Post.

In an adjacent conference room, a Juda County sheriff's deputy pushed down the stop button on the recorder that was used to tap the day room's telephone. He took the earphones off his head and jotted down the locator number where the tape had stopped. Next to the locator number he put the words, "Ending point of Mary Sue Fellows' telephone conversation with Joseph Fellows via the phone in the Juda County jail day room."

Then the deputy put the tape in a large evidence envelope, sealed it, and hustled down to detective Otis Tracher's office. The secretary greeted him.

"I am sorry, Otis is out of town at a funeral. He won't be back till tomorrow."

"This is a rush," the deputy said. "Try to get ahold of him if you can. I have a hot tip on the Mary Sue Fellows case. Did he leave anybody in charge while he was gone?"

"Not that he told me," the secretary said. "He's been working this one alone. I have a contact number for him. I'll see if I can run him down."

The deputy handed the evidence envelope to the secretary.

"Tell him I think we have a definite bead on Mary Sue Fellows. We need to act on this right now."

He left, and the secretary turned to her notepad.

"Alright," she said to herself with exasperation, "now where did I put those contact numbers for Otis?"

36

I T WAS STRANGE TO SEE AN ANGEL in a jail cell.

First there was the female angel. She was a black woman, pretty and dressed in a business suit. She looked familiar, but he could not recall a name.

And then there was the other angel. He was a white man, dressed like a jail guard.

The black female angel was bending down and smiling, but with a sorrowful look, as if she was experiencing his pain.

She said, "Get up—we're going to take you out. Get your shoes and coat on."

The white male angel bent down and unlocked the handcuff on his wrist.

Supporting him under the arms, the angels helped him out of the cell. As they walked down the corridor, they turned a corner.

There was the desk.

And there was the television, still blaring rock videos. But the nameless guard was no longer there.

At some point, some indistinct moment, Will became aware that it was Jacki Johnson and guard Thompson who were escorting him out of the overflow pen. He was in pain, but he was alive.

Will drifted in and out of consciousness.

As things began becoming more distinct and clear, Will realized he was in a hospital bed—a clean bed—in the Delphi hospital. There was a bandage across his face, and he felt pain and pressure behind his eyes. And, of course, his whole head was throbbing violently.

Then he noticed Jacki Johnson sitting patiently in a chair next to him. She smiled.

"You broke your promise, Will."

"What?" Will replied weakly.

"You told me you didn't need a baby-sitter anymore. No more bailing Will Chambers out of trouble. Remember?"

Will started chuckling, but stopped as he grabbed his head in exquisite pain.

"Just don't make me laugh again," he groaned. "Has anybody told Fiona?"

"Oh, yes," Jacki replied. "She's been given the whole story."

"And?"

"Well—she did freak a little bit. Not much. The woman is a trooper—although she did tell me something I'm not sure I should share with you."

"Huh—what?"

"Well," Jacki explained, "she said something about Jesus, and a whip, and driving out the money changers. And she added that she figured it would be okay if she brought a bullwhip and took off the hide of the guys who did this to you."

Will laughed out loud and then grimaced as he grabbed his head again.

"That's my Fiona," he said, smiling in spite of the pain. He took a few sips from a Styrofoam cup of ice water and then put it down on the tray next to him.

"So how did you get me out of that hellhole?"

"Well, Hilda gave me the *Reader's Digest* version of your message. I called the court, got a copy of the court record and the judge's order confining you to jail, and filed an urgent petition with Georgia's Supreme Court. It took them less than three hours to kick out an order reversing Judge Mason and ordering your immediate release."

"Great work," Will said as enthusiastically as he dared.

"I did file another motion—to force the state Supreme Court to remove Judge Mason from the case. But they haven't ruled on the motion yet. I must be honest and tell you it doesn't stand much of a chance."

"Don't worry about that," Will replied. "If we have to try the case before Judge Mason, so be it. Has anyone heard from Mary Sue?"

"She called the office a couple of times trying to track you down. That was before we knew you'd been locked up in the county jail."

"I've got to get out of this hospital and start preparing for the custody trial. I've lost track of time—what's the trial date?"

Jacki leaned forward and put her hand on Will's arm.

"I suggest you ask the court for an adjournment so you can do a little bit more recovery."

"No…no, I can't afford to do that. I don't think time is on our side," Will replied.

That was when Harry Putnam strode through the door of Will's room. His hands were thrust in his pockets, and he stopped short at the end of the bed. He bounced on the balls of his feet nervously and nodded in Will's direction.

"One thing you should know," Jacki interjected. "Mr. Putnam here was very helpful in getting you immediately released from the overflow pen. As a matter of fact, he was outraged when he found that you had been transferred."

"That is right," Putnam said, his voice rising to make the point. "Look, Chambers, I fight hard—maybe too hard—but I never try low blows against another attorney. I would never submit you to this kind of treatment. You've got to know that. When I found that someone had transferred you, I blew a gasket. I gave your associate here all of my attention when she presented the order from the Supreme Court. I helped her track you down and get you out of jail pronto."

"Harry," Will spoke up, "I owe you a debt of gratitude."

"Don't get mushy on me," Putnam countered. "I still plan on beating you in this case. Don't forget that. I just don't want to see one of my legal brethren treated like this. And one more thing…"

"What is it?"

"We've been investigating that Neanderthal who worked in the auxiliary jail. A grand jury just issued an indictment against him for abuse of authority, battery—you can imagine all the charges. We're going to need your testimony. I assume you'll be more than happy to provide it."

"You figured that one right," Will replied firmly. "On the other hand, maybe prison would be too good for that guy."

"How so?"

"If you want real punishment, forget prison—instead, let my girlfriend, Fiona, go after him."

Will and Jacki had a good chuckle, at the expense of Will's aching skull.

Then the attorney narrowed his eyes and looked straight at Harry Putnam.

"I want those two thugs put away—the guard *and* the motorcyclist. I'll be watching you to make sure that happens. And I expect you to find out who was *behind* their attack on me."

Putnam nodded nervously.

After his two visitors said their goodbyes, Will was alone in the room—but only for a few minutes. Out of the corner of his eye, he saw someone stop in the doorway. It was a woman. Then he noticed the dark hair and radiant smile.

Fiona ran to the bed with a huge basket of flowers. She hugged him and kissed his forehead gingerly.

"Thank you, God. Thank you for keeping Will alive."

She was laughing and crying, and after a moment she had to grab in her suit pocket for a Kleenex to blow her nose. She executed that task so loudly that both of them burst into belly laughs.

With that, Will's head began splitting again, but he kept laughing and wincing all the same.

After sitting down next to him, Fiona raised his hands to her face and kissed them.

"It's funny," she said wistfully, "how all of the things that bothered me—that upset me about how things were between us...the things you forgot to do...even my questioning whether you were really over Audra's death. They all seem so small and stupid now when I realize how easy it is to lose someone you really love—someone you love more than life itself."

Will stared into her dark eyes, taking in her face, and her dimples, and the funny way her lips turned when her feelings were coming to the surface.

"Do you realize," Will said slowly, "what you just said...it's the first time you told me you loved me like that?"

Tears were streaming down Fiona's face, and she laughed about her make-up smearing. But Will was indifferent to that.

"How in the world did you get here?"

"The minute I found out you were in the hospital I told my producer it was an emergency—I needed twelve hours off. I chartered a private plane. That was a miracle of sorts. All the charters are getting booked up. Everybody thinks there's going to be a big airlines strike. The pilot is sitting downstairs, so I'm afraid I have less than an hour."

Will didn't care. He told Fiona how much he loved her—and that, when he returned to Virginia after this case, how the two of them needed to do some serious decision-making.

The two of them talked a little more about their lives, and then, too soon, Fiona rose slowly, saying she had to go. When she kissed him again, he could taste the hot tears that were running down her face.

"Better check your make-up on the way out, dear," Will said with a smile. "I can't wait till we're together again."

And then she was gone.

Glancing over to the other side of the room, he realized for the first time that he was not entirely alone. There was another patient sleeping quietly in the other bed, behind the curtain.

Father Godfrey, at the hospital on visitation, entered the room slowly, threw a casual smile and nod in Will's direction, then pulled the curtain fully around the bed of the other patient.

A nurse breezed into the room to check Will's vital signs.

The nurse turned to the drawn curtain. "There's Father Godfrey again. He sure is faithful to his people. He's here all the time."

"How's the other guy doing? He's not getting the last rites, is he?" Will asked a little apprehensively.

"No, nothing like that—just a hospital visit. In fact, I think he'll be ready to be discharged tomorrow. And I think you will too," the nurse replied.

From behind the curtain, Father Godfrey was speaking in low, gentle tones and the patient was responding, but Will couldn't make out any words. The nurse finished her work and hurried out of the room.

Some of the pain pills were kicking in. With the muffled sounds of the conversation across the room in the background, he drifted off. For a little while, at least, he could forget about vindicating Mary Sue Fellows—or wondering who was behind the attack in the jail and really wanted to locate her.

Will's eyes closed as he fell into a deep sleep, oblivious to the ritual of confession being administered discreetly behind the nearby curtain.

37

Tɪɴʏ Hᴇꜰᴛʟᴀɴᴅ, all two hundred thirty-five pounds of him, was tired and hot.

As the private detective sat in his new Cadillac convertible, he wiped his brow and loosened his tie. Then he checked the notepad lying on the passenger seat next to him, thanking his stars again that he'd decided to drive to Georgia rather than fly, now that the big airline strike was almost certain to occur.

Pursuant to Will's instructions from a week before, Tiny had followed up a number of leads in the Mary Sue Fellows case.

His contact with attorney Stanley Kennelworth had been a bust. By the time Tiny had talked to him, Kennelworth had been fired by Joe Fellows as his attorney, and was in no mood to talk.

But Tiny did follow up on the ownership of Continental Motors, the car dealership from which the local attorney had gotten his brand-new Jaguar.

Continental Motors was owned by a two-man partnership consisting of Ambrose Deacon, a flashy multimillionaire and owner of several sports franchises, and Jason Bell Purdy.

Social worker Liz Luden had been surprisingly cooperative when Tiny had contacted her. According to the written demand that Will had served before his incarceration, Luden had to permit Tiny, as an official investigator, to peruse through her file on Mary Sue Fellows.

Most notable in Tiny's review of the four-inch stack of documents was a small, handwritten phone message. The name of the caller was absent, but the note had been taken by "LL" (Tiny presumed that was Liz Luden), and it documented a phone conversation. The caller had indicated that he or she had some reason to believe that Mary Sue Fellows was "poisoning her little boy Joshua—with hydraulic brake fluid."

Bob Smiley, the insurance agent, had been playing a persistent game of dodgeball with Tiny, not answering his phone calls, and complaining that he was just on his way to a "meeting" the one occasion Tiny had cornered him at his office. The agent had indicated he'd been unable to locate the file he'd discussed with Will Chambers but would continue looking for it.

Tiny finished jotting down a few notes, glanced at his watch, and then decided he would breeze by the Delphi hospital to give his greetings to Will, thinking he ought to pay the injured man his respects.

As Tiny maneuvered his huge frame through the hospital room door, Will had just finished dressing and was ready to be discharged.

"My oh my," Tiny exclaimed, "aren't you a sight for sore eyes!"

"Hey—I've been out of things for a while. So I hope you have some great news about our case."

Tiny walked up closer and checked out Will's black eyes, his gauze-covered broken nose, and the bandage around his head. After a few seconds of solemn silence, Tiny spoke up.

"Will, my man, there's one thing they did not teach you in law school."

"What's that?"

"How to duck." Tiny enjoyed his own joke with a belly laugh.

"Well, I *thought* I was glad you'd stopped by," Will remarked. "But anyway, I need a drive over to my car at the courthouse. I hope it hasn't been towed away."

On the way over, Tiny reviewed the results of his investigation. The lawyer was particularly interested in the anonymous telephone message accusing Mary Sue of poisoning her child.

After he'd studied a photocopy of the note that Tiny had obtained, Will muttered something.

"What was that?" Tiny asked.

"Just something that keeps going around in my mind. Something on this note. Something that's at the bottom of this case. *Hydraulic brake fluid.*"

As they got within a few blocks of the courthouse Will turned to him with an idea.

"Tiny, before you drop me off, let's go out to the Fellowses' farm. There's something I want to look at."

Tiny pulled into the drive of St. Stephen the Martyr Catholic Church. As he was turning the car around, Will noticed a sign that announced the time of daily masses. Below, the sign also bore a pastoral message, which Father Godfrey would post for the encouragement or edification of passersby.

This week's message read,

CONFESSION IS GOOD FOR THE SOUL

Tiny pulled his big Cadillac back on the road, and they headed out to the countryside and the farm.

Tiny unlocked the house with the key he'd picked up from the jail, where Joe Fellows' belongings were being kept. The two men walked in. The two-story farmhouse had the musty smell of not having been occupied for several weeks. The windows were closed, and everything was silent.

They walked up to the second floor, and as they reached the top of the stairs, Will noticed a pair of child's yellow plastic binoculars lying on the carpet and glanced out the hall window that gave a good view of the winding dirt road that led from the main highway to the front yard. Will and Tiny looked through each room—not knowing exactly what they were looking for, but finding nothing significant in any event.

Walking downstairs to the kitchen, they noticed a few dishes in the sink from some forgotten breakfast.

It was then that Will walked to the garage, which was connected to the kitchen by a door that had been left ajar. The two-car garage contained only one vehicle there—an older-model pickup truck. The front hood had been left propped open and two oily red rags were lying over the radiator.

Will stood staring at the truck, until he noticed Tiny's large bulk looming behind him.

"Okay, chief—what's the deal?" he asked.

"Joe and Mary Sue had two trucks."

"So?"

"The other truck was the one that broke down on the highway when Mary Sue was trying to escape. I know that truck was impounded by the sheriff's department. It says so in their report."

"Well—what's the big mystery?"

"No mystery," Will said. "It's just that Mary Sue never mentioned the second truck. This truck was being worked on before the deputies arrested Joe."

Tiny did not see the connection or the point and simply shrugged.

They locked up the house, climbed into Tiny's big Cadillac, and headed back to Delphi, where Will would pick up his Corvette.

He was anxious to get back to the houseboat, take a shower, and then start his frantic last-minute preparation for Mary Sue's trial, which was now only a few days away.

38

As Tiny was pulling up to Will's Corvette in downtown Delphi, he was suggesting something to his passenger.

"Look, I've got a room in a motel here, but maybe I'd better stay on the houseboat where you are. You may need a bodyguard."

"Bodyguard? Where were you when I really needed you?" Will asked with a chuckle.

"I'm serious," Tiny protested. "Look, can't you tell I've dropped twenty pounds? I've been trying to exercise—get back into shape. You know there was a time in my former life, when I was a cop in the military—you know, I was a lean, mean, fighting machine!"

"Thanks anyway," Will replied. "I really don't need a bodyguard. On the other hand, if you like the Huckleberry Finn life of living on a high-class raft, why don't you join me? There's only one bed, though—you may have to try to make yourself comfortable on the couch."

"Me on a couch?" Tiny said with a laugh. "Look, if you don't need protection, I think I'll pass on that and stay at the motel."

Tiny headed off while Will climbed into his Corvette and gunned it off in the direction of Eden Lake. It seemed as if he had been gone for weeks. He recognized the familiar "Tex, the Flying Cowboy" sign and the road that led down to the water.

It was late afternoon, and the sun was getting low on the horizon over the quiet surface of the lake when he pulled up to the dock, looking forward to getting settled back into something normal.

He unlocked the houseboat and threw open the windows to get fresh air. Suddenly feeling exhausted and a little dizzy, he thought he would lie down for a minute. Although his skull wasn't fractured, as the doctors had originally feared, he had had a serious concussion and a broken nose. He stretched on the couch in the small living room that overlooked the lake.

He was just dozing off when the phone rang next to him.

"Is this Will Chambers?" a young female voice said on the other end.

"Yes, it is. What can I do for you?"

"You can't do anything for me, but I might be able to do something for you."

"Like what?"

"You represent a woman by the name of Mary Sue Fellows?" the young woman on the phone asked.

Will sat up quickly—so quickly that his head gave him an immediate reminder of his injuries.

"Yes—do you know her?"

"Never met her in my life."

"Alright—do you have some information on her case?" Will asked.

"I am the anonymous caller."

"Okay—can you explain that?"

"I'm the one who called the Department of Social Services. I told them about Mary Sue Fellows poisoning her little boy."

"I am sorry, I didn't catch your name..." Will prompted.

"You're not going to get my name. I want no part of this case. And I don't want any trouble."

"Then why are you calling me?"

"Because someone did me wrong. I had a perfectly good job, and now I've been fired. He's mistreated me and taken advantage of me—I've been harassed and treated like dirt. I don't appreciate that. So I took the information about how to contact you with me."

"Wait a minute," Will said, trying to put the pieces together. "Who did you wrong?"

There was silence at the other end. Will decided to probe a little further.

"You said that you made the phone call. But you've never met Mary Sue Fellows. Why did you accuse her of poisoning her child?"

"I was told to. He told me that I could make the phone call—no one would have to know who I was—and the law protected me as an anonymous caller reporting a child-abuse incident."

"When you made the phone call, you knew that those allegations were basically untrue?"

"Look, like I said—I know nothing about Mary Sue Fellows. I don't know anything about her poisoning her kid. I was told to say those things and that's it."

"Why would you have made a false allegation against someone you didn't know?"

"Very simple—money. And there were other issues. Anyway, I'm sorry I did it and I wanted you to know. I'm hoping this could be helpful."

"It isn't going to be very helpful," Will replied, "unless you give me a name and give me some way to contact you so I can interview you. I need to find out who put you up to this and why. And then I need to convince you how important it is to be a witness in this case."

"Oh no," the young woman said, "there's no way I'm going to get involved in this case. I'm not going to give you my name and I can't afford to testify. You're just going to have to run with the information I've given you."

"I don't think that's enough," Will said gently but firmly. "An innocent woman may lose custody of her child. And there's still a criminal case pending against her—she may even go to prison when this is all over. Can you live with that?"

There was a tense pause at the other end. Will continued to push.

"Can you tell me who put you up to this?"

"I…I don't think I can tell you that. I really don't want my life destroyed. He can really mess up your life."

"Isn't there anything else you can tell me?" Will asked, passion rising in his voice.

He heard noise in the background as the woman remained silent. It might have been as long as a minute. It sounded like she was calling from a telephone booth or a store, or perhaps a restaurant.

Finally she spoke. "Do you ever give confession? Are you Catholic?"

"No, I've never given confession to a priest, if that's what you're wondering."

"Well, ask a guy named Henry Pencup. He gave a confession. I can guarantee you that."

"And what does that have to do with Mary Sue Fellows?"

"That's what you'll have to figure out," the young woman said. Then she hung up.

Will quickly jotted down the name she'd given him on a magazine, spelling it several different ways—Pencupp—Pencup—Penkupp—Penkup.

Then Will noticed the telephone number on the caller ID and called it immediately.

After a number of rings, a man answered the phone.

"Delphi Café."

"I think a young woman just called from your phone. Is she still there?"

"Haven't got a clue. If she is, I don't know what she looks like. We've been real busy here."

"Do you think you could find her in there in the restaurant?" Will asked.

"Locate who—what's her name?"

"That's just the problem—I don't know her name. She just called me from your telephone," Will said.

"Look—we're real busy here. Sorry I can't help you." The man hung up.

Will quickly plugged in his laptop and went on-line. After searching a few news sources under various spellings, he came up with a small article in an Atlanta newspaper. It was an obituary.

Henry Pencup had been the president of the Delphi National Bank. The obituary indicated that he was memorialized in a service at St. Stephen Catholic Church in Delphi.

Following the obituary, Will also located a number of articles mentioning an ongoing investigation into several million dollars missing from the Delphi bank. Auditors had so far failed to uncover the reason for the missing funds. The death of Henry Pencup, who had suffered a massive heart attack, had become a major obstacle in the investigation.

That was when Will remembered the sign outside the St. Stephen the Martyr Catholic Church.

Confession is good for the soul, the attorney thought to himself. He decided he needed to visit the church.

It was time to find out *whose* confession.

And—whose soul.

39

FATHER GODFREY WAS BEHIND the rectory at St. Stephen's, working on his garden. He was wearing a wide-brimmed straw hat that he took off occasionally to wipe off the perspiration trickling down his pale, withered face.

He was resting for a moment on a stool, hoe in hand, when Will rounded the corner of the rectory and called out to him.

"Are you Father Godfrey?"

"Yes, sir. You look familiar. Have we met?" the priest replied.

"I am Will Chambers, a lawyer from Virginia. I was a patient at the Delphi hospital. You visited my roommate yesterday. I'm here in Georgia working on a legal case, and I'm wondering whether I could take a few minutes of your time."

"Your timing is good—I just decided to sit down for a few minutes and catch my breath."

"Do you know a man by the name of Henry Pencup?"

"I did. I presided over his funeral. He was a member of my parish."

"Do you happen to know if he gave a last confession at the Delphi hospital before he died?"

"That is a very strange question—why do you ask?"

"I represent a woman by the name of Mary Sue Fellows. She is a mother of a small boy named Joshua. Happily married. Her husband is a farmer by the name of Joseph Fellows. They live outside Delphi on the farm they own and operate.

"Mrs. Fellows has been charged with committing child abuse against her son. I don't believe those charges are true. I believe she is innocent, but I have only a short period of time to prove that. If I don't, they are going to take her child away from her—possibly permanently—and she may end up going to prison."

"That is a rather amazing situation you describe. What did you say your name was?"

"Chambers, Will Chambers. I am her attorney."

"I think I may have read something about this in the local paper. The name doesn't ring a bell. But then—I don't think they publish the names of people involved in those juvenile cases, do they?"

"No—no they don't," Will said.

"But I don't see how this concerns me," Father Godfrey went on.

"I have reason to believe," Will explained, "that a confession was given to you by Henry Pencup right before he died, and that it may have something to do with my client's case. It may help me prove her innocence."

"I can tell you this—I did take the last confession of Henry Pencup. And it was at the Delphi hospital. I can tell you that much."

"Is there anything else you can tell me?" Will asked.

"Being a lawyer, you know better than I do that this involves a legal privilege of confidentiality. I can't share anything with you. And more than that, there is a sacred trust between his priest and his penitent. I am afraid I cannot be of much help to you."

And with that Father Godfrey rose slowly from his stool, leaning on the hoe for support.

Will was about to leave, but then he thought of a question that he thought the priest might be able to answer.

"Was there anyone else in that hospital room with you when Henry Pencup gave you his last confession?"

Father Godfrey paused for a moment. He took his straw hat off and wiped the perspiration from the thin strands of his white hair.

"Now that you mention it—I believe there was."

"Can you remember anything about that person?"

"She was a nurse, I believe."

"Would you recognize her if you saw her again?"

"I think so. My memory isn't what it used to be. But I think I might be able to recognize her."

Will felt around in the pocket of his sport coat and pulled out a snapshot of Mary Sue and handed it to the older man. After a prolonged silence, holding the photograph close to his eyes, the priest finally replied.

"This could be her. I am not positive. But I think this could be the same woman. Immediately after I gave Mr. Pencup his last rites, his heart stopped. And then—all the alarms and bells—you know, the medical equipment starting going off. She pulled open the curtain because she was right there in the room and started to perform CPR as she was calling for the rest of the staff. In a few seconds there were doctors and other nurses there, but they could not revive him."

"Do you think she heard any of Henry Pencup's last words to you?"

"Oh, I doubt that," the priest replied quickly. "Henry didn't have much energy. He was speaking very quietly—I had to strain to hear him."

"Is there anything more—anything at all—that you recall about your last contact with Henry Pencup, or with that nurse, that you can tell me?" Will asked.

Father Godfrey searched his memory for a few seconds, but then shook his head.

Thanking the older man for his time Will turned to leave.

"Good luck on your garden here. It looks like you have a green thumb."

"I may have a green thumb," Father Godfrey replied, "but I also have something else."

"What's that?"

"Well, I thought I had rabbits. My vegetables were being eaten at night. And I did see rabbits in the area. So I put up this little two-foot fence to keep them out. But I kept noticing that my vegetables were still being eaten at night."

"Did you find out what was doing it?"

"Well, one morning I came out, and I noticed something bound out of the garden and over the fence in one easy leap. It was red, with a bushy tail."

Will was fishing in his pocket for one of his business cards.

"Which just goes to show you..." Father Godfrey said—and then his voice trailed off.

"Goes to show you what?" Will prompted.

"Well," said the older man, gathering his thoughts, "it shows you that you shouldn't be looking for rabbits when you have a fox."

The attorney smiled and handed his business card to the priest.

"This is my card, but I have written my local number on the back because I'm staying here in the Delphi area at a houseboat on Eden Lake. If you think of anything more that you can tell me that might relate to Mary Sue Fellows or Henry Pencup, please do not hesitate to call."

"Eden Lake? Did you say Eden Lake?" the priest asked, suddenly becoming animated, his voice rising.

"Yes—is that important somehow?"

Father Godfrey leaned on his hoe and studied Will for a few seconds.

"Mr. Chambers, that is an interesting lake. I used to fish it when I was a boy. Have you visited the grounds of the Eden Lake Resort there?"

"No, I can't say that I have."

"You really ought to. You really ought to get a boat and go over there and take a look at the resort."

"I wasn't aware there was a resort on the lake. The whole area looked pretty quiet to me. A few cottages here and there. But I certainly didn't realize there was a large resort area."

"You go over there. You take a look at the Eden Lake Resort," Father Godfrey said with urgency in his voice.

"I certainly will," Will replied respectfully, but a little mystified.

Then he thanked the elderly priest again and returned to his car, glancing at his watch, feeling the crushing pressure of time. The trial date for Mary Sue was approaching fast. Every hour had to count. And Will was beginning to wonder whether the mystery woman who'd called now had him chasing rabbit trails that led nowhere.

40

As Will pulled up to the dock on Eden Lake, he thought back to what Father Godfrey had said.

He wondered if the elderly priest's reference to the Eden Lake Resort was simply an irrelevant, wandering comment—or if it had some relevance to Mary Sue's case.

There was a small aluminum fishing boat anchored off the houseboat he could use. Will checked his watch again. Did he really want to waste time taking a boat ride, only because of Father Godfrey's odd statement? How could a lake resort hold the key to proving Mary Sue's innocence?

Well, why not, he thought to himself. *Stranger things than that have happened.*

He climbed into the boat, which had a modest seven-horsepower motor, similar to the one he'd used as a boy during his summers on the lake in Maine.

After untying the boat from the dock, he yanked the pull rope and started out across the lake. With no other boats in sight, the water was calm, and its surface like glass. Here and there he heard a plop at the surface, as a fish jumped. It took him almost an hour, running along the bank, until he saw some log buildings, docks, and outbuildings tucked behind some pine trees at the other end of the lake. A sign on one of the swimming floats offshore said, "For Use By Eden Lake Resort Guests Only!"

Will cut his engine as he slid closer to shore. After he tied up the boat, he walked down the wooden plank dock toward the buildings, noticing a large "No Trespassing" sign at its shore end.

Every building, though beautifully crafted, was boarded up and the doors were padlocked. As he cast his eyes over the scene, he noticed winding sidewalks connecting the structures and a large pavilion at the top of a pine-covered hill—which Will figured was intended to contain a theater and restaurants, judging by the signs.

Then he realized there were written notices on the doors, giving public notice of a bankruptcy sale of the resort property.

Glancing between the boards over some of the windows, he saw that each building was empty. As he returned to the manicured path, a raccoon scampered out from under one building marked "Ultra Spa and Beauty Center."

There were signs pointing the way to an eighteen-hole golf course, horse stables, a "Cultural Arts Center," "Children's Fantasy Area," and a business-conference complex. All were closed, some in varying degrees of incompletion, with a few tractors and a backhoe stationed off in the distance.

Then he heard the sound of a motor—and it was getting closer.

A man in a green maintenance uniform, driving a golf cart, scooted up to Will's position. He got off and approached Will.

"This is private property. Got to leave," he said curtly.

"No problem," Will replied. "But I'm here on some related business. I'm a lawyer."

"Bankruptcy sale on the personal property is already long past."

"I'm not interested in that."

"Then what kind of business you got?"

"I'm wondering what real-estate development group owned this resort."

"Why do you want to know?"

"That's confidential."

"You can give me your name and telephone number—I can have someone call you," the man said, eyeing Will and glancing over at his boat at the dock.

"I don't think that will work," Will replied.

"Then you got to get out of here—now."

Will smiled and walked back to the boat. As he was pulling away from the dock, the man took a cell phone from his golf cart and tapped a number into it.

In a few seconds there was an answer at the other end.

"Howley, this is George, down at the resort."

"What is it—I'm busy."

"Some guy came over here snooping around."

"Who was it?"

"Don't know. Some lawyer. Didn't give me his name. But he's pretty recognizable. He's got a couple black eyes and a bandage across his face. He just left in a boat."

"Where's he heading?"

"Over toward the other side."

"Watch him. See where he goes. Then call me back," Howley ordered.

The groundskeeper picked up a pair of binoculars from the cart. He watched Will as he traversed the lake, the rolling ripples from the boat's wake fanning out over the calm surface of the water.

Will was enjoying the clean lake air. Even though his head and nose were still hurting badly, his mind was clear. He knew now what Tiny Heftland's next lead would be.

Then the comment Father Godfrey had made sprang into his mind—about the fox in his garden. Something he'd read in the Bible. Jesus had called someone a "fox." Who was it?

The lake was quiet as Will cut his motor and glided up to the houseboat. The only sound was the mournful warbling of a loon out on the water somewhere.

As soon as he got inside, he picked up the phone and called Tiny at his motel room.

"Tiny, I want everything you can tell me about who owned the Eden Lake Resort, which is now bankrupt," Will said. "Check out the bankruptcy petition. Find out who the principals were. Keep an eye out for someone by the name of Henry Pencup, a bank president. See if he had an interest in the venture."

After he hung up with Tiny, Will walked out onto the deck of the houseboat. The sun was setting over the great pine trees that ringed the lake.

Who was the "fox" that Jesus talked about? he wondered again.

And then he remembered.

It was one of the Herods. Jesus called him a "fox" because he was devious, clever, and devoid of scruples.

As he went inside for the night he also recalled that the Herod who was denounced by Jesus was a blood relation to the very same Herod who had sought, unsuccessfully, to hunt down Mary and her infant child, Jesus.

Have I been looking for rabbits when I should have been hunting for a fox? Will asked himself.

He had no answer to that—yet.

41

WILL SLEPT DEEPLY THAT NIGHT. When he woke, it was almost noon. He was starting to feel a little more like himself, despite the headaches from his concussion and the tenderness of his broken nose.

He poured himself a cup of coffee and went out onto the deck with the medical records from Mary Sue's case. He reviewed them again, particularly noting the blood test from Dr. Parker, the chief pathologist at the Delphi hospital. The report was dated nearly three weeks after Joshua's admission to the emergency room for one of his spells of vomiting and lethargy, when his blood had been taken for a routine CBC. Will figured the lab results should only have taken a few days at the most.

Then the phone rang. It was Tiny.

The private investigator had gone to the bankruptcy court when it opened for the day. He had already reviewed the court file and was calling from his car in the parking lot.

"Any reference to the bank president—Henry Pencup?" Will asked right out of the gate.

"We have a great big zero on that one, chief," Tiny answered. "Believe me, I looked real hard for that."

"What did you find then?"

"There were some general partners in on the resort at the beginning," Tiny said. "This was a huge project. I'm talking 170, 180 million dollars. And that was only for phase one of the development. There were two more phases planned. Somebody must have thought this was going to be the next Disney World.

I suppose they figured it was close enough to Atlanta to draw the big-city folks—and it looks like they were planning to make part of it a business conference center. They even had long-range plans for a major sports arena. Anyway, the whole thing started collapsing when they couldn't squeeze their investors for a measly few more million dollars to pay off some of the subcontractors."

"How much were they short?"

"About three million—something like that. The project was mortgaged up to the hilt—no banks would extend any more credit after the subs started filing liens and the lawsuits started piling up. And all of a sudden—bango—the whole deal collapsed like a house of cards."

"Are you sure Henry Pencup's bank didn't lend any money on that project?"

"Positive. There were no mortgages listed in the name of his bank—and that bank was not listed as a creditor. Most of the banks were the big Atlanta lenders, and a couple were out of state—you know, New York banks, that sort of thing."

"This doesn't add up," Will commented, with some exasperation in his voice.

"Why's that?"

"I don't see how any of this relates to Mary Sue Fellows being accused of child abuse."

"Yeah—well, either do I. But then, you're the legal genius—I'm just the P.I."

"Father Godfrey, the priest that took Henry Pencup's last confession, suggested I take a look at the resort. I took that to be some kind of hint—a clue that he was not free to fully explain. Now I'm thinking it was just an irrelevant comment. He's getting pretty old, after all."

"Well, look—if you won't be needing me any more on this, I'll drive back to old Virginny," Tiny said.

"I'm not sure. I may still have some work for you on this. But go back a second—you mentioned the general partners. There were several?"

"In the beginning. But by the end there was just one—with a whole long list of limited partners."

"Who was the last remaining general partner on the project?"

"Some guy named Jason Bell Purdy."

"'I've heard about him. Well-known local hero. He even dated Mary Sue Fellows in high school. I think he comes from old money here in Georgia," Will said.

"If he came from big money, then why didn't he bail out his project with his own cash?"

"I don't know," Will replied. "But I'd like you to find out."

"You said he was well-known in the Delphi area?"

"Yeah. I think he went to a ritzy private school in the Delphi area—he was some kind of football star when he was in high school. There's a street in Delphi named after some prominent ancestor of his."

"Then," Tiny concluded, "I think it's time for me to get a haircut in one of Delphi's fine barber shops."

"I don't get it."

"Will, I'll let you in on a little trade secret. In small towns, if you want the scoop on a well-known local man—go to the local barber shop and strike up a conversation. You'll hear a goldmine of info. If you're checking on a local female socialite, head for the best beauty salon in town."

"Tiny, you're letting go of the tricks of the trade," Will said with a chuckle.

"Look, I trust you. You've been good to me, Will. But just don't be sharing my stuff with anybody else!"

"Oh—before you go, how about the list of limited partners in the resort?" Will asked quickly.

"Sure. It's a long list—I'll e-mail it to your laptop."

After Tiny hung up, Will returned to his coffee, by now grown cold. He glanced out the window. The water of Eden

Lake was being whipped up by a stiff breeze, and the waves were causing the houseboat to rock a little.

He thought back to the phone call he'd received from the woman who said she'd called in a false child-abuse allegation against Mary Sue. It seemed like a flip of the coin—but Will felt he had to accept that message at face value.

He had no other choice. Outside of the protestations of innocence from Mary Sue—and of course from Joe, that phone call represented the first real corroboration of their story by an independent source.

On the other hand, Will could not use this hearsay information as proof at trial. Without the caller as a witness to identify who had put her up to the false accusation, Will was left only with using her scoop as a lead in his investigation. If justice was to be obtained, it would have to be through other facts, other witnesses, other evidence.

But there was something else about the woman's anguished call to Will. She had somehow known that Henry Pencup's confession had a bearing on the accusations against Mary Sue.

That had led Will to Father Godfrey. And from the best of the elderly priest's memory, Mary Sue was the nurse who was in the hospital room at the time of the confession.

One thing was now quite clear. Someone was concerned that she might have overheard Pencup's last words. If that was true, then was that a motivation to try to silence his client? Was that the reason behind the pressure put on the woman—whoever she was—to place a phone call to the Department of Social Services accusing Mary Sue of poisoning her own child?

Will could think of one possible scenario. If Mary Sue Fellows were found guilty of plotting the death of her son in return for life-insurance money, that would certainly destroy her credibility forever—particularly in the eyes of the Delphi community. Her value as a potential witness would then be destroyed permanently. But, potential witness against who? Will knew of no other legal cases that would involve her as a possible witness.

Who was it, then, who was so fearful of what she might know about Henry Pencup?

Will was convinced there was a connection there. There was a picture forming within in the mass of seemingly unrelated factual fragments in front of him—if only he could connect the dots. Will had to ask himself—*Was there a fox somewhere in this picture? And if so, who was that fox?*

42

THE FOLLOWING DAY, Will wanted to make a jail visit to Joe Fellows. Since the imprisoned man was now representing himself, that meant Will was ethically free to contact him directly—rather than having to deal through the very unhelpful Stanley Kennelworth.

Before heading over to the jail, Will went on-line for a few minutes to check out news stories on the Eden Lake financial collapse.

He reviewed several of them but gained no new information. The final one he scanned was mildly interesting only because it added one small detail. Jason Bell Purdy—apparently the perennial entrepreneurial optimist—was quoted as saying that, because of recent promises of additional investor capital, he believed he could come up with the additional funding to resolve the contractor lawsuits. All contractor liens would then be removed, thus satisfying the primary mortgage lenders who were all poised to file foreclosure.

But later news articles indicated that the investor capital either never materialized, or it arrived too late to resolve the massive loss of lender confidence in the project that had developed.

A glut of foreclosure suits was then filed, and bankruptcy ensued.

Will then checked his laptop e-mail. As promised, Tiny had transmitted the list of limited partners in the Eden Lake development.

Limited partners, by definition, possessed only very narrow rights in a real-estate investment deal. Their risk was limited to the amount of their financial investment—they had no additional personal liability. But they had no control over decision-making in the project, in a formal sense. Their only interest was in recovering—if all went well—a substantial profit beyond their original investment.

A *general* partner—like Jason Bell Purdy—stood to gain huge profits. But he could also suffer titanic personal losses if the project fell apart and the partnership property was insufficient to cover all debts.

Looking over the list of limited partners, Will was astounded. There were more than one hundred of them. He printed out the list, closed down his laptop, and then sat down with a pen, ready to mark any names that were significant.

He found only two. The first was that of Dr. Parker—the pathologist from the Delphi hospital, who would be testifying for the county that Joshua's blood test showed he had been poisoned. At first, Will thought he'd hit gold. But then he reviewed the list again and saw that, in addition to Dr. Parker, there were seventeen other physicians who had also invested in the project.

The second name was a surprise. Bob Smiley, the insurance agent who'd issued the $100,000 life-insurance policy on Joshua's life, was listed as an investor. But according to the list that Tiny had pulled from the bankruptcy court file, Smiley had put in only six thousand dollars—an insignificantly small share.

As Will drove to the county jail, he called Tiny on his cell phone. Yes, the detective assured Will, he had indeed sat down for a haircut at Delphi's busiest barber shop.

Tiny then reviewed all of the gossip he'd heard when he raised the name of Jason Bell Purdy. Most of it concerned Purdy's notorious divorce from a southern-belle beauty-pageant queen by the name of Magnolia. The general consensus, Tiny discovered, was that Magnolia had been a gold digger who'd landed on hard times. She'd hunted down Purdy like a lioness that hadn't eaten for a month. Because she'd been only after Purdy's money, so it was thought, the sympathy vote in the crowded barbershop inclined toward Purdy.

There'd also been quite a bit of raucous humor when Tiny had asked about Purdy's dating life since the divorce. Apparently he'd been romantically linked to half the female population between Delphi and Atlanta.

Tiny further discovered that Purdy had two older sisters. Susan Purdy, the middle child, had been committed to a long-term psychiatric hospital in San Francisco.

The oldest of the siblings was Lori Lou Purdy—a flamboyant character now residing with the jet set in Lucerne, Switzerland—but who continuously hopped from there to the French Riviera, to Paris, and to the casinos in Gibraltar and Morocco.

But Tiny was also quick to add that Purdy, his father, and his grandfather were still considered to be of heroic proportions in the greater Delphi area.

As far as Purdy's finances, however, there was a little bit of a surprise. Tiny said it was widely known that most of his money came from a "spendthrift" family trust. The trust kept a tight lock on the money, dispensing a huge annual interest and investment income—but gave Purdy no control over the mammoth "corpus," or principal, of the trust.

Will immediately understood why Purdy had not been able to use any of his personal fortune to cover the few million dollars he needed to put his real-estate project back on track. It had been locked up tight in the family trust—beyond his control.

By the time Will finished with Tiny he was parked in front of the jail. He felt an eerie sense of recognition as he passed through security and into the lobby. The stocky, bald jailer was reading a crossword puzzle magazine at his desk. He recognized the attorney immediately and made a hasty call.

In a few minutes, deputy jailer Thompson arrived. He came over to Will and shook hands warmly.

"I need to have your driver's license and your wallet before you enter," the bald jailer called out.

"No you don't," Thompson barked out. "I'll vouch for him."

"Regulations say that—"

"Those regulations are about to change," Thompson replied, cutting him off and then passed Will through the security door.

Once inside a clean, well-lighted conference room, Will turned to Thompson.

"I get a *conference room* with Joe—no glass between us?"

"There are a lot of changes going on here," Thompson said, lowering his voice.

"Oh?"

"Yeah. Ever since I called Harry Putnam and told him you'd been transferred over to the auxiliary jail—or should I call it the overflow pen? Anyway—this is not for public consumption—the head jailer is on the way out. I'm being appointed interim head of the jail. And that goon who was responsible for what happened to you—he's facing criminal charges."

"Yes, so I've heard. Justice does happen," Will said with a smile.

Thompson eyed the bandage over Will's broken nose. "Look—I am sorry about what happened. You got a raw deal—you really did."

"Maybe," Will said. "But I know a mother out there with a little boy, who may be getting the rawest deal of all."

Thompson nodded, but added only, "I'll get Joe Fellows. If you need anything, let me know."

When Joe entered the room he broke into a big grin that took over his handsome, but now slightly gaunt face. But it quickly faded as he studied Will's nose and the black-and-blue streaks under both eyes.

Brushing off Joe's questions about his injuries, the attorney jumped into the facts of Mary Sue's case.

Joe was quick to answer questions about the truck that Will and Tiny had spotted in the farmhouse garage. He explained that the brakes needed fluid. It really was not a big thing for him to do it—it was just that he was always behind in his work on the farm. He figured it was the older truck anyway, and if Mary Sue ever needed transportation—for her part-time nursing work, or to take Joshua to the doctor, or whatever—he always gave her the newer truck.

"Was the newer truck the one she used to take off the day the sheriff's deputies and social services showed up?"

"Yeah. And then," Joe added with chagrin, "the engine ends up overheating, and Mary Sue is almost stranded. Figure that one out."

"But the older truck that was in the garage with the hood up—you're saying you never filled the brakes with fluid?"

"No, never got around to it. It's stupid, really. It hardly takes any time to do it. Looking back, I wished I had. Then maybe they would be saying *I* did the poisoning—rather than going after my wife."

"But there were several containers of brake fluid in the garage. I saw them myself," Will said.

"Sure. Along with fuel oil, cleaning solvents, engine oil, oil for my tractor, bar oil for my chain saw, gasoline. There are containers all over the garage."

"Did Mary Sue add the brake fluid to the truck?"

"No. I never asked her to. She's always got a million things to do. I figured I would get around to it myself."

"Then how did brake fluid get in Joshua's cup in the kitchen? And how did it end up in Joshua's bloodstream?"

"Look, Will," Joe said loudly, "like I've said from the beginning, this is a nightmare that doesn't make any sense. None of it. You've asked Mary Sue the same thing…"

"I have. And she told me she doesn't know how the brake fluid got where it did—or why the blood tests indicated what they did."

Joe just shook his head and ran his strong hands through his greasy, blond hair.

Will decided to change subjects. He asked whether Mary Sue had ever talked about Henry Pencup.

"Sure," Joe replied, "I think she was on duty when he died."

"Did she ever tell you anything Henry Pencup said?"

"No. Don't remember that."

"Anything about being there when a priest—Father Godfrey—took his last confession?"

"No. Never. Is this something I should know about?" Joe said with some concern in his voice.

"Not really."

"Is there something you think Mary Sue should have told me—but didn't?"

Will looked at Joe and tried to reassure him.

"No, not at all. I'm just trying to put together a puzzle."

"What puzzle?"

Will then revealed to Joe that he had received a call from an unknown woman who had said she'd been pressured into making the initial child-abuse allegation falsely.

Joe was elated that, at long last, their innocence seemed to be emerging. But his excitement faded as Will explained that the hearsay information he'd received—from a woman he could not identify—was far from a "smoking gun."

"This woman seemed to believe that somehow the Pencup confession was linked to Mary Sue's case," Will continued. "Do you know of any connection?"

Joe just shook his head.

Before leaving, Will wanted to touch on one more subject—Jason Bell Purdy.

"Sure, I know him," Joe said with reservation in his voice. "He dated Mary Sue for a while. A very short while. That was way before we got engaged. Mary Sue—in case you haven't noticed—is beautiful, and is quite a woman. I still wonder, sometimes, why she married me rather than him."

Will looked Joe in the eye.

"Mary Sue tells me you're the greatest husband to walk God's green earth."

"She would. That's just like her."

"You went to public high school in Delphi?"

"Yeah."

"I hear you were a pretty fine linebacker on the football team."

"I did okay. I made All-Conference."

"You were the same age as Jason Bell Purdy?"

"Right. Course he didn't go to the same school. He went to the private school—Exeter Academy. They played us in the play-offs. Jason was their star quarterback."

"And?"

"They beat us by one touchdown. Jason threw a forty-yard pass. He made All-State that year—I often wonder what would have happened if I'd have blitzed him, rather than hanging back like I did."

Joe paused and looked down at the table. Then he added, "Rich boy makes All-State. I admit to you, Will, I've had some feelings about the guy—dating Mary Sue and everything."

"But she picked *you*," Will said. "That's the most important fact here."

Joe smiled at that.

As Will was about to leave, Joe asked him one more question.

"Do you think God corrects injustice?"

"Why don't you ask him?" Will responded.

"I have. You know, in the past, Mary Sue was always the real spiritual one. I was busy trying to make the farm survive. Keep food on the table. Trying to build a future for us. Now I'm sitting here in this hole...my hands tied...not knowing where she and Joshua are, or exactly how they are doing. And she tells me, when she called here to the jail the other day, that Joshua is doing real bad. Been hospitalized."

"Recently?"

"Yeah, about the same time they threw you in here."

"How is he doing now?"

"I haven't heard. So I cry out to God. Every day. I ask him for protection for my wife and child. And for justice. For these lying charges against us to be dropped. You know, Will, I feel pretty helpless. I want to save my wife from this—to do something for her. But all I can do is sit here in this miserable jail."

Will embraced Joe, surprising him with a quick hug. There were no more words he could give him. The other man was going down a road of shadows—and he would have to go down it himself.

Meanwhile, Will was scrambling down his own dark alley in trying to prove Mary Sue's innocence. Time was running out. And with each new turn that appeared at first to be promising, the light seemed to be fading even more quickly.

43

WILL WAS HOLDING ON THE LINE, trying to be patient. This was the second day in a row that he had tried to contact Dr. Parker, the Delphi hospital pathologist, in an effort to gain an interview with him before the trial.

After several long minutes, the receptionist came back on the telephone. Dr. Parker's schedule would not permit an in-person interview. But he did have just a few minutes, right now, to talk.

When the doctor came on the line, Will introduced himself. The other man indicated he was expecting the call.

Will first asked him about the blood test on Joshua. The doctor gave a measured, confident, account about the test results showing the presence of ethylene glycol, an ingredient found in hydraulic brake fluid, among other industrial and machine uses.

"Why did you take two weeks to write up that lab report?"

"Mr. Chambers, this is a busy hospital. As I recall, we had a number of rush evaluations we needed to do. I was short-staffed."

"Is that why you did the blood test report yourself—rather than one of your lab assistants?"

Dr. Parker paused, then said, "That was probably the reason."

"Who did you talk to about this?"

"I notified our chief of staff when I saw that the blood test indicated possible poisoning. I called our social services director here in the hospital. She contacted the Department of Social Services for the county, and the sheriff's department."

"Why didn't you entertain the possibility of accidental poisoning—as opposed to intentional poisoning?"

"We did, of course," the doctor replied quickly. "But after consultation with the authorities—and I believe they brought the family physician, Dr. Wilson, in on it—coupled with a phone call they received from someone reporting child abuse—all that tipped the scales."

"Do you know the name of the caller?"

"No, they never give me a name."

After Will paused to jot down a few notes, he decided to return to a prior question.

"Anyone else you talked to about this case?"

"Mr. Putnam, and that guardian lawyer for the child—"

"Harriet Bender?"

"Yes, that was her."

"Did Putnam and Bender come to you together?"

"That's right."

"Anyone else you talked to?"

"Maybe some of the staff here."

"Do you remember their names?"

"No, not really. Just mentioning the case in passing."

"Anyone else?"

Dr. Parker cleared his throat. "I do have some matters to attend to here at the hospital, Mr. Chambers."

"Certainly. I'm almost done. Who else did you talk to?"

After pausing, Dr. Parker continued.

"Possibly a concerned friend or two of the Fellows family, and a few news reporters."

"And that would be who?"

"One reporter from Atlanta, one television news-magazine host—a woman—and some reporters from Delphi and the papers in the county and surrounding areas."

"Actually, doctor," Will said, "I meant the family friends. Who were they?"

"I recall one, Jason Purdy. There were some others that may have tried to call me. I didn't return their calls."

"Jason Bell Purdy?"

"Yes. I think he said he was a longtime friend of Mary Sue Fellows—during his college years, I think. He called because he wanted to help her out, see if there was something he could do. He was sure there had been a mistake."

"What did you tell him?"

"I told him that, regrettably, there had been no mistake. It was in the hands of the authorities. There was nothing I could do—or he, for that matter—to stop Mary Sue from being prosecuted."

"So Mr. Purdy was calling as a friend?"

"Yes."

"On the telephone?"

After a few seconds, Dr. Parker corrected himself.

"I think he actually stopped by, if I remember correctly."

"Did the two of you discuss anything else?"

"No. We didn't. Now if you will excuse me—"

The attorney threw out one last question, "Doctor, I made a written request for Harry Putnam to have you produce the remaining portion of Joshua's blood sample to me, so I can have my own expert test it. Has he mentioned that?"

"You'll have to talk to Putnam about that," Dr. Parker snapped.

Will thanked the doctor for taking the time to talk. Unfortunately, he had not had the chance to question the doctor about his investment in Eden Lake, but that seemed to be of only marginal interest in any event.

After hanging up, he checked his e-mail. There was a short note from Tiny.

> Will: I checked the probate file on Henry Pencup. Found nothing that seemed to help. He had only modest hard assets. But his estate also listed a $750,000 life insurance policy. It was written by Bob Smiley, that local insurance guy. No other players in your little drama seem to be involved in the Pencup estate. Everything went to his widow. See ya.
>
> Tiny
>
> P.S.—Stay out of jail!

Up till then, Bob Smiley had successfully evaded a follow-up interview with either Tiny or Will. But Will decided to send a quick return e-mail to his detective, asking him to try to tie down the insurance agent one more time before trial.

Dr. Parker had aroused Will's curiosity about Jason Bell Purdy. Perhaps Purdy had never gotten over his romantic interest in Mary Sue. Or perhaps there was something else.

Picking up the phone, Will glanced at the telephone number that Tiny had obtained for him, and began dialing Purdy's corporate office in Atlanta.

After two layers of receptionists passed his call through, he was finally connected to Purdy's appointment secretary. He said he wanted a meeting with Mr. Purdy as soon as possible in regard to Mary Sue Fellows.

She said she would check on that and call him back.

Wanting to clear his mind so he could start focusing on the final push of trial preparation, Will strolled down the dock and skipped a few rocks in the lake, which had calmed considerably since the day before. Since he didn't expect a call back from Purdy's office any time soon, the question then became, what stones had he yet to turn over?

But before he could answer that, the phone in the houseboat rang.

He ran in and picked it up. It was the appointment secretary calling back.

To Will's surprise she indicated that he "was in great luck. Mr. Purdy is just finishing up a meeting at his home—and after that he has a small window open in his schedule. He will meet you there in two hours. Do you want directions to the Purdy mansion?"

After jotting down the directions, Will hung up and tried to call Fiona, but only connected to her voice mail. He then called his office to check in.

Hilda said she had last talked to Fiona right after Will had been released from jail.

"Yeah—I got a surprise visit from her in the hospital. Do you think she'll still love me, now that I'm not just another pretty face?" Will said with a laugh.

"Oh, Will—when Jacki got back here she said you looked like you had rented out your face for a punching bag. But I don't know why we are making a joke out of this," she said, suddenly serious. "What happened to you was just plain ugly. And it could have been a tragedy."

"Yes, *Mother*."

"Good thing I know how to handle you," Hilda retorted. "Now here is something important. Mary Sue called here yesterday. She said she wanted to call you there at the houseboat today, and she is going to call me back today to confirm."

"Tell her to call me in exactly five hours from now. I'm on my way to interview a guy by the name of Jason Bell Purdy. That should give me plenty of time to get back here."

"Oh, isn't that the fellow who is going to fill out the rest of the term of that Georgia senator who died?"

"Where did you hear that?"

"INN news last night."

"Huh—that will be good to know for the interview. I'm glad you mentioned it," Will responded. "And if you hear from Fiona before I do, tell her I'm trying to connect with her."

"She's en route back from the recording session today, flying into BWI airport. I think she made it just under the wire with the strike. If I hear from her, I'll tell her."

After about an hour-and-a-half drive through the Georgia countryside in the direction of Atlanta, Will located a sign arching over a private drive that came off a county trunk highway.

The black metal sign, ornately detailed with delicate scroll-work, contained one word in gold letters—"PURDY."

A half-mile down a long driveway that was lined with peach blossom trees, Will encountered a guardhouse.

The security guard checked his ID, then made a call to the mansion. After a few minutes he waved Will through.

Will drove another mile through the green, rolling landscape. Several chestnut-colored horses grazed peacefully beyond the cleanly maintained black horse fence. Off in the distance he caught glimpses of an equestrian course.

As the mansion came into view, a black stretch limo, followed by a smaller limo, blew past him on their way out.

The mammoth white antebellum edifice was perched on a hill. Two huge columns on each side of the front entrance helped support a full porch wrapping around the second floor, all crowned by a fantail window on the third floor.

The front of the mansion was graced by a semicircular, red-brick drive-through.

Will pulled his car to the side of the road for a minute to take in the full view of this spectacular house that was sending his mind back to the past.

It brought back his memories of Generals' Hill, the much smaller antebellum mansion that he and Audra, his artist wife, had purchased in Virginia. But theirs had been in disrepair. The couple had been halfway through the renovation when they'd separated. Against Will's desires, Audra had moved to George-town. Shortly after that, she'd been found murdered in her apartment.

Will had never recovered enough from that to complete the work on the house. Instead, he'd spent several years immersed in self-pity, living alone at Generals' Hill and drinking himself into an emotional abyss. He'd allowed his law practice to disintegrate and his personal life to hit bottom.

That was when Angus MacCameron had walked into his office. The unique issues in the preacher's case had forced Will to come to grips with spiritual realities that he had, up to then, successfully avoided. Ultimately, his life was transformed by a divine encounter. At first, even his friend and several-year associate,

Jacki Johnson, had doubted this. But the evidence for the complete spiritual renovation of his life had become undeniable.

And of course, that same lawsuit brought Fiona, Angus' daughter, into Will's life. That was a second kind of miracle.

But Generals' Hill had not survived. It was burned to the ground in an act of arson, which had been committed by powerful enemies whom the attorney had created during his handling of the MacCameron case. And instead of trying to recreate the burned-down structure, Will had settled on building a large, rambling log house on the same spot.

Now, seeing the Purdy mansion as he sat in his idling car, Will felt old, powerful feelings emerge. He had not thought about Audra for quite some time. Fiona had totally eclipsed those memories, it seemed.

Until now. It was odd, he thought, how merely seeing this house could suddenly sweep the ghosts back into his head.

Reminding himself that he was there for Mary Sue Fellows, he pulled the car into the circle drive in front of the carved-oak double doors at the front of the mansion.

After parking, he strode up to the entrance and rapped the brass door knocker.

After a moment, Will could hear someone approaching. Footsteps were echoing and getting louder within the massive entranceway on the other side of the door.

44

THE IMMENSE DOUBLE DOOR OPENED. At first, Will was unable to see who was there.

He stepped into the vast marble-floored foyer. Two spiral staircases, one at each side, led to a second-story balcony. In the middle, there was a round, velvet settee with a stone figurine in the center that looked vaguely Roman.

Suddenly, from behind one of the doors, a figure stepped out.

Will had to keep himself from gasping. In front of him was a smiling young woman—pretty, blond, with crystal-blue eyes. She was laughing almost the same kind of quirky laugh that Will's wife, Audra, would when she would tease him.

Though this young woman was not a complete likeness, her similarities to Audra were remarkable.

"I'm Suzanne Purdy Black. I'm Uncle Jason's niece." With that she thrust a slender hand into Will's. Laying her other hand on Will's other arm, she began gently leading him toward the end of the foyer.

"Won't you come with me, Mr. Chambers? Uncle Jason's going to be a couple of minutes—he's been exercising. I'm just going to entertain you for a few moments out here in the sunroom, if that's alright."

Will was taken aback—and slightly embarrassed—by her forward approach, but he dutifully followed her to a large glass-enclosed sunroom that lay through several arched doorways, at the end of the house.

She seated Will on a padded rattan chair, still holding his hands.

Suzanne leaned close to his face and smiled. "Now I've got some iced tea over on the table and I'm going to fix you a glass right now. My, my, what happened to you? Your eyes are both black and you've got a nasty old bump on your nose. Did you get your nose broken, Mr. Chambers?"

Will tried to lean back in his chair and release her grip.

"Yes, I had a run-in with some bad folks."

"Well, I'm sure they got the worst of it—you look like a man who can take care of himself."

"Actually, I'm happy just to be conscious right now. But thanks for asking."

"Well," Suzanne said flirtatiously, "then that must have been a very, very unfair fight!" And with that she laughed, stood up straight, and tossed her hair back.

"Do you live here with your uncle?"

"Yes, off and on," she said as she poured a glass of iced tea from a crystal pitcher on a glass table. "I dabble in art, and I come and go. Uncle Jason is sort of a replacement father for me. There's always a place for me here in the mansion."

"Did you say you were an artist?"

"Yes," Suzanne said, flashing a wide smile, "do you like art?"

"I used to," Will said, staring at Suzanne's pretty face and trying to shake the feeling that there was a connection, somehow, between his life and Suzanne's.

He took a few sips from his glass and then asked, "Is your uncle going to be long?"

"Oh, with Uncle Jason you never can tell! Why—don't you like talking with me?"

"It's just that I have some business with your uncle."

"*Everyone* has business with Uncle Jason! And now that he's going to be the newest senator from the state of Georgia…well, I'm sure he's going to be busier than ever!"

"You must be very proud of your uncle."

"Of course, but do you know what he told me this morning?"

"No, what did he say?" Will asked.

"Mr. Chambers—may I call you Will? Well, Uncle Jason said I don't look like I'm twenty-five years old. Do you think I look twenty-five years old? Uncle Jason is always joking and saying that I look like I'm much younger than that. But I don't want to look younger than that! I'm a grown woman. What do you think?"

"I've never been very good at guessing ages."

"You know what—neither am I!" Suzanne said with a laugh. "Now take you for example, Will—I suppose you are older than me by several years but I've always said that age really doesn't matter. Besides, sometimes a man your age is so much more attractive—so much more mature and together, you know what I mean—so much more appealing than these boys I have to run around with. Particularly back here in Georgia when I visit Uncle Jason. By the way that reminds me of something—guess what?"

"What," Will said, feeling increasingly embarrassed and wanting to extricate himself from Suzanne's flirtations.

"There's a wonderful party at the country club tonight—and I have absolutely no one to go there with. It's for couples only—this is a very silly question to ask you, I really shouldn't…"

"Then maybe you shouldn't—"

"If you are absolutely doing nothing and are bored out of your mind, and if you would like to have a good time at the country club tonight, I would love to have a chaperone," Suzanne said smiling.

"You said you were an artist?" Will asked, something having suddenly occurred to him.

"Well, I certainly did, and you asked me that already."

"What is your medium?"

Suzanne gave a somewhat listless smile and cocked her head, "My what?"

"My wife was an artist. I'm just wondering what your medium is. Oil—acrylics—sculpture? What is it?" he went on.

"Oh, just about everything. I dabble in everything," she replied.

"It sounds to me like you'd love the paintings of Stravinsky," Will suggested.

"Oh, yes. I absolutely adore them!"

"On the other hand, I love listening to classical music as well," Will said. "Cézanne is one of my favorite composers. How about you?"

"I can't say that I've heard of him. But I'm sure his music is beautiful."

There was an awkward silence as Suzanne struggled to continue her engaging smile.

"Suzanne, tell me something. Why did your Uncle Jason have *you* meet me at the door? I'm sure he's got butlers and servants all over this mansion."

After a few more moments of silence and a smile that was beginning to tighten around the corners of her mouth, she replied, "Well, some of the staff is off today. Besides, I thought it might be nice to meet you."

"In other words, Uncle Jason thought it might be a nice idea for you to meet me."

"I don't know what you are talking about," Suzanne said, dropping her smile at last and throwing Will a concerned look.

That was when Jason Bell Purdy stepped into the room, slightly short of breath. He was in jogging shorts, jogging shoes, and a Princeton jersey with the sleeves cut off. A vintage Atlanta Braves baseball cap was on his head. He was sweating and smiling confidently.

"Hey there, Will Chambers. I'm Jason Bell Purdy—it's great to meet you." He approached Will quickly and gave him a strong handshake. "Forgive the exercise outfit, but I like to be informal when I'm holding meetings in my house. What do you think of the place? I just love this old mansion. I prefer to conduct meetings here whenever I can, rather than in downtown Atlanta."

"It's a beautiful place." Will remarked. "Now if we could talk about a few things, then I'll let you get on with your other business."

Purdy smiled and agreed, and he dismissed Suzanne with a "Run along now."

As she turned to leave, Will called to her. She whirled around quickly.

"It was good to meet you," Will said. "And I thought you should know—Stravinsky's not a painter, he's a composer. And Cézanne is not a composer, he's a world-famous painter."

Suzanne Purdy Black flashed a final, flustered smile and then quickly exited the room.

Jason Bell Purdy led Will into a wood-paneled library. The two sat down across from each other in overstuffed chairs, and Will quickly got down to business.

"Mr. Purdy, I represent Mary Sue Fellows. I think you know something about her and her case."

"Yes, I certainly do. Mary Sue and I go back a long way. As you probably know, I dated her for a while. She was the one that got away. Too bad. She's a beautiful person and a very charming lady. Joe Fellows is a very lucky man."

"And you found out about her case? And had a conversation with Dr. Parker, the pathologist at the Delphi hospital, about her legal situation?"

"Yes," Purdy confirmed. "I learned about the problems that she was having with Social Services regarding Joshua. They seem to involve Joshua's declining health. Social Services sounded very suspicious, and it sounded to me like they were not being very helpful to Mary Sue. So I thought I'd talk to Dr. Parker, who I knew had evaluated some of Joshua's tests at the hospital."

"How did you find out about Mary Sue's ongoing dispute with Social Services?"

"Hey—I'm surprised she didn't tell you, being your client and all. I learned it directly from her. She and I talked about it. In fact, she called me up and asked for my help."

Will was thunderstruck. Mary Sue had never indicated that she'd talked about her case to anyone else, and certainly not Jason Bell Purdy. As Will tried to hide his surprise, the other man continued filling in the blanks.

"That family doctor had called Social Services because he said that Mary Sue was not following his orders and that she had made some comments that sounded strange to him. He was worried about Joshua's health. I knew that she was just the best mother in the world, so I thought maybe, with my influence, I could help straighten things out before they got out of control. That's why I talked to Dr. Parker."

"And what did he say to you?"

"I'll tell you something, Mr. Chambers, by the time I talked to Dr. Parker, the cement was already dry on this deal. He told me that Social Services had talked to him and that he had evaluated the blood samples and had come to the conclusion there was some kind of poison in Joshua's blood that only would have been there if someone had given it to him. I told him I thought Mary Sue was as pure as the driven snow—but he told me there was nothing they could do. He said they'd put together some evidence that made it look pretty clear Mary Sue had been poisoning her son, and they were going to go after her. I have to tell you, Mr. Chambers, that just broke my heart. It really did."

"Do you know anything about the identity of the person who called in a report to Social Services accusing Mary Sue? You don't know the name, do you?"

"Mr. Chambers, I haven't the faintest idea what her name is or who she is."

Will paused a minute, keeping his eyes riveted on Jason Bell Purdy.

"Who said it was a woman?"

"I thought you said it was a woman—but never mind, I simply haven't got any information about that. Look, Mr. Chambers," and with that Purdy leaned forward and pointed his finger directly at the attorney. "I have never doubted that Mary Sue

Fellows is innocent, not once. And I have never done anything against her, but only tried to help her in this thing. And that is the absolute truth."

Then Purdy narrowed his eyes and studied Will. "Why? What has she told you about me? I'm sure she will vouch for exactly what I just told you, right?"

"Sorry," Will said, "what my client tells me is confidential. I can't share that with you."

"Hey, I can relate to that. You lawyers are all the same. I have a whole army of lawyers working for me—they drive me crazy! But I can respect that—attorney–client privilege, and all that."

"Now that you mention your lawyers," Will went on, "tell me, how long has Stanley Kennelworth been doing work for you?"

"Oh, just recently. You know I like to make sure I use local professionals from the Delphi area. I believe in giving back to a community that has given me so much. So I don't just hire the big guns from Atlanta. Every once in a while I'll put a guy like Stanley Kennelworth on retainer."

"He must be doing quite a bit of work for you," Will remarked.

"Oh, odds and ends. You know Stanley. Maybe you don't. He does a little bit of this and a little bit of that."

"Well, the little bit of this and little bit of that must be very expensive, because I hear Kennelworth got a new Jaguar out of his relationship with you."

"Exactly what are you getting at, Mr. Chambers?" Purdy demanded, his voice now becoming emphatic.

"I'm just wondering if you hired Stanley after Joe Fellows was charged. And I wonder whether, having him on retainer as your attorney, you also pumped him for information about what was going on with the defense for Mary Sue and Joe."

"I'm shocked," Purdy responded loudly. "You are insinuating, Mr. Chambers, that Stanley Kennelworth violated his code of ethics by sharing confidential information about his representation of Joe Fellows with me. Now you know as well as I do that it would be highly improper for him to do that."

Will knew now that Purdy's patience was running low. "One more question. You knew Henry Pencup, the president of the Delphi National Bank?"

"Sure did. Longtime friend. Did a lot of financing for the Purdy family over the years."

"Well, which is strange. I wonder why his bank was one of the few not on record for having loaned you money for the Eden Lake Resort project."

Now Purdy was clicking his teeth together. He stood up abruptly. "I was mistaken—I thought you wanted to talk about Mary Sue Fellows. Mr. Chambers, I believe our conversation is done. You be safe now."

And as he turned to leave, he shouted over his shoulder, "You know the way out." But Will threw one last question at him.

"You knew my late wife, Audra, was a painter and a blond, didn't you? That's why you had your niece meet me at the door and flirt with me. Did you really think I'd fall for that one?"

Purdy did not turn or stop, but walked quickly out of the sun-room and disappeared within the cavernous halls of Purdy mansion. A moment later, a butler and another man appeared and quickly led Will to the front door.

45

ON HIS WAY BACK TO DELPHI, Will clicked on the radio. He needed to clear his mind and detox after his interview with Jason Bell Purdy.

He hit the top-of-the-hour news. The Dow Jones and the NASDAQ had taken a beating.

In Mexico, a terrorist cell group had been discovered that had been planning attacks against the United States.

Billionaire Warren Mullburn—self-exiled in Switzerland while under investigation by U.S. authorities—had reached an agreement with the Department of Justice through his attorneys. Mullburn had agreed to give an extensive interview to Justice lawyers regarding what he knew about several high-profile Washington scandals—one involving the former Undersecretary of State—in exchange for a promise of "no extradition." He would be free to travel in his continuing global economic pursuits.

Lastly, the long-anticipated national strike by airline pilots had finally taken place. The President and Congress were planning to quickly intervene in an effort to avert a transportation tie-up of nightmare proportions. As of news time, there were no flights in or out of any major commercial airports.

Will was back at the houseboat when the expected call from Mary Sue came in.

"Will," Mary Sue began, "Joe told me in our phone call that the jailers had transferred you to some horrible place. Are you all right?"

"I am now—and I'm scrambling to get things pulled together for your trial. How's Joshua?"

"I'm really worried. Joshua's not doing well. We thought we had him stabilized, but his vital signs have been getting worse. We need a diagnosis so we know how to treat him."

"How are you planning on doing that?"

"Dr. Bill, the family doctor I've been dealing with here in South Dakota, took some blood samples of his own. He indicated there were some abnormalities, but he can't be definite yet. He knows a specialist in pediatric metabolic diseases, a Dr. Forrester. From England. He's agreed to take a look at the blood samples and give his diagnosis. The only problem is, he's down in the Bahamas right now doing mission work on Grand Bahama island."

"How in the world are we going to get a blood sample down to a doctor in the Bahamas when every commercial airplane has been grounded?" Will asked urgently.

"I honestly don't know." Mary Sue's voice was quivering. "I was just hoping you could figure something out. That's why Andrew and I decided on a plan—I hope it's not a waste of time."

"What plan?" Will asked.

"Andrew has to start his teaching duties again in New Mexico. Since he's going by car, he's offered to drive to Georgia first and bring the blood sample. Dr. Bill had some reservations about it—it's just not usual protocol to have private parties transporting blood samples. But in this case, because of the urgency of my trial date, and the need to get a diagnosis for Joshua, he made an exception. Andrew is already on his way down south to see you. He has the blood sample in a special refrigeration unit—it looks about the size of a mini-cooler."

"Mary Sue," Will said, "I'll take the blood sample, but I can't guarantee I can get it down to Dr. Forrester. I think we need some kind of a miracle."

"That's exactly what I've been praying for," she replied.

"Let me change gears here for a minute," Will said. "It's been a while since you and I have had a chance to talk about your case. We've got a trial in three days. Am I going to have you by my side at counsel table? I need you to testify clearly and convincingly about your innocence. If I don't have you sitting next to me in trial, I don't know whether it will be possible to win this custody fight."

"I've talked to Andrew about that. And I hear what you are saying—you want me return to Delphi."

"Yes. Not only for your case, but for Joshua's safety as well."

"All I can say is that I'm considering it. I'm praying about it. And it will probably be a last-minute decision."

Will wanted to press the point further. It would be a mind-boggling effort to prove Mary Sue's innocence if she herself refused to appear before the court and explain her side of the events. But he also needed answers to other questions.

"I went to visit Jason Bell Purdy today," he announced.

"Jason? You saw Jason Purdy?" Mary Sue said, clearly stunned.

"Yes. And it looks to me like there's quite a bit of information you never told me," Will added. "Like the fact that you sought Purdy's assistance at the early stages of this, when the Department of Social Services was beginning to hassle you about the way you were handling Joshua's medical care."

"That's true. I didn't tell you. And there are some reasons for that," Mary Sue said passionately.

"Reasons? Like what?" Will asked in irritation.

"Joe was always jealous of Jason. I never wanted Joe to feel like he was a second choice, or second-class compared to Jason. And I certainly never wanted to do anything that would hurt Joe, or make him feel betrayed."

"Betrayed? About what?"

"I didn't want to tell you, because I didn't want anyone else to know. And I was afraid that, somehow, since you were working closely with Joe on his case as well as with me, he might find out. I just wanted to avoid that if at all possible."

"Find out what?" Will pressed. "Mary Sue, you've got to tell me *everything*."

"I'm not sure I can. Not now. If you go into court and you somehow win this case, then it's done and it's over with. Joe doesn't have to be hurt by finding out. That's what I'm hoping for."

"Mary Sue, I'm tired of you tying my hands!" Will replied forcefully. "You can't expect me to defend you while handicapping me at the same time. You are cutting the legs out from under my ability to prove your innocence—and free your family from the grip of the government."

There was only silence at the other end.

Will continued pressing in, trying to get his client to open up.

"Mary Sue, I want you to think about something. If you come down here voluntarily, if you come down and tell the truth—the whole truth behind everything that happened—that is the best chance you have of winning your case. On the other hand, if they end up finding you—if they end up capturing you while you are on the run—what kind of impression is that going to give the court? The judge will conclude you were running because you thought you were guilty. That's the conclusion he will reach—and nothing you can then say, after being apprehended, will make any difference. Can't you see what I'm trying to do for you?"

"Yes, I do see," she said quietly, "but that doesn't change my decision. I can't commit to returning to Delphi right now. I'm taking this thing one hour at a time."

Will tried to get answers from his client about the truck in their garage. He asked her about her access to brake fluid, and about Joshua's cup that was found in the kitchen. But with each question, Mary Sue's voice got quieter and more troubled. She told him she simply could not supply details right now. She was going to bank *everything* on Will's ability to get the blood sample down to Dr. Forrester and get a favorable diagnosis that would not only prove that she had not poisoned her son, but would provide a key to his cure.

As Mary Sue explained that strategy, Will began to feel the threads—the threads he'd carefully begun to weave into a picture of the truth—starting to unravel.

"Mary Sue," Will said slowly, "what you're asking me to do is get a blood sample down to the Bahamas within twenty-four hours, when the entire country has been locked down in an airline strike. I just don't know if I can do that."

After Mary Sue hung up, Will immediately called his office. He put Hilda onto the task of contacting every private-charter air carrier that Will had ever used in the past. He instructed her to try to round up some pilot—anywhere—who would fly down to the Delphi area, pick up Will with the blood sample, and transport him to Grand Bahama island. He also asked her to check the medi-vac services in the Atlanta area.

Will tried to review his now voluminous file on Mary Sue's case, but he was too distracted. He finally strode out onto the deck of the little houseboat. The sun was setting on the lake. Looking at it, he prayed for divine intervention—the means to make an impossible trip under impossible conditions and then return with proof of Mary Sue's innocence in time for the trial.

Then the phone rang. Will picked it up expectantly.

"Will," Hilda said, "it's me. I've called all four of the private-charter air services you've used in the past. All of their pilots are tied up with other flights because of the strike. I then went to the Yellow Pages."

"And?"

"I'm sorry—I had absolutely no luck at all. It appears that every private pilot around here has already been hired for other flights. I also tried the medical transports. They are taking only critical patients or organ transplants. Your blood sample doesn't qualify."

Will thanked Hilda, broke the connection, and then tossed the phone down on the table with a clatter. Frustration was now being added to disillusionment.

And then he had a thought. He wanted to call Fiona that night anyway. On her concert tours she took some private chartered flights. Maybe she knew someone.

He quickly dialed Fiona's number, and she answered.

She was glad to be home from the recording session but missed him terribly, she explained. Now that she was back home in Baltimore, she certainly wished he could see her soon.

Will explained that the Fellowses' custody trial was coming up in three days, and he would be locked into trial preparation until then. And then the trial itself would take several days. He simply did not know when they would see each other next.

Fiona's tone changed as she heard the news.

"By the way," Will asked, "do you know of any private pilots or charter air services I could use? I've got some evidence for the case that has to be flown down to the Bahamas immediately."

"Not really," Fiona answered. "The only one I remember is Gil Rowling. He flew that private charter for me to visit you in the hospital. But he said he was booked solid after he squeezed me in."

"Thanks anyway," Will told her.

"So how's the case coming?" Fiona asked with an effort at enthusiasm.

"Long, difficult—no, make that impossible," he replied.

"Any regrets about taking it?"

"This is probably the worst time to ask me that question," Will remarked. "All the interviews I've been doing are turning up dead ends, so it seems—even my talks with my client. And then something really odd happened today."

Fiona asked, "Can you tell me about it?"

"I hope you'll understand," Will said. "I visited an antebellum mansion down here—it reminded me so much of Generals' Hill. And then I met someone. A young woman—and suddenly all of my thoughts about Audra came rushing back. It really took me by surprise."

"*Audra.* There's a name I haven't heard you mention for a while. I thought God had brought you through a healing about her death. Maybe not," Fiona commented quietly.

"It's not that I haven't gotten over her." Will was struggling to explain. "It's almost like someone contrived fake scenery in a movie set—recreating this memory of Audra. It really hit me out of nowhere."

"Like I said," Fiona continued, "perhaps you haven't finished getting closure over Audra—or maybe it's something else. Is there anything about this woman you need to tell me?"

"No—it's nothing like that. I just think she was purposely trying to impersonate Audra when we were together…"

"Will, this whole thing sounds a little strange. And, honestly, more than a little hurtful. One minute you tell me you want to spend the rest of your life with me, and the next minute—this. I guess I'm having a hard time understanding you. When we talked at the hospital, everything seemed so clear. Now—I don't know."

After an awkward silence and a few unsuccessful attempts to repair things, Will said his goodbyes and hung up. And then he started wondering.

He asked himself how he could be so skilled at legal communication—but so lousy at interpersonal connection.

46

IT WAS EVENING, and Will was at the small kitchen table in the houseboat, struggling to prepare for trial.

But he was also faced with a whirlpool of conflicting feelings.

If he was so in love with Fiona and she with him—why did things always seem so hard? Their schedules were impossible, their communication ended in disaster half the time, and emotionally, they never seemed to be at the same place at the same time. Would their relationship ever get on track?

And then there was Mary Sue's case. Will's client was hiding information from him—the unforgivable sin in litigation. He kept asking himself, over and over again, *What was it that was going on between Mary Sue and Jason Bell Purdy? And why wouldn't she answer questions about her access to the brake fluid?*

His concussion headaches had persisted, and he rose, walked into the little kitchenette, and downed several aspirins with a glass of water.

He walked to the front window and looked out at the lake. The moon was out, and there was a shimmering, sparkling trail of golden light that played on the surface of the water.

Turning away, he sat down at the table again. He also had another decision. When Andrew White Arrow arrived from South Dakota with the blood sample, what was he going to do with it? He had toyed with the idea of trying to locate an expert in the Delphi or even Atlanta area to examine the sample, but there were two problems with that.

First, according to the curriculum vitae that Will had obtained, Dr. Parker, the chief pathologist of Delphi hospital, had numerous connections with hospitals and clinics throughout the greater Atlanta area. Will was afraid that this would taint the willingness of other doctors to get involved.

Second, he had done a check on pediatric hematologists in the area, and none came close to Dr. Forrester in their credentials. Did he really want to risk a second wrong opinion?

Will was convinced that the only way out for Mary Sue was to get a definitive diagnosis from the best available expert. If that meant going to the Bahamas to track down Dr. Forrester, then that would be his task. But there was one seemingly insurmountable problem—how on earth would he get there in the middle of the airline strike?

As Will sat concentrating at the table he thought he heard a sound outside. He listened intently, but everything was silent except for a few loons out on the lake, the occasional groan of the houseboat straining against its moorings, and the lapping of the waves.

A hundred feet away from Will's houseboat, Howley Jubb and Linus Eggers sat in the black Hummer. The engine was turned off, and the two were talking in hushed tones.

"Remember, don't close the door when you get out. I don't want *any noise* that he could hear," Howley said.

"And tell me again," Linus asked, his hand shaking as he raised a cigarette to his mouth to take a draw, "why am *I* sticking my neck out on this deal?"

"Just keep thinking about your momma sitting in that stinking, rat-infested, flies-on-the-food nursing home you've got her in right now," Howley continued. "When you go into the sweet hereafter, don't you want to know that she's been transferred to a nice, clean nursing home that will take care of her—don't you want to know that you've been a good son?"

"How do I know I can trust you?" Linus said, beginning to choke up and covering his mouth.

"Hey, keep it quiet, Linus. How do you know? Because I've already showed you the contract and one of the Purdy retirement homes. It's all set and ready to go. When I verify that this deal is wrapped up, your mother gets transferred."

"And how about me? You're my brother-in-law—are you going to make sure that I get taken care of when things start going bad?"

"When things *start* going bad? Linus, have you taken a look in the mirror? You're not listening to what your doctors are telling you. You've had full-blown AIDS for how long now? They've been telling you to get your act together, wrap up the loose ends of your life. You gotta wake up, Linus. I'm one of the few people who's going to make sure you get the care you need when you start really falling apart."

Linus took one final drag on his cigarette and then crushed it out in the ashtray.

"Okay then—I guess that's it. I guess I'm ready. Let's do this thing."

"Just remember—the first thing we do is find out where Mary Sue Fellows is, and then we find out what she told Chambers. After that we take care of the rest. You got it?"

Linus nodded his head. Howley passed a black ski mask over to him and pulled out his own. He then gave the other man a .38 revolver. Linus stuffed it into his belt buckle and covered it with his shirt. The two slipped quietly out of the truck and padded down the path to the dock, ski masks in hand.

Howley bent over and whispered, "You make a noise at the back of the houseboat. Meanwhile I'll come around to the front door and bust my way through. Then you get in as fast as you can run."

As they reached the beginning of the dock, Howley heard something and froze in his tracks. He grabbed his partner by the arm so hard that he almost cried out.

Linus had already put his mask on halfway but was able to see. Howley put his finger to his lips and started to turn slowly toward the noise. By now both of them could hear the sound of heavy footsteps coming down the gravel driveway.

When they had fully turned around, they were confronted by a looming human figure, standing only a few feet away in the shadows.

It seemed enormous. In its right hand appeared to be some kind of an ax. In its left hand, it looked as if it was carrying a bucket.

The figure spoke in the deep voice of a man.

"What business do you have here?"

Linus remained silent, and Howley was about to speak but changed his mind. After another few seconds of silence, the man in the shadows spoke again.

"I feel in my spirit that you are up to no good. I think you have come to do harm to a prophet of truth. You are not the first one to try that. Listen to the words of the Lord:

> So he sent and had John beheaded in prison. And his head was brought on a platter and given to the girl, and she brought it to her mother. Then his disciples came and took away the body and buried it, and went and told Jesus.

Howley began reaching toward his pocket for his revolver but then thought better of it. He motioned to Linus that the two of them should leave.

"No harm done, my friend," Howley said. "We were looking for a surprise party, but I guess we came to the wrong place."

The two men walked around the figure in the shadows, giving him a wide berth.

As they reached the Hummer, Linus began whispering excitedly.

"Did you see that guy with the ax? Man, he must be some kind of nut case. Walking around with an ax, talking about chopping some guy's head off named John. Hey, come to think of it— didn't your mom used to call you John?"

Howley stopped for a second and threw an angry glance at his partner.

251

"That's my middle name. That's what she used to call me. Now shut up and get in the truck."

When the black Hummer had left the premises, Andrew White Arrow stepped out of the shadows and started walking toward Will's houseboat. In his right hand was a long-handled ceremonial tomahawk, and in his left he was carrying the small refrigeration unit.

By that point Will had heard the voices and had walked out of the houseboat with an inquisitive look on his face.

Andrew strode over to him and explained who he was.

"Do you mind if I give you a big, brotherly hug?" Andrew asked, embracing the attorney.

As the two of them entered the houseboat, Andrew explained that the tomahawk was a gift from Tommy. Then he showed Will the portable refrigeration unit with the blood sample.

"You need to keep this thing shut. You can plug it in here and recharge it. If you charge it overnight, it will be good for another twenty-four hours at least," Andrew explained.

As the two settled down to talk, Will asked him about the visitors he had encountered.

"There were two of them. Very strange," Andrew added. "I felt in my spirit they had some real evil in mind."

"Do you have any idea who they were?"

"Not at all. Two men. They apparently drove up in a big black Hummer. There was a silver skull-and-crossbones on the bumper. One of the guys was actually wearing a ski mask."

"How did you get rid of them?" Will asked.

"That's also sort of funny. On the way here from South Dakota, I was listening to my Bible CDs. I was up to Matthew 14 when I pulled up here—you know, the part with John the Baptist in prison. The beheading."

"And?"

"Well, I just told them I thought they were up to no good. Then I felt led to recite a couple verses from Matthew fourteen. That must have done the trick because they left rather quickly."

Andrew gave Will a big smile, and the two had a cautious chuckle together over the incident. But there was little question in Will's mind who was behind the two ominous visitors.

He invited Andrew to spend the night before he left for New Mexico. Andrew gladly agreed, saying he would sleep in the living room.

"That way I can be close to the front door, just in case there is any more trouble."

Double-checking the lock on the front door and the windows, Will crawled into bed. He tossed and turned for several hours, but finally, somewhere around two or three in the morning, he fell into a deep sleep.

But right at 6 A.M., Will sat up in bed with a start, his eyes wide open. The words of a sign had just flashed in front of him while he was sleeping.

He jumped out of bed, grabbing his head after propelling himself a little too quickly for his injuries.

"It's an idea. It's a chance. I've got to check it out," he muttered to himself loudly.

Throwing on his clothes, Will grabbed his shaving kit and put a few things in. Then he snatched the part of the case file that contained his trial-preparation materials, including the medical records Andrew had brought down from South Dakota, and threw it into his briefcase.

His visitor was up by now, and was standing in the middle of the living room with a quizzical look on his face.

"I take it you are going somewhere, my friend. Am I right?" Andrew asked.

"Andrew, I'm sorry to run. But I had a thought. Actually some kind of a dream—or maybe I was awake, I don't know. Anyway, I've got to chase down this possibility. If it doesn't work out, I'll be right back, and you and I can have breakfast together. Otherwise, there's food in the refrigerator. I'm sorry I may not be able to have a chance to chat with you about Mary Sue and everything."

As Will reached out to shake hands before leaving, Andrew put both of his big hands on Will's shoulders.

"I pray a blessing on you, Will Chambers," he said with a smile.

Will quickly loaded his belongings into his Corvette. Then, running back to the houseboat, he collected the most important item of all—the little metal refrigeration unit with the vial of Joshua's blood.

"Just close the door behind you when you leave," he shouted back to Andrew. "It'll lock on its own. Remember, the authorities are still looking for *you*, as well as Mary Sue. Keep that in mind."

Will gunned his engine and sped off down the road that led from the lake to the county highway.

47

AFTER DRIVING FOR A FEW MINUTES on the county highway, Will spotted what he was looking for. He turned off onto a side road marked by a red windsock that was billowing in the breeze. Right next to the windsock was the sign he'd remembered in his sleep.

He sped down the narrow road, kicking up gravel, until a large red arrow pointed to a turnoff on the left.

Driving into an open field, he saw several outbuildings and a large, wooden barn that had been converted into an airplane hangar. The barn had a large American flag painted on its side. Along a makeshift landing strip were two rows of bleachers—enough seating for maybe a hundred onlookers. On the landing strip there was a vintage biplane that was painted in red, white, and blue.

Will parked his car and stepped quickly through the open doors of the hangar. On a step stool, peering over the engine of a small, single-prop Cessna was a man with dirty cowboy boots, grease-stained blue jeans, and a cowboy hat.

Will shouted out, "I'm looking for Tex—Tex, 'The Flying Cowboy.'"

The lanky man turned around and looked at Will with an amused expression on his face. He looked to be in his late 40s and had a tan, rugged face with a gray mustache.

"Well sir, seeing as I'm the only one in this place wearing a cowboy hat, I guess that would be me," he quipped.

"Tex, I've got a problem," Will said.

"That goes for just about everybody. What's yours?"

Will launched into an abbreviated, rapid-fire explanation of Mary Sue's case and Joshua's medical condition. How time was of the essence because of the impending trial date and Joshua's deteriorating health. Dr. Forrester in the Bahamas was the most qualified expert to not only diagnosis Joshua's *real* medical condition but also to exonerate his client. The only problem, of course, was getting an immediate flight out to Grand Bahama island.

"I don't think I got your full name," the man responded. "My name is Tex Rhoady. What's yours?" he asked, extending a callused hand in Will's direction. The lawyer shook his hand readily.

"Will Chambers. I'm an attorney from Virginia here in Delphi on Mary Sue Fellows' case.

"Virginia? That's a fair distance from the Peachtree State. I suppose that means your client must have thought you were worth bringing all the way down here."

"I guess so," Will replied, "And while I appreciate my client's confidence, what I need now is quick transportation down to the Bahamas to deliver this blood sample to Dr. Forrester who's waiting for me there."

"Well, I tell you, Will," Tex explained. "I've got three planes. One is a Learjet. It's a pretty little thing, but I've leased it out to some other pilots—for a fair chunk of change, I might add. You can imagine with the strike that private planes are being snatched up pretty quickly. The second plane I've got is this Cessna. Nice machine, but it's got engine problems right now. And then I've got that old biplane, the Stearman out there, that I use for stunt flying."

There were a few moments of silence, and then Will looked out toward the airfield. Walking out to the opening of the hangar, he took a long look at the red, white, and blue biplane. It had two open cockpits and a single propeller.

Then Will turned slowly back toward Tex.

Tex caught his glance and began to chuckle.

"I assume you are an experienced pilot?" Will asked.

"Well sir, I've been around planes all my life. My daddy was a pilot. I flew quite a few missions in the Gulf. I did some commercial flying after that, flew for the civil air patrol. I even did fly-throughs on forest fires for the Forest Service. Then, when the Afghan war started, I was reactivated and called up. I flew a couple recon missions, and after that I told the military I was hanging it up. Ever since I've been back here, stunt flying and crop dusting, just like my sign says."

"Stunt flying?" Will asked.

"Yeah. You know—'aeronautical high jinks that will amaze and astound you'—just like my brochure says." Tex laughed a little at that.

Will gazed out through the open doors of the hangar.

"What about that?" he said, motioning to the biplane.

That was when Tex stopped laughing.

The pilot swept his hat off his head, wiped his brow, and hopped off the step stool. Putting his cowboy hat back on, he strode over to Will and stared him in the eye from just a foot away.

"You're serious, aren't you?" he asked.

"I'm afraid I am," Will answered.

"You aren't a pilot, are you?"

"No, I'm not. And I only have a thimble's worth of knowledge about aeronautics. I handled a few small-airplane cases years ago in my law practice—a string of crashes involving a certain model of dual-engine plane. And, then I also fly quite a bit because my practice takes me here, there, and everywhere. So that's all I know."

"Well, let me give you the quick course," Tex began somberly. "You are talking about taking a vintage biplane—single-engine—out over the Atlantic. Out to the Bahamas. Now this plane here, it's got a nine-cylinder, 450-horsepower Pratt & Whitney power plant as a retrofit. I've staked my life on it doing stunt flying. It's an absolutely reliable workhorse of an engine. But you are talking about going over the *Atlantic*—this time of year—with a plane like *this.*" With that, Tex walked outside and stared at the biplane. Then he turned around.

"You're talking about updrafts, downdrafts, wind shear, water-spouts, hurricanes—that's the kind of stuff you get the minute you leave land and hit ocean atmospherics."

"Look," Will said, "I'm not asking you to do a Lindbergh and get us to Paris. I'm only asking you to fly to Grand Bahama island. I've checked the map—what is it, fifty, a hundred miles off the Florida coast?"

"Yep," Tex replied, "that's about it, depending on where you leave land."

"Let's put it this way—if I'm foolish enough to be a passenger in this thing from here to the Bahamas—are you gutsy enough to be the pilot?"

"Wrong approach, counselor," Tex replied firmly. "Don't pull that macho stuff on me. I don't have to take risks in an airplane to prove that I'm a he-man. Do you know how many sorties I flew in the Gulf? Have you ever flown through antiaircraft fire? Have you ever seen your squadron buddies flame out and crash right in the thick of it?"

"Tex, you do aerial stunts for a living. That's got to be a hundred times more dangerous than taking this flight," Will countered.

"If you're not a flier, I guess you don't understand. I do all of that 'daredevil' stuff—but I will tell you something—it's all calculated, calibrated, and controlled. It looks real risky, but I know exactly what I'm doing up there for my audience. But flying over varying terrain and open water is a whole different thing."

"Then let me put it to you this way—you are my last chance. If you don't do this flight for me," Will said, "then Mary Sue Fellows is probably going to lose custody of her child for the rest of her life. She may even go to prison for a crime she didn't commit.

And worse than that, a little boy might end up dying because we didn't get a diagnosis in time. Can you live with that?"

Tex gave a big sigh and thrust both hands in the pockets of his blue jeans. After a period of silence, during which he appeared to be visualizing some unseen scenario, he started in.

"Man-oh-man," he said with a rueful smile, "I sure thought my momma raised me smarter than this."

Then the pilot ambled over to an old wooden desk in the corner that had several greasy engine parts on it. He pulled open a drawer that squeaked, and retrieved a piece of paper. Walking over to a tall tool chest, he propped his elbows on it.

"Okay, come over here, Mr. Lindbergh. You need to sign this. Agreement and Release. You being a lawyer, I'm sure you know all about these."

Will hurried over to Tex, read the paper hastily, and scribbled his signature at the bottom.

"We leave here in one hour. I'm going to do a systems check. I'm also filing a flight plan. That way, if we go down into the water—and let me remind you, this is *not* a seaworthy plane— then they can look for whatever is left of us after the sharks get through."

Will gave an uneasy smile.

"An hour is fine. I'll go over to my car there and make a couple of calls."

"One more thing," Tex added. "You're going to be charged my standard rate for a coast-to-coast charter flight. And I don't come cheap. And I'm also adding a twenty-percent surcharge."

"What's the surcharge for?"

"For the additional risk factor. If we end up getting some weather," Tex explained, "you better make sure your seatbelt's on. Because in that case there's going to be a whole lot of 'bouncy-bouncy,'" and with that, he made a wild flapping motion with his hand. Then he let out a chuckle and disappeared into his office at the rear of the hangar.

Will hurried over to the car and called his office.

Hilda answered. "I've got some good news for you," she said.

"I could use some."

"Jacki said we just received a fax from the Georgia State Supreme Court. They ruled on her motion for recusal of Judge Mason."

"And?"

"They just issued an order removing him from hearing the trial."

"That's terrific news," Will exclaimed. "Have we gotten notice of who the new judge is going to be?"

"Yes," Hilda said. "I've got an order from the Juda County Circuit Court right here. It reads, 'The Honorable J. K. Trainer has been appointed to hear the trial In The Interest Of Joshua Fellows, A Minor Child.'"

"Do we know anything about this judge?" Will asked.

"We're checking into it—we don't have anything yet."

"I'm going to be out of pocket for about a day or so."

"How can I reach you?" Hilda asked.

"Actually, I'm not sure if I'm going to be able to get reception on my cell phone. I doubt it. I'm going to be…in transit."

"That sounds rather mysterious," Hilda commented, probing a little.

"It's meant to. I'm trying to get this blood sample down to a Dr. Forrester from England, who is currently on Grand Bahama island."

"Anything else you want to tell me?" Hilda inquired.

"Well," Will said, "if things don't go well—tell everybody they can make memorial donations to my church, and I want Fiona to sing 'A Mighty Fortress Is Our God' at the service."

Hilda was quiet on the other end, struggling for a response.

"Will, I just don't know when you are joking and when you are serious anymore."

"Don't ever lose your sense of humor, Hilda," Will said with a smile.

Will then asked his secretary to go down the list of other phone calls to the office.

At the end of their conversation, Hilda remembered one more message. "Oh, I almost forgot. The attorney from the State Department. They want to talk to you again about that lawsuit against General Nuban."

"Do me a favor, Hilda—would you call him back and ask if it's time-critical? If not, I can just talk to him when I get back into the office after the trial."

After hanging up with Hilda, Will gathered up his briefcase, the refrigeration unit, and his shaving kit. He locked up his car and walked over to the plane, where Tex was doing his final walk-around.

Tex opened a small door to the hold in the bottom of the plane, where they stored the briefcase and shaving kit.

"I want the case with the blood sample here in the seat with me," Will insisted.

"Look, Will," the pilot explained, "you know what happens to stuff on your lap when you take those really wild roller-coaster rides—you know, the ones that go upside down and around and do curlicues? I think you want that case down in the storage hold."

"And what happens if the door flies open?"

"Never happened yet."

"This is too important," Will said. "It has to stay with me."

Tex rigged up a restraining strap for the refrigeration unit. He then hooked it to a metal loop in the rear cockpit where Will's feet would be.

The attorney climbed into his seat, and Tex showed him how to harness in. Then he gave him a pair of goggles.

"These are no joke," he said about the goggles. "When we're clipping along, particularly on takeoff or landing, it's amazing the stuff that smacks you in the face. And at those speeds, a big bug, a twig dropped by a bird—something like that could take your eye out."

As Will got settled into the rear seat, Tex took a look at the bandage on his nose and the little black, blue, and green streaks under his eyes.

"I was meaning to ask about your nose there," Tex said, "not that it's any of my business."

"Let's just say that I was handcuffed when it happened."

Tex smiled. "They must practice law pretty rough where you come from."

"Say," Will interjected, "did you really mean what you said about the risks of this trip?"

"Oh, well…" Tex said, chuckling a bit, "the thing about that is this—I guess I wanted to see how serious you were about doing this, that's all. Actually, I've taken this plane down off the Florida coast, and along the Keys. I was thinking about a trip down to Nassau once, but it didn't pan out."

"So you were exaggerating—right?" Will said.

"Let me tell you two things. First of all, this is a Boeing PT-17 Stearman. They used these to train pilots in World War II. This would have been the first plane a cadet would have learned to fly. It's a stable aircraft—strong—reliable. I put my life on the line with this plane. I've done every kind of maneuver—loops, rolls, hammerheads, Cuban eights—you name it, I've done it in this old lady."

"That's good to know," Will said. "What's the second thing?"

"Flying over open water, out over the ocean—it's no joke. Things whip up fast, weatherwise. So it could get rough, that's all. You can expect a fair amount of, well—"

"'Bouncy-bouncy'?" Will asked with a grin.

"You're catching on," Tex said. "About that bandage on your nose—I don't think it will last the trip. Things might get a little sore. There's a whole lot of wind coming at you—you'll think you've gotten the world's toughest facial…"

Then the pilot explained a few final details. He showed Will how to use the headset and mike to communicate with him in the front cockpit. He then gave him a set of earplugs.

"This Pratt & Whitney really screams," Tex said. "Feel free to use these plugs. If I need to talk to you on the headset I will give you this signal," and Tex pointed to his right ear.

"What happens if you've got the earplugs in and I want to talk to you?"

"I don't use them."

"Why not?"

"If the engine stalls, or changes pitch, or starts coughing a little—I want to hear it."

"Yeah—exactly," Will responded. "You listen for that stuff!"

Tex smiled and climbed into the plane. He punched the starter button, and a magnificent, bone-shaking roar came from the engine as the prop came up to speed in front of them.

As Tex throttled the plane down the little runway, and the tail began to come up, Will felt a mounting sense of excitement.

The Stearman lifted up into the sky, and Will could see, off in the distance, his houseboat and the water of Eden Lake glittering in the sunlight. Even farther off, there were the church steeples of Delphi and the top of the courthouse. They reminded Will a little of home—of the old buildings and church steeples of Monroeville, Virginia.

Suddenly, he was slightly homesick but also exhilarated. After all, he thought, this little adventure just might turn Mary Sue Fellows' case around and help cure her little boy.

Will felt good as they kept climbing higher—until he looked down at the decal on the panel in front of him.

It read,

GET IN
BUCKLE UP
HANG ON FOR DEAR LIFE

48

Is THERE ANYTHING ELSE? You've confessed your sins—are there any more matters on your heart?" Father Godfrey asked.

Otis Tracher sat quietly in the confessional and thought.

"Not exactly a matter of sin, Father."

"Then what is it? Is something troubling you?"

"Yes—it's not really a personal matter."

"Something else?"

"It's more like a professional problem, but it is bothering me."

"Would you like to talk about it?"

"I have an arrest warrant for a woman. I now have a pretty good idea where she is. I think if I act on this right away, I can apprehend her. But there is something about it...something that bothers me."

"Something about her guilt or innocence?"

"Yes. That would be part of it, but something else..."

"And what is that exactly?"

There was another pause. Tracher shifted uncomfortably in the wooden chair. Suddenly, it was as if he was back in the principal's office at St. Stephen the Martyr Catholic School, having been taken there by his instructor, a young Father Godfrey.

"I'm troubled. My job is not to decide innocence or guilt. We leave that up to the lawyers and the courts and the juries. But I'm uneasy about this. It's as if all of my efforts—doing my job well, which I was taught was a good deed—all of this will be used to do an unnatural harm."

"This woman—does she have...a lawyer who is protecting her interests?"

"Yes, she has an attorney."

"Then if the system works—if she has a fair opportunity in court and the judge operates according to the law—you are without moral blame for your actions. You harbor no personal malice against this woman?"

"No. No—far from it."

"Is this a matter you can discuss with the woman's attorney?"

"Absolutely not. That would be against policy."

"I see," Father Godfrey said. "Is this something you can discuss with your superiors—perhaps with the county prosecuting attorney? With the judge?"

"That is something for me to think about."

After lunch the detective met with Harry Putnam. Putnam was conducting trial preparation—a brainstorming session with Liz Luden from Social Services and Harriet Bender, guardian ad litem for Joshua.

When Tracher arrived, they were already well into their meeting. Tracher sat quiet in the discussion until Putnam addressed him.

"Otis—you've been quiet. What do you have to add? We're talking about the order of witnesses here—what do you think?"

"I have a very definite lead on Mary Sue Fellows. South Dakota. Probably on an Indian reservation up there."

Putnam was flabbergasted.

"That's incredible news. Let's snatch her—now. And let's get the little boy. I think that's great timing. I'm sure Chambers is now going to ask for an adjournment, but we're going to fight tooth and nail to avoid that."

Liz Luden was next. "Joshua has got to be a priority in this. We've absolutely got to get physical control of him and get him into this jurisdiction."

"Assuming he's still alive," Harriet Bender said. "I'm betting there's more than half a chance that Mary Sue Fellows has got that kid buried somewhere in a shallow grave."

Putnam turned quickly back to Tracher.

"Pronto, Otis. We need this done now. Get ahold of the South Dakota authorities and—"

The detective broke in. "I've been thinking…"

"That's a dangerous thing to do," Putnam said with a chuckle.

"No, really, I was just wondering whether—with the trial date so close—we shouldn't plan our apprehension *after* the trial, rather than before."

"Not smart. Not smart at all," Putnam responded. "Bad idea."

"That's just plain nuts," Bender chimed in.

Tracher explained his thought. "And what if we get the mother—and the child. And the child is perfectly well. And what if you do some tests on him and you find out he hasn't been poisoned at all. And now you've got a mother in the lockup who's been on the run—and a child suspected of being poisoned who is perfectly fine. How is that going to look for Juda County?"

The three others grew thoughtful. Putnam finally broke the silence.

"That's just a chance we're going to have to take. I just want you to remember who's in control here. It's Harry Putnam—not Mary Sue Fellows or her attorney," the prosecutor said.

The detective nodded, rose, and walked down the hall to his office. He called the local authorities in South Dakota, explained the situation, and told them he would be flying up in the airplane owned by the sheriff's department. No arrests were to be made, he emphasized, until he was there with them. He would leave in an hour.

Tracher hung up the phone. The uneasy feeling was still there, in the hollow of his gut.

That was the part that always gave him the biggest problem. To Otis Tracher, law enforcement had always been a business of concrete actions and easily perceived consequences. Suspects were either apprehended or they weren't. Crimes were either charged or they were not charged. Defendants were found either guilty, or not guilty. But moral responsibility—that was a problem. To the detective, that issue seemed to be part of an abstract netherworld of maddening ambiguity.

When he arrested Mary Sue Fellows and pulled her little boy from her arms, he knew he would feel that restless gnawing in the hollow of his gut. And he also knew, just as surely, that he would probably choose to ignore it when he placed the handcuffs on her wrists.

49

So FAR, THE FLIGHT HAD BEEN flawless.

As the late-morning sun climbed higher, the Stearman threw its speeding shadow down over little country roads, across the tops of barns, over the red dirt of plowed fields.

Occasionally, Will could see children running along, looking up, and waving.

Tex was taking a logical and careful route—around Augusta, Georgia, and toward the delta plains of the coast.

He slowly turned them east-southeast toward Savannah.

Eventually they took a wide sweep around Savannah and used the eastern seaboard as their bearing toward Jacksonville, Florida.

Will found the ride a refreshing change, though monotonous after a while. From time to time he would glance down at the metal case between his feet.

Continuing south, they flew over the boundaries of the great green cypress-and-water expanses of the Okefenokee Swamp.

As they swung clear of Jacksonville, Tex motioned for Will to take his earplugs out.

"What is it?" Will asked.

"Did you hear that?"

"What?"

"The engine just stalled—for about two seconds."

"What are you going to do?"

"There's a little airstrip between here and Gainesville," Tex said. "I'm going to put down there and make sure there's no problem. I can also double-check our fuel supply before we head out over water."

Tex seemed unconcerned. But Will was still glad he was going to check out the engine before they left the coast behind.

Although the sky was blue, with billowing white clouds, they started experiencing some turbulence as they neared the little airport. The plane pitched and rolled slightly, then hit a few unexpected jolts that shook Will down to the spine.

Then the airstrip came into view. Tex glided them down effortlessly onto a short blacktop runway with a single, small building for a control tower.

When the plane came to a stop, the pilot hopped out and said he was going to check in at the tower.

Within a few minutes he was back. He mounted a portable stepladder, cranked open the hood, and started looking over the engine. Will said he was going to stretch his legs, and he headed into the only building on the airstrip.

There was an ancient-looking soda machine—Will actually retrieved a drink from it in a bottle, not a can. He gulped it down, then went into the men's room to throw some water on his face.

When he got out, the air controller handed him a two-page fax with some kind of weather configuration on it.

"Give this to your pilot," he said with a drawl.

As Will walked out to the tarmac, Tex was revving up the engine. He turned slightly, talking more to himself than to his passenger.

"Well, I did a mag check—carb heat was off...maybe I had some plugs flaring out for a few seconds...I'm not positive. But I'm sure not seeing anything combustion-wise..."

Will waited for his diagnosis.

"Well," Tex said slowly, "I think we're fit for sea duty—let's put it that way."

"The guy in the tower gave me this—he said you should take a look at it." Will handed him the fax.

Tex straightened up stiffly and read it. His face was expressionless.

"We got some thunderheads massing, a little off to the west," he said. "It looks like we can stay ahead of them if we keep our airspeed up. The tops of those clouds are pretty high—there's going to be a big blow, alright. But I think we can miss it if we get out of Dodge right now—and I can keep our speed up to par. It's really up to you—it's your nickel, and your deadline." He looked at his passenger.

"What do you think?" Will asked him.

"I just told you the odds," the pilot said. "We can probably miss that storm as long as I can maintain maximum airspeed. But we've got to go now—right now, partner. I mean you've got to decide *right now*."

"What happens if we wait out the storm?"

"Who knows. Maybe that storm will be out over the ocean and gone in half a day—or a day—who knows…and maybe it will stall out…and you and I will be sitting here in this little garden spot of the universe for a day or two waiting for an opening in the sky. There are no guarantees."

"I don't have that kind of time—neither does my client—and neither does her little boy."

Tex walked close up to Will and stopped.

"Counselor, it sounds like you've just made up your mind. Let's crank 'er up."

Both of them climbed in quickly and buckled up.

Tex taxied them rapidly down the airstrip—but unlike in the first takeoff, he was now accelerating much faster. The plane nosed down momentarily and pitched a bit as they rolled and then straightened up against the mounting crosswind.

After the pilot had leveled off, he kept glancing off to the west. They could now see the edge of the thunderclouds building like a wall, inland, as the Stearman headed out over the waters of the Atlantic.

As they flew, Will looked back over his shoulder. Back at the disappearing Florida shoreline behind him. Where the safety of land was. And where the uncertainties and dangers of ocean weather had begun for them.

At the point when they'd completely lost sight of land and the biplane was surrounded by water, Tex motioned for Will to listen on the headset.

"Just did it again."

"What?" Will said loudly against the droning of the engine and the rising wind.

"I said," Tex shouted, "the engine just stalled again. I'm going to have to bring my RPMs down a bit—see if that helps."

Minutes went by slowly, as the plane bounced as if on an invisible water slide and Tex brought the speed down.

"Not enough," he shouted out. "I'm going to have to keep bringing the RPMs down until I don't hear the stall any more. And if that doesn't work, we may have to turn back."

Will turned around again, but to his dismay, the wall of storm clouds seemed to be gaining on them. Perhaps it was just his perspective, he thought. In the short time they'd left the coast, how could the storm line have moved so rapidly?

After half an hour, with the plane increasing its swaying and pitching in the advance of the storm that was chasing them, Tex finally called out again.

"Okay," he shouted, "I've got a smooth airspeed now—the engine purring—I think I've got it under control..."

"Great!" Will answered.

"One problem..."

"What?"

"I'm way under the airspeed I wanted."

"How much under?" Will yelled.

"Too much under," Tex shouted back.

"What happens now?" Will asked at the top of his voice.

"Looks like we're going to be riding the rodeo bull—whether we like it or not."

Will checked his seat belt and harness. Then he checked the tether strap that secured the little refrigeration unit at his feet.

But minute after minute, the flow underneath the biplane seemed to be growing more and more turbulent.

The air around them seemed to be alive with energy—bouncing then jarring, then finally slamming the vintage Stearman up—drifting for seconds as if lacking any control—and then plummeting it downward.

That was when Will began to doubt their mission—and his decision to go forward and try to outrun the storm.

Tex seemed frozen in the front cockpit, responding to each unpredictable side slap or downdraft with unflappable poise.

How the storm front had moved in on them—like an alien army of wild air current and boiling dark clouds with only blackness within—was not apparent to Will.

But one thing he knew—it was happening. The wild mass of weather was gaining on them—and it would be enveloping them.

The Stearman was soon caught in a full-fledged fight for life. There was mounting darkness around, rain was coming from somewhere—everywhere—the fabric of the wings was shuddering in the battering and howling of the storm.

The plane dove, then tried to climb. Tex was struggling—Will could see that.

The pilot's shoulders were arched as he attempted to keep the plane on an even keel, but every maneuver was met with a wilder reaction—first a plunge downward to the point that Will thought he would certainly retch—then buffeting sideways—then all-but-uncontrolled rolling, pitching, diving.

Jagged streaks of lightning were all around them—and then cataclysmic booms with pelting, punishing rain.

Tex looked up and around in a futile attempt to find a hole in the cloud bank—some opening to get relief—to thread the needle through to somewhere.

Anywhere.

Then lightning crashed and blinded them in one unearthly explosion that seemed to have struck just above their heads.

The plane shuddered—then pitched madly about. Then downward, sideways, and then plunging straight down—like a diver doing a jackknife—the engine screaming.

Tex was yelling something wildly, but Will could not—or would not—hear.

All sense of direction was gone. The laws of physics seemed to have been ripped and shredded—and lost in the screaming wind and wall of water all around them.

They were hurtling down. And then Will knew the depth—the numbing reality of their plight. As he looked upside down, over his head, he saw it.

The metal case was dangling in the wind above him like a balloon at the end of a string.

It was at the very end of its tether line, floating in the air above, shining and silver against the black sky and flashes of lightning—as the plane dived straight down, the engine screaming, then sputtering, and screaming again.

Will yelled a prayer in a choked scream—was it a prayer? A psalm?

Quickly—quickly—remember! he yelled to himself in the center of the dark.

Then it came.

UNDER HIS WINGS YOU MAY SEEK REFUGE

Will was shouting it out, his eyes blinded in the pelting rain and raging wind. He tried to grab the tether line connected to the case.

But up and down were indistinguishable.

He reached and missed, unable to see it.

There was no plane—no direction—only chaos and fear.

UNDER HIS WINGS YOU MAY SEEK REFUGE

Will shouted it—over and over—but then, no sound came out.

The Stearman was going down and down, twisting and turning in a corkscrew as it fell toward the sea, faster and faster. And Will, bleary and overcome, had one last thought.

Blacking out. I'm blacking out...

50

Aʟʟ ᴏꜰ ᴛʜᴇ ꜱǫᴜᴀᴅ ᴄᴀʀꜱ were there at the rendezvous point, about ten miles down the highway from Tommy White Arrow's ranch.

There were two squads from the county sheriff's department and two state patrol cars.

Detective Otis Tracher had arrived in a sheriff's vehicle driven by the sheriff himself. He briefed the officers on the situation and stressed that the primary objective was to secure the child, Joshua—if indeed he was still with the mother.

The second objective was to apprehend the mother, Mary Sue Fellows.

It was to be done without the use of firearms, if at all possible. Tracher had been given authority to make that judgment call. Only upon his directive would sidearms be unholstered—unless, of course, any of the officers were fired upon first.

The detective had been warned by the sheriff that Tommy White Arrow, while he had no criminal record, was known to harbor strong antipolice and antigovernment sentiments.

He'd also learned that Tommy—and others on the White Arrow ranch—had access to weapons. A registration check had yielded the finding that they were properly licensed.

Tracher gave the word, and the five law-enforcement vehicles moved out. When they arrived at the entrance of the long ranch driveway, one of the State Patrol vehicles parked across it, blocking it. The other squads headed quickly down the dirt road, kicking up a cloud of dust as they approached the main ranch house, where Tommy lived.

The cars swerved tightly to a stop in front and two officers sprinted out of their vehicles to secure the rear. The rest surrounded the house, their hands on their holsters. All except detective Otis Tracher.

He walked, alone, up to the front door, no weapon drawn. In his hand were the arrest warrants for Mary Sue Fellows, the order from Judge Mason transferring custody of Joshua Fellows, and an emergency order from the local South Dakota judge permitting the apprehension of Joshua and Mary Sue, pending a hearing on a Governor's Warrant.

The detective was about to knock on the door, but to his surprise, it swung open quickly—so quickly that the officers in back of him latched their hands to their holsters.

Tommy White Arrow walked out the front door. He was smiling.

"Good day, officers," he said. "I presume you know that this is an Indian reservation, protected under federal law. If you are here on state law business, and are coming after me, I think you may have a jurisdictional problem."

"Mr. White Arrow, I am Detective Otis Tracher from the Juda County sheriff's department, State of Georgia. We have no quarrel with you. We are here for a male child named Joshua Fellows, and we are also looking for Mary Sue Fellows, his mother."

"You won't find them here."

"No?"

"No."

"Where are they?"

"I'm not really sure where they are this minute."

"Where is the boy—Joshua?"

"Airlifted."

"What?"

"Airlifted to a hospital in your hometown, I believe."

"By whose order?"

"By order of his attending pediatrician here in South Dakota."

Detective Tracher paused for a few seconds to assimilate the information he had just received.

"But Joshua was here?"

"Yes. But his doctor here felt he needed continuity of care—back at his hometown hospital."

"Mary Sue was here?"

"Yes. But not any more."

"So—she fled?"

"No."

"No?"

"No. She was moving very calmly and slowly when I last saw her. Not *fleeing* at all."

"Where was she last headed?"

"I'm not sure. She didn't tell me."

"You have no idea where she is going?"

"Not really. She said she was still trying to figure things out."

"Was she with anyone?"

"Yes. My sister."

"What's her name?"

"Katherine White Arrow."

"Mr. White Arrow—"

"Call me Tommy."

"I am going to ask that you not leave this area for a while—until we can get this all sorted out."

"Where am I going to go? I've got three horses to break for customers. And I have several riding lessons to give. I'll be right here."

Tracher asked one of the officers to go inside with Tommy and get identification information on Katherine's vehicle.

The sheriff approached detective Tracher.

"Why don't I put an all-points out. We can get roadblocks and border checks at all the highways leaving the state. She can't be that far away—we'll get her."

But Tracher just looked at the sheriff. Then he walked back to the car and got in.

The sheriff climbed into the driver's side. He looked over at the detective.

"Look, this is your show. But I think you've wasted a trip up here if we don't secure the roads along the state line right now and grab this lady."

After thinking it over a couple minutes, Tracher explained himself.

"Sheriff, I don't want any roadblocks. Or border checks. Or roundups. No dragnet. This is it. I'm going home. I have a strong feeling I know where Mary Sue Fellows is going. And I also get the feeling I know exactly how things are going to end."

Then he looked over at the sheriff and asked, "You ever get those kind of feelings about a case?"

"No," the sheriff said. "I never have."

Then he started up the engine and headed out of the White Arrow ranch.

51

FREEPORT, THE CAPITAL CITY of Grand Bahama Island, would see the aftermath wash up on its white shores.

Like the other towns of the Bahama Islands, its history was strewn with the flotsam and jetsam of hundreds of years of ill-fated attempts to navigate its waters.

There were pirates. And slave traders. And Confederate ships that had used the islands during the Civil War as a place from which to run the Northern blockades.

But those who lived there would always search the beaches. After naval battles. After storms. After ships sank with valuable cargo, which would float to the sandy beaches.

And sometimes there were the bodies that washed ashore, bloated and disfigured.

Then came the airplanes. But sometimes, like the ships, the aircraft would lose the battle with wind or weather. And bits of wreckage would float ashore.

Sometimes the pilots or their passengers would arrive, face-down, on the shores.

Several children were along the beach, not far from Freeport, looking for wood, cans, and other debris from the storm.

That was when they witnessed the fate of the Boeing PT-17 Stearman that was carrying Tex Rhoady and Will Chambers.

A black child wearing white swimming trunks, his torso still wet from swimming, yelled to his playmates.

"Look, look!"

His friends ran over to where he was standing.

And then they saw what he was looking at.

"I saw it first," the little boy in the white trunks yelled out. He pointed wildly with his index finger. "That's what I told you."

The other children huddled together, growing quiet in amazement.

Then they could only yell and whoop at what they saw.

The Stearman biplane, engine whining, was flying so low that it was nearly skimming the water—limping, with its wings unstable and rocking slightly back and forth.

Then it buzzed directly over their heads in its brilliant colors of red, white, and blue. Tex was waving to the children as they flew over.

Will, in the back cockpit, gave an exhausted salute.

The children on the beach cheered.

The plane made its way over the trees and the small, brightly colored cement houses until Tex spotted the small airstrip at the end of the island.

As the Stearman set down on the cracked concrete landing strip, a flock of chickens scurried out of the way. When the plane had finally taxied up to the airport building, a handful of locals, smiling and wondering, came to the edge of the strip to look at the antique plane that was painted in the colors of the American flag and had just come in.

Will, his hands shaking a little, unhooked the tether line. Then he picked up the metal case and climbed out.

The attorney had often seen pictures of people kissing the ground after returning home from a war, or finishing a perilous journey. He had wondered at that gesture—and had always thought it was a little foolish.

As Tex was climbing out, he turned around—and then laughed out loud as he saw Will Chambers kneeling on the airstrip, kissing the ground.

The two shook hands, looking each other in the eye for a few seconds, but saying nothing at first. Then they walked into the tiny airport. After going through customs under the amused gaze of officers dressed smartly in white British uniforms, they passed through to a lobby that was filled with local families, a few tourists, and a boy leading a goat by a rope.

A thin, distinguished-looking man in a white island shirt and khaki pants quickly came up to them. He had white, thinning hair and a large, gentle face.

"I'm Dr. Forrester," he said in a crisp British accent. "You made it through that tropical blow we just had? Amazing. It just came and went. Out of nowhere. They get those here. Oh good, you've brought the box with the blood sample. I told customs to be on the lookout for someone bringing in a medical sample."

Tex introduced himself and then said, "Counselor, I think I'll see if I can rustle us up a couple clean rooms. And then I'm going to have me a sit-down in a nice quiet cabaña. Doctor, good to meet you."

The Englishman handed a card to Tex as he left.

"I've written down the number and address of the office where I'm working here. You can get hold of us there."

Dr. Forrester took the box and led Will to a waiting taxi, a converted minivan with the sliding door replaced by a piece of fishing net that was latched over the opening with a hook.

"We had a tough flight," Will said. "This box got tossed around pretty violently, and I'm worried that the vial is all smashed up inside."

Dr. Forrester smiled but didn't respond. Finally he said, "With the airline strike, I suppose that old biplane is the best you could do. Remarkable. Truly remarkable. I can't believe you're here."

"Neither can I," Will quipped.

In less than thirty minutes they were in downtown Freeport. Going past the international bazaar that was thronged with shoppers, the taxi stopped at the opening of a narrow alley. After the doctor had paid the cab driver, he and Will began walking down the tiled sidewalk between two rows of small businesses and shops, some painted green, some white, others yellow, each with a wooden sign hanging out in front.

They ducked into one with a medical logo. Dr. Forrester warmly introduced Will to the local staff and took him into a back room that was filled with lab equipment.

He opened the top of the silver box carefully. Will looked in and saw that it was filled with a thick gel-like material—that looked like petroleum jelly, but with much more density.

"This stuff is marvelous," the doctor remarked. "You can put an egg inside of a box, surround it with this, drop it off Big Ben to the sidewalk, and it wouldn't crack."

He reached in and pulled out a smaller metal tube, which he opened.

"Give me an hour," he said, taking the vial containing Joshua's blood.

"That quick?"

"I already have an impression of what we are dealing with, based on the symptoms Dr. Kendoll described and on his evaluation of the blood. By the way, do you have a copy of Joshua's medical chart?"

Will fished the file out of his briefcase. A nurse came in with a note and handed it to the doctor, who passed it on to Will.

"Your pilot found some rooms at the Driftwood Hotel. Here's the address."

After thanking Dr. Forrester again, Will caught a cab over to the hotel.

When he arrived, he found Tex sitting at the curved bamboo bar by the pool.

"Pull up a chair, counselor. I'm drinking an island screwdriver—what's your poison?"

"Ginger ale with a slice of lime," Will said to the bartender.

"Oh," Tex commented, "you're ridin' the wagon?"

"Your drink there used to be my drink once," Will replied. "During the daytime, at least. Then nighttimes it was Jack Daniels. All through the night."

"Yeah, it can be a problem. My last two wives said that to me. It was more than that, though—a whole lot more. Anyway," and with that Tex lifted his glass, "to us who land softly—and to those who don't."

He swung around on his stool and looked out to the azure ribbon of ocean on the horizon.

"I did you a favor."

"What? You mean in addition to not killing me on that flight?" Will exclaimed, laughing.

"Yeah, that was a mean old Brahma bull we were ridin'," Tex said. "No—I mean something else."

"Oh?"

"When's your doctor going to do his thing?"

"He's looking at the blood right now. I'm expecting a call any minute."

"Then it should work out."

"What?"

"Did you think about how you're going to get back to the mainland?"

"How's your plane?" Will asked.

"Don't really know. I thought I'd mosey over there later and take a closer look. Anyway, you said you've got the court case coming up."

"Right."

"So I checked around. There's an Air Mexico flight sitting here on Grand Bahama island. Late this afternoon it'll be taking off for Miami and then going on to Atlanta. They're holding a seat for you. They're not affected by the strike, of course."

Will thanked Tex warmly.

"Now it's not at the little airstrip *we* landed on," Tex explained. "It's over at the international airport, just down from Freeport. That's the one that actually *looks* like an airport—sort of."

Tex put down his drink and rubbed his hands together.

"So let me ask you something," Tex said quietly. He paused and then continued. "What you were saying—spouting off up there…"

"What do you mean?"

"When we were up there, and coming down in the middle of all of that. We were in a free fall. I was figuring we were going to buy the farm right there. I did every stick and rudder trick I knew. But it just wasn't happening. We were going down."

Will was listening intently.

"So the thing is this," Tex went on. "The thing is—what were you reciting up there? Was it something from the Bible, or what?"

"Psalm ninety-one."

Tex was studying Will.

Then Will recited the passage:

> He will cover you with His pinions,
> And under His wings you may seek refuge;
> His faithfulness is a shield and bulwark.

"Pinions?" Tex asked.

"Those are the feathers of the wing. The feathers that create flight."

After a few moments of silence Tex said, "So, you're a religious man?"

"I didn't used to be," Will explained. "Not really. I just didn't think about it. Then my life started taking a nosedive…"

Tex grinned a bit.

"And then one day this particular lawsuit came into my office. Well, it was much more than just the legal case. Anyway, things came in on me. I was cornered. It was like I was chased into this corner by someone who was trying to catch my attention. I was there in the box and I had to look—really look—at all the evidence there was about the life of Jesus. What He said. How He died. And the stories in all four Gospels about the resurrection. I really had never thought about it before. You might say I was forced to render a verdict. On who Jesus really was."

"I had an uncle like that," Tex said. "My dad left us when I was young, and my mom got killed in a car accident. I was raised, from about twelve on, by my uncle. Now he was a cussing, fighting, drinking kind of a guy. He worked in the oil fields. They called those guys 'roughnecks.' And they sure were."

"What happened?"

"One day he goes to this revival. He comes back and says he just got saved. Says he's invited Jesus into his heart as savior. Sins forgiven. You probably know the line. I didn't think much of it. But he sure caught on. Suddenly, he is this churchgoing, amening, Bible-reading, going-to-heaven fellow. 'You have to come to Jesus, Gerald,' he used to say to me all the time."

"*Gerald?*" Will remarked with a smile.

"You don't think I was born with the name 'Tex,' do you?"

"So, after your uncle became a Christian, where did that leave you?"

"He dragged me to church until I was too old to be dragged—and I finally left the house. Went out on my own."

After a pause, Tex added, "My uncle—his name was Warren. He was a good man, though."

A hotel clerk approached Will.

"Are you Mr. Chambers?"

The attorney nodded.

"A call for you. You can take it at the phone here," he said, and he pointed to a telephone on the bar.

Will picked up the phone and greeted the caller.

"Mr. Chambers, Dr. Forrester here. I've looked at the sample. And the records. It confirms my suspicions. What you've got here is methylmalonic acidemia."

"What?"

Dr. Forrester repeated the name of the condition and then continued. "It's one of a group of metabolic diseases that cause the accumulation of methylmalonic acid in the body. It can cause severe episodes of acidosis and ketosis—and it can be fatal."

"You say this is a *disease?*"

"Yes. I find no evidence of poisoning. Though it is possible for a physician to mistakenly assume that a child with this disease has been given a poisonous substance."

"Is there treatment for this?"

"Oh yes, several regimes. But it is a nasty medical condition. A low-protein diet helps. Avoiding general infection is also good. There are shots—hydroxycobalamin if there is a cobalamin defect—and other things that can be done."

"You need to get your diagnosis to Dr. Kendoll—"

"Already done," Dr. Forrester said. "He will get it to the treating physicians."

"Doctor, I need your testimony. The trial starts tomorrow in Mary Sue Fellows case."

"I wish I could. But my mission down here is too important. I simply can't leave."

Will thought for a moment.

"It may be possible to present your testimony by satellite tele-conferencing. Let me figure this out…"

"I do know they have those facilities over in Nassau. Last year I participated in a video medical forum from there. I would be willing to go down to Nassau on the day you need me for the trial."

Will thanked the doctor and immediately called his office. He instructed Hilda to arrange for a video satellite hookup from the courthouse in Delphi to Nassau, Bahamas. He suggested she try the video companies in Atlanta first.

"Then have Jacki file a motion for me," Will continued, "naming Dr. Forrester as our expert witness and asking permission to present his testimony via live satellite feed. By the way, where are we on our demand to have a local expert evaluate the blood sample that Dr. Parker used at the Delphi hospital?"

"Bad news," Hilda said. "District Attorney Putnam says that they will not be able to allow that—for reasons they will reveal on the first day of trial. Jacki did line up a hematologist in Decatur to look at the sample—he was very reluctant—we really had to twist his arm. He knew Dr. Parker and did not want to get involved. But now it looks like there is nothing for him to evaluate anyway. That's probably for the best—it didn't sound like he was very happy with our case."

Will concluded and hung up the phone.

"Good news?" Tex asked.

Will nodded. "Our trip down here was worth it. I think we found what we came for."

He told Tex he was going to take off for the airport to catch the Air Mexico flight. He would rent a car in Atlanta and could be back at the houseboat by evening. Trial would start the next day at one-thirty in the afternoon.

"But how about you?" Will asked.

"I think I'll hang around the island for a few days. Take it easy. Besides, I need to check out the Stearman for damage."

After the two shook hands one more time, Will left to catch his plane. Tex put his cowboy hat on, hailed a cab, and headed for the little airstrip at the end of the island.

When he arrived, he wandered over to the biplane, which was still parked where he'd pulled up, in front of a tall, tin-covered hangar.

He walked around it, inspecting the havoc the storm had caused. The fabric of both wings was damaged. Reaching the rear, he looked at the tail flaps. Then he looked more closely. They were swinging completely loose and inoperable.

"This old Stearman never should have made it...not in this shape," the pilot muttered to himself.

As he ambled thoughtfully across the airstrip he gazed up into the blue sky. It was clear, with a few white wisps of clouds thinly streaked across it.

Then he put his hand to the brim of his cowboy hat, and tipped it to the sky.

"Thank you, Sir," Tex said. "Maybe it's time to talk—you know, catch up on things."

52

THE DELPHI COURTROOM was jammed with court personnel, extra bailiffs, and new reporters. Inside the chambers of Juda County Circuit Judge Trainer, an informal pre-trial conference was being conducted.

Judge Trainer was a middle-aged man of medium height and bland expression. Cautious and studious, he was not prone to overblown emotion or exaggeration. As he sat at his desk, he was pinching the bridge of his glasses with two fingers, readjusting them minutely.

"We have some preliminary matters," he began. "But first I want to address the media issue. I have instructed all of the news reporters that, because this case involves a minor child, they are to use only the initial of his first name. Furthermore, the last name of the family involved is not to be used in any media reports. I have also ordered that no cameras be allowed in the courtroom, nor are any interviews to be given in the courtroom, even during the breaks. All media interviews are to be done out in the hallway—and if that becomes a problem, I'm going to move all of the reporters and their equipment to the front lawn. Now, counsel, do you have some preliminary matters of your own?"

Harry Putnam, Harriet Bender, and Will Chambers were sitting in a row in front of the judge's desk. Joe Fellows, in his jail suit and appearing for himself, was next to Will. A court reporter was in the corner, putting everything on the record.

Putnam spoke up first. "I believe Mr. Chambers has two matters."

The judge nodded in Will's direction.

"Your Honor," Will said, "the first matter relates to discovery. The county bases much of its case on a blood sample from the minor child, Joshua. It was taken some time ago when he was treated as an inpatient at the Delphi hospital. A while after Johsua's treatment, Dr. Parker, the chief pathologist, rendered a report indicating that the blood sample showed the presence of ethylene glycol. That's a substance contained in many industrial products and oils, and in hydraulic brake fluid specifically. Their case rests on that blood sample. I have made a demand to have our own expert, a hematologist down in Decatur, take a look at the sample from which Dr. Parker arrived at his conclusions. If Dr. Parker's conclusions are wrong, then there is no absolute proof that Mary Sue Fellows poisoned her child by having him ingest brake fluid. Yet the district attorney, Mr. Harry Putnam, has refused to allow us to evaluate the rest of that blood sample."

The judge turned to Harry Putnam, who launched into his explanation quickly and diplomatically.

"Your Honor, no one in this room loves justice more than I do. Our system thrives on it. I believe in giving everyone a fair trial. Now, we do have a problem with this blood sample."

"What type of problem?"

"Well," Putnam continued, "Dr. Parker advises me that the blood sample is no longer available."

"Why?" the judge followed up.

"We really aren't too sure. Somehow—and we don't know exactly how—this sample has disappeared. Dr. Parker has turned the hospital upside down. He has talked to everyone that has had access to the lab. The sample simply cannot be located."

"This is outrageous, Your Honor," Will responded. "I move first that the results of Dr. Parker's evaluation be excluded from evidence. It's unfair for the county to be able to admit into evidence the results of this examination but deny our due-process right to check the same blood sample and see if our expert comes up with the same results."

"Your Honor," Putnam said, now more emphatically, "it was not the county's fault that this sample disappeared. We did not have control and possession of it. And the hospital and Dr. Parker—neither of those entities are parties to this action. If this were a piece of evidence we had in our evidence locker at the sheriff's department, and it disappeared—*then* we could be charged with the failure to maintain that evidence."

"That's a distinction without a difference," Will said in response. "The county is prosecuting this case. The county and Mr. Putnam knew full well that the sample is at the heart of the issues in the case. If their primary witness can't control the evidence for the county's case, why should Mary Sue Fellows' defense be punished as a result?"

The judge nodded toward Harriet Bender.

"Judge, you know my attitude in these cases," Bender said with a smile. "It's all about the best interest of the child. That means the best interest of Joshua. If he is being poisoned, then we've got to know about it. That means that the report of Dr. Parker should come in even though it is unfortunate that the blood sample is not available for Mr. Chambers' expert to take a look at."

"This is a tough one," the judge replied cautiously. "Mr. Chambers, I can sympathize with your situation and your desire to have a full, fair defense for your client. On the other hand, are we to prevent the county from prosecuting a child-welfare case because an independent expert not entirely under its control, or the hospital, may have misplaced a piece of evidence? I think not. I will do this for you, Mr. Chambers—I promise you that I will consider the misplacing of this evidence as a factor bearing on the credibility of Dr. Parker and the district attorney's case against Mrs. Fellows. I will do that in considering the evidence."

That was a major setback for the defense. It was certainly an appealable issue, but Will did not want to have to take the case up on appeal while Joe and Mary Sue were deprived of the custody of Joshua—and possibly convicted of a criminal offense. At this point, though, there was nothing he could do about the judge's ruling. He also knew that he had a fallback position—Dr. Forrester's evaluation of the more recent blood sample.

Will carefully explained the sequence of events—Dr. Bill's taking the blood sample from Joshua in South Dakota and Will's trip to Grand Bahama island with it, followed by its evaluation by one of the world's foremost experts in pediatric metabolic diseases. He then went through the diagnosis of Joshua's condition by Dr. Forrester and his exclusion of ethylene-glycol poisoning as a cause. He concluded by asking for an opportunity to permit Dr. Forrester to testify by live, satellite-fed video. He explained that arrangements had already been made for the equipment to be set up in the Delphi courtroom and that there was corresponding equipment available near Grand Bahama island.

Harry Putnam waded into the argument with both fists.

"Your Honor, Mr. Chambers did not list his expert until yesterday. We've had no chance to have discovery from him—this is a complete surprise. Moreover, we do not stipulate to the use of live video conferencing in this case. We either want live witnesses, where we can all take a look at their demeanor and appreciate the physical aspect of their testimony—or we don't want their testimony at all."

Harriet Bender was next. She spoke sharply and cut the air with her right hand as she spoke, as if she were wielding a hatchet.

"I strongly object! Strongly object!" Bender exclaimed. "And I am going to tell you why, Judge. We don't know that this blood sample was really taken from Joshua. Are we supposed to take Mr. Chambers' word for it? He said he hand-carried it. Where did he get it from? Has he proved chain of custody for this sample?"

"If the court will bear with me," Will said, "I can bring in each of the witnesses from the chain of custody to prove that."

"But that's not my main point," Bender snapped back, now heading in a new direction. "My main point is that Mr. Chambers' client flees from this jurisdiction and takes that little boy with her. That little boy is my client. His name is Joshua, and I am his lawyer, appointed by the Juda County Circuit Court to represent him as guardian ad litem. I have never—*never*—consented to have a blood sample taken from my client and submitted to Dr. Forrester for evaluation. I should have been consulted first."

"And would you have agreed, if I had asked your permission—which I don't think I needed to do?" Will asked.

"I'm sure I would *not* have agreed to allow the blood sample to be taken," Bender shot back.

Judge Trainer mildly scolded both counsel for arguing among themselves rather than directing their arguments to him. His ruling, on the issue of Dr. Forrester's testimony, he explained, would be deferred. He would wait, possibly until the end of the county's case, to make that decision. But he invited Will Chambers to make a narrative offer of proof as to what the doctor's testimony would be.

Will painstakingly went through Dr. Forrester's qualifications. His technique for the evaluation of the blood sample. His diagnosis, to a reasonable degree of medical certainty, of the metabolic disease affecting Joshua and his opinion that the sample did not show the presence of ethylene glycol.

Further, Will continued, Dr. Forrester would testify that it was possible that a physician could mistakenly assume the presence of ethylene glycol in the blood of a patient suffering from that disease. Dr. Forrester would also indicate that, if Joshua had been poisoned with brake fluid and it appeared in Dr. Parker's blood test in sufficient amount for Joshua to be sick, it was likely there would be some trace of ethylene glycol still left in his blood at the time the later sample had been drawn. And yet Dr. Forrester had found none.

The judge then adjourned the chambers conference, asking Harry Putnam if he was ready to proceed. Putnam said he was.

"Okay," Judge Trainer announced. "Then let's get started."

53

ONCE THE THREE ATTORNEYS were settled in the courtroom, Putnam addressed the judge.

The district attorney explained that he would rely on the factual background laid out in his written trial brief and would waive any further opening statement. Guardian ad litem Harriet Bender followed suit.

Will reserved his opening statement until the close of the county's case.

Joe Fellows, sitting at the defense table next to Will in his orange jail suit, indicated he wanted to address the court. Judge Trainer motioned for him to rise.

As he began to speak, intensely and passionately, Joe held his hands open in front of him, pleading.

"Your Honor, I just want to say that both my wife, Mary Sue, and I are totally innocent of any abuse against our son Joshua. We love him—more than our own lives. We would never hurt him on purpose—*ever.*"

"Thank you, Mr. Fellows—but I would remind you that this is not a criminal trial. We are not trying to decide guilt or innocence. We are here to determine whether child abuse *probably* took place—the county need only prove its case by the lower civil standard of proof—and if so, whether it is in the best interests of Joshua to grant the county's request to permanently transfer his custody to the Department of Social Services.

"Of course, you are also facing criminal charges relating to these same facts. But that's a separate case. That trial is scheduled

292

next month. And your wife still has outstanding criminal warrants against her. As soon as she is apprehended—or turns herself in—then her trial date will also be set in her criminal case. Now, do you understand all of that?"

After nodding, Joe sat down and folded his hands in his lap, momentarily closing his eyes and bowing his head. As he did, Will placed his hand on his shoulder.

As his first witness, Putnam called Liz Luden of the Department of Social Services. Luden explained the background of the case. She had received a phone call from Dr. Wilson, the general practitioner for the Fellows family. He had indicated some concerns to her about Joshua's medical treatment. He also expressed concerns about Mary Sue Fellows' compliance with his treatment requests, and Mary Sue had also made some comments about Joshua that deeply concerned him. He suspected child abuse, but wasn't sure.

Luden then indicated that the department had contacted Mary Sue, who they knew was a nurse doing part-time work at the Delphi hospital. At first, Luden testified, she was cooperative, though somewhat confused as to why Social Services should be involved.

Luden had requested access to Joshua's medical records just to verify that everything was being done for him that should be done. Mary Sue had reluctantly agreed. But shortly after that, she had said that she was going to seek a second opinion from another doctor because she did not feel that Dr. Wilson had the skills to diagnose Joshua's problems. She was given a short period of time to secure a second opinion from a qualified physician.

"When Mary Sue neglected—or failed—to secure a second opinion or have Joshua's medical care taken over by a competent doctor, my suspicions were confirmed that we had a problem going on."

"What kind of problem?"

"It was my feeling," Luden said, "that the mother's lack of cooperation was not just accidental—that she might be trying to cover something up. Something about Joshua's medical status. Something about his health."

"And did something very significant happen then?"

"Yes," Luden continued, "our department received a phone call from a third-party abuse reporter."

"Exactly what do you mean by that?" Putnam asked.

"Someone other than the parents and someone other than the department called in to us and gave us a very detailed complaint describing exactly how Joshua was being poisoned by his mother."

Will objected to the testimony as hearsay but added, "Unless, of course, Mr. Putnam agrees that he is not presenting this for the *truth* of the accusations—but simply to set the stage."

Putnam acknowledged that that was exactly his intent, and the judge overruled the objection.

"And what did the caller indicate?"

"The caller indicated that Mary Sue was poisoning Joshua with hydraulic brake fluid."

"And what did you do after that?"

"We contacted Dr. Parker, the pathologist at the Delphi hospital. He confirmed the presence of a substance in the blood sample taken from Joshua earlier—a toxic ingredient present in brake fluid. I then proceeded to contact the sheriff's department, and we arranged for the immediate issuance of warrants and the filing of the petition for transfer of custody on an emergency basis. Judge Mason held an ex parte hearing temporarily taking custody away from Mary Sue and Joseph Fellows and transferring it to the county—*pending* this final hearing, of course."

"Were you with the sheriff's deputies the day they tried to apprehend and take custody of Joshua?" Putnam asked.

"Yes, I was," Luden said. "But Mary Sue had just escaped with Joshua. Joseph, the father, was there. He appeared rather combatant—and angry. He declared he was glad his wife and child 'got away'—those were his words. He was immediately arrested."

Will began his cross-examination by asking Ms. Luden for the identity of the caller.

"As you know," she replied, "I cannot disclose that. That's protected and privileged. We treat all incoming calls about child abuse as anonymous."

"But you know who called?"

"Yes, we have a name."

"And the caller was a young woman, wasn't it?" Will asked in a voice loud enough for everyone to hear.

"And exactly how did you come by that information?" Luden exclaimed. "This information is confidential. I think the court ought to get an explanation from you immediately, Mr. Chambers."

"I'll tell you how I found out," Will replied. "The caller called *me*. A young woman called me and told me that her anonymous tip to you regarding Mary Sue was entirely bogus. False. Untrue. She said she was motivated to do it by a person who had some kind of financial control over her—" But Will was unable to continue. Harry Putnam and Harriet Bender were both on their feet objecting.

"Mr. Chambers," the judge said, "confine yourself to question-and-answer format. You are not a witness here. What you may or may not have heard in your investigation or preparation for this case, is not evidence."

Will nodded in acknowledgment of the judge's ruling and plowed ahead.

"Did you ever doubt the caller's honesty or accuracy in reporting this to you?"

"Not really. I had no reason to."

"Why hydraulic brake fluid? Doesn't that strike you as a bit odd?"

"No, not really. Mary Sue is a nurse. She knows, presumably, what types of toxic substances could be administered to a child and be difficult to differentiate from actual health problems."

"So you carefully thought through all the ways that the caller's report could be consistent with Mary Sue's *guilt?*"

"Yes, that's true," Luden said.

"But did you ever think of the reasons why Mary Sue might be *innocent?* Did you ever think through all the evidence that was consistent with her *innocence?*"

Luden's eyes darted around a little a bit as she thought.

"I'm really not sure what you are getting at."

"In other words, did you put as much energy into trying to determine her innocence as you did into trying to establish her guilt?"

Putnam and Bender were both on their feet again, shouting out objections that Will's question was argumentative.

"It's getting close to argumentative," the judge ruled. "I'll give you only a little bit of leeway here—that's all. Please proceed."

"Do you understand my question?"

"Yes—and I resent the implication that you are making."

"So you really devoted a substantial amount of energy and thought to trying to figure out whether this caller was really telling you the truth?"

"I absolutely did. We certainly would not want to take a child away from a parent who is not guilty of child abuse—or neglect or some other parental misfeasance."

"You are sure about that?" Will asked.

"Absolutely," Luden answered.

"You provided me with a copy of your notes relating to your investigation of Mary Sue Fellows, is that correct?"

"The only thing we did not provide was a copy of the intake message when the caller made the telephone call to our department."

"And your thought process was carefully laid down in your notes as you investigated this?"

"Just the main things—the important things."

"Did you ever stop and ask yourself this—how would this caller have possibly known?"

"What do you mean?"

"I mean this," Will explained. "There were only three people on that farm. Little Joshua, too young to be able to describe anything about hydraulic brake fluid. And then there was Mary Sue, and then there was Joe. Those are the only three who were living on the farm. How in the world did this caller find out that Mary Sue was allegedly giving brake fluid to her son in an effort to poison him?"

"I'm sure we considered that. We reviewed that. I can't remember offhand, but I'm sure it's in my notes."

"Please review your notes. I have a copy of them in front of me. And I will represent to you, Ms. Luden, that there is nothing in your notes indicating that you ever raised that question. That you ever recognized that there was a major problem with the story the caller had given you. The caller gave absolutely no facts upon which you could determine that she had ever had an opportunity to observe the family, or see Mary Sue giving brake fluid to her child—or to even *hear* that it could have been done. Review your notes, Ms. Luden, and see if it ever appears there."

Luden thumbed through her records, and after several prolonged minutes of silence, she answered.

"Apparently...I do not see anything in my notes about that."

"Would that not have been an important question to ask yourself the very first minute you received the call from this anonymous person?"

Luden paused for another moment. Then she gave her answer.

"Yes, I assume it would have been a good idea."

54

WILL STEPPED OVER to his counsel table, wondering briefly if the tide was turning with this witness.

When he turned back toward Liz Luden, he had a large, black notebook in his hands.

"Did you use a CRAM in Mary Sue's case—in evaluating her as a potential child abuser?"

Luden took a few seconds to eye Will and study the notebook he was holding.

"A what?" Judge Trainer asked, with subtle confusion on his face.

"Child Risk Assessment Manual, Your Honor," the attorney responded.

"It is our practice to use the guidelines in that manual in all our investigations." Luden answered confidently. "But Mr. Chambers, that is only one tool in our procedure. And it's only a tool—it's not Holy Writ"—and with that she smiled.

Harriet Bender guffawed loudly.

"No, I don't suppose you would consider *anything* Holy Writ," Will commented, "including Holy Writ itself."

However, before the Putnam and Bender tag team could leap up with mutual objections, Will launched into his next question.

"But how about someone who *did* believe in Holy Writ—someone who is a Bible-believing, churchgoing person with strong—even 'absolutist'—spiritual beliefs?"

"Like?" Luden inquired.

"Mary Sue Fellows. You did evaluate her in light of her religious beliefs?"

"We don't discriminate on the basis of religion, if that's what you're asking."

"No—I'm not asking that. But isn't it a fact that, according to Risk Factor Seven in the manual, a parent who holds—and I quote—'rigid, authoritarian religious beliefs' should be treated with a *higher* index of suspicion for child abuse?"

"Mr. Chambers," Luden responded with a tinge of sarcasm in her voice, "I know what the manual says. It says thousands of other things too. And they don't relate to this case—just as Risk Factor Seven doesn't either."

"It doesn't relate? Mary Sue's strong beliefs in the Bible—her 'rigid' moral beliefs—her use of spanking as a form of discipline according to Scripture—none of those things relate to this case?"

"We decided to prosecute her and to seek custody of Joshua for his protection because of evidence she was *poisoning her child.* You don't seem interested in talking about that."

"Oh, Ms. Luden," Will said somberly, "we will certainly be talking a lot about that. But you seem uncomfortable with my questions about how you assessed Mary Sue's Christian beliefs."

"I didn't assess them," she snapped back.

Harry Putnam jumped up. "There is a limit, Your Honor," he said in his most deferential voice, "to adversarial zeal. I can appreciate Mr. Chambers trying some kidney punches against our first witness here." By then, Putnam was rocking on the balls of his feet like a basketball player ready to make a free throw. "But this is way out of line—he's accusing the department—a Juda County Department—of religious bigotry. Now that simply will not stand. No sir, it will not stand."

Judge Trainer was unperturbed.

"If that was intended to be a legal objection, Mr. Putnam— and that would be a rather wild assumption on my part, because it sounded more like a Fourth of July speech—if it was, it's over-ruled."

Will dug in.

"Ms. Luden, do you *deny* indicating to Julie, your intern at the Department of Social Services, that Mary Sue was 'rigidly religious,' and that as a result she met the criteria for a 'heightened risk of child abuse'?"

Luden's eyes narrowed. She spotted her intern in the audience section of the courtroom and glared in her direction.

Before she answered, Will added, "And we have subpoenaed Julie to testify. She is here in the courtroom. If your memory is bad, I can simply call her and have her relate what she told my investigator, Tiny Heftland."

"That won't be necessary," Luden said with a manufactured smile. "I may have indicated something to that effect regarding Mary Sue Fellows."

"Thank you," Will said and he jotted a small plus sign next to his notes.

Harriet Bender indicated she had no questions, but Joe asked to also cross-examine.

Will held his breath.

"You were saying how I said some things when I was arrested—was that said to you, or to the officers—wasn't it to the officers? And didn't I say some things also to you?"

Putnam jumped up and Bender followed, both objecting to the question being compound.

"Sustained," Judge Trainer said and commented, "I know you are not a lawyer, Mr. Fellows—but if you insist on representing yourself, you'll be bound by the same rules as everybody else. Ask single, separate questions."

Joe tried again.

"What else did I say to you..."

"I believe that you were muttering something about a government conspiracy—and then you asked me something. You asked me—and this is a quote—'Why did you come to my farm in an automobile—don't you usually ride on a broomstick'?"

Will cringed and jotted two minus signs on his notes. Several reporters in the audience broke into laughter.

Judge Trainer gaveled the courtroom into silence and admonished the reporters.

Putnam was grinning. He paused for a minute—wondering whether to let things end there, or whether he should try to put the icing on the cake.

"Just a few more questions—on redirect," Putnam announced.

"Ms. Luden, you said that Mrs. Fellows had fled from the farm and that Mr. Fellows said he was glad about it, and then angrily accused you of being part of a government conspiracy—do I have that correct?"

"Exactly," Luden answered.

"Had you announced your arrival? In other words, had you warned the Fellowses why you were coming that day—or indeed, *that* you would be coming?"

"No—we didn't want to take the chance. We arrived without notice."

"So," Putnam asked, "can you explain then what caused Mrs. Fellows to run away so fast—and drag little Joshua along with her—if she couldn't have known why you were there?"

Will objected, but the judge overruled him.

"Yes, I have an explanation."

"Please share that with us."

"She fled from the farm because she knew she was guilty of child abuse—and Joshua was the proof of that, so she had to take him along."

"Thank you," Putnam said, and sat down with a flourish and a grin.

"Re-cross?" Will inquired.

The judge nodded.

"No notice to Mr. or Mrs. Fellows?" Will asked.

"That is correct. The sheriff's deputies and I arrived at the Fellows farm without prior notice."

"But let me see if I understand—Mary Sue had been cooperative previous to that in giving you access, at your request, to Joshua's medical records?"

"Yes."

"And she had permitted you to interview her and her family physician, Dr. Wilson?"

"That's right."

"And she had articulated some reasons why she had lost confidence in Dr. Wilson and was seeking a second opinion?"

"Correct."

"And you knew that money was tight for the family and that it would take some time to raise the money for a second opinion that wasn't covered by insurance. Right?"

"That was our assumption."

"So when you felt enough time had gone by and Mrs. Fellows hadn't secured a second opinion, that's when you and two squad cars came swooping down?"

"Hardly—by that time, we had also received the anonymous phone call and secured the lab results from Dr. Parker, the pathologist," Luden responded. And then she added, "You make it sound sinister, Mr. Chambers. It was an emergency situation— we had to act immediately to rescue Joshua."

"An emergency?"

"Absolutely."

"To rescue Joshua?"

"Yes, that is what I said."

Will pulled out his copy of the Social Services file, and glanced at it.

"That's interesting," he commented, "because the anonymous call came in a full four days before you swept down onto the Fellows farm—correct?"

Luden looked at her file, then answered curtly, "Yes. Correct."

"And Dr. Parker's report was given to you a full three days before you decided to bring the sheriff's deputies over to the farm in an attempt to grab Joshua and place the parents under arrest?"

"'Grab' is not the right word. But yes, your timetable is correct."

"During those full three days you had left, you could have called Mary Sue and asked to interview her—and get her side of things first?"

"Anything is possible," Luden snapped.

"You could have done that?" Will demanded, his voice ringing.

"Yes."

"But you chose not to?"

"We chose not to."

"And then, when your county vehicle and the two squad cars approached the house, was it slowly—or did you arrive at high speed?"

"We were making good time."

"The three vehicles drove down the driveway so fast, in fact, that they were spinning tires, spitting gravel, and sending clouds of dust up in the air?"

"Probably."

"And then after you had seen that Mary Sue was gone and Joe Fellows had been arrested, there was a court appearance?"

"Yes."

"An ex parte hearing—without notice to me as Mary Sue's attorney?"

"There were reasons for that…"

"And you knew, and the district attorney's office knew by then, that my office was representing Mary Sue—yet you met behind closed doors with Judge Mason—you, and Mr. Putnam, and Ms. Bender here—*without notice to or participation by me as Mary Sue's attorney?*"

"That is why it is called an ex parte hearing, yes."

"And you actually wonder—and Mr. Putnam here wonders—why Mary Sue, a mother whose whole life is her family, panicked after being treated like that, and took flight with her little boy?"

Putnam and Bender leaped up, but Will cut them off.

"Your Honor, that was admittedly a rhetorical question—I withdraw it."

Liz Luden was excused, and as she whisked past Will's spot at counsel table, he could feel the polar winds blowing.

Joe gave Will a hopeful, searching look. But it was too early—the attorney had no definite feelings about the case yet.

He took his legal pad and jotted down a plus sign.

And then he followed that with something else—an even larger note on his legal pad.

It was a question mark.

55

THE SECOND WITNESS called by the county was Dr. Wilson, the physician for the Fellows family.

He was a general practitioner in the Delphi area and had been for fourteen years, he testified. He had treated Joe Fellows, Mary Sue Fellows, and of course Joshua.

The doctor listed the symptoms for Joshua—some developmental delays, listlessness, low-grade fever, problems eating, nausea, loss of appetite. He admitted that such symptoms were not entirely uncommon—the point was to diagnose and treat them, he emphasized.

"Are those symptoms consistent with certain kinds of poisoning?" Putnam asked.

"All except the developmental delays—that symptom not so much, unless the poisoning was done incrementally, over a long period of time."

"Did you prescribe a series of tests?"

"Yes."

"Blood tests?"

"Yes. At one point we had Joshua admitted to the Delphi hospital as an outpatient to do some tests. Blood tests."

"Did you recommend to Mary Sue Fellows some other tests?"

"Yes. I wanted to do a moderately invasive gastrointestinal procedure to rule out some differential diagnoses..."

"Did you have a specialist who was going to do that?"

"Yes," Dr. Wilson replied, "but it did not happen."

"Why not?"

"Mary Sue refused to permit it."

"Did you consider talking to her husband to convince him—or even seeking a court order?"

"At the time, no. In retrospect, I wish I had come to you people sooner."

"What reason did Mary Sue give for her refusal?"

"She said she didn't think I knew what I was doing. She was fearful of complications for Joshua, and the painfulness of the procedure. And she didn't think it was gastrointestinal."

"Did she say anything else?"

"Yes—something that really bothered me."

"What was that?"

"She said—and I recall this very well—Mary Sue said she was 'giving Joshua to God.' That's exactly what she said."

"Do you know what she meant by that?"

"Objection—speculation!" Will rapped out.

The judge overruled the objection.

"I was afraid that she might have made a decision—a very frightening decision—that somehow Joshua would be better off in heaven with God."

"Is that when you called the Department of Social Services?"

"That's what I did, yes."

Putnam concluded his direct examination and sat down with a satisfied smile.

As Will began his examination, he walked to the lectern and opened a large notebook of medical records in front of him.

"The symptoms you noted for Joshua—you mentioned them for Mr. Putnam. Do you recall them?"

"Yes, I do," the doctor responded.

"All of them—taken together as one constellation of physical symptoms—would be consistent with a medical condition known as methylmalonic acidemia, is that correct?"

"Actually, I've never treated any child with that condition. It's rather rare."

"Exactly. You were not looking for that condition, right?"

"It was not the first thing on my radar screen, diagnostically, that's right."

"But you must have read the medical literature about that condition? Let's call it by its first letters for short—MA."

"I had read—once, I believe—something about methylmalonic acidemia. But remember, Mr. Chambers, I am board-certified in *family* medicine—not in the more esoteric diseases. That is for the specialists."

"So—do you agree that Joshua's symptoms were consistent with MA?"

After a moment, Dr. Wilson nodded in agreement.

"Yes, to the extent I understand that particular medical condition."

"Now. Mary Sue's comment about God—did you take it literally?"

"I'm not sure I understand..."

"Well, a few seconds ago you used the phrase 'on my radar screen,' did you not?"

"Yes. A figure of speech."

"Right. Exactly," Will said. "But you really don't have a radar screen in your office, do you?"

"Of course not," Dr. Wilson said, turning to the bench for some relief from what he considered an absurd line of questioning, but finding none.

Judge Trainer continued sitting expressionless.

"So why," Will continued, "didn't you simply interpret Mary Sue's comments about 'giving Joshua to God' in the same way? In other words, that she was committing Joshua's medical problems to God through prayer, in addition to the medical care she was seeking? Why, instead, did you insist on believing she might kill her own son? Did you really think she would put him on a stone altar and sacrifice him to God?"

Bender jumped up first this time, with Putnam coming in second.

"Argumentative! Compound question also! We object to this—"

Judge Trainer motioned for them to sit down.

"The question does have some problems, Mr. Chambers. But I see where you're heading. Doctor—why did you take Mary Sue so literally?"

"You really had to be there, Your Honor. This woman had refused the GI procedure I wanted to have done, she was hostile toward me, and the look in her eyes when she said it all—it really sent chills down my spine."

The judge nodded for Will to continue.

"*The look in her eyes?* You invoked the police power of the County of Juda upon the life and domestic tranquility of this family because of *the look in her eyes?*"

"It was not just that..."

"But it included that. You just said that."

"Yes, her look, her presentation of herself, everything."

"But there was something else, wasn't there?" Will followed quietly.

"I don't know what you mean."

"There was another reason you called Social Services down on this family, is that not correct?"

"I'm still baffled, sir, by your question," the doctor responded, now shifting a little in the witness chair, but being careful to hold himself upright, shoulders back.

"Is it a fact that you called Social Services because you did not want to be sued for medical malpractice—again—for another child-abuse case?"

"Absolutely not! And I deeply resent that insinuation. I was not sued for malpractice for a child-abuse case."

"Oh, is that true?"

"Yes. I was not sued."

Will pulled some papers out of his file.

"Would it refresh your memory to review the Civil Complaint filed in The Estate of T.O., A Deceased Minor Child, By His

Guardian, Versus The Delphi Family Clinic, And Dr. Ruttaluse, And Dr. Wilson?"

"I'm familiar with that lawsuit, but I need to explain..."

"The fact is that your partner, Dr. Ruttaluse, was the treating doctor for a child brought in repeatedly with bruises and injuries, who was finally killed by the live-in boyfriend of the mother. And it hit the news—and your clinic, including you as partner, were sued. Correct?"

Putnam objected wildly, but since Bender was talking and waving her arms at the same time, pointing to Will, the only words that could be deciphered in the melee were "outrageous" and "admonish."

Judge Trainer ruled quickly and decisively.

"We are not going to rehash that Estate of T.O. case—I am well aware of it. And I am sure Dr. Wilson is too. Doctor, please answer the question."

"Yes—a child treated by Dr. Ruttaluse was killed. It was child abuse—our clinic was sued—and I was named in that suit merely as a technicality."

"And so you vowed that you—and your clinic—would not be involved in another debacle like that again. So you figured you would always err on the side of calling Social Services—and whenever you had the least problem with the parent of a pediatric patient, you would always just throw the ball to Social Services. Am I right?"

"I don't like the term 'throw the ball...'"

"How about *'throw the parent'*? You tossed Mary Sue Fellows to the Department of Social Services because of your concern over malpractice suits—and your malpractice-insurance premiums?"

"I *referred* Mary Sue Fellows over to Social Services. I don't appreciate being sued, Mr. Chambers. No doctor does. It is a sad fact that we have to practice defensive medicine occasionally."

"You were practicing defensive medicine with Joshua, then?"

Dr. Wilson lowered his gaze toward the medical file that lay in his lap. And then he answered.

"I did what I had to do..."

"As did Mary Sue," Will concluded.

56

THE FINAL WITNESS of the day was Otis Tracher. The county called him to recount the forensic evidence that had been taken from the Fellows house.

Tracher sat down in the witness chair slowly. He rubbed his chin and then straightened up the police file on his lap.

The Juda County Sheriff's Department veteran described how, a few hours after the arrest of Joseph Fellows, the department had performed a forensic sweep of the inside of the house—and particularly the kitchen. One item of note, he indicated, was a plastic child's cup that was found near the kitchen table.

The detective recounted a statement that Joe Fellows had made immediately after being taken into custody. After Joe was read his rights, he was asked if Mary Sue was the one who always fed little Joshua.

"Joe Fellows indicated," Tracher said, reviewing the supplemental report in front of him, "that Mary Sue always fed Joshua—and that she did indeed use the little plastic cup to give him orange juice."

"Now, that forensic sweep of the kitchen—did it also include taking that little plastic child's cup into evidence?"

"Yes, it did."

Harry Putnam held a plastic bag up, high enough for everyone in the courtroom to see. Inside the plastic bag there was a white plastic cup.

Then he had the detective identify the evidence bag and the cup inside.

"That is the same cup we removed from the kitchen," Tracher confirmed.

From his table, Putnam retrieved a written report from the state forensics lab that had already been marked with an exhibit sticker. The prosecutor had his witness identify it as the report generated by the crime lab after their examination of the cup.

"What were the results of that test?" Putnam asked.

"Two substances were present on the cup."

"What were they?"

"One was residue from a fruit-based liquid, high in acid, noted to be orange juice."

At this point Harry Putnam walked to front and center in the courtroom. His arms were folded across his chest.

"Would you also tell the court what else the crime lab found in the cup?"

Tracher glanced down at the report. Then he looked up.

"The report also notes the presence of hydraulic brake fluid—including a component called ethylene glycol."

"So, both orange juice—and poisonous brake fluid—both found in the same cup?"

The detective's mind seemed to be wandering. He asked for the question to be repeated.

"Orange juice—found to be in that cup?"

"Yes," he confirmed. "I'm sorry, I was thinking of something else. Yes. Orange juice was noted in the cup."

"As well as hydraulic brake fluid?"

"Yes. That was also found on the cup."

Then the prosecutor lifted the plastic bag with the white cup up high again.

"Detective, did you note that this was a child's cup—a cup used by a little child, in fact a little boy?"

"Yes."

"How did you know that?"

"Because of the markings."

"What markings?"

"It had a picture of a little teddy bear on the outside."

"Anything else?"

"The name 'JOSHUA' was printed on the outside—like the way you can get a child's name put on a toy."

"So a little teddy-bear picture and little Joshua's name are on the cup—the same cup with the hydraulic brake fluid?"

"That's correct."

Putnam rested, and Harriet Bender had just a few questions.

"Did you take steps to ensure that you did not contaminate that cup during the forensic sweep of the kitchen?"

"We took all of the standard steps to make absolutely sure there was no contamination."

"In other words," Bender continued, "if Mr. Chambers here argues that maybe that brake fluid got in the cup accidentally—by you picking up some oil or brake fluid on your hands in the garage of the Fellows house and then inadvertently touching the cup—you have an answer for that?"

"Yes, Ms. Bender. I am sure we did not contaminate the cup. We put it into the plastic bag exactly the way it was when we found it."

"And the plastic bag—the one you put it in—was it clean?"

"We use one-hundred-percent sterile evidence bags. The cup was not contaminated in any way by the law enforcement folks who went through the house."

Bender rested by giving a kind of salute to the detective and sitting down noisily at the counsel table next to Harry Putnam.

Will thought back momentarily to his interviews with Mary Sue. She had never given him any information about how brake fluid had gotten near the cup. And Joe Fellows had said flatly that he'd intended to put brake fluid into the truck—but had never gotten around to it.

Further, there was no doubting the validity of the crime-lab report. Will had gone over it in excruciating detail while preparing for trial. He had to reconcile himself to the fact that his client had given him nowhere to go on this line of questioning.

He glanced at Otis Tracher. The detective was certainly giving the impression he wished he were anywhere else but there. At the bench, the judge was stretching and sitting himself up straighter. One of the onlookers in the courtroom coughed.

Then Will looked down at his notes again.

He examined what he'd written down during Tracher's testimony and compared it with the questions Putnam had asked.

Then Will's head snapped down to his legal pad—this time so quickly that Bender and Putnam glanced over at him curiously.

"Are you cross-examining, Mr. Chambers?" the judge asked.

Will nodded. Then he rose to his feet with his yellow legal pad in hand.

"Mr. Putnam asked you—repeatedly—about what was *in* the cup according to the forensic report. Do you recall that?"

"Yes. He just asked me about it all."

"And you said that the liquid identified as orange juice was *in* the cup, as determined by the crime lab?"

"That was my testimony."

"And Mr. Putnam asked you whether the presence of hydraulic brake fluid was noted *in* the cup. Right?"

"He did ask me that."

"But," Will went on, "according to my notes here—you answered that the brake fluid was noted *on* the cup. Is that correct?"

Tracher glanced over at Putnam. There was fatigue—or something like it—on his face. Then he looked back at Will.

"The crime-lab report itself does not indicate precisely where the toxin—the brake fluid—was found."

Will could have stopped there. The point was to create some doubt about the exact location of the toxin in relation to the cup. If he stopped there, it might raise a sufficient doubt so that the judge would conclude that, somehow, the brake fluid had gotten on the cup accidentally.

But he didn't stop there. This was not a by-the-book case. He had no client sitting next to him. Instead, he had the husband of his client sitting next to him—in jail orange.

And his client had fled the state.

Will was about to ask the question. The question you're not supposed to ask—at least, not if you are an experienced trial attorney.

"Never ask a question that you don't know the answer to," he was told in law school.

But now he was going to do exactly that.

"Detective," he continued. "About that last statement you made..."

Tracher's eyes were now riveted on Will.

"Do you know *where*—in reference to the cup's exterior or interior—the brake fluid was found to be present?"

"Yes—I did find that out."

"How did you determine that?"

"When I saw that the crime lab report *did* specify that the orange juice was found *inside* the cup—but did *not* specify whether the *brake fluid* was inside or outside the cup—I went over to the crime lab myself to talk to the head of the forensics unit who did the test. And that's when he told me."

Putnam had his hands planted down on his counsel table, elbows out, as if he were an Olympic sprinter ready to fly out of the blocks. Bender was staring, blank-faced, waiting to see if Will was going to ask the question.

There was no sound in the courtroom.

Will cleared his throat. This was it.

"Detective," he asked, "what did the head of the crime lab tell you about where in relation to the cup the brake fluid was found?"

Chaos broke out. Putnam leaped up, and his feet actually came off the ground for a moment. Bender also tried to jump up, but in doing so she knocked her chair over.

"Don't you say a word," Putnam yelled at Tracher. "Your Honor, we object. Hearsay. This is hearsay. This is a question that cannot be answered except by having the head of the crime lab here personally. We did not call him because we are admitting the report under the rules of evidence."

"Then I'll call him," Will said.

"Can't," Putnam shouted out. "He is out of the country traveling for several weeks."

"Then," the judge asked, "doesn't that bring into play the exceptions to hearsay when the declarant is not available?"

"No sir—no sir, Your Honor," Bender jumped in loudly. "None of those exceptions apply here. None. None of them."

The judge looked at Will. But this time—perhaps for the first time during the entire Mary Sue Fellows case—he had to agree with Harriet Bender.

"I'm afraid that Ms. Bender is correct on that," the attorney said quietly.

The judge leaned back in his chair and glanced over the courtroom—but he was looking nowhere in particular.

"However," Will added, "there is one final consideration. The rules of evidence list numerous exceptions to hearsay. We are all familiar with them. But the rules have also created a catch-all exception. Often argued, but rarely applied. The rules talk about 'other circumstantial guarantees of trustworthiness.' I think that means this—if we can all look at the statement that detective Tracher is about to share and know that it came from a highly reliable source, under circumstances that are virtually guaranteed to be trustworthy—then the purposes behind the hearsay rule have been met. Justice is done. The statement can be described by the detective to this court. After all, this is about justice, Your Honor. My client's fundamental right as a parent of Joshua is a hollow right if a healthy measure of justice is not applied to protect it."

Judge Trainer pursed his lips together and thought for a few long seconds.

Then he ruled.

"Detective," he said.

"Yes," Tracher answered.

"Answer the question."

Bender stood up.

"I doubt he remembers the question after all this," she said with an attempt at a laugh. "Perhaps Mr. Chambers should resubmit the question in a different form. Have another go at it. That way defense counsel could ask the question in a way that *we all could understand* this time."

"I remember the question exactly," the detective stated.

Then, after another slight pause, he answered.

"The fact is, the crime-lab chief told me that the brake fluid was found on the exterior portion of the cup, and a minute amount was found on the lip of the cup. But there was *no brake fluid at all inside the cup*."

Joe Fellows hung his head down, muttering something and smiling.

Judge Trainer adjourned for the day, but he warned the audience to be more compliant with his directives about noise when they resumed the next day.

When the judge and court reporter had exited, Harriet Bender took a few steps toward Will Chambers as guard Thompson was escorting Joe out of the courtroom and back to this cell.

Then Bender opened up.

"All of that..." she said, waving vaguely around the courtroom, "this afternoon. Your cross of the witnesses. Of detective Tracher. Nothing—a big lot of nothing. A lot of noise. Two facts remain. First, Dr. Parker's opinion places the brake fluid *in Joshua's bloodstream. In his bloodstream.* Only one thing explains that. Someone fed it to that kid. And you and I both know who did that. Maybe Mary Sue washed the brake fluid out of the inside of the cup to hide her tracks. Don't know. Don't care. Dr. Parker's opinion is going to nail this thing. We both know that."

"What's your second fact?"

"Your client's not here. If that isn't a picture of guilt, I don't know what is."

"What's really on your mind, Harriet?" Will asked.

"I came over here to offer you a deal. I think that Putnam would be willing to drop this whole thing if your client simply agrees to stipulate to cause for a temporary extension of child custody by the department. We will give your client the standard list of conditions she has to meet—parenting classes, counseling, supervised visitation with Joshua for a couple months. If she's a good girl and does everything to our satisfaction, she and Joe will get custody of Joshua back."

"I'll tell you what I think," Will replied. "My client did not do this thing. But someone is trying hard to make it look like she did."

"You really are nuts." Bender shook her head athletically, grabbed her briefcase, and walked hastily out of the courtroom.

57

As WILL RETURNED TO THE houseboat for the night, he was feeling momentarily optimistic about the course of the trial. He still had reservations, though, in two areas.

First, there was the problem of Dr. Parker's opinion about Joshua's blood test. Harriet Bender *was* right about that. If Judge Trainer felt there was any credible evidence that Joshua's blood contained an unexplained toxin, then the burden shifted. The defense would have to account for it. They could do it with Dr. Forrester's testimony, but Judge Trainer still had not decided whether to permit that testimony.

The only other way, it seemed, was to have his client testify in court—to explain, if she could, how the poison made its way into Joshua's bloodstream. It could not have been accidental—Mary Sue had assured Will that Joshua was never out of her sight. And that he was certainly never allowed to be near the chemicals and other dangerous materials in the garage.

Here was the mystery—almost as opaque and incomprehensible as the reason why Mary Sue had not been open and forthright with Will about the facts of her case.

In any event, it seemed that she would not be appearing at trial. That created the indelible impression—like it or not—that his client was hiding something.

Will threw a frozen dinner into the microwave and sat down at the little table in the kitchenette, waiting for the timer to let him know it was done.

He rubbed his eyes. Suddenly he was very tired. Things were catching up to him. Maybe he should make a quick call to Fiona, he thought, before it got too late—patch things up again—*maybe*.

His headaches were back with a vengeance. Maybe he would lie down and sleep for a while. Then call Fiona, when his mind was clear, and he was less liable to put his foot in his mouth.

Outside, the sky had turned gray and the air was heavy. A breeze started blowing through the houseboat's small windows. Within minutes a light rain started drifting down onto the lake, followed by the rumbling of distant thunder.

Then the phone rang. It was Mary Sue.

Through the poor reception on the line, Will told her it was urgent that they talk before the second day of trial. He gave her a thumbnail sketch of how court had gone that day.

"I will not be there to testify," Mary Sue responded.

While this did not surprise Will intellectually, something in his insides started churning at the thought of having to win this case with no client to tell her story.

The question was—what was her story?

"You've got to tell it to me straight," Will said firmly. "Everything. I need to know the whole story—now."

Mary Sue launched into a prolonged introduction—an apology of sorts. She knew that Will might think that the reason for her nondisclosure of facts was silly—even stupid—and mindless. But long after this case was over, she would still have to do everything possible to ensure a happy marriage with Joe.

Will listened patiently, but he urged Mary Sue to tell him some facts that would help him make sense of the case against her.

She had called Jason Bell Purdy, she started out. She hadn't talked to him in a while. The last time before that had been at a benefit dinner for the Delphi hospital. A new wing was being opened, partly due to a generous donation from the Purdy Trust. Mary Sue and the rest of the nursing staff were there. Jason, in tux and black tie, was also. He was given a ceremonial key to the hospital and made a few comments that charmed the crowd.

Then the group had retired to the banquet hall. Jason had deliberately moved his place card to her table so he could sit with her. They made small talk, she said. Nothing significant. But he was, she commented, "the same old Jason—still on the prowl.

"Because Henry Pencup had died on my shift recently, someone at the table—one of the nurses—made a point of talking about it. I didn't think it was appropriate to be talking about a patient's care at the banquet table—even if he had died.

"Then one of the nurses—I think it was my supervisor, Dorothy Atkinson—she has a thing against me anyway—says loudly, 'Hey Mary Sue—didn't he die on your shift? You were right there in the room with him and that priest, weren't you?'"

His client's voice grew very strained.

"Jason gave me a really funny look. He bent over, close to my ear, and tried to talk a little about it. But I just avoided the issue. The whole thing was very uncomfortable.

"Then a few days after the banquet, Jason called me at the hospital and left a message with Dorothy, my supervisor. But I didn't return the call.

"It wasn't long after that call that Dr. Wilson called Social Services, which brought the county down on us. I pleaded with Joe to hire an attorney to try to resolve things over their interference with Joshua.

"But Joe was adamant," Mary Sue continued. "Money was tight. That was his same refrain, all the time. We simply couldn't afford to get legal counsel. In fact, he kept saying he didn't know how we could afford a second medical opinion for Joshua, considering it wouldn't be covered by our insurance."

"So you got back in touch with Purdy and asked him for money?"

"No," Mary Sue answered quickly. "It wasn't that. I kept saying we needed a lawyer to get Social Services off our backs. Working in the hospital, I had seen what happens when things go bad in a Social Services custody case. But Joe said no. I sulked. He kept saying no. So—then I did what I now regret."

"What?"

"I called up Jason at his office in Atlanta. I told him a little bit about it. I said we couldn't afford a lawyer—but we needed someone with clout to straighten things out with Social Services before things really got out of hand. Frankly, Jason knows everybody in high places in this part of the state. I figured that he could just pick up the phone and make things happen."

"So what did he do for you?"

"Well, apparently he made some calls. He told me he was talking to people—he didn't say who. But he said he had to meet with me to discuss it."

"Did you?" Will asked.

"I remember the day all too well. It was about a week before the sheriff's deputies and Social Services came tearing up to our house. Jason said we had to meet. It was urgent. It was about Joshua, he said."

"What happened?"

"Jason wanted me to drive to his mansion. I knew that was not a good idea. You have to realize how crazy jealous Joe has always been of Jason and me. I knew he would absolutely freak if he knew I was talking to Jason, let alone driving to his house. But I was really scared about Social Services. I kept telling myself that pretty soon Jason would take care of it—and it would be all over."

"Did you go?"

"I tried to. Joe was going to be gone all day at a meeting of the farmers' co-op board. He was taking the good truck. The older truck was still in the garage. He'd said all it needed was some brake fluid—it was dangerous to drive otherwise because the brakes were so mushy. But he just never got around to it."

"So you put the brake fluid in yourself?"

"Yes," Mary Sue said with a deep sigh. "Spilled it. Made a huge mess. I was so angry. Mostly at Joe, I guess. That he hadn't taken care of the truck like he promised. But then, the real irony is this—I try to start the truck and the battery is dead. I was furious and frustrated. I called Jason crying. I said we couldn't meet because of the truck. I pleaded with him to help. I was so incredibly naïve. Jason says in that smooth, good-little-boy voice of his—'Mary Sue, you have no worries. I'm going to drive over to your farm myself. So you and I can work this Social Services stuff out.' Of course he suggested that when I told him Joe would be gone all day."

"Did he come—to your house?"

"Certainly. And I told him about the truck. About spilling brake fluid all over myself. Tracking it into the kitchen. I'd cleaned it up the best I could. I must have touched Joshua's cup. Anyway, Jason was right there listening to me spill all of this information. I told him Joe would do something drastic if he found out that Jason was in our house. Jason just smiled and said, 'Nobody needs to know I was here.'"

"For heaven's sake—why didn't you tell me this at the beginning?" Will demanded.

"And then explain everything about Jason?"

"What do you mean?"

"When Jason was at my house he didn't want to talk at all about Social Services or helping me. He kept asking me about Henry Pencup. And the priest. And everything that Pencup had said before he died. On and on about that."

"What did you tell him?"

"I told him the truth—at first. That I really hadn't heard much of anything. I'd just happened to be there when the cardiac arrest took place."

"Did he believe you?"

"I don't know. Because then he started getting…this is very tough for me to say."

"I need to hear," Will said gently but firmly.

"He tried to put his arms around me. Joshua is sitting right there on the floor playing. I'm in my jeans and work clothes, and he starts pawing me. I really couldn't believe it was happening. His hands were all over me. Like I was a cheap date he'd picked up at a bar. I pushed him away. He kept coming at me, touching me. Finally I hauled off and slapped him. Hard, too. I think I left a mark."

"How did it end?"

"That was the scary part. I thought I knew Jason. I was aware he was always going after the ladies. And me. But I figured that down deep he was a gentleman—just consider the family legacy he came from. Well, that day I learned differently. He looked at me with such a look—almost demonic. That's the only way I can describe it. He says, 'I'm going to ask only one more time—what did you hear Henry Pencup say?' And this is where I was so wrong. So stupid. I wanted to get his goat."

"What did you tell him?" Will asked.

"I led him on, just to get back at him. I said, 'Wouldn't you like to know?' As if I really knew something. The fact is, I didn't."

"He left?"

"Like a snake slithering out of the house. He gets in his Porsche and zooms off."

"Is that the last you saw of him?"

"That is the last time we talked."

There was a long pause. Then Mary Sue spoke again.

"Where does this leave us?"

"I have a feeling that if we checked the Unemployment Department records in the Atlanta district, we would get the identity of a woman fired by Jason Purdy—terminated shortly before she called me and gave me that ambiguous tip. It's all falling into place."

"Will, do you have any idea how I struggled with telling you this?"

"I think so," Will said. Then he added, "Honestly, I'm having a problem figuring it out."

"I tell you, then my husband finds out. He never trusts me again. And you can't use Jason to prove any of this to help my case—because he would lie on the stand without blinking. He would deny it."

"That last bit I can certainly agree with."

"And after all of that—what would I be gaining?" Mary Sue said, pleading in her voice.

"I'm your attorney, not your marriage counselor," Will said. "But I'm going to give you some advice. You need to tell your husband all of this. No matter what happens. It also sounds like Jason may have committed sexual assault—"

"Will, come on. Do you really think that a simple farm wife like me, accused of child abuse, could make a charge like that stick against Jason Bell Purdy?"

"There is nothing simple about you," Will replied. "You love your husband. You are deeply devoted to your son. You've tried to follow God's leading on this. And you've been facing a horrendous injustice almost entirely on your own. My hat's off to you. But you do need to do something else."

"Why do I think I know what you're going to say?"

"You need to come home."

"Joshua is already there."

"In Delphi?"

"At the hospital. We had him airlifted. Joe's mom is staying with him."

"But he needs his mother."

Mary Sue started weeping. Then she said, "I know."

"Where are you now?" Will asked.

"Still on the road. Do me a favor and just win that case for me tomorrow. I need my family."

The static on the telephone line was getting worse. Now the rain was coming down hard over the lake, in sheets.

Will quickly reviewed with Mary Sue the remaining witnesses for the county, who were scheduled for the next day: Bob Smiley, the insurance agent—Dr. Parker, the pathologist—and Dorothy Atkinson, Mary Sue's nursing supervisor.

As he wrapped up the conversation, a final thought popped up.

"Did you remember any words—anything that Henry Pencup said?"

Mary Sue thought for a few seconds. "There was only gibberish. He was in tremendous pain."

"What kind of gibberish?"

"Actually, there were two kind-of-nonsensical things he kept saying to me. What were they?"

Mary Sue took a minute or two. Will watched the upper reaches of the sky flash with lightning, deep within the storm clouds.

"I think it was…'insecure'…and the other one—let's see—it was 'unsign.'"

"You're sure?"

"Pretty sure."

Will thought for a minute. He wanted to get clarification. Something more—anything. But the telephone line crackled, and then it went dead.

As the thunder rolled and rumbled, Will went to the window. He could smell the water in the air, and the pines, as he listened to the shimmering waves of rain falling on the surface of the lake.

Insecure.

Unsign.

Will repeated those words over and over. There was a message inside those cryptic references made by a dying bank president. A message perhaps as clear as the confession he had made to Father Godfrey.

It was late when Will stumbled his way into bed, exhausted. He had not had a chance to call Fiona. And he still was trying to figure out Jason Bell Purdy's enigmatic involvement in Mary's Sue's case. He knew that Purdy wanted to destroy her credibility—at all costs. But why? There were no connections between Henry Pencup—or his bank—and the Eden Lake Resort. So, why Purdy's obsession with Pencup?

One thing he did know. Unless he performed a legal vivisection on each of the county's witnesses the following day, his client might never enjoy the security of her family again.

58

Bob Smiley was not smiling. His face had the look of a turkey before Thanksgiving. He fidgeted in the stand, stretching his neck out and tugging at his tie.

"Now you were telling us," Harry Putnam said, "about the insurance policy. Mary Sue asked for it to be written up."

"Yes."

"And you wrote it for $100,000?"

"I sure did. Did it myself. Submitted it to the life insurance company per Mary Sue's request."

"And the policy was issued?"

"I'm not sure. I think that the full premium wasn't paid—so it may have been cancelled, ultimately."

"But as of the date that Joshua was sick, and they took him to the Delphi hospital and took blood from him—you'll recall that we established that date?"

"Yes."

"About that same time is when Mary Sue made the insurance application for $100,000 on the life of Joshua—listing herself and her husband as sole beneficiaries in the event of Joshua's death?"

"I think you've got that right. Correct."

"Did your insurance company have concerns about that?"

"Well, that particular company wasn't doing physical exams for children's life-insurance policies. We just asked the parents to check a list of boxes about a whole long list of disabilities, and whether they knew the child to have any—you know—cancer, AIDS, things like that."

"As you mentioned, was the insurance policy cancelled—you think—for nonpayment of premiums?"

"Yes."

"When?"

"Well, after Mary Sue left the area and Joe was arrested, the remaining portion of the premium was not paid. So it got cancelled."

"So Mary Sue fails to pay the premium after she knows the police are looking for her and the gig is up, right?"

Will could have jumped all over that one—but he deliberately let it go.

"It sure looks that way," Smiley confirmed.

"Is $100,000 an unusually high life-insurance policy to have on a young child?"

"I don't sell many that high on children—that's right."

Putnam rested. Harriet Bender waived any questions and then glared at Will.

Will began his cross-examination by asking permission to approach the witness. Once it was granted, he strode up to a position directly in front of the insurance agent. Then Will held out his hand, palm up.

Smiley gave him a strange look.

Will kept his hand outstretched.

"Did you bring it, Mr. Smiley?"

"What?"

"The very thing we demanded in the subpoena we served on you," Will answered.

"Oh, that?"

"Yes, Mr. Smiley. Your file on policy number 000258HGB, on the life of Joshua Fellows in the name of Joseph and Mary Sue Fellows."

"Not here I don't have it," Smiley replied.

"Where is it?" Will asked.

"It's on the bench there where I was sitting."

"Then please fetch it, Mr. Smiley. By all means."

The agent scurried down, grabbed the thin green folder, and returned, clutching it in his hand firmly.

"May I see it, please?" Will asked as courteously as he could. Smiley handed it over, throwing Will the kind of look one would expect from a schoolboy whose secret note to his girlfriend had just been intercepted by the teacher.

Will paged quickly through the file.

"Mr. Smiley, you took the information from Mary Sue, wrote up the application, and then submitted it to the insurance company?"

"That's exactly the way we do it."

"These application forms are standard?"

"Yep. Standard forms. I always use the same ones from that company. I am an independent insurance broker—so I can offer a range of different insurance products through different companies, depending on the individualized needs of the insured."

"The insured—that would be Mary Sue?"

"Technically—in the insurance industry—Joshua would be considered the insured. Mary Sue is one of the owners of the policy."

"What insurance needs did Joshua have, then?"

"Oh, that would be hard to say."

"What insurance needs did Mary Sue have?"

"That also is hard to say at this point—I can't recall."

"Those standard forms. Is it important to fill them out properly?"

"You bet it is. Otherwise the company sends the application right back."

"And with your experience, I'll bet you know exactly how to fill out those application forms?"

"Sure do."

"Dot all the I's and cross all the T's?"

"I think I do a pretty good job at it."

"Anything missing from this application form?" Will asked, handing the green file back to Bob Smiley.

The agent glanced at it.

"No, I think this is just about right. Uh-huh. Yep. This one's up to snuff."

"Sure?"

"Yes. It's all filled out correctly. Yep."

"What's at the bottom?"

"What do you mean?"

"There," Will said, pointing to the bottom of the application form.

"That," Smiley said, "appears to be a line."

"A blank line?"

"Yep."

"A line for Mary Sue Fellows' signature?"

"Yes sir, it does appear that way."

"Does her signature appear on that line?"

"Well...not on this one."

"What do you mean—*this* one?"

"This is not the original. The original is sent to the insurance company."

"But this is a carbonless copy, right?"

"Yes."

"The signature—if it was ever signed, which I think it was not—the signature would go through to the copy marked 'Agent's Copy.' Is that correct?"

"Ah...well, now—you have a point there."

"And the form says in bold letters, 'TO THE AGENT— MAKE SURE SIGNATURE GOES THROUGH ALL COPIES.'"

"Yes. It sure does."

"Mary Sue never signed this application form, did she?"

"Hard to tell. Very hard to tell."

"By the way, Mr. Smiley—did you win the sales contest this year for your company?"

"Not this year, I'm afraid. I came in runner-up."

"What was first prize?"

"An all-expense trip to Hawaii," and with that Smiley gave a faded smile.

"How do they tally the total volume of life insurance sales for that contest? By the amount applied for—or the amount actually issued out in the final policy after the premium is paid?"

Smiley paused and bounced his head a bit from side to side.

"Amount applied for."

"So if you send in an application for a $100,000 insurance policy for Mary Sue Fellows, the company gives you credit for that in the sales contest?"

"Yeah, that's right."

"Even if the client would later come back and say, 'Hey—I really only wanted $10,000—reduce the policy.' By then, you would have already been credited for the $100,000 you submitted. Right?"

More head-bouncing by Smiley.

"I guess so...I suppose so."

"Didn't you approach Mary Sue to sell her some insurance?"

"I may have actually made the originating call."

"And you told her that the cost of covering the funeral of a child would be about $10,000—so why didn't she think about taking out a policy in that amount?"

"Possibly. I can't recall everything..."

"And you said, 'It's the cheapest policy in the world—literally just a few dollars—and we'll bill you, no need to pay now—and by the way, I'm trying to win an insurance sales contest and I sure would appreciate your getting a policy.' That's about how it happened, correct?"

"Um...it may not have been in that order, exactly."

Will stared Smiley in the eye.

"But it was something like that."

The attorney continued. "You were an old high-school friend of Mary Sue's, weren't you?"

"Yeah. That's true."

"You liked her back then?"

"Yeah. A lot of people did."

"She was the kind of person that always liked helping people out, correct?"

"Oh, yeah. Softhearted. That was Mary Sue."

"In sales lingo—you would call her a 'soft touch'? An 'easy mark'?"

"I'm not sure I understand you there."

Will knew that Bob Smiley understood—and so did the judge, who at this point was adjusting his glasses and looking intently at the witness.

Before the agent retreated from the stand, Harry Putnam tried one more charge through the barricades.

"Is it a fact, Mr. Bob Smiley, that you signed up an insurance policy for $100,000 on the life of Joshua Fellows, with Mr. and Mrs. Fellows as beneficiaries—true or false?"

"True!" Smiley shouted out, as if it were a game show and he had finally heard the TV host call out a question he could nail with ease.

When the judge excused him, Bob Smiley scampered off the stand and walked directly out of the courtroom.

Without looking back.

59

"DOROTHY ATKINSON, MSN. Nursing supervisor at Delphi Hospital. I was Mary Sue's day supervisor."

After the preliminaries, Harry Putnam led the nurse into a series of questions that established her knowledge of Mary Sue's situation.

"Did you ever hear her despair over being able to continue handling her son's medical problems?"

"Several times."

"Can you give us one instance?"

"Yes—about the time Joshua was admitted for tests at the hospital as an outpatient. She seemed overstressed. Upset. She complained about the pressure on her marriage. She said she was tired of trying to manage Joshua's medical problems "

"Did she say that more than once?"

"Yes, quite a few times."

"Did she seem desperate?"

"I would say so."

"Did she get teary-eyed when she complained of being tired of handling Joshua's problems?"

"Yes. I believe she was crying."

"Did she complain of having to take care of her son's health problems all by herself—with not enough help from her husband?"

"I recall her saying that her husband was busy with the farm—and that the burden on her, handling things alone, was too much."

Harriet Bender rose slowly.

"Do you occasionally handle children who have suffered abuse at the hands of their parents?" she began.

"Unfortunately, I do."

"And you have dealt with parents of pediatric patients—parents who have committed child abuse or neglect?"

"Sadly, that also is true."

"Do you see any similarities between Mary Sue's emotional state and such parents?"

Will objected, expressing his disbelief that Bender would try to qualify Atkinson as a de facto expert in child abuse. But to his consternation, Judge Trainer seemed unmoved by the argument Will had advanced and calmly overruled the objection.

The nurse continued. "Yes, I would say that most of the abusive parents exhibit the same kind of frustration, despair, and exasperation as shown by Mary Sue. Those kinds of feelings often lead the unskilled parent into taking their frustrations out on the child."

Bender, though she looked tired, seemed satisfied enough with those answers, and she sat down.

Against a strong temptation to do otherwise, Will decided to avoid any mention of Atkinson's discussion of Henry Pencup's death at the hospital banquet, where she and Mary Sue had been in the presence of Jason Bell Purdy. At least with this witness, that would be wandering in the wilderness. He needed instead to stay focused and controlled.

"Do you deal with pediatric patients—children—who have chronic health problems?"

"Quite a few."

"And you work with the parents of such afflicted children?"

"Yes, of course."

"Would you agree that the vast majority of parents of children with chronic serious health problems exhibit 'frustration, despair, and exasperation' to the same degree that Mary Sue has?"

"I don't think that is a fair comparison."

"But you are familiar with the nursing literature that indicates that caring for a chronically ill child places a tremendous emotional, physical, and financial drain on the average parent?"

"I do read the nursing journals—that is true."

"If we assume that Joshua has MA—methylmalonic acidemia—would that qualify as a chronic disease?"

"From what I know about it, it would."

"And Mary Sue would be expected to display the same kind of emotional fatigue that parents of other chronically ill children display?"

"Well," the nurse responded, "that's an assumption—we don't know that Joshua has MA."

"But he is now back in your hospital, is he not?"

"Yes."

"He is?" the judge exclaimed, whirling toward Will.

"He was airlifted to the hospital at the directive of Mary Sue and her South Dakota doctor."

"That is where she was—South Dakota?" the judge asked.

The attorney nodded.

"So," Will continued, "Joshua is in your hospital, in your pediatric unit. Surely you know what the working diagnosis is, right?"

"We have the consulting report from Dr. Forrester...It was faxed to our unit—"

But before she could finish, Putnam was up, waving his arms to object. By that point, Bender seemed to have lapsed into fatigue and did not bother to rise to the occasion.

Judge Trainer cut to the chase. "Mr. Putnam, you called this witness—you opened the door to this area. And even if you hadn't, now that I know that the child is at the Delphi hospital, I certainly would have opened the door to this area of questioning myself. Please finish, Ms. Atkinson."

"Dr. Forrester's credentials are impeccable. His report indicates MA for Joshua—that's our working diagnosis."

Dorothy Atkinson was excused.

Now Will knew that the most important witness of the trial was about to be called.

But the judge looked at the big clock on the wall of the courtroom.

"Ladies and gentlemen, it's almost noon. Let's break for lunch—till one-fifteen. Then we will take the testimony of Dr. Parker."

The courtroom rose in a clatter of feet and chairs as the judge slipped into his chambers.

Will pressed his way through the crowd with files and notebooks under each arm. He jumped into his car and made it out to Denny's Log Cabin restaurant in time to beat the lunch crowd.

He ordered a steak sandwich and ginger ale while he made notes for his cross-examination of Dr. Parker and plotted out the argument he was planning to give at the close of the county's case.

The restaurant started filling up. Stanley Kennelworth trotted in with what appeared to be a client, smiling—until he locked gazes with Will. Then he quickly looked away.

In the noise of the crowd, Will was still grappling with his questions about Dr. Parker. And how Jason Purdy fit into the big picture. And he still had no idea about those last words of Henry Pencup—"insecure" and "unsign." What on earth could they mean, if anything?

He was finishing up when the waitress whisked by and dropped the check on the table. After he put his credit card out, she scooped it up and was back in a second with the charge slip.

A few minutes later she came by again. "Ready for me to take this, hon?"

Will nodded, distracted by the tangle of loose ends in the case.

"Say, hon," the waitress pointed out, "you forgot something."

"What?"

"You forgot to sign the slip. If I tried to pass this off to my boss I'd be in a whole lot of trouble."

Will nodded, took out his pen, and was just about to sign the slip—a contract authorizing his credit-card company to pay the sum of $7.43 to Denny's Log Cabin, which represented the value of a steak sandwich and a ginger ale. And by the terms of which Will agreed to pay that sum back to his credit-card company, with interest.

Then something opened up—a door of some kind.

Will stared at the unsigned slip.

Then he leaped to his feet and thrust it in front of the waitress.

"What if I were to *keep* this credit-card slip and not sign it—maybe even stick it in my pocket and throw it away at my house? And you agreed not to tell your boss, and I just walked out of here—what would that be?"

"That don't sound like too good an idea, hon," she replied with a confused look on her face.

"What would that be?"

"Theft, I guess," the waitress said sheepishly.

"Yes, it sure would be!" Will said exuberantly. "But—theft from whom?"

"My boss?" the waitress answered with a raised eyebrow.

Will was now talking excitedly under his breath, to no one in particular. "Why didn't I see it before? It wasn't '*insecure*'—it was '*unsecured*,' as in a multimillion-dollar *unsecured loan* from the Delphi bank, courtesy of poor Henry. But it never showed up on the records. Why not? Because, ladies and gentlemen, it was an *unsigned* loan—a phantom loan that didn't exist except in a private deal between Jason and Henry. Jason promised to return the several million he'd borrowed in a week or two, after he had quieted his angry subcontractors down—all in return for a huge under-the-table profit for Henry. Only one problem…"

By then, the waitress was looking around the room, wondering whether it might be wise to ask for help.

"But here's the problem… A week or two grows into several weeks, and then months, and the bank examiners start asking questions—'Henry, your bank is short several million dollars—where is it?' Henry has a heart attack, and when he dies, Jason figures his problem is over because there's no documentation for the secret deal. But there is a problem…"

The waitress was still standing there, stunned by her customer's indistinct rambling and not knowing whether or not to just leave him to his own self-absorbed narrative.

"The problem is," Will continued muttering to himself, "Henry wanted to tell someone the truth—anyone—because he was being accused of stealing the money himself. In truth he had made illegal loans—which is also criminal—but when you're a bank president I guess you still have your pride…"

By now the waitress was retreating toward the jukebox.

"So here is where Mary Sue comes in—of course! Jason thinks she's heard Henry spill the beans—he figures the word may leak out. He's got big political plans. Can't afford a scandal. Has to put Mary Sue away—stain her reputation—destroy her credibility. How to do it?"

The waitress was gradually edging farther away from her babbling customer.

"And then it happens. Mary Sue calls on him to help. She spoon-feeds him the actual evidence—the business about the brake fluid. Jason gets his staffer in his corporate headquarters—probably some poor girl he's promised a raise—to make the call to Social Services. Presto—child abuse."

The waitress had now moved off to what seemed to be a safer distance—and was pointing to the still-unsigned credit-card slip in Will's hand.

"But one call to Social Services wouldn't do it. He needed something else. Proof of poisoning. Lab results…Dr. Parker…"

Finally realizing he still had not signed the slip, Will scribbled his signature on it and walked up to the waitress. Taking her hand in his, he gave her the piece of paper and then thanked her.

"I want to express my deepest appreciation for everything you've done for me…" he told the waitress sincerely.

"Listen, hon—I'm married, okay?"

"And I hope to be married too—soon," the attorney replied.

Then he glanced at his watch, grabbed his files and notebooks, and ran out of the restaurant.

As Will drove out of the parking lot, the waitress was still staring in bewilderment at the door through which he had run.

60

Dr. Parker had run down his impressive list of credentials, to be followed by his testimony about Joshua's blood tests that had been performed at the Delphi hospital.

Prefacing these remarks, he declared firmly, "I am absolutely certain about the validity of my findings—"

"And what exactly are those findings?" Harry Putnam asked, punching each word as if he were socking a blow-up clown.

"My findings are that Joshua's blood contained dangerous levels of ethylene glycol—a chemical ingredient of hydraulic brake fluid."

"You're certain?"

"I am certain."

Before resting, the prosecutor spent thirty minutes having Dr. Parker describe each place the staff at the hospital had looked for the missing blood sample, each person interviewed, and each attempt to unearth the misplaced evidence. "We are as upset as you are," Dr. Parker intoned solemnly, "that we cannot find that sample. If it were found, then any expert in the world could verify the correctness of my findings."

Putnam sat down. Bender did nothing, having now almost completely relinquished the courtroom to the district attorney. The battle was now between Putnam and Will.

As Will rose to cross-examine Parker he had one huge challenge. He had to get the pathologist to retreat from the certainty of his conclusions. And it had to be a substantial retreat. Anything less would not do.

The attorney also knew that he had only one line of attack against Dr. Parker. But if he overplayed his hand by going directly after Jason Bell Purdy, the judge would undoubtedly admonish him.

If, however, he didn't get Parker to feel the heat, the court would never see the light.

"Most blood tests—simple ones of the kind that you did here—take just a few days. Is this the case?"

"Give or take—that's true."

"This one, however—this report—was not signed by you until weeks after the blood draw. Correct?"

"That is true. But it's not too remarkable—I believe we were understaffed and overworked at the time."

"Now, you were visited by someone in regard to Mary Sue Fellows' case?"

"You mean Mr. Putnam and Ms. Bender?"

"No."

"You mean the reporters?"

"No," Will said. "I mean Jason Bell Purdy."

"Yes—well, he is a longtime friend of Mary Sue's. He had heard of her problems with Social Services. Felt sorry for her...found out nothing could be done."

"The timing of your blood-test report is interesting. It is dated the day after Jason Bell Purdy came to talk to you, right?"

"Coincidentally, that is true."

"Was there an earlier blood-test result—one that was changed after Mr. Purdy met with you?"

Judge Trainer, almost uniformly impassive throughout the trial, was now almost aghast.

"Absolutely not!" Dr. Parker exclaimed. "How insane. Do you know what you are insinuating?"

"You were an investor in Eden Lake Resort—the development primarily owned by Jason Bell Purdy?"

Harry Putnam bounced up, sending a few pens and papers flying.

"No, Your Honor. Not in a million years...do I think this court will allow Mr. Chambers—who does not know, apparently, the rules of decorum of the courts in our State of Georgia—to besmirch the reputation of innocent people. Persons of high standing in not only our community, but our state. I think this is quite sad, for it really shows how desperately Mr. Chambers is trying to win this case, though knowing he has absolutely no defense."

"Your Honor," Will began slowly and cautiously, "I understand how fragile this line of questioning is. How careful I must be not to drag in unrelated issues. But there is an issue here of motivation—what motivated Dr. Parker to write the blood-test report the way he did. Please give me a limited opportunity to explore that."

Judge Trainer was not pleased. Somehow this unusual case was starting to metamorphose—to mushroom out of control.

"Only *very limited* opportunity, counsel," he said in a voice that bordered on scolding.

Will turned back to the witness.

"You were an investor in that project?"

"Yes. Along with dozens—maybe even hundreds—of others."

"Yet you were special?"

"I don't follow you."

"Mr. Purdy treated you differently."

"I was listed along with all other creditors in his bankruptcy," Dr. Parker replied. "How does that make me special?"

"Just this," Will said. "Reaffirmation."

"What?"

"The debt to you, though forgiven in bankruptcy, was later reaffirmed by Jason Bell Purdy. The other creditors received about twenty cents on the dollar—but you, Dr. Parker, because your debt was reaffirmed, were ultimately paid back one hundred cents on the dollar. I find that remarkable."

"Not really. I believe that Mr. Purdy was simply appreciative of my having been one of the original investors—that's why I received the preference."

"You did nothing else to gain the special bankruptcy privilege you just mentioned?"

"I'm not sure what you are driving at…" And with that Dr. Parker flexed his shoulders in an effort to relax.

"Your connection to the Eden Lake Resort. Your writing your lab report about Joshua Fellows—but only *after* a meeting with Jason Bell Purdy. And the ongoing criminal investigation into Delphi National Bank's missing money—money that folks are trying to trace, but to where? Where? These are all the things I'm driving at—"

Harry Putnam began shouting an objection, but what finally came out was only a sputtering, incomprehensible tumble of words, beginning with "fantasyland" and ending with "Barnum and Bailey."

Will Chambers knew the moment. Each case had one—sometimes several. The linchpins. Sometimes they came through precise calculation. Sometimes they appeared suddenly—like some kind of natural wonder. But as a trial lawyer, Will knew how to recognize them.

"Your Honor, I would rather not go into this line of questioning. Investments gone bad. The Eden Lake financial collapse. Bank fraud—illegal loans—business partners who come to hospitals asking questions about child-abuse investigations. This is a sordid business—it really is. I would rather not scandalize the entire Delphi community with this kind of evidence."

Then Will turned, not to the judge, but again to Dr. Parker—the witness—lest there be any mistake whose call this really was to make.

"So if Dr. Parker were to admit that his report may have been inaccurate, that the results were prone to invalidity—then of course this whole other line of questioning would be irrelevant. His motivation would not be material to the case. But as long as he clings to his opinion that his report was absolutely accurate—well then..."

Judge Trainer could see the widening abyss—between a case with measured justice and a case that was on the verge of perhaps imploding the political structure of much of the State of Georgia. It was his job to determine which kind of case this would become.

And his ruling would determine that.

"Dr. Parker," the judge said, addressing the witness directly, "are you aware that working diagnosis for Joshua is now..." and with that he looked at his notes "...methylmalonic acidemia?"

"I am."

"In light of that, do you believe that your blood test—as fine a job as you may have done in performing it—may have mistakenly noted the presence of ethylene glycol when in fact the real condition detected was this other one—MA, as it has been called?"

There was no noise in the courtroom. Somewhere down the stairs, on the first floor of the courthouse, someone was talking. Outside a few car horns were sounding.

But there in Judge Trainer's courtroom, a vacuum had sucked all of the sound out. There was dead silence.

"I do believe," Dr. Parker said slowly, "there is a possibility that my report might have missed the MA condition—and erroneously attributed the abnormal finding to poisoning instead."

While not entirely satisfied, Will knew that was the best he was going to get.

The county rested its case.

Will rose to argue his motion to dismiss the case.

"Just three minutes," the judge said, admonishing Will. "That's all I want you to take."

Will was concise—even brutal—with the facts. There were two pictures being drawn, he argued. The county was, so to speak, saying that it had displayed a clear picture of abuse—but it was only a cleverly constructed pattern of random bits of evidence.

"It is as if," Will explained, "we have just been taken into a modern art museum. The director of the museum shows us an abstract mural—a huge, imposing canvas. On it are a scattering of unrelated lines, colors, and shapes. The director assures us that this is a picture of a rabbit, if only we could see it through his expert eyes. We should trust him. If we do, we will conclude that the rabbit is, indeed, in the picture.

"Mr. Putnam and Ms. Bender and, yes, even Dr. Parker—they are the proprietors of the power structure here. They say they have put forth a picture of a rabbit. But in fact, Your Honor, it is only unrelated lines and colors and shapes. No honest evaluation of this evidence can conclude that a picture of abuse has been presented. No sane definition of justice can cause the state to take the custody of Joshua away from his parents—and certainly not on the basis of the picture that Mr. Putnam and Ms. Bender have put forth.

"As for the other picture, that is the defense portrait, Your Honor. It is as plain and simple—and as identifiable—as those 'hunt' paintings you see hanging at country clubs here in Georgia. We have shown, not a rabbit, but a fox. There is a clever, very devious aspect to this case. Someone has caused a false allegation of child abuse to be called in—a blood sample is missing—medical records are mysteriously unfinished until after conversations with business partners. A clever fox is behind this case. We need not name him or even officially recognize him, but the fact of his existence is real—and it has caused untold harm to a decent farming family, to caring, loving parents in your community.

"Therefore, I ask that you dismiss the custody petition of the county."

Judge Trainer announced a thirty-minute recess, after which time he would rule on the defense motion to dismiss.

As the judge retired to his chambers, the courtroom rose, this time quietly. As quietly as the onlookers sit just before the music swells and the bride comes down the aisle—or just before the black-draped casket is carried down to the front of the funeral home.

61

JUDGE TRAINER WAS ON THE BENCH. He was shuffling—and reshuffling—the notes and papers on the bench in front of him.

The court was called to order, and all noise in the courtroom evaporated.

"First, as to the motion for this court to take the testimony of Dr. Forrester of England, currently residing in the Bahamas, by video satellite hookup. I deny that request. Opposing counsel have not stipulated to it, and I feel it would unduly burden the county's case."

At that point Will was trying to keep his mind clear—despite the sinking feeling that all hope of winning Mary Sue's case had now been lost.

"As to the defense's motion to dismiss..." Judge Trainer's voice trailed off. Then he resumed.

"Your 'picture of the fox' analogy is interesting, Mr. Chambers. But ultimately unconvincing. The evidence I have is simply insufficient to conclude that there is any kind of intentionally wrongful or malicious motivation behind this child-abuse petition filed by the county.

"Now, as to the 'picture of the rabbit' argument. You have raised it, so I will address it."

The judge was now adjusting his glasses and once more straightening his papers.

"I have carefully studied the picture of evidence presented by the county. I should add that, to a single witness, each of the witnesses presented by the county is an upstanding, credible member of the Delphi community. I believe they are honest, and I have

347

considered their testimony carefully. We are here for the protection of Joshua. Let's not forget that. To make sure that he—and other children in our community—can be safe from harm, injury, or abuse. There is no greater task in the law than that.

"I have looked at the picture drawn by the county…"

He paused for a moment as if trying to recollect some thought. Then, grasping it, he continued.

"And it is my considered opinion—" and with that Judge Trainer took off his glasses and wiped the sweat from his eyes. Then he put his glasses back on.

"It is my conclusion that there is simply no rabbit in that picture."

Will, whose gaze had been fixed on the counsel table in front of him, now raised his eyes and looked over at Joe Fellows sitting next to him.

Joe, afraid of misconstruing the ruling, tried to restrain a smile—but he saw the hope that was springing to life in Will's eyes.

"The picture," the judge continued, "does not convincingly show me that rabbit. I see only unrelated bits of evidence—some coincidentally related, but only barely so, and most of it hanging together by a thread. Some not hanging together at all after Mr. Chamber's cross-examination.

"I spoke of the right of children to be free of abuse. But I am also concerned about the abuse of good parents by a system that doesn't always respond the way it should. The right of parenting is a fundamental right. To overcome it, the harm to the child must be real, not imagined—the threat must be imminent—and above all, the procedures used against the parents must be scrupulously fair.

"Ex parte hearings without notice to the parents or their attorneys—police sweeping down onto a farm family when lesser measures could have been used—a case carefully built to prove abuse rather than to search for truth—these are not the hallmarks of fairness. This case should not have been brought. Period. If you want to know where the system went awry, then I suggest that you, Mr. Putnam, and you, Ms. Bender—as honest and hardworking as the two of you are—I suggest that when you get up in the morning you look in the mirror. You will see where the system failed the Fellows family.

"This custody case is dismissed. The order transferring custody of Joshua to the county is hereby vacated. Mr. Putnam, there are still criminal charges outstanding against both Mr. and Mrs. Fellows, are there not?"

"Yes, Your Honor," the prosecutor responded, not bothering to stand.

"If you can't prove abuse by a civil standard, then you can't prove it by a criminal standard—right?"

"That's true—though Joe Fellows is actually charged with obstruction of justice."

"Yes. And that case is assigned to my courtroom. Do you know what I intend to do with those charges?" the judge asked sternly.

"Actually, judge," Harry Putnam said, finally rising to his feet, "I will be withdrawing all criminal charges against both Mary Sue and Joe."

"Today?"

"Ah…yes. That's right. Today."

Joe Fellows was weeping openly and unashamedly, his shoulders heaving with sobs.

In the pandemonium that followed, the judge swept down from the bench and then slammed the doors to his chambers so firmly that the picture of George Washington hanging over the judge's chair began swinging to and fro.

The crowd in the courtroom was on its feet—reporters were shouting for Joe and for Will. But Will was being drawn, inexplicably, out of the courtroom. Out through the cacophony and the pushing and shoving, and the sea of faces. Will made his way through them. Guard Thompson rushed to Joe and offered to escort him to his cell so he could remove his jail clothes, don the shirt and pants he was wearing the day he was arrested, and get ready to be released into the daylight.

As Will muscled his way out, the crowd of reporters was spilling out into the hallway—and soon it was packed with onlookers and members of the press.

"Mr. Chambers!" a woman's voice called out.

Will glanced in the direction the voice had come from.

"There he is—go on!" said an older woman he didn't recognize. She was propelling a younger woman with blonde hair and light-blue eyes toward Will.

And then the attorney realized who the younger woman must be.

The crowd parted in front of Mary Sue as she made her way toward Will Chambers, smiling, crying, and laughing all at the same time, and wiping the streams of tears away in big swipes.

She reached out her arms to Will, who accepted her tender hug.

"Thank you for giving me back my family," she whispered, in a voice choked with tears.

Guard Thompson was smiling and opening up the crowd for his former prisoner. Then Joe Fellows saw his wife. When his eyes met hers, she gave a little convulsed sob and began running toward him.

"Mary Sue!" Joe yelled out in joy.

But in the chaos there were others.

Beth, Jason Bell Purdy's former secretary, was in the crowded hallway, making certain for herself that the terrible mistake she had made would be corrected. She covered her mouth and disappeared quickly into the human tide in the hallway.

And there was also another, there in the hallway. In the mass of people. And as Joe ran toward Mary Sue, he realized it first.

Suddenly the elation rushed out of him—replaced instantly by fear. Stunned, he looked closer, to his right. He saw a gun barrel appearing out of the crowd.

Behind sunglasses and a hat, Linus Eggers held the revolver with both hands to steady it. It had a full round. More than enough for both of his targets—Mary Sue Fellows and Will

Chambers, her attorney, who was assumed to be the repository of all of her knowledge about Henry Pencup.

Eggers aimed at Mary Sue's chest and started to squeeze the trigger.

Joe screamed wildly and dove toward the gunman, flying at him like a crazed linebacker who was using his body like a human missile to prevent the final, deadly play.

The gun discharged with a terrible reverberating bang as Joe's arms reached the barrel and knocked it downward.

The bullet hit the marble floor and ricocheted into the ceiling.

People were screaming and running away. Will was trying to push Mary Sue out of the line of fire. When he whirled around, he saw Linus Eggers on his back, sunglasses knocked off—pointing the gun toward his face.

There was a bang as the barrel was directed at Will's left eye.

Immediately a second shot rang out with a terrible, hollow echo.

But Will was still standing.

Deputy Thompson, his revolver pointed at the gunman's chest, had squeezed off two rapid-fire rounds before Linus could pull the trigger a second time. Eggers was dead on the cold marble floor, still clutching the revolver.

Joe scrambled up off the floor and rushed over to Mary Sue. He embraced her, checking her face, her hair, her body, to make sure she was unhurt.

Will stood stunned for a moment, taking a few seconds to process it all. Deputy Thompson was calling on his walkie-talkie for an emergency vehicle—and additional backup in case there were more gunmen.

They would find no other assassins.

Will walked over to the deputy. He reached out and the two men clasped hands firmly. The attorney could only shake his head—he had no words at first.

Thompson was smiling.

"Give me fifty years or so," Will finally said, "and I will think up some way to thank you."

62

THE PRESS CONFERENCE had been adroitly planned to take place on the front steps of the Georgia Statehouse. A bevy of news reporters and cameras were all focused on Jason Bell Purdy, who was smiling confidently while concluding his remarks.

"For those reasons," Purdy said, "I support the quick action of Congress, as well as the President, in ending the airline strike that was threatening to paralyze our nation."

Then Purdy pivoted ever so slightly and looked directly into the cameras, with polished sincerity and honed poise.

"Later this week I'll be releasing my position paper on the recent developments in the Middle East, the ever-present threat of terrorism, and even more importantly, the need for a geo-political partnership with the community of nations. Global unity and goodwill are not options in the twenty-first century, they are mandates. That will be a major theme of mine as I represent the fine state of Georgia in the United States Senate, finishing the term of Senator Jim Boggs Hartley, a truly great American whose death was a blow to us all. I am leaving this press conference and going directly to his widow so I can confer with her and get a true sense of those matters that weighed most strongly on his heart—those matters she thinks her late husband would most want me to complete on his behalf."

A raft of hands appeared in the crowd as the reporters began pelting Jason Bell Purdy with questions.

"What about the allegations of wrongdoing in the Eden Lake Resort project? What about the questions that were raised in the child-abuse case over in Delphi?"

Purdy smiled with assurance and raised his hand to quiet the group.

"As you know," he responded, "you were told in advance I was not going to take any questions except in regard to those matters in my prepared remarks, but I will say this: Because these wild accusations have been raised, tomorrow, at noon, my office will release a statement answering all of your questions and putting to rest this ridiculous allegation that was thrown out by a desperate trial lawyer. Of course, you all know the reputation of trial lawyers!"

A few chuckles came from the press corps.

The new senator fielded a few more questions from the media group and then excused himself with a smile and a wave to the cameras.

Jason Bell Purdy would be right about one thing—the statement released from his office, carefully prepared by political and legal strategists, would quiet the questions raised about the Eden Lake Resort project.

Bank examiners would be unable to trace the several million dollars missing from the Delphi National Bank.

Father Godfrey, who was spending more and more time fishing and tending to his small garden, would never reveal the confession of bank president Henry Pencup.

The overflow pen was permanently closed, and the brutal guard pleaded guilty on a negotiated plea and was sentenced to ten years in prison. And the Juda County jail overall, both in its procedures and its facility, would be updated.

On the whole, the predictable and safe patterns of life in Delphi continued as before. However, metal detectors were installed at all the entranceways of the courthouse—particularly when it was realized, after the Linus Eggers shooting, that the Delphi facility was one of the few remaining courthouses that had not installed them.

Eggers had died immediately in the shootout. At the autopsy, high levels of cocaine were found in his blood. That, coupled with the fact that Eggers was in the final stages of his battle with AIDS, created a comfortable conclusion for most of the community—that his attempt to assassinate Mary Sue Fellows and Will Chambers was an aberration caused by a brain dysfunction.

Harry Putnam had had hopes of being a circuit judge, but he was rightly concerned about the outcome of the Mary Sue Fellows case and felt it did not bode well for him politically, at least in the near future.

Not long after the trial, Putnam called Will Chambers at his office in Virginia to confirm the final dismissal of all the criminal charges against Joe and Mary Sue.

"Will, trying the Mary Sue Fellows case against you was—well, let's just say it was *educational*. Do me a favor and don't come up against me again anytime soon."

Will thanked him for the compliment and wished him farewell.

After he hung up with Putnam, Will contacted the legal counsel for the State Department. The attorney told Will that the Department appreciated his cooperation in delaying the lawsuit against General Nuban for the Sudan atrocities. As a result, they wanted to offer him some information.

The lawyer indicated they had received information that General Nuban would be making a short stop on American soil for a meeting of international arms dealers in Miami. That would give Will Chambers and his legal team a perfect opportunity to serve the lawsuit papers on the general while he was within the borders of the United States, which would remove some of the jurisdictional objections the general and the nation of Sudan might have to the legal action.

After finishing the phone call with the State Department, Will stepped over to Hilda's desk with the carbonless copy of a credit slip that documented a lunch at Denny's Log Cabin for $7.43. Handing the slip to Hilda, he asked, "Do me a favor—get this framed, will you?"

Hilda gave him a look of total bewilderment. "You are kidding, of course—right?"

Will smiled, and then he declared, "Hilda, I've never been more serious in my life."

63

So where does that leave you?"

"With a little different perspective, I suppose."

"You mean, regarding Mary and the welfare of her little boy?"

"Yes. A different paradigm. A shift of focus."

"How so?"

"Well, I'm trying to figure this out—put myself in her shoes. She sees a tyrannical abuse of government power—obviously. But I really believe she was mostly thinking much like any loving mother would—she was trying to figure out how to protect her little boy."

"But with obvious differences from the usual case, right?"

"Oh, yes. Absolutely."

"In this case, the little boy is what the whole story is about."

"Sure. But the idea is the same. That's why I said a different paradigm, or focus. I was trying to approach the miracles in the Gospel accounts from the viewpoint of my old intellectual rationalism. I was approaching this story as if the real question were this—does God really protect us through supernatural acts?"

Len Redgrove thought for a minute about what Will had just said. Then he asked another question.

"Is that what you think was on Mary's heart?"

"I'm not sure," Will replied, finishing the last bite of his apple pie. "But we have to assume she would be feeling and thinking like any mother—or any parent. Or any one of us, for that matter."

"And how is that?"

"Well, it seems to me we just *think* we struggle with the question of whether God will really protect us. In Mary's case the question would have been, 'Will God protect my boy, Jesus—protect him from the murderous plans of Herod?' We tend to think that is the actual question. But it really isn't."

With that last comment, Will was waving his fork for emphasis.

"Well, what's the actual question?" Redgrove asked.

"It seems to me that the question that plagues us is really not *if* God is willing to protect us—because we really know the answer to that question already. We know it through the promises in the Bible. We know it through the inner spiritual voice we have when Christ has come to live in us through his Spirit. And we know it from experience, from answered prayer—numerous ways. No, the real question we are asking, but perhaps don't want to admit it, is this—*how* will God protect me? Is he going to protect me in the way *I* want—from tragedy, injustice, false accusations, disease, accidents, injuries? In other words, *how* will he do it?"

"Can you give me an example?"

"Well," Will said after thinking a minute, "a little boy gets a toothache. His mother wants to protect him from dental problems, so she takes him to the dentist. The dentist fills the cavity, but in the process he causes some pain. The mother knows she's protected her boy from tooth decay. But the little boy is upset because all he wanted was some protection from having to experience any pain.

"Most of us are like the little boy. We know, down deep, that the Father loves us and will take care of us—but we want to settle for much less. We want the form of protection to be *our* way—according to our shortsighted desire to avoid pain—rather than *his* way. And he has the welfare of the whole universe in his plan."

Redgrove listened quietly, smiling.

"What our flesh feels—what our heart says to us when it's breaking—is usually about the pain, rather than God's plan for the human race," the professor noted. "As long as we recognize the difference, then it's okay to want to run from the pain—or to clench our fists and cry out when we lose loved ones. God gave us souls, but he also gave us bodies with nerve endings."

Will reached for the check that the waitress at the Diner had just dropped off at their table, but Redgrove grabbed it first.

"Oh no. You paid last time."

As the two walked out to the parking lot Will said, "I've got to hit the sack. I'm getting up really early tomorrow. Fiona is driving down from Baltimore and dropping her car off, and then the two of us are going to take a long drive."

"Say," his friend asked inquisitively, "when in the world are you going to ask her to marry you?"

Will kept walking to his Corvette and then said over his shoulder, "Dr. Redgrove, that is the best question you have asked me all night."

((((((

In the countryside outside of Delphi, Georgia, it was hot, and the bugs were droning in the fields. The cattle on the farms had waded down to the nearest pond or creek.

But the sun was getting lower in the sky and there was a bit of a breeze, which, coupled with shade from the clouds overhead, was welcome relief to those down below on the farm.

Long tables in the farmhouse's front yard were covered with checkered tablecloths and filled with platters of food—corn on the cob, barbecued ribs, mashed potatoes, steaks, fresh green beans, not to mention salads, bowls of Jell-O, and pies—more than enough to feed the crowd that had gathered at the home of Joe and Mary Sue Fellows.

Andrew White Arrow had traveled back from New Mexico to be there. Tommy, Danny, and Katherine had come all the way from South Dakota. Among the group were Madeline, Joe's mother, and many friends from the Fellowses' church.

A few miles away, Will was driving his '57 Corvette with the top down, approaching the farm on the county highway. Next to him, Fiona had a baseball cap pulled down snugly on her head to keep her hair in place.

"What finally caused Mary Sue to return to Delphi when she did?" Fiona asked.

"That was really remarkable," Will replied. "She had given the go-ahead to Dr. Bill to arrange for a medical airlift for Joshua, who was seriously ill by then, to the Delphi hospital. And Joe was in Delphi, but still in jail. And of course, her farm—her home—was back there. Further, she had to face the legal system sooner or later. She knew, I think, that the time had come. But there was something else."

"Like what?" Fiona asked, checking the directions that lay in her lap to the farm.

"She asked God for a sign."

"Really? What kind of a sign?"

"Anything, I guess. She told me she never felt comfortable doing something like that. But she was desperate. So she was in her cabin on Tommy White Arrow's ranch, praying about it."

"And?" Fiona asked, urging Will on.

"And there's a sound at the door. It was Danny White Arrow."

"Danny—oh, the one who was disabled from the head injury?"

"Right," Will said. "Danny is the youngest of the three brothers. Anyway, he trots into the room, gives his favorite yo-yo to Mary Sue, and says, 'This is for Joshua to have after your trip back home.'

"Mary Sue looks at him and says, 'Trip?'

"And Danny says, without skipping a beat, 'There's never been a better time to go home.' His exact words."

"So, Mary Sue took that as the final cue from the Lord?"

"That's it. Say—" Will turned slightly to glance around the car. "We didn't forget the flyers for the concert, did we?"

"These?" Fiona asked, pulling them out of the manila folder in her shoulder bag.

Will smiled as he glanced at the sheets in Fiona's lap. They were glossy color versions of the ads that had been placed in several magazines, describing "a Special Benefit Concert with Dove-Award-Winning Gospel Singer FIONA CAMERON— in Honor of the Bravery of Deputy Hugh Thompson of the Juda County Sheriff's Department."

"This whole idea of yours was remarkable. You are an amazing woman!" Will declared.

Fiona held up a flyer and pointed to the words "Deputy Hugh Thompson," and then she grinned, with her dimples showing.

"This man," she said, "saved the life of my future husband. Are you kidding?"

As she held the sheet up, she couldn't help noticing the sunlight playing in brilliant flashes off the large diamond on her left hand.

Then she glanced at the last sentence of the flyer—"All Proceeds Will Be Donated for the Treatment and Cure of Methylmalonic Acidemia."

Suddenly Fiona snapped up her head. "There, Will, turn there—that should be the farm."

"I was there once, but this doesn't look like it..." Will replied vaguely.

"Will, dear—the directions say to turn *right here*."

Will slowed the Corvette down and pulled onto a gravel road. That was when they noticed the bunch of balloons tied to a post at the opening of the driveway.

"See?" Fiona said, smiling triumphantly.

Up ahead, at the farm, there were two pairs of legs churning at full speed. A man was running through the field.

Joe Fellows slowed down to half speed.

The other set of legs, however, was still running at top speed—but because they were very small legs, they were making little headway despite a heroic effort.

Joe was catching up. Then, when he was right there, he slowed his stride a bit, swooped down, scooped up Joshua as he was running, and took him in his arms, swinging him around like an airplane.

Joshua burst into exuberant laughter, and Joe began belly-laughing himself.

At one of the tables in the yard, Tommy White Arrow was talking politics with a friend of Joe's from the farm co-op. Under a spreading tree, Andrew White Arrow was sipping lemonade and discussing something with the pastor of the Fellowses' church.

Mary Sue paused for a minute in the front doorway, surveying the front yard, the friends who had come, and her husband frolicking in the field with their son.

Inside the farmhouse, Katherine White Arrow was helping in the kitchen, and Danny, taking a break from the activity outside, was watching television.

A promotional ad from the National Airline Association, which had been playing since the time of the airplane strike, had just appeared on the screen. It showed a tired man and woman in an airport, checking in their luggage. Then the man called on his cell phone to his son and daughter at home. "Mommy and I are on our way home," he said. "We'll be there soon. You can count on that." As the music in the background swelled, a deep, soothing voice closed the ad by saying,

AMERICA'S AIRLINES ARE HERE TO SERVE YOU

And then, as the voice concluded, Danny lit up in a huge smile and repeated the words by heart along with the ad—

THERE'S NEVER BEEN A BETTER TIME TO GO HOME

As the Fellows family's farmhouse came into view, Will and Fiona caught sight of the group that had gathered outside.

Pulling to the side, Will came to a stop. He pointed out to Fiona where Andrew was standing under the tree.

Then he said, indicating one of the long tables, "That must be his brother, Tommy." He also spotted Joe, who by then was carrying Joshua on his shoulders toward the front door—where Mary Sue was wiping her hands on her apron, standing and waiting for them with an expression of quiet peace on her face.

When Will pointed to Joe, and Joshua, and Mary Sue—there on the threshold of their home—that was when Fiona, with the finger of one slender hand, delicately wiped away the tears forming in her eyes. And then, as the car was parked with the motor running, she turned to Will Chambers, placed her hands on both sides of his face, and spoke to him—softly and tenderly.

When the crowd at the house finally noticed the Corvette in the driveway—and the couple in it, embracing—a great cheer rose up. It echoed from the heart of the farm through the fields and hollows, all the way down to the little creek at the very edge of the land.

The Accused
by Craig Parshall

Attorney Will Chambers has fought for justice for his clients in the popular Resurrection File *and the harrowing* Custody of the State. *But now, in* The Accused, *Will must grapple with the terrifying temptation to execute justice for himself—by avenging the brutal crime that shattered his past.*

A honeymoon in Cancún. What could be more romantic? But the happiness of attorney Will Chambers and his wife, Fiona, is ambushed by two unexpected events: a terrorist kidnapping of a U.S. official...and a phone call telling Will that a link has been found to the previously unidentified murderer of his first wife.

As the newly married lawyer struggles with these terrible events, one of them thrusts him into a new legal case. A secret U.S. team had tried to thwart the Cancún kidnapping, and the Marine colonel who led it, Caleb Marlowe, has now been court-martialed for the murder of unarmed civilians—disavowed and hung out to dry by the White House.

At the mercy of international politics, Marlowe is ping-ponged from a military court to both a Senate subcommittee and the International Criminal Court, with Will arguing his defense. And when the disguise is ripped away from past treachery and callous betrayal, both Will and his client must ask, *Is forgiveness real?*—or face a debacle ending in bloody vengeance.

The Accused *is a legal thriller that recounts a man's epic confrontation of evil from his past—and reveals the power of God through forgiveness.*

THE RESURRECTION FILE—

THE EXCITING FIRST NOVEL
IN THE CHAMBERS OF JUSTICE SERIES

"Powerful...*The Resurrection File* is one of the most fascinating books I have read in years."

—Tim LaHaye, coauthor of the
bestselling LEFT BEHIND® series

A Respected Professor...
A Take-No-Prisoners Lawyer...
A Small-Time Preacher...
WHO IS TELLING THE TRUTH?

Depressed, down on his luck, and dropped by his law partners, Will Chambers is an attorney whose troubles are starting to exceed even his considerable talents.

When Reverend Angus MacCameron asks Chambers to defend him against accusations that might destroy not only the man's ministry but the very foundation of the Christian faith, everything in Chambers' nonbelieving heart says "run away."

But Chambers can't resist the preacher's earnest pleas, the presence of his lovely and successful daughter, Fiona, and the chance to go up against high-powered attorney J-Fox Sherman.

Quickly caught in a conspiracy involving terrorism, top-level government intrigue, and wild legal maneuvering, Chambers is in for the ride of his life—a ride whose destination he never could have imagined.

"*The Resurrection File* has action, adventure, and very good courtroom scenes. The characters are real. The dialogue is compelling. The story situations keep the reader riveted and—it's a cliché, but I will repeat it—'I couldn't put it down.'"

—Ted Baehr, publisher of MOVIEGUIDE®
(Web site: www.movieguide.org) and Chairman
of the Christian Film & Television Commission